P

"The cozy villa

inhabitants make the holidays bright."

—*Library Journal* on *An Irish Country Christmas*

"Taylor masterfully charts the small victories and defeats of Irish village life." —*Irish America* magazine

"Taylor continues his charm streak with this latest dip into Ballybucklebo, Ireland, spinning out the story of Kinky Kincaid. . . . Taylor, like Kinky, is a bang-up storyteller who captivates and entertains from the first word."

—*Publishers Weekly* on *An Irish Country Girl*

"Full of stories and vivid characters, [*An Irish Country Village*] recalls a good night in a pub. Good, light entertainment." —*Booklist*

"Patrick Taylor, M.D., is a man of words and a healing physician, too. . . . Written with compassion and hilarity about a community whose inhabitants are as wonderful and loony as any on earth. A grand read from a grand man."

—Malachy McCourt, *New York Times* bestselling author of *A Monk Swimming*, on *An Irish Country Doctor*

"Wraps you in the sensations of a vanished time and place."

—*The Vancouver Sun* on *An Irish Country Doctor*

"At last! Here is an authentic Northern Ireland voice. A full cupboard of delightful characters, both human and animal, enriches every page. Quirky, funny, and deeply moving by turns, Taylor's writing perfectly captures the language and character of Ulster in times gone by. I promise you will enjoy this book immensely; I did."

—Morgan Llywelyn, *New York Times* bestselling author of *The Last Prince of Ireland*, on *An Irish Country Doctor*

"With an unerring eye for detail, the talents of a natural storyteller, and the ability to pepper his anecdotes with large doses of wit and humor, Patrick Taylor has written a delightful novel."

—*Calgary Herald* on *An Irish Country Doctor*

Also by Patrick Taylor

Only Wounded
Pray for Us Sinners
Now and in the Hour of Our Death

An Irish Country Doctor
An Irish Country Village
An Irish Country Christmas
An Irish Country Girl
An Irish Country Courtship
A Dublin Student Doctor
An Irish Country Wedding
Fingal O'Reilly, Irish Doctor
The Wily O'Reilly: Irish Country Stories
An Irish Doctor in Peace and at War
An Irish Doctor in Love and at Sea
An Irish Country Love Story
An Irish Country Practice
An Irish Country Cottage (forthcoming)

"Home Is the Sailor" (e-original)

An Irish Country Christmas

PATRICK TAYLOR

A TOM DOHERTY ASSOCIATES BOOK
NEW YORK

AN IRISH COUNTRY CHRISTMAS

Maps by Elizabeth Danforth

A Forge Book
Published by Tom Doherty Associates
175 Fifth Avenue
New York, NY 10010

www.tor-forge.com

ISBN 978-0-7653-6685-6

First Edition: November 2008
First Mass Market Edition: November 2010

Printed in the United States of America

0 9

To Dorothy

ACKNOWLEDGMENTS

Doctor Fingal Flahertie O'Reilly made his first appearance in 1995. His gradual development was gently supervised by my friend Simon Hally, editor of *Stitches.*

O'Reilly's growth to maturity has been nurtured by some remarkable people. Without the skilled editorial advice of Carolyn Bateman, my editor and friend, I would not consider submitting a manuscript. Adrienne Weiss was my editor at Insomniac Press of Toronto, which first published the work in 2004 as *The Apprenticeship of Doctor Laverty.* My agent, Susan Crawford, represented the first two books in the series, and Rosie and Jessica Buckman of England handled foreign rights.

Natalia Aponte, then an editor with Tor/Forge Books of New York, saw value in my efforts and persuaded Tom Doherty, publisher of Forge, to share her confidence. She has always had unswerving faith in the inhabitants of Ballybucklebo. Now as my agent and my confidante, she constantly encourages me when my faith falters.

My Special thanks go to Pat Phelan, copy editor Extraordinary.

During the writing of *An Irish Country Christmas* I was stricken with anaemia. My haematologist and friend, Doctor Linda Vickars, of Vancouver, not only dealt with my condition, but also clearly explained the arcana of disorders of the blood to an old gynaecologist.

Doctor Tom Baskett, obstetrician, and my oldest friend from medical school days, advised me on the finer points of breech delivery.

The bulk of *An Irish Country Christmas* was completed in a suite in North Vancouver, Canada, rented to me by Duncan and Kathy Campbell. No author could wish for a better place to work or for more considerate landlords.

To you all, Doctors O'Reilly, Laverty, and I tender our unreserved thanks.

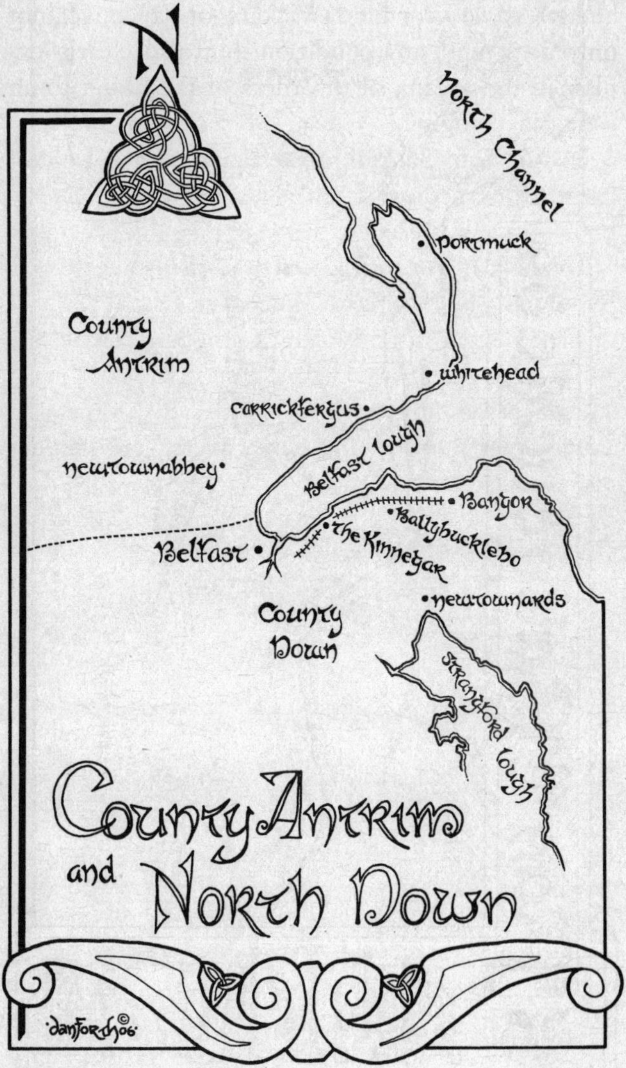
N
North Channel
Portmuck
County
Antrim
Whitehead
Carrickfergus
Belfast Lough
Newtownabbey
Bangor
Ballyhucklebo
The Kinnegar
Belfast
Newtownards
County
Down
Strangford Lough
County Antrim
and
North Down
danforth06 ©

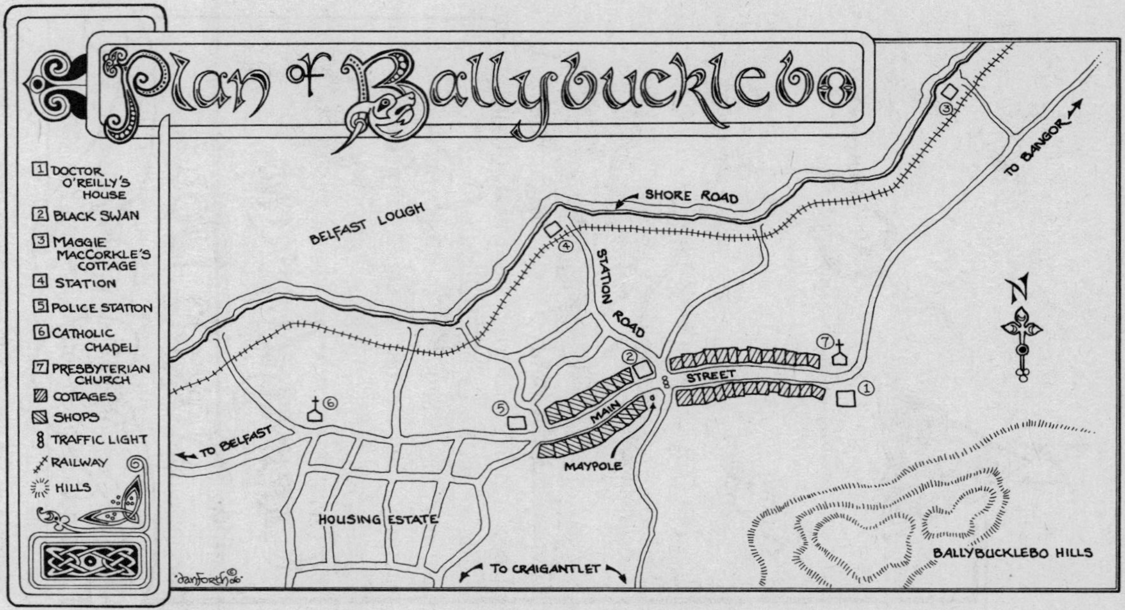
Plan of Ballybucklebo
1 DOCTOR O'REILLY'S HOUSE
2 BLACK SWAN
3 MAGGIE MACCORKLE'S COTTAGE
4 STATION
5 POLICE STATION
6 CATHOLIC CHAPEL
7 PRESBYTERIAN CHURCH
COTTAGES
SHOPS
TRAFFIC LIGHT
RAILWAY
HILLS
BELFAST LOUGH
SHORE ROAD
STATION ROAD
MAIN STREET
MAYPOLE
TO BANGOR
TO BELFAST
TO CRAIGANTLET
HOUSING ESTATE
BALLYBUCKLEBO HILLS
N
danForth © 06

1

Recommend the Old Inn *to Ev'ry Friend*

Barry Laverty—*Doctor* Barry Laverty—slammed the door of Brunhilde, his elderly Volkswagen Beetle. He hunched his shoulders against the sleet and hurried across the car park of the Old Inn in Crawfordsburn, County Down. Night comes early in December in Northern Ireland, and at four-thirty in the afternoon it was barely light enough for him to make out the leafless branches of trees tossing and swaying in the gale, but he could hear the wind battering its way through the glen behind the hotel.

He pushed through the inn's double front door and went down three steps into a well-lit lobby. Blinking at the brightness, he twitched his shoulders up and his neck down as a trickle of water found its way under his collar.

"Hello, John," he said to the manager, who stood behind a reception desk at the far side of the lobby.

The middle-aged man looked up and smiled. "Good afternoon, Doctor."

A little more than a year ago he would have said,

"How's about ye, Barry?" The Old Inn was only a few miles away from Barry's parents' home in Bangor. During his years as a medical student, he'd often popped in here for a quick pint, and John had been standing in reception for as long as Barry could remember.

"Dirty day out there," John observed.

"I'm half foundered." Barry rubbed his hands together.

"There's a nice cosy fire lit in the Parlour Bar, sir."

"I'm going to the reception."

"The Donnelly-MacAteer party's in the Guests Lounge, but Doctor O'Reilly's just gone into the Parlour Bar. He said to tell you if you came in."

Typical, Barry thought, of Fingal Flahertie O'Reilly, the senior man in the practice where Barry worked, to be slipping out to the bar for a quick drink. He knew Julie MacAteer's parents were Pioneers—teetotalers—so the party would be what was called in Ulster an orange juice reception.

"Thanks." Barry shrugged out of his raincoat. "I'll just park this and then nip in and get warm."

He caught a glimpse of himself in a mirror mounted at the back of the coat stand. Blue eyes with dark rings beneath looked back from an oval face. At twenty-four he was too young for the dusky half circles to be a permanent feature, but he'd attended a confinement for most of the night. Although he might be tired, he thought the woman he'd just delivered of a healthy seven-pound five-ounce boy would be a lot more so.

He yawned. His fair hair was darkened, soaked, and plastered to his scalp. At least his cow's lick wasn't sticking up like the crest on a tufted duck.

Barry hung his coat, ran his hands over his hair, turned, and walked along a short, carpeted corridor to the bar. He wondered if Colette the barmaid, a big, motherly woman, would be on duty tonight.

This part of the building, he knew, had been an old coaching inn built in 1614, and generations of owners had very sensibly preserved the whitewashed daub-and-wattle walls and the heavy, rough-hewn, black ceiling beams. C. S. Lewis had stayed here in 1958 with his wife, Joy, for what he called "a perfect fortnight."

Barry went through a door to his left into a low-ceilinged room where a turf fire blazed in a wide grate. After the bitter cold of the day outside, the heat was stifling, but the scent of the burning peat was familiar and comforting to him. There were several men in the room, most standing at the bar, a few in booths beside the wall. Barry heard a murmuring of conversation. The smells of damp tweed and cigarette smoke mingled with the aroma of peat. He could hear the sleet outside rattling off the curtained windows.

"*You,*" roared Doctor Fingal Flahertie O'Reilly, who stood leaning against the bar, "look like a drowned rat. Come on in and have a jar."

"Thanks, Fingal."

"What'll you have?"

Barry rapidly rubbed his hands together, feeling

them tingle as the circulation returned. "Hot Irish, please."

O'Reilly turned to the barmaid, who stood behind the marble-topped bar polishing a straight pint glass with a dish towel. "Do you hear that, Colette?"

"Hot half-un it is, Doctor."

"Half-un be damned. Give him a double."

"How are you, Colette?" Barry asked, turning his back on O'Reilly, shaking his head at her, and mouthing silently, "Just a half." A double whiskey on top of his tiredness could be the end of him.

Her smile was wide and welcoming as she nodded her understanding of his order and said, "Grand, so I am. Haven't seen you in for a wee while."

"I've been busy—"

"Jesus, lass, would you give the young fellah his jar?" O'Reilly said.

"Coming up." She moved away and switched on an electric kettle.

"Now, Doctor Laverty," growled O'Reilly, "where the hell have you been?"

Barry looked at the big man's florid, craggy face, bushy eyebrows, and his bent nose with a distinct list to port. O'Reilly was in his shirtsleeves, red braces holding up his tweed pants. A glass—a large glass—of what Barry knew would be Irish whiskey was clutched in one hand.

"Working."

"Working? When I left the house for the wedding, the door to the surgery was still shut, but there were only a couple of customers in the waiting room. Nuala Harkness never takes long."

"Maybe not for *you,* Fingal. You've known the woman for nearly twenty years."

O'Reilly grunted. "And Harry 'The Boots' Hawthorne."

"Who?"

"Harry 'The Boots' Hawthorne. They call him that because when he was first married his wife told her best friend he was so virile that when he came in from the fields and feeling his oats, wanting her, he wouldn't even take the time to get his boots off."

Barry laughed. "I've read Napoleon was like that with Josephine."

"Maybe Harry'd read it too. Anyway the wife's friend told her husband, and he told . . ."

Barry nodded. He had already experienced just how quickly news could fly around the village of Ballybucklebo.

"So now the lads won't let him live it down, and they call him Harry the Boots. He usually comes in for a tonic, and you can finish with him in five minutes."

Barry shook his head. "*You* can, Fingal, but I've only been here for a few months, and if I want to know the patients as well as you I have to spend a bit of time getting to know them."

"I suppose so," O'Reilly frowned. "But two more shouldn't have taken you until now. We expected to see you at the service."

"Harry took longer than I expected; then Jeannie Jingles phoned. She thought her wee Eddie had croup and—"

"And you went to see the lad?" There was a hint of paleness in the tip of O'Reilly's nose, a sure sign that his temper was not entirely under control.

"I know you're meant to be on call today for emergencies, Fingal, but—"

"You thought you'd do me a favour?" The pallor spread.

"Not a favour. You were already in the church. It made sense to me to call in and see the kiddie. I thought it would only take a minute."

"Huh. Some minute. The service was over at two thirty. You should have been there."

"I'm sorry." Barry held one hand at shoulder height, palm out. "If I'd known I was depriving you of the pure delights, the immensely satisfying medical moments of seeing one more case of common croup, I'd have sent a police escort to haul you out of your pew."

O'Reilly managed a chuckle. "Alright. Have it your own way. Work yourself into an early grave if that's what you want. See if I give a tinker's damn." The laugh lines deepened at the corners of his eyes.

"Jesus, Fingal, I just thought it made sense."

O'Reilly clapped Barry on the shoulder. "You're right this once, Barry, but . . . but . . . an agreement's an agreement." O'Reilly swallowed a mouthful of whiskey. "We decided in August, when you were ready to work on your own, we'd split the work."

"And haven't we? One of us in the surgery to see the minor cases, the other one out doing home visits and taking calls at night. I thought it was working fine."

O'Reilly grunted. "You were up half the bloody night. *I'm* on call today."

One thing Barry had learnt. He must never cave in to O'Reilly. He looked the older man right in the eye. "It was a bloody good thing I went. The little lad had a raging pneumonia. I had to get him up to the Royal Victoria Hospital immediately."

"Had he, by God?" O'Reilly's eyebrows met above his nose as he frowned. "Lobar was it?"

"As best as I could tell without an X-ray."

O'Reilly took a deep swallow of his whiskey, clapped Barry on the shoulder, and said, "Maybe you did do the right thing."

"I think so."

"So do I." O'Reilly nodded. "But as of this minute, Doctor Barry Laverty, *I'm* on call." At least his nose tip was its usual plum colour.

"Fine, Fingal."

"And Kinky knows where to find me if anything crops up."

"She's not at the reception?" Barry was surprised. Mrs. "Kinky" Kincaid, the Cork woman who was O'Reilly's housekeeper, was usually very much a part of the Ballybucklebo social scene.

"She was invited. She came with me to the service,

but she said she was feeling a bit snifflish and didn't want to be out in that bloody awful gale. She went home. She asked me to apologize to Julie."

"Is Kinky all right?"

"Kinky? Right as rain. She has the constitution of an ox, that woman." He lowered his voice. "I think there was a program on the telly she really wanted to see."

Barry smiled at his mental picture of Kinky, who was as she once described herself "very tall around," curled up with a cup of tea in front of her television set. He wondered if Lady Macbeth, O'Reilly's white cat, would be keeping Kinky company. His thoughts were interrupted by "Here y'are, sir." Colette handed Barry a steaming mug. "Two and six, please."

"Here." O'Reilly threw coins on the bar top. "But I thought I called for a double."

"A wee half's just fine, Fingal." Barry sipped, savouring the flavours of a mixture of Irish whiskey, sugar, and lemon juice topped off with boiling water. He noticed a couple of cloves floating on the surface. "*Sláinte*."

"*Sláinte mHath*." O'Reilly finished his whiskey and put the glass on the bar. "Being as it's me on call, I'd better go easy on the grog." He clapped Barry on the shoulder. "But you're not, so you can enjoy the reception"—he stepped back from the bar—"which is where the pair of us should be now. Come on."

"You go on, Fingal. I'll catch you up."

O'Reilly frowned. "Where are you going?"

"Jesus, Fingal. A policeman wouldn't ask you that."

O'Reilly laughed. "Need to shed a tear for the old country?"

Barry nodded and finished his drink. It wouldn't be polite to bring a whiskey to a teetotal reception. He left the bar, crossed the main corridor, and slipped into a small bathroom. He unzipped.

This would be, he thought, the second wedding he'd attended since he'd started working in the village of Ballybucklebo, which lay seven miles west of Crawfordsburn. He remembered, would always remember, his first trip there and his introduction to O'Reilly. The date of that meeting, July 1, 1964, was, as he had heard the older man say when referring to another never-to-be-forgotten moment, "tattooed on the inside of the front of his skull."

Barry had been standing outside the front door of O'Reilly's house when O'Reilly himself had appeared and bodily flung a patient into a rosebush, with the bellowed admonition, "The next time you come here after hours on my half day and want me to look at your sore ankle, wash your bloody feet!" Barry had almost turned tail.

He was glad now he hadn't. In the five months during which he had gone from probationary assistant to assistant, with a view to a full partnership in one year, he had learnt a great deal about the practice of medicine in a rural setting. He had also come to know and like many of O'Reilly's patients.

He rezipped his pants. The last wedding he'd been

to, in August, was of Sonny Houston to Maggie MacCorkle, both sixty-plus, both odd as two left feet. Sonny had a Ph.D. but preferred to live in an old motorcar. Maggie had at one time complained of headaches that were two inches *above* the crown of her head. Barry had initially thought she was mad as a hatter, but O'Reilly had known better. He usually did.

Barry chuckled and headed for the Guests' Lounge. Today's happy couple had originally planned to have a double wedding with Sonny and Maggie, but Julie, who was already pregnant at the time, had miscarried before the big day, and the event had been postponed until now.

Today, he thought as he opened the door to the lounge, Donal Donnelly has finally made an honest woman of Julie MacAteer. It had to be expressed that way because the odds of Julie making an honest man of Donal were *very* remote.

To Barry's knowledge, Donal was paying for the reception with money he had accumulated in July from a suspiciously fixed bet made on his racing greyhound, Bluebird, and from a more recent scheme selling Irish coins embossed with the image of a racehorse for eight times their face value. Donal had managed that by persuading an unsuspecting Englishman the coins were valuable medallions struck in honour of the great Irish steeplechaser, Arkle. It would not surprise Barry if Donal Donnelly tried to sell the Ballybucklebo maypole to an American tourist. It would only be surprising if the attempt failed.

The door closed quietly behind him, and he moved

close to O'Reilly at the back of a small group of formally dressed folks. Donal Donnelly stood at the far end of the room. He had changed out of his morning coat into a suit of dark blue worsted serge. His carroty hair was slicked down with Brylcreem. He was grinning widely, his buckteeth shining in the light from a cut-glass chandelier. A large glass of orange juice was in one hand, and he made broad gestures with the other, swaying quite markedly as if the gale outside was affecting only him in the warm and draughtless room.

Barry laughed and whispered to O'Reilly, "The groom's looking well."

"Huh. He should be. He was half stocious at the altar, and he's been topping off his orange juice with gin."

"Donal? I know he likes his jar but—"

"Sure can't we give him a fool's pardon for today? It's not every day he gets married."

"I'm not going to lose any sleep over it." Barry took a look at the wedding guests who stood round the room. All had glasses of soft drinks in hand. All had their backs to Barry. The atmosphere was redolent of pipe tobacco. The wedding had been a small affair, and only the happy couple and the invitees were here at the reception.

Barry saw Julie, the bride, in her going-away outfit, a neatly tailored cream suit over a maroon silk blouse. She looked well recovered from the miscarriage of three months ago. Her cornsilk hair was bright and shone to match the gleam in her green eyes. She was, as it was believed to be the duty of every bride, looking lovely. She was paying no attention to Donal but was engrossed in conversation with her maid of honour, Helen Hewitt, whose red hair was tied back with a green ribbon. Helen wore a matching green jacket and short skirt above a pair of wickedly high stilettos that accentuated her shapely legs. He was pleased to see she had not had any recurrence of the eczema behind her knees, and wondered for a moment if she was still seeing his best friend, Jack Mills.

O'Reilly bent closer and muttered to Barry, "'Two girls in silk kimonos . . .'"

"'Both beautiful, one a gazelle.' William Butler Yeats, 'In Memory of Eva Gore-Booth and Con Markiewicz.'" Barry seemed to have been playing this dueling quotations game with O'Reilly since that day he'd arrived back in July. "One a gazelle," he repeated, and for a moment his thoughts strayed to another beautiful young woman, but Patricia Spence was in Cambridge, had been there since September studying civil engineering. He wished she wasn't, but she'd be coming home soon for Christmas. Barry was counting the days.

His daydreaming was interrupted by the sound of Donal's voice carrying above the otherwise muted conversations. "Anyway, Willy, there's your man explaining to Mrs. Murphy that her husband has drowned in a vat of Guinness . . ."

Donal stood with one arm around the shoulder of his best man, Willy Dunleavy, landlord of the Black Swan pub in Ballybucklebo. It was hard to tell if Willy, who was shifting from foot to foot, was uncomfortable in his morning suit or with Donal's obviously more than happy state. Donal had originally wanted Seamus Galvin, the man O'Reilly had hurled into the rosebushes, to stand up for him, but Seamus and his wife, Maureen, and their infant son, Barry Fingal, the first baby Barry had delivered in Ballybucklebo, were now in California.

Barry saw Willy glance at an older couple sitting in chairs at the front of the room, and he guessed they were Julie's parents down from Rasharkin in County Antrim. By the look of her mother, who now had grey among the gold, Barry could tell where Julie had got her gorgeous hair. Julie's father was hunched forward, taking short breaths and scowling at his new son-in-law. The Pioneers took their abstinence very seriously. Willy must have noticed. "Wheest now, Donal." He smiled nervously at the elder MacAteers.

Oblivious to his friend's efforts at being tactful, Donal continued in a contrived stage Dublin accent, "'Jasus,' says Mrs. Murphy. 'Drownded is it? In Guinness? Did he suffer?'"

"Wheest now, Donal."

Unabashed, Donal delivered the punchline. "'Not at all, dear,' says your man." Donal took a prolonged count before announcing, "'He got out three times to take a piss.'" He guffawed loudly.

Barry had difficulty controlling his own laughter. He noticed a second older couple sitting beside the first. The man was as buck-toothed as Donal. Barry guessed he was Donal's da, and judging by the way he was guffawing, he might have had something fortifying in his orange juice too. Beside him the older MacAteer sat more rigidly and, in Barry's opinion, was feeling, like Queen Victoria, distinctly not amused.

Ignoring his new father-in-law, Donal bowed to the audience, clearly relishing being the centre of attention. Then he straightened and noticed Barry. He strode over, hiccupped, and said, "How's about ye, Doc?"

"Sorry I missed the service, Donal." Barry shook the outstretched hand.

"Never worry. Better late than never. I'm sure you'd someone to see to." He stepped back. "Come on now, you with me," he hiccupped, "and say hello to Julie."

"I'd like that, Donal."

Donal giggled. "It's Missus Donnelly now to you, Doc, so it is."

Barry followed a weaving Donal past the others, acknowledging their greetings as he passed. Finally the two men reached where Julie stood. "Julie," he said, "you're looking lovely. I'm sorry I missed—"

"Thank you, Doctor Laverty. No apologies needed." She smiled at him.

"Are you not . . . *hic* . . . are not going for to . . . *hic* . . . kiss the bride?" Donal gave Barry a shove, and he found himself just that bit too close to Julie. He laughed and took a step back. "Easy, Donal."

"Well, if you're not going to, I bloody well am." O'Reilly now stood at Barry's shoulder. "Come here, me darlin' girl." O'Reilly stretched out one big hand, took Julie's, and pulled her to him. Even in her high heels, the top of her head barely reached the big man's shoulder. He wrapped her in a bear hug and gracefully kissed the very crown of her head. "I wish," he said, and his words were solemn, "for both of you, long life, good health, prosperity, an always stocked larder, a full crib, and may your praties never know the blight."

"Thank you, Doctor O'Reilly," Julie said, blushing. She stood on tiptoe and whispered something in his ear.

"Well, I'll be damned," said O'Reilly, glancing sideways at Donal. "Well, Mrs. Donnelly, you pop in and see Doctor Laverty or me when you get back from your honeymoon."

"I will."

"Now," said O'Reilly, inclining his head toward the door, "Doctor Laverty and I have some business to attend to." He strode off, Barry at his heels. As soon as they were in the hall, he said, "Julie's up the spout again. I'll say that much for Donal. He doesn't let the grass grow under his feet."

Barry frowned. "Fingal, is it not a bit soon after her miscarriage for her to be pregnant?"

O'Reilly shrugged. "Hard to say, but I think it's great news, so great in fact that if you'd like to join me in the bar we could drink to it."

"I thought, Fingal, you'd said, seeing you are on call . . . you wouldn't be having anymore." Barry couldn't resist having a dig at his senior colleague.

"Did I say that?" O'Reilly asked. "Boys-a-dear, whatever was I thinking of?" He headed toward the bar and was just about to open the door when John, the manager, rushed along the hall.

"Doctor O'Reilly, there's a Mrs. Kincaid on the phone. She'd like to speak to you."

"Bugger," said O'Reilly.

"This way, please, sir."

"What's up?"

"I'll tell you when I get back." He vanished into the lounge, leaving Barry alone. Well, Barry thought, Fingal was right about one thing. Julie's news did call for another drink. He'd pop into the Parlour Bar, get himself a small whiskey, drink it, and go back to the party for half an hour or so to be polite. Then he'd head back to Ballybucklebo.

He opened the bar door. Just another half hour here at the Old Inn, then home to Number 1 Main Street with its big bow windows and grey pebble-dashed walls. Home to Kinky and her superb cooking. Home to Lady Macbeth, and home even to Arthur Guinness, O'Reilly's daft dog.

Barry let the door close behind him and yawned. It had been a long night last night. He was looking forward to one other thing at home: his bed in the attic bedroom, snug under the eaves, warm and protected from the gale that raged outside.

"Another one, Barry?" Colette asked.

"Just a small John Jameson, please."

"Right."

As he waited for his drink, Barry wondered what kind of case had sent O'Reilly rushing off into the night. None of his business. He wasn't on call, and as

O'Reilly was fond of saying about others, Doctor Fingal Flahertie O'Reilly, M.B., B.Ch., B.A.O., Physician and Surgeon, was big enough and ugly enough to look after himself.

2

A Little Snow, Tumbled About

The Rover shuddered as it was broadsided by a gust that came funneling through a gap between the houses. O'Reilly gripped the steering wheel more tightly and swore at the gale. "Bloody weather!" With nightfall the sleet had turned to snow.

He wondered what the trouble might be at the Gillespie farm. All Kinky had been able to tell him was that the call had come from Mrs. Gillespie, she was hysterical, and she wanted the doctor to come at once. There was something wrong with her husband.

He had to slow down because the windscreen wipers of his elderly vehicle could barely cope with the accumulation on the glass and he had difficulty seeing. O'Reilly felt the arse end of the vehicle slide sideways as he nudged her out of a turn, had to steer into the skid, and nearly went into the ditch. He wrenched the car back on course. "Bloody weather!" But it would take more than a bit of snow to stop him getting to the Gillespies' place. Molly Gillespie was usually an unflappable woman. She was unlikely to have sent for him for anything trivial on a bloody awful night like this. He'd find out when he got there, but damn it, getting there was going to take longer than he had anticipated.

At least there'd be no cyclists to get in his way on a god-awful night like tonight, and he'd certainly seen worse weather at sea on the old *Warspite* during the war, nearly twenty years ago now. He missed the camaraderie of the battleship's wardroom, and his friend Tom Laverty, the navigating officer.

Funny coincidence, young Barry being Tom's son. Of course during the war Barry would have been in nappies, and Tom, while being a convivial companion and a damn fine navigator, was, like many men of his generation, reticent about his family life. He'd never mentioned he had a son, and since the war he and Fingal had gone their separate ways, just the way the bloody Rover was trying to do by sliding toward the ditch again. O'Reilly hauled it back on course by brute force on the steering wheel. Tom Laverty was in Australia now on sabbatical. Probably kept in touch with Barry by letter. Perhaps, O'Reilly thought, he'd ask Barry for Tom's address and drop the man a line himself, let him know how well young Barry was doing as a GP.

He hoped Barry would be doing all right tonight, driving back to Ballybucklebo in that funny little German car of his. It made you wonder, O'Reilly thought. Twenty years ago the Germans and the British were trying to hammer the living bejesus out of each other. Now the same Germans were happily telling us, as they had done a year ago, in 1963, that we could whistle if we thought we were getting into the European Economic Community. Their antipathy on the trade front didn't stop them selling us a model of car originally demanded as a "people's car" by Adolf Hitler.

Their little car might be built for the people, but it hadn't been designed to cope with the narrow winding roads of Ulster in midwinter. That was what cars like the old Rover were for.

O'Reilly turned left off the main Bangor-Belfast Road, dropped into third gear, and began the grind up into the Ballybucklebo Hills. The snow had stopped falling, but all he could see ahead was an unbroken sheet of pure white covering the road. No one else had been up here to leave tracks. On each side of the road the hedges, white-crowned, black-branched, stood stark and frigid. It was a good thing the snow had only been falling for about half an hour. It couldn't be more than an inch deep.

He passed a crossroads. The lane to the Gillespies' farmhouse was a mile further on. The road would slip down into a hollow, then climb again to crest a hill, at the top of which was a stand of sycamores. The gate to the lane was just past the trees and to the left. The last time he'd been here was—he had to try to remember—three, no, four years ago.

The sycamores that now appeared to his left had been in full foliage back when Molly had given birth to the twins. Those trees tonight stood out gauntly against a backdrop of moon-silvered clouds.

He stopped the car at the lane and climbed out to open the five-bar gate. The fresh snow crunched under his boots, and the wind sighed in the trees. He felt the chill of it on his cheeks. He looked up through a gap in the clouds and saw the black of the sky and three bright stars. He'd not be seeing them if it was still snowing, and for that he was grateful. He'd not like to be stuck at the Gillespies' overnight. Deep snowdrifts were rare in Ulster but they could happen.

The gate was difficult to shove against snow, but he was able to ram it far enough open. As he guided the Rover past the gate, he was tempted to leave it open and save himself the trouble of having to reopen it on his way home. He stopped the car and walked back. Neither Molly Gillespie nor her husband Liam would be impressed if their stock wandered out through an open gateway. Come to think of it, neither would he.

The Rover jolted along the tyre-rutted lane. The bouncing dislodged some snow from the sides of the windscreen where the wipers didn't reach. O'Reilly grabbed a chamois leather from the dashboard and used it to wipe condensation from the inside of the glass.

He could make out lights from the farmhouse up ahead. One was shining through an unshuttered upstairs window. A single glass-encased bulb burned above the front door. The shutters were closed over the downstairs windows, and only errant rays crept through the chinks where the panels didn't quite meet.

He parked the car outside the front door. He'd not be sorry to get inside, and the sooner he left the car the sooner that's where he'd be. He grabbed his black bag and got out.

"Get away to hell out of that," he said sharply to the border collie that appeared from the darkness and crouched, belly low to the ground, lips curled, throat quivering, as it snarled.

"Go on. Away to hell." O'Reilly strode past the dog and was about to hammer on the door when it was thrown open by a large thirtyish woman who wore a calico pinafore and fluffy carpet slippers. He could see a little girl, thumb in mouth, peeping round the hem of her dress.

"Come in, Doctor O'Reilly." She stepped back and pushed the little girl away. "Run you away on and play with your brother."

The little girl, thumb still in her mouth, walked across the floor. O'Reilly noticed how she turned her left toes in. She stopped from time to time to stare at him with the biggest blue eyes he had ever seen. He winked at her, crossed the threshold into a spacious kitchen with a tiled floor, and said, "And what's the trouble with Liam, Molly?" He started to shrug off his coat. The room was stifling from the heat coming from a cast iron range in the corner of the kitchen. "Kinky said you sounded upset."

"I'm better now," she said. "I lost the bap when I

seen Liam lying there out in the barn. I tried for to lift him, but he's a big man and I couldn't budge him so I ran in here and phoned." She held one fist in her other hand and, resting her chin on top, pursed her lips and stared at the floor. Then she looked O'Reilly in the eye. "I thought he was dead, so I did."

O'Reilly stopped with his coat sleeves halfway down his arms. "Is he in the barn yet?"

"No." She raised her eyes to the ceiling above. "He's in bed up there. By the time I was off the phone and heading back to the barn, Liam was on his way here."

O'Reilly finished taking off his coat. "Can you tell me exactly what happened?"

"For the life of me, Doctor, I don't know. We'd brung the cattle in out of the snow. Liam was getting a bale from the hayloft. I'd my back turned to him. I heard a thump, turned round, and there he was . . . out like a light. I couldn't rouse him, so like I said, I phoned you."

"Ma-aa . . ." The four-year-old came in through the kitchen door. "Ma, Johnny's just shit his pants."

"Just wait a wee minute, Jenny. Mammy's busy."

"Liam got back here under his own steam?"

"Aye. He wanted me to phone back and tell you not to bother coming."

Typical of countryfolk not wanting to put anyone to trouble, O'Reilly thought, "It's all right, Molly. Liam's in your room, is he?"

"Aye."

"Ma-aa . . . he's shit himself."

"Mother of God, go and get your brother into the bathroom. I'll be along in a wee minute, so I will."

"I'll find my own way up there. You see to the kids."

"Thanks, Doctor." She stepped across to the four-year-old, grabbed her by the hand, frowned, and said, "I've told you before, don't you say shit."

"It's what Daddy says, so it is . . ."

The debate was continuing as O'Reilly left the kitchen, climbed a flight of stairs, went along a landing, and let himself into a bedroom where on one side of a double bed Liam Gillespie lay propped up on a couple of pillows on top of the eiderdown. "Come on in, Doc. I'm sorry we'd to trouble you on a night like this."

Liam was indeed, as Molly had said, a big man. O'Reilly guessed he'd be about six and a half feet tall and would weigh a good fourteen stone. He looked pale and was sweating.

"It's no trouble, Liam." O'Reilly sat on the edge of the bed. "What happened?"

"I was stupid. I was lifting down a bale of hay from the hayloft, and I slipped and fell, so I did."

"Hit your head, did you?" O'Reilly peered at the man's eyes, noticing that both of the pupils were the same size.

"Divil the bit. No. I hit my ribs, here on the left . . ." He pointed to just above where his shirt disappeared beneath the thick leather belt that held up his moleskin trousers. "I must have hit myself a ferocious dunder, for I passed out. I don't know how long I was out for."

"Can't have been very long. You were heading back here by the time Molly phoned me."

"Right enough. So it was only a wee short turn I took?"

"Did you pass out before or after you fell?" O'Reilly reached for Liam's wrist and took his pulse. The skin was clammy.

"After. I remember hitting the corner of a workbench. The pain was ferocious in my ribs for a wee second, and then I was coming to lying on the floor."

The man's pulse was rapid and thready. "Still sore in your side?"

"Aye. But I can thole it."

"Let's have a look." O'Reilly had long ago learnt of the stoicism of many of the countryfolk. If one of the important diagnostic symptoms of any condition was pain, having a man like Liam Gillespie say he could put up with it did not necessarily mean that the pain was not severe. Fourteen stone falling on the corner of a bench would probably have cracked a rib or two, and of more consequence the spleen lay beneath the lower left ribs.

Liam started to pull his shirt out of the waistband of his trousers, but then flinched, sucked air between his teeth, and gasped, "Ah, Jesus."

"Sore?"

"Bloody right."

"Here, let me." O'Reilly unbuckled the man's belt, unbuttoned his shirt, then pulled out the faded blue shirt. There was a bruise as big as a soup plate. O'Reilly stood to face the patient. "This may hurt a wee bit,

Liam." He put the flat of one hand on top of the bruise and slipped the other hand under the man's chest. Liam whimpered when O'Reilly squeezed, and he felt a grating sensation. "Sorry about that. You've a rib or two bust there."

Liam nodded but did not speak. His forehead glistened in the light from the overhead bulb.

Pain could certainly make a man sweat, and O'Reilly had no difficulty being empathetic with anyone with broken ribs. A bloody great boot from an opposing forward had caved in three of his own ribs during a rugby game years ago, and he could still remember the grating pain every time he took a deep breath.

He also remembered vividly another game when a player had taken a thumping, gone to the sidelines to rest for a few minutes, come back to play out the rest of the game—and collapsed in the dressing room. He'd had a ruptured spleen.

Were Liam's broken ribs alone sufficient to account for his rapid, thready pulse? O'Reilly shook his head. He moved one hand beneath Liam's ribcage on the left side and tried to depress the muscles of the abdominal wall. They were stiff as a board and unyielding. "Am I hurting you, Liam?"

"By Jesus, you are, Doc." Liam's words had difficulty getting past his clenched teeth.

O'Reilly lifted his hand gently away. "Can you stand up?"

"I can try." He started to swing his legs over the side of the bed.

O'Reilly waited, hoping the man would succeed. If

Liam couldn't make it under his own steam, O'Reilly wasn't sure he was strong enough to carry the two hundred-pound man downstairs. O'Reilly was sure the man had a ruptured spleen. The giveaway was his pallor and rapid pulse, along with the rigidity of the abdominal muscles caused almost certainly by blood in the peritoneal cavity. And there was no guarantee that the bleeding from the damaged organ would stop. Death from haemorrhagic shock was a real risk.

"Jesus, Doc," Liam said, "I'm weak as a baby." He breathed in short gasps.

"We've to get you downstairs." O'Reilly lifted Liam's right arm and draped it around his own left shoulder. "Come on. I'll oxter-cog you."

A ruptured spleen had to be treated at once by surgical removal of the damaged organ. That meant Liam must be taken to the nearest hospital, and it was unlikely that an ambulance, with the necessary attendants to carry him out to the vehicle, could get here in under four hours—if at all with the snow on the roads. If O'Reilly was right, Liam could bleed to death in less time.

God, he weighed a ton, but he was doing his best to help. Together they made it to the top of the stairs when Liam gasped, "Can we . . . rest for . . . a wee . . . minute?"

O'Reilly himself was panting, and each indrawn breath burnt his lungs. He coughed. Maybe there was some truth in what Barry and young doctors like him were saying about tobacco smoking being bad for your health. "Can . . . can you manage a bit more, Liam?"

Obviously too weak to speak, Liam nodded.

O'Reilly steadied them by putting his hand on the banister and slowly descending, one step at a time. An ornamental wooden bench stood in the hall below. O'Reilly debated sitting Liam down on it so they both could rest but decided against it. He might not get the man back on his feet again. "Come on, Liam . . . almost there," he said, as they reached the hall. He was more than supporting the man now. Liam's legs were limp, and his feet dragged.

In the kitchen Molly looked up from a sink where she was rinsing a pair of boy's short pants and underpants. "Jesus, Mary, and Joseph."

"It's all right, Molly. If you could just . . . open the back door, the back door of the car, and then go and get . . . a couple of blankets . . ." O'Reilly heard his chest wheezing.

She hurried to the door, threw it open, and ran outside.

O'Reilly felt the chill and saw snowflakes being blown inside.

"I'll get the blankets." She dashed past him, leaving behind her a trail of wet footprints on the tiles.

O'Reilly hauled in one last deep breath, pursed his lips, and forced himself to march ahead, through the kitchen, out the door, and through the lying snow and the once more flying flakes that reflected the rays of light coming from the bulb above the back door. Liam's head lolled against O'Reilly's shoulder.

Thank Christ Molly had opened the Rover's back door. It took his last reserves, but O'Reilly managed to stuff Liam into the back of the car. He stood, hands on the roof, ignoring the chill in them, head bent, mouth gaping as he pulled in lungful after lungful. He could only nod when Molly appeared with blankets, but by the time she had tucked them around Liam, O'Reilly was able to speak.

"You stay with Liam for a minute. I've to make a phone call."

"The phone's in the kitchen."

He didn't reply but headed straight back to the house, picked up the phone, and dialed the Casualty Department of the Royal Victoria Hospital.

"Hello. Who's that? Registrar on duty? Great. Listen, I need an ambulance sent to the Holywood Arches on the outskirts of Belfast. I'll need six units of O-positive blood and . . . I beg your pardon? Who do I think I am?" He could feel the blood draining from the tip of his nose. He knew he should be polite, but Liam Gillespie could die if he wasn't treated soon. "Son. I don't *think* I'm anybody. I bloody well *know* who I am. I'm Doctor—did you get that, son?—*Doctor* Fingal Flahertie O'Reilly from Ballybucklebo. I'm at a farm at the arse end of nowhere up in the Ballybucklebo Hills, and I have a patient with a ruptured spleen. That's right. No, I don't want the ambulance here. I've the patient in the back of my car, and I'll have him at the Arches by the time the ambulance gets there . . . You're not sure you can arrange that? You're too junior to order an ambulance on your own authority? Jesus.

Who's your boss tonight? . . . Sir Donald Cromie?" Sometimes, O'Reilly thought, honey catches more flies than vinegar. He lowered his voice from its quarterdeck-at-sea-in-a-gale level and gently said, "Well look, son, you give old Numb Nuts . . . that's right, Numb Nuts . . . he and I played rugby together years ago . . . give him a call right away, tell him who phoned and why, and I'll be surprised if the ambulance isn't waiting for me at the Arches . . . You will do that? Good lad."

O'Reilly hung up and looked round for his overcoat. He'd have a quick word with Molly, tell her what was going on, send her back to her kids. Then he'd drive up to the Holywood Arches and make sure Liam was safely transferred to the ambulance and transfused if necessary.

O'Reilly lifted the coat from the peg and paused as a sudden gust whirled fresh flakes in through the open door. He'd better get a move on. If it started to drift up on the country roads, even the Rover could have difficulty getting through, and he wasn't sure how long Liam could live if they got stuck. O'Reilly's jaw muscles tightened. By God, Liam Gillespie was going to survive for the rest of his natural span if Fingal O'Reilly had anything to do about it.

He hauled his coat on, strode to the door, and headed back to the Rover.

"Go in and get warm, Molly."

He climbed in, started the engine, and waited as Molly dropped a small kiss on Liam's forehead.

"Go on," O'Reilly said. "He'll be fine. I have to

go." The second Molly shut the back door he put the car in gear, hunched his shoulders when the tyres spun for a moment before gripping the icy mud of the farmyard, and then relaxed as the big car lurched forward.

As the car jolted down the farm lane, occasional snowflakes dancing in the beams of the headlights, he chided himself for taking things so personally. He'd done everything possible for Liam—more by driving him. If the weather conspired to frustrate his efforts and he did lose his patient, it would hardly be his fault. Every doctor should bloody well know that.

O'Reilly stopped at the gate and unlatched it. Then he wrenched it open so forcibly that he bent the top bar. Lose Liam? A few weeks before Christmas? He snorted, and his breath clouds made a little smoke screen.

"Hang on," he called to the backseat as he drove through the gate and onto the road. The gate would just have to stay open. Getting Liam to the ambulance was a damn sight more important than a few stray beasts—and anyway weren't they in the byre?

The going was easier on the road. He'd get through all right so he could stop worrying and concentrate on his driving, and if all went according to plan, O'Reilly grinned, he'd be back at Number 1 Main Street in a couple of hours. His tummy rumbled. He hoped Mrs. Kincaid would keep him something decent to eat. Of course she would, unless young Laverty, who should be home by now, had scoffed the lot.

3

The Cobbler's Children Are the Worst Shod

Somebody opened the front door, and Barry felt the draught in the dining room. Boots clumped in the hall and then paused. O'Reilly would be hanging up his overcoat. Barry was curious about what had taken the man out into this gale and wondered what would be considered a decent interval before asking. O'Reilly's main preoccupation, quite naturally, would be his stomach. The dining room door flew open, and the big man, blowing on his fingers, stamped in. O'Reilly, Barry thought, never so much entered a room as took it with all the enthusiasm of a storming party assaulting a breach in a castle wall. O'Reilly slammed the door behind him.

"Good evening, Fingal," Barry said. He noticed the snowflakes in O'Reilly's hair. As O'Reilly clumped past to dump his bulk into his usual chair, he grumbled, "There's bugger all good about it. It's cold as a witch's tit, and snowing again out there to beat Banagher. I damn nearly didn't make it back from the Holywood Arches." He coughed, a dry hacking sound, pulled a steaming tureen to him, and ladled stew and a lonely suet dumpling onto his plate. "Decent of you to leave me *one* of Kinky's dumplings," he remarked, with his mouth already full.

"I thought you might appreciate it. They were *very* good." It was childish, Barry knew, but he remembered a night not so long ago when he'd been out on a case and had come home famished to discover that O'Reilly had polished off a whole roast duck. Barry had, after all, left the senior man a dumpling.

Barry heard the door open and half turned to see Mrs. Kincaid, carrying a dish. She had a soft look on her face. "I heard that, Doctor Laverty. I am glad you enjoyed them, so." She moved to the head of the table and lifted the lid of the tureen. "There's only a shmall, little bit of the stew left, but enough to wet these with the gravy." And so saying, she lifted the dish in one beefy hand and put more dumplings into the tureen.

"You, Kinky, are a miracle worker," said O'Reilly, grabbing the tureen and dumping the entire contents onto his plate. He hacked again.

"And you, Doctor O'Reilly, sir . . ."—she glanced at his ample waistline—"need to go a bit easier on the starches but, och, it is a dirty night out and a body needs a good inside lining."

"Indeed, Kinky. Indeed." O'Reilly impaled the last dumpling on his fork and used it to mop up the remainder of the gravy. "Your stew would give a man the inside lining that beats the cold." He stifled another cough.

Barry saw Kinky's eyes narrow as she bent to peer more closely at O'Reilly's ordinarily florid face. "Is it a chill you have, Doctor dear?" she asked.

"Me? Not at all . . . a bit of a dumpling went down the wrong way."

She sniffed, as she herself would say, with enough force to suck a small cat up a chimney. "It sounds like a chill to me."

O'Reilly's laugh ended in another dry hack. "Mrs. Kinky Kincaid, when I come into your kitchen and advise you on the baking of a ham, you can start the doctoring. Is that fair?"

She pursed her lips and shook her head at him, turned, and started to leave, saying, "I expect you two gentlemen would like some coffee and a slice of cherry cake?"

"Kinky," said Barry, "you are a mind reader."

"Well, trot on upstairs the pair of you, and I'll bring something up to the lounge. There's a fire lit and it's cosier." She hesitated at the door. "It'll be better for that chest of yours, Doctor O'Reilly, so."

"My chest's fine, Kinky." Barry heard the edge of finality creeping into O'Reilly's voice and was surprised when Kinky said, "It's not my place to say, I know, but I've heard it remarked that doctors who doctor themselves have *amadáns* for patients." She left before O'Reilly could answer.

Barry, who had no Gaelic, asked, "What's an 'omadawn,' Fingal?"

"An idiot," said O'Reilly. "If anybody else called me that, I'd . . ."

Barry shuddered.

"Sure," O'Reilly said, rising, "it's only her way of showing she's concerned. And I'm right as rain." He walked past Barry. "Come on up the stairs and I'll tell you about the case I'm just back from."

Kinky was right. It was cosy in the upstairs lounge. The curtains over the windows were drawn to keep the heat in and the night out. One curtain fluttered each time a strong gust hit the house, and the old window sashes weren't completely airtight, but the warmth from a coal fire burning in the grate kept the winter chill at bay.

Lady Macbeth, O'Reilly's white cat, had preempted the space on the rug directly in front of the grill of the grate. She was what O'Reilly called "inside out." Her pink nose was tucked into her belly, her tail curled over the top of her head, and in this posture she had somehow managed to manoeuver herself so that she lay on her back.

Arthur Guinness, O'Reilly's black Labrador, lay flopped at the edge of the rug, his big square head on his paws. He looked dolefully from Lady Macbeth to O'Reilly, as if to say, "That *thing* is in *my* place."

O'Reilly bent and scratched the big dog's head. Arthur's tail flopped from side to side. "I let him come into the house when the weather's really nasty, but he's meant to stay in the kitchen. Aren't you, sir?"

"Arf," said Arthur, giving not the slightest indication he was going to move.

O'Reilly parked himself in one of the big armchairs.

Barry took the other. He leant back and stretched his legs out in front. God, but it was comfortable. As curious as he was about O'Reilly's patient, if he wasn't careful, Barry could easily fall asleep. His head nodded onto his chest, and his eyelids drooped.

He heard the scraping of a match on sandpaper and smelled the sharp aroma of O'Reilly's pipe tobacco. His half-doze was shattered by O'Reilly's paroxysm of coughing. Barry sat bolt upright and stared at his older colleague. O'Reilly bent forward in his chair, arms crossed in front of his stomach, eyes so tightly shut that Barry could see tiny trickles of water being squeezed from their corners.

The outburst scared Lady Macbeth, and Barry was distracted by the white blur of her fleeing from the room and almost colliding with Kinky, who was coming in. He saw Kinky's eyes widen as she shoved her tray onto the sideboard. She pointed at O'Reilly and, eyes fixed on Barry's, jerked her head in O'Reilly's direction. He nodded and rose, intending to go to his senior colleague and perhaps examine him.

O'Reilly straightened up, wiped the back of his hand across his eyes, took a deep breath, blew it out, and said, "Boys-a-boys, maybe those English experts are right." He stared at his weakly smoking briar, still grasped in his left hand, "This tobacco isn't all that good for you. Particularly when a fellah's been out on a night like this, lugging a great heavy man around and straining his own lungs."

O'Reilly's remark about tobacco not being good for you was something of an understatement, Barry thought, as he peered into O'Reilly's face, hoping the big man had not noticed his sudden frown of concern. Seven years ago the British Medical Research Council had come down heavily in favour of the cause-and-effect relationship between cigarette smoking and lung cancer. He'd taken the warning seriously enough to have quit a year ago. But the same scientists didn't seem unduly concerned about pipe tobacco, so there was probably nothing sinister happening to O'Reilly. Barry's frown vanished.

His speculation was cut short by O'Reilly coughing loudly once more. He took another deep breath and stared up at Barry and across to Mrs. Kincaid. "Jesus," he said, "by the faces on the pair of you, you'd think you'd both seen Lazarus rising from the dead. Would you sit down, Barry?"

Barry said levelly, "Fingal, you had the next bloody thing to an asthmatic seizure a minute ago. We were worried about you."

O'Reilly cleared his throat. "Nothing to worry about. Sit down."

"We *were* worried—"

"Well, you can stop worrying. Right now. I told you, I must have inflamed the tubes a bit hauling in great lungfuls of cold air when I was half carrying Liam Gillespie to my car. I'm fit as a fiddle. I'll be over this in no time." O'Reilly's cheeks were more florid than usual, but his nose tip was alabaster.

Barry realized it was useless to argue. He sat.

"Now," said O'Reilly, dumping his pipe in the ashtray and rubbing his hands together, "is that the coffee and your cherry cake, Kinky?"

"Aye, so."

"Then let's be at them. Will you pour, Kinky?"

Barry heard Mrs. Kincaid sniff for the second time that night, and to his surprise he heard O'Reilly add an uncharacteristic "Please?"

"I will," she said, starting to pour. "And will I maybe get a kettle warmed to fix a bit of friar's balsam for you to inhale?"

O'Reilly seemed to consider the offer, then said, "All right, but just bring up the boiling water and the brown bottle."

Barry was surprised to see the big man cave in so readily to Kinky's suggestion. It would be something to see, O'Reilly sitting at the table with a jug of boiling water and aromatic herbs, towel over his head like a primitive oxygen tent, inhaling the reputedly beneficial fumes.

"Right," said Mrs. Kincaid, bringing her tray with two cups of coffee and a plate with slabs of her cherry cake over to the coffee table. "I'll go and see to it." She left the room.

Barry lifted his coffee cup.

O'Reilly grabbed a slab of cherry cake, took a large bite, and coughed. "Bejesus," he said. "I've a powerful tickle, so I have." He winked. "But it's not Kinky's balsam that'll be the cure of it." He eyed the decanter on the sideboard, and Barry thought of the hot whiskey he'd had himself not so very long ago. You couldn't make a hot Irish without boiling water.

Arthur had stirred himself and now sat directly in front of O'Reilly, head tilted, black eyes fixed on every move of the hand that held the cherry cake, twin strings of saliva hanging from the corners of his mouth.

"You should never feed a gun dog people food," O'Reilly said quite seriously, as he shoved the last piece of his cake into Arthur's mouth. "Now," he said, "if my little bit of a hirstle is of no further interest, I suppose you'd like to hear about who I went to see?"

"Yes, I would. I didn't know we'd patients as far away as the Holywood Arches."

"We don't. I went to see the Gillespies. They farm up in the Hills. When I saw Liam, I was pretty sure he had a ruptured spleen so I arranged for an ambulance—"

"To meet you at the Holywood Arches, and you ran him up there in your car." O'Reilly's habit of transporting his patients no longer came as a shock to Barry; indeed he himself occasionally ran someone to the hospital if the urgency was great enough. Back in August he'd driven today's bride, Julie, to the Royal when she'd been miscarrying.

"Bloody good thing I did too," O'Reilly said. "Liam was flat as a pancake when I got him there, but the ambulance was waiting and we were able to get him aboard and a blood transfusion started. His blood pressure came up after we'd got a couple of pints into him."

"And he'll have his spleen out tonight?"

"I would imagine—" Whatever he was about to imagine was interrupted by a crash.

Barry jumped at the sudden sound and tried to understand what had happened. Lady Macbeth must have crept back into the room, jumped onto the tray to try to get at the milk jug, and tipped the whole shebang over. The tray had fallen from the coffee table, and the milk jug lay overturned on the carpet. Lady Macbeth, howling like a banshee, tail fluffed like an electrocuted lavatory brush, was halfway up a window curtain and heading north to the pelmet. Arthur Guinness, without a by-your-leave, was finishing the last slice of cherry cake.

"Jesus," said O'Reilly, shooing Arthur away. "It's like feeding time at Whipsnade bloody Zoo." He turned and stared at Lady Macbeth, where she now sat on the pelmet above the curtains, washing her paws. "And you, madam, can stay there. You clawed me the last time I had to get you down."

Barry, bending to recover the tray and its contents and then setting them on the table again, remembered the incident. He was making a mental note that he too was not going to volunteer to rescue O'Reilly's cat when O'Reilly hacked loudly and said, as if the carnage of a moment ago simply had not happened, "Aye. Liam would have his spleen out tonight, I'm sure, and with a bit of luck he'll be home and up and doing in time for Christmas." He coughed and spluttered again, hauled a hanky from a trouser pocket, and dabbed his eyes.

"And," said Barry, as gently as he could, "I'd think by the sound of you that all that gallivanting around in a snowstorm in that old Rover car has given you a touch of tracheitis. Do you think we'll have *you* up and doing in time for Christmas?"

"Course we will," O'Reilly said. "I'll have to be. Christmas is only three weeks away. We could be busy in the surgery for the first two weeks; the customers'll want to get their aches and pains sorted out before Christmas week. It's flu and sniffles and coughs and colds season. It could take the pair of us to manage the practice." He coughed and frowned.

"I could cope by myself for a few days, you know." Barry rather relished the thought of even more independence.

"I don't doubt it for one minute, son, but it's not just the practice. The whole village goes daft."

"Oh?"

"What with Rugby Club parties, the kiddies' Christmas pageant, His Lordship's open house . . . dear God, even the Bishops have a do on Boxing Day . . ."

"Councillor Bertie Bishop has a party?" Barry's eyebrows and the tone of his voice shot up. Bertie Bishop was the meanest man in all of the Six Counties.

"I think," said O'Reilly, "he must watch *A Christmas Carol* with Alastair Sim on the telly every year. What happens to Scrooge probably bothers him for a day or two, so he tries to act like a Christian gentleman. He's like most people. His Christmas spirit soon fades. It usually lasts until about Twelfth Night; then he reverts to his usual great gobshite self."

"I'll be damned."

"I don't want to miss out on the fun, and I don't want you to miss out on it either, but I'm going to be bugger all use until this clears up." O'Reilly strangled a small hack. "But that won't take long."

"Fingal, I told you. I can manage."

"Well, that's a mercy that one of you two gentlemen can." Barry turned to see Kinky coming into the room. She carried a folded towel over one forearm the way a waiter would in a classy restaurant. She set a large tray on the sideboard. He could see a steaming kettle, an assortment of bowls, and a bottle of brown fluid. "I suppose you've a notion that spilled milk tidies itself up?" She glowered at the damp stain on the carpet.

"Sorry, Kinky," Barry said.

"Men." But she had a grin on her face. "All right," she said, "we'll get you seen to first, sir." She lifted a small bowl off the tray, set it on the sideboard, and carried the rest over to a larger table in the bay of one of the windows. "Will you please come here, Doctor O'Reilly?" She busied herself spooning the brown, glutinous liquid into the bowl and then pouring boiling water over it. The room filled with dark, pungent fumes that made Barry's eyes water. "Now, Doctor O'Reilly, dear, sit you here . . ." She indicated a chair beside the table.

O'Reilly rose, wandered over, and sat.

"Put your head over the bowl . . ."

Barry could see how the rising steam enveloped O'Reilly's bent head.

"And get in under this." She took the towel off her

arm and draped the material over his head. Tendrils of the vapors escaped around the edges of the towel. He looked, Barry thought, like an Arabian sheik in a London pea souper. "Now," she said, "that'll loosen your chest, so. Mind you, my granny would have given you an infusion of carrageen and nasturtium seeds to drink with it."

O'Reilly muttered something that Barry missed, but Kinky must have heard. "All right, all right," she said. "Don't I know what you are after? And haven't I brought the makings? You'll get your hot whiskey. It'll be just right for you to have one after you've been in there for fifteen minutes." She wagged a finger at the crouched O'Reilly. "And not one minute less, do you hear, Doctor dear?"

Barry heard a muffled "yes, Kinky" coming from under the towel.

"Now," she said, taking her tray back to the sideboard, "Doctor Laverty, do you have it in you to make himself a wee hot half?"

"I do."

"I'd be grateful if you would, sir, while I trot downstairs to get the things to clean up the stain on the carpet." She tutted. "How you managed to spill it—"

"Kinky, would you look up?" Barry pointed to the pelmet where Lady Macbeth was now scenting the air, her pink nose whiffling as the balsam's fumes drifted in her direction. "There's the culprit."

Kinky's round face broke into an enormous grin.

"Och, well then, she's forgiven." She called directly up to Lady Macbeth, "For you're nothing but a wee dote, so. Y'are, y'are." And with that she left.

Barry rose and busied himself making a hot Irish for Fingal. He decided against having another drink himself. He really was getting sleepy. He spooned sugar into a mug.

"Barry?" O'Reilly's voice was muffled by the towel.

"Yes, Fingal?"

"About you managing on your own?"

"Yes." Barry added a measure of John Jameson's from the decanter on the sideboard.

"See if you think we're maybe a tad less busy than we used to be."

Barry hesitated as he was about to squeeze some lemon juice into the mug. "Do you think we are? I'm not sure. I haven't really thought about it."

"I just wondered," O'Reilly said. "I hear we may have a bit of competition."

"Oh?"

"Aye. Some new doctor's moved into the Kinnegar since Doctor Bowman retired in September."

"And you think he might be pinching some of our patients?"

"Not if I'm on my feet he won't."

Barry stiffened. "Do you not think the patients will stay for me too?" The lemon juice dripped into the whiskey. Christ, Barry thought, I sound as bitter as the bloody juice. "Forget I said that, Fingal. I understand what you're saying. Of course the customers are more used to you. They bloody well ought to be after twenty-odd years." He threw a couple of cloves into the mug. "Anyway," he said, pouring in the almost boiling water from the kettle, "we *will* have you on your feet in no time. And I will be able to manage on my own for a few days. And Fingal? I'm on call tonight." A gust buffeted against the windows. "You're not going out again in that lot."

"Thanks, Barry."

"I'm glad you agree." Barry was just about to carry the whiskey to O'Reilly when Kinky reappeared. "I believe," she said, "it was to be a full fifteen minutes before we gave that to himself?"

Barry replaced the mug on the tray and glanced at his watch. "Sorry, Kinky."

She was marching to the place where the milk had stained the carpet when Barry heard a plaintive mew drifting from above. He and Kinky both looked up to see Lady Macbeth huddled at the furthest end of the pelmet, clearly trying to escape the ever-increasing miasma of balsam fumes. "The poor wee craytur." Mrs. Kincaid moved under the pelmet and stood close to O'Reilly. "Come on now, jump you down and Kinky'll catch you. She will, so."

Lady Macbeth crouched, hunched, sprang—and missed Kinky completely, but the towel over O'Reilly's head served as a safety net. The scene unfolded before Barry's eyes like a slow-motion film loop. Lady Macbeth hitting the fabric and disappearing into its folds.

The towel being pulled from O'Reilly's head, allowing Barry to watch as his senior partner was bent forward by the combined weight of cat and towel until his nose was forced into the bowl of balsam. The film loop had a soundtrack: a cat's eldritch screech, a doctor's basso roar. O'Reilly rose to his feet, hand clutching his nose. Arthur trotted over, head thrown back, yodeling, tail going ninety to the dozen. Mrs. Kincaid clapped one hand over her opened mouth, and Barry Laverty, bent double with laughter, had to turn his back on the entire assembly.

Oh dear, oh dear. He tried to collect himself. In such a household as this, where the unexpected was the norm, how could he possibly worry about O'Reilly's cough, the new doctor in competition, or the fact that he was all alone right now to run the practice. And even if he wasn't called out tonight, he'd be on his own in the surgery tomorrow. He would continue to be alone until O'Reilly, who he could see standing and using the towel to dry his nose, was figuratively as well as literally back on his feet again.

4

The Daily Round, the Common Task

O'Reilly was definitely not on his feet yet. Forty minutes earlier when Barry had walked softly past the big man's bedroom door, he'd heard distinct rumbling snores, noises akin to the purring of a pride of lions he'd seen in a TV documentary by Armand and Michaela Denis. Now he was finishing his breakfast alone.

"You've time for another cup of tea. It's Twinings, so." Mrs. Kincaid fussed with the teapot, pouring the tea through a silver strainer into Barry's cup. "Here's the milk."

Barry knew better than to refuse. "Thanks, Kinky."

"Now get that into you like a good lad, and I'll trot upstairs in a minute and see how himself is doing."

Barry saw the twinkle in her agate eyes and the deepening of smile lines at their corners. Someone in Kinky's ancestry, he thought, must have been a close relative of Florence Nightingale. Nothing seemed to make her happier than ministering unto her charges.

He added milk to his tea as Kinky cleared his breakfast dishes and left. Barry yawned and sipped. Thank the Lord there'd been no emergencies after they'd gone to bed last night. Barry hadn't minded taking calls for O'Reilly, but he'd needed his night's sleep. The weather probably explained why no one had summoned him last night. If they thought the roads were blocked, they'd not want to drag him out unless it was an absolute emergency. And perhaps, the thought nagged, if they lived closer to the Kinnegar they might be giving the new doctor a try.

Between laughing at the mayhem caused by Lady Macbeth and plummeting into a deep and dreamless sleep there had been little time for worry, but the appearance of the competition O'Reilly had mentioned did have to be taken seriously. Barry was no health economist, but the question remained. Were there enough patients in the territory of Ballybucklebo and the Kinnegar to sustain three busy doctors who were paid an annual fee by the Ministry of Health for every patient who belonged to their practices? Old Doctor Bowman had been no threat, and his practice list had been small. He'd been semiretired. But a new man? Och, well, Barry thought, "Sufficient unto the day is the evil thereof." And Saint Luke should have known. He was a physician.

Barry swallowed more tea. He looked through the window at six-inch-deep ridges of snow on the wall of the churchyard opposite. In Ulster snow was rare, and a fall like last night's, which would be brushed aside as irrelevant by a North American prairie dweller, could paralyse rural Ireland.

It had stopped falling sometime through the night, and this morning the sky was bright, eggshell blue. The sun was already making water drip from icicles hanging from the eaves of the Presbyterian church opposite O'Reilly's house. One of the icy stalactites caught and refracted the sun's rays, and Barry smiled to see the frozen water sparkle on one side and release a tiny perfect rainbow of colour on the other.

Shiny black slates peeped wetly through the snow that clung to the roof. As he watched, a snow floe slithered off the north side of the tilted steeple.

The boughs of old yews in the churchyard were bent, and from their white and dark green branches drops and drips pattered to the ground, digging small pits in the otherwise even carpet. Like a scene from a Christmas card, a single robin redbreast perched on a lower branch, its scarlet feathers in cheerful contrast to its wintry surroundings.

Barry wondered why so many Christmas card publishers favoured scenes with a Dickensian flavour. Probably because when Dickens had been writing *A Christmas Carol* and Currier and Ives were producing their famous prints, all of Europe had been in the grip of what meteorologists refer to as the Little Ice Age. Lord alone knew the last time the Thames had frozen over in modern times, but it certainly had back then.

Barry glanced at his watch. He would be five minutes early, but with Doctor O'Reilly *hors de combat*, today was going to be the first time he would run the practice alone. And he wanted to get started. Barry rose, wiped his lips on his napkin, crumpled the Belfast linen square on the tabletop, and went into the hall.

The door opposite lay open to what had been the downstairs lounge when Number 1 Main Street had been a private house. He knew that had O'Reilly been a specialist, the facility would be referred to as his "consulting rooms," and had he been an American it would be his "office." In Irish general practice, the time-hallowed term for the place was "the surgery," and it was in the surgery he would be spending the morning dealing with the kind of patient O'Reilly often called the "worried well." Few if any would have serious ailments, but all would be concerned enough to have taken the trouble to come here.

He walked to the waiting room and opened the door a crack. Even though he had been here for five months, the god-awful roses on the wallpaper still had the power to make him wince. He could picture Oscar Wilde, for whom Barry's senior partner Fingal Flahertie had been named, uttering his famous last words: "Either that wallpaper goes, or I do."

He'd once heard of an incautious senior consultant at the Royal Victoria Hospital in Belfast paraphrase the lines during a spat with the hospital's senior nursing officer, the matron. "Either you go or I do." Matron was still there.

Barry opened the door fully.

"Morning, Doctor Laverty," several voices said. It was a muted greeting. Only about a dozen of the wooden chairs were occupied. Was it simply because the roads were bad and anyone with a relatively trivial complaint was waiting until the weather improved before coming in? Or was it that . . . ? Bugger it, he told himself. Stop worrying about the new doctor and get on with your job.

"Right, who's first?" he asked, wondering if one day somebody might think to introduce an appointments system.

An angular, middle-aged woman rose. She was wearing a stylishly cut navy blue raincoat, the lines of which were not exactly complemented by her massive rubber galoshes. Her pepper-and-salt hair was pulled back into a severe bun. Her hatchet face wore a scowl that Barry thought might have been stitched on by a plastic surgeon bearing a grudge. She did not use the customary "Me, Doctor," but merely glared at the other occupants as if daring them to challenge her priority.

"Miss Moloney," he said. "How nice to see you." You hypocrite, Laverty, he thought. "Please come this way."

Miss Moloney was the proprietress of the Ballybucklebo Boutique, the local ladies' dress shop. No one had seen her in the village since she'd had an unfortunate run-in with Helen Hewitt, the redhead who had been Julie MacAteer's bridesmaid. Back in August, Miss Moloney had acquired new stock to be sold to the ladies of the village for a wedding—Sonny and Maggie's wedding. She'd not bargained for her shop assistant Helen, whom she had been persecuting mercilessly. The day before the big sale Helen had removed every single hat from its box, lined them up on the floor—and stamped every one of them flat.

Helen had quit, and the eczema that had been plaguing her for months had cleared up. Miss Moloney, rather than face the derision of the villagers, had made a diplomatic and prolonged visit to her sister, who lived in the village of Millisle on the Belfast Lough side of the Ards Peninsula. Now, Barry thought, she's come back.

He followed her into the familiar, thinly carpeted room with its examining couch, folding screens, and instrument cabinet along one green-painted wall. At least the Snellen eye-testing chart above a wall-mounted sphygmomanometer no longer hung crookedly. He'd straightened it a couple of months ago. If O'Reilly had noticed, he hadn't commented.

Above the old rolltop desk, Barry's year-old 1963 diploma from Queen's University, Belfast, signed by Sir Tyrone Guthrie, its script clean and fresh, kept company with O'Reilly's 1936 degree from Trinity College, Dublin.

"Please have a seat." He indicated one of the hard wooden chairs.

Miss Moloney sat on the edge of the chair, back erect, hands primly clasped in her lap. Barry moved past her to take the swivel chair on casters. "Welcome back," he said. "How was Millisle?"

She sniffed. "Cold, damp, windy, and desolate."

"Well, it is winter, you know."

"How astute of you to notice, Doctor."

He cleared his throat. It would seem that the milk of human kindness was still curdled in Miss Moloney.

The sooner he got this conversation on a professional level, the better. "So what seems to be the trouble?"

"I'm very tired."

"I see. And anything else?"

She shook her head.

Not a lot to go on. Tiredness could simply be a reflection of not enough sleep, or overwork, unlikely in her case, or it could be a clue to almost any disorder in the entire medical textbook. Barry sat back. He steepled his fingers, just as he'd seen O'Reilly do a thousand times, and looked at her face.

She was extraordinarily pale. "Hmm," he said to himself, as he leant forward and took her hand in his. It felt cold and clammy. He held it palm down and looked at her neatly trimmed fingernails. They were a most peculiar shape. Each was concave, like the bowl of a shallow teaspoon; the technical term for this was *koilonychia*, and it was usually associated with iron-deficiency anaemia. Interesting.

"Just look into the distance, please." He used one thumb beneath each of her eyes to pull the lower lids down. The membrane that lined them, the conjunctiva, was transparent and allowed for inspection of the fine blood vessels beneath. There should be a healthy red colour, but in Miss Moloney's case Barry saw a very pallid area. He now was sure she was anaemic. Simple laboratory tests would confirm it.

He sat back. "I'm pretty sure, Miss Moloney, that you are suffering from thin blood."

"Oh, dear. Is that bad?" Her narrow eyebrows arched upward. Her lower lip trembled.

The truth was that indeed it could be, if, for example, the anaemia was a reflection of blood loss. Some of its causes could be very serious, although in women the most common cause was heavy periods. "How old are you, Miss Moloney?"

She bridled. He knew that in some circles it was considered impolite for a gentleman to ask a lady her age, but heavens above, he was her doctor. "Miss Moloney?"

"Fifty-one."

"I see. Thank you." He pursed his lips. Time enough at the next visit to ask if she had experienced "the change of life." He swivelled to the desk, made a note on her record, filled in a laboratory requisition form, and then spun back to face her. "Now, Miss Moloney. I don't think you need worry about this," he said, because he, her doctor, was quite able to be concerned for her. "The first thing we have to do is make sure that you *are* anaemic."

"But you said you *were* sure." She frowned and tightened her thin lips.

"Pretty sure, but I need to be absolutely certain, so I'd like you to go to the lab at Bangor Hospital and have some blood tests." He handed her the pink form.

"All right."

"And I'll see you next week to give you the results." And if you are anaemic, I'll decide how to investigate you for any possible underlying cause, he thought, but he kept a gentle smile on his face. He stood to indicate the consultation was over.

Miss Moloney rose and followed him to the door.

"I'll see you next week," he said, as she let herself out through the front door. With any luck, he thought, as he walked back to the waiting room, she'll have a simple iron-deficiency anaemia due to poor dietary intake. He really didn't want to have any very ill patients, particularly not at this season.

Barry opened the waiting room door. "Next, please."

"Me, sir." He knew Cissie Sloan, the very large woman who spoke and rose to her feet. She wore a headscarf over pink, plastic hair curlers, and a gabardine raincoat that Barry thought had probably been built by Omar the tentmaker.

"Good morning, Cissie." Barry stood aside to let her precede him along the hall to the surgery. "Go on in," he said. "Have a pew."

Cissie Sloan sat heavily on one of two plain wooden chairs facing the desk. Barry took the swivel chair on casters in front of the desk. "How are you, Cissie?" he asked, knowing that the question was an invitation for the opening of her verbal floodgates.

"You remember," she said, in her hoarse voice, "when I come 'til youse first and youse found out I was short of that wee thyroxine thingy in my blood, so I was?"

Barry nodded. He did indeed remember. O'Reilly had missed the diagnosis of hypothyroidism and had been giving her vitamin B_{12} as a tonic. The hoarseness in her speech was a result of her hypothyroidism.

"And Doctor O'Reilly prescribed me that thyroid

extract." She peered round. "Where is the big fellah the day anyway?"

"He's got a bit of a cough."

"Has he, by God? What's he taking for it?"

"Now, Cissie," Barry said gently, "I can't discuss Doctor O'Reilly with you. You know that."

"Aye, right enough, but—"

"Now, what can I do for *you* today, Cissie?"

"It's my throat, so it is." She leant forward toward him. "Now I know my voice is a bit crakey ever since I got the thyroid thing, but for the last two—no, I'm wrong—for the last three days, or mebbe it's four . . . no, no, three . . . I remember now. It was the day the milkman, Archie Auchinleck . . . him with the son a soldier in Cyprus . . . Archie dropped my milk on the doorstep, and the bottle broke, and the milk froze, and my cousin Aggie slipped on it and fell on her arse and . . ."

Barry hoped she hadn't noticed him rolling his eyes to the heavens, but something had brought her back on course.

"Anyways," Cissie continued, "it's been raw and sore something chronic." She leant forward and whispered, "And it hurts to talk."

Barry had to stifle a smile. There could be no greater imposition in Cissie's life. "Have you been coughing?" he asked.

"Only a wee bit."

"Have you taken anything for it?" Countryfolk, he knew, often used honey for a sore throat, and he had once seen a child whose mother applied a hot potato in a sock to the front of the neck.

"I did try tying some Saint Brigid's cotton around my neck." She opened the collar of her coat, and Barry saw a rough piece of cotton cloth knotted around her throat.

"I'm sorry, Cissie, but I'm not familiar with the treatment."

She tutted. "You leave the cloth outside the door of the house on the night before February first, that's Saint Brigid's Day." She crossed herself. "The saint herself passes by that night and blesses the cloth." She rubbed the makeshift scarf. "I've had this bit since last year, so I have, but it's not doing me no good, so it's not."

Barry rose and pulled a small penlight from the inside pocket of his jacket. "I'd better have a look." He went to the instrument trolley and returned with a wooden tongue depressor. "Open wide and put out your tongue."

She obeyed.

He used the wooden spatula to shove her tongue toward the floor of her mouth and shone the beam of the little torch inside her mouth. "Say, 'Aaaaah.' "

"Aaaaah."

He could see the back of her pharynx and noted *en passant* that she had no tonsils or adenoids. The beam lit up the normally pink membrane in her throat. It was an angry red, flecked with yellowish spots, and looked for all the world like a ripe strawberry with yellow instead of white seeds. Bacterial, probably streptococcal, pharyngitis. He removed the tongue depressor and felt the sides of her neck. Good. There were no enlarged lymph glands. "Your gullet's a bit inflamed, Cissie."

"Bad is it?"

He shook his head. "A bit of penicillin and a gargle, and you'll be right as rain in no time."

"Am I going to need an injection?" She eyed the instrument trolley. "I've my stays on."

"Not today." Barry could picture the day he'd first met Cissie. O'Reilly had given her an injection through her dress and hit the whalebone of her corset, and the syringe ricocheted across the room like a well-thrown dart.

He returned to the chair, swiveled round to the desk, and wrote a prescription for penicillin V to be taken orally four times daily for five days. "Here." He handed her the scrip. "And can you make up a gargle of table salt and warm water?"

"Och, aye."

"Good. Use it three times a day, and go easy on the talking. You mustn't strain your voice."

"I will, sir. And will I keep wearing the Saint Brigid's cotton?"

Five months ago Barry would have told her it was a superstitious waste of time. "Absolutely," he said solemnly, "and for a couple of days after you're all better." He knew by the great grin that creased her face he had said exactly the right thing.

He rose and gently took her arm to help her to her feet. There were other patients waiting. Barry knew that once Cissie Sloan got comfortable in a chair, she could be a hard woman to budge, even if the chair was one of Doctor O'Reilly's specials with an inch sawed off the front legs so that patients kept sliding down the seat. He steered her to the door to the hall. "If it's not all better in six days, next Monday, come back in and see me."

"It'll have to be better. If you could see the amount of work we've to do to get the chapel hall ready for the kiddies' Nativity play . . ."

"I'm sure you'll be fine, Cissie." Barry increased the pressure on her arm. "It'll take more than a tiny wee germ to knock the stuffing out of a powerful woman like yourself."

She blushed at what Barry supposed she saw as a compliment and playfully punched his shoulder. He knew he should take such familiarity as an indication of total acceptance by Cissie Sloan, but he rubbed his shoulder and wondered how Cassius Clay, the new world heavyweight champion, would fare after three rounds with the woman. Cissie would probably have destroyed him in the second round.

"I believe you, and thanks a lot, Doctor Laverty," she said. "It's early, I know, but if I don't see you before, you have a very merry Christmas."

"Thank you, Cissie, and the same to you."

He was about to leave her to make her own way out the front door when she asked, "And will you be coming to the Nativity play? It's Christmas week. The Monday."

"I will." He opened the surgery door.

Cissie lowered her voice. "And will you be bringing the pretty wee lady that's over at her studies in England?"

Barry laughed. There were no secrets here in Ballybucklebo. "I will, Cissie. She's coming home." And it couldn't be soon enough for him. He just hoped O'Reilly would be back on his feet so he, Barry, could have as much time off as possible to spend with Patricia Spence, the pretty wee lady who was studying at Cambridge.

He bade good-bye to Cissie and headed back to the waiting room. At least, he thought, the time passed more quickly when he was busy, and trying to solve the patients' problems left little time for worrying about Patricia. She'd told him she loved him and that should be enough, shouldn't it?

He opened the door to the waiting room. "Who's next?"

He was not prepared when Santa Claus, resplendent in his red fur-trimmed suit, black boots, and vast white beard lumbered to his feet and announced, "Me, Doctor sir."

Barry chuckled, glanced around to make sure his next patients wouldn't be a bevy of elves, and escorted Saint Nick along to the surgery. He wondered how O'Reilly would deal with this; indeed he wondered, as he shut the door behind him, how O'Reilly was getting on this morning.

5

A Memory of Yesterday's Pleasures

O'Reilly reckoned he could be doing a damn sight better. He fidgeted in his armchair in the upstairs sitting room and stared at his unlit pipe in the ashtray. Christ, he wanted a smoke, but the flaming cough refused to go away, and it had kept him awake for half the bloody night.

He twitched his plaid dressing gown shut, tightened the waist tie, and scowled at his pyjamaed legs and slippered feet sticking out from under a blanket where they were propped up on a footstool. He cleared his throat, spat into a big linen handkerchief, and looked at the results.

The sputum was clear and sticky. There wasn't a large amount. Classically sputum was expected to be like that with early bronchitis, which was almost certainly what ailed him now. Last night he'd had a sore tickly throat and Barry had been right about tracheitis, but by the early hours of this morning O'Reilly's entire chest had become tight and wheezy.

Acute bronchitis, while hardly life-threatening, was a bit more serious than tracheitis, and it might take just that bit longer for him to recover. He frowned at the gob in his handkerchief. If there were lots of pus cells, the stuff would have a greenish-yellow colour. It didn't, so he'd not have to worry about acute bacterial bronchitis or pneumonia. In the latter case, there would be a rusty tinge as well. He peered more closely. No blood. Excellent.

Blood in sputum meant one thing and one thing only until proved otherwise. Last night, the expression on young Laverty's face had told O'Reilly what Barry was thinking, as clearly as if he had spoken his thoughts aloud. He probably assumed that his senior colleague hadn't read about the connection between smoking and lung cancer. But he had, by God, and as things stood in the research community, cigarettes were definitely implicated. Pipe smoking didn't seem to be so bad. O'Reilly looked at the gob once more. Definitely no blood. It was a relief. Even doctors were not impervious to worrying about their own health.

He heard the front door slamming below. Young Barry was at his work, showing one patient out and going to get the next. Good for Barry. O'Reilly certainly didn't feel up to facing the multitudes this morning. He heard the telephone in the hall ringing. No doubt somebody who wanted a home visit, and that would keep Barry occupied for part of the afternoon. O'Reilly half listened to Kinky's voice coming from below as she answered the phone. It seemed odd that after all the years when he'd had nobody to share the work, he could now happily delegate some to his new assistant.

He yawned, coughed again, stuffed his handkerchief into the pocket of his dressing gown, and with his eyes half closed, lay back against the cushion at the back of the chair. He was sleepy and, he realized, bored.

He heard a quiet "Ahem," opened his eyes, and turned his head. Kinky came in through the doorway, head cocked to one side, a steaming mug held in one hand.

"Yes, Kinky?"

"Is yourself feeling a bit better, sir?"

"A little, thanks."

"Huh." Mrs. Kincaid shrugged. O'Reilly thought she looked as believing as a mother who, having just caught a child out in some minor peccadillo, asks, "What are you doing?" and gets the sheepish reply, "Nothing."

"Well, my granny used to say, 'Feed a cold and starve a fever,' so I've made you some beef tea." She set the mug on the coffee table, stood back with arms folded, and glowered down at O'Reilly. "Here."

He knew he had no choice but to drink from the mug. He lifted it, and the tangy, meaty smell of the bouillon filled his nostrils. He sipped. "By God, that's powerful stuff, Kinky." He was relieved to see her expression soften. "Made it with Oxo, did you? Bovril maybe?" He knew at once that that had been a stupid thing to say. Kinky would *never* use a proprietary brand of anything if she could make her own.

"I did not." She frowned. "Indeed not, sir. It's made from the grade A beef, and—"

"Sorry, Kinky. I should have known, but I'm not altogether myself today." He took a deeper swallow.

"I'll forgive you," she said. "Thousands wouldn't" —she looked at his mug—"but get that down you, and get the good of it into you."

He thought she was going to add "like a good little boy."

"And I've a great big bowl of chicken broth for your lunch, so."

O'Reilly smiled weakly. "And I thought it was the Jews who believed in chicken soup?"

"Well, maybe they do and maybe they don't, but the Cork people do, so." She moved closer. "Sit forward."

He did as he was bid, and she grabbed the cushion, pulled it free, fluffed it up, and stuck it behind his back. "Now lean you back against that," she said.

O'Reilly leaned back and handed her the now empty mug. "Thanks, Kinky." He coughed, shook his head like an irritated stallion trying to dismiss an annoying cleg-fly, and said, "Who was on the phone?"

"The new doctor from the Kinnegar; he says his name's Fitzpatrick. He wants to come calling. He said it would be a courtesy visit."

"I hope you told him not today. I don't feel much up to having visitors."

"Of course I did." Kinky bent and arranged O'Reilly's blanket more tidily. "We've to get you back on your feet, so." She frowned. "I hope I convinced him for he seemed bound and determined to come today. If he does, I'll see to him."

O'Reilly smiled. This new Doctor Fitzpatrick might *sound* bound and determined. However, if anyone ever produced an illustrated dictionary, a photo of Kinky, arms folded on chest, multiple chins thrust out, would accompany the entry for "determined." Doctor Fitzpatrick would have his work cut out if he imagined he could get by Kinky.

She snorted but smiled back. "Now is there anything else you'd be needing?"

"Just one wee favour?"

"What?"

He pointed to the big wall-mounted bookshelf. "Fourth shelf up, halfway along. The book in the orange cover."

She went to the bookshelf. "This one? *The Happy Return* by C. S. Forester?"

"That's it."

She brought the book and handed it to him. "About birthdays, is it? Like 'many happy returns'?"

He took the slim volume and managed a little laugh. "No. It's a story about a sea captain in Lord Nelson's navy."

"Nelson? And him the fellah with one eye and one arm on top of the column in Dublin City?"

"Right. They have one of him in London too. In Trafalgar Square."

She shrugged and said, with a tinge of disapproval, "Huh. No doubt he keeps the London pigeons as happy as the ones in Dublin."

O'Reilly knew Mrs. Kincaid was no respecter of English heroes. He pointed at the book. "This is a great read."

"Well, I'm sure if it's a story about the navy it'll do

grand to keep your mind occupied, an old sailor man like yourself."

O'Reilly coughed. "Sure that was more than twenty years ago, Kinky."

"And don't I know it very well? And haven't I been housekeeping here since you got off that big battleship when the war was over and you came here?"

"You're right."

"Neither the one of us is getting any younger . . . and . . ."—she headed for the door—"neither is my chicken soup. I'll have to tend to it at once."

"Kinky?" O'Reilly settled back against the cushion. "Thanks for the beef tea."

"It's nothing." She hesitated in the doorway. "I'll be bringing your soup up on a tray. Would you like me to ask young Doctor Laverty to join you for his lunch?"

"I would."

"I'll see to it, so." She left.

Fingal O'Reilly smiled. Not for the first time he wondered just how an old bachelor man like himself would have managed without her. She could be as fussy as a mother hen, authoritarian as a sergeant major, and diplomatic as an ambassador. Although *he* ran the practice, there was no doubt about who ran Number 1 Main Street, Ballybucklebo.

He cleared his throat, reached over to the coffee table, picked up his half-moon spectacles from where he had left them, stuck them on his nose, and opened the book. He hadn't read the Hornblower stories for years, and when he saw the handwriting inside the front cover, he gasped. *To Fingal on our engagement. With all my love, Deidre.*

He let the book fall into his lap.

He swallowed hard. Closed his eyes and felt the prickling behind the lids. Christ Almighty, you idiot, he berated himself, how could you have forgotten *she* gave you that book? How could you have forgotten *when* she gave you that book? Of all the books on the shelves, why in the name of the wee man did you ask Kinky to get you that one, when you're not at your best and the last thing you need to be reminded of is why you are still a bachelor. As if you didn't remember every bloody day, the golden girl, your bride of six months, snuffed out by a German bomb in 1941. Twenty-three years ago.

What did Kinky call you last night? An *amadán*. She was right.

He opened his eyes, lifted the book, reread the inscription, and firmly closed the cover. He knew that amputees, years after losing a limb, could for a fleeting moment be vividly conscious of its presence. But they must accept it is gone, as must he.

And yet . . . and yet, he still thought of her. Deidre, named for the Celtic princess, Deidre of the Sorrows. On their honeymoon night she'd quoted a line from the *Táin Bó Cúailgne—The Cattle Raid of Cooley*—the first epic in European history. He could remember her every word. "Deidre saw a raven drinking blood on the snow, and she said . . . 'I could love a man with those three colours: hair like a raven, cheeks like blood and body like snow.' And I do love you, Fingal."

Bugger it. It must be the bloody bronchitis that had knocked some of the stuffing out of him, letting in these melancholy thoughts. He'd be all right once this damn chest had cleared up and he was back in harness. If medical practice was no substitute for a wife, it was certainly a demanding mistress and had filled the empty spaces for him, along with his lifelong interest in rugby football and his enjoyment of a day's wildfowling with Arthur Guinness for company.

He wriggled to a more comfortable position. As soon as his chest was better, he'd see if Barry would look after the shop for a day, and he, O'Reilly, would go down to Strangford Lough for a day's duck hunting. When Barry had had his knickers knotted about his love life and his professional life the first month he'd been here, hadn't O'Reilly suggested a day's trout fishing to the boy as a good way of clearing his mind?

And maybe, just maybe, it was time to go and see Kitty O'Hallorhan again. Ever since he'd taken her to Sonny and Maggie's wedding, they'd met once every week or so to rehash old times. He'd been a medical student and she'd been a student nurse back in Dublin, and he admitted to himself he'd been not a little in love with her. He might have married her if Deidre hadn't come along but, och, he told himself, if she hadn't he'd never have had those few months.

He felt the drowsiness starting to overcome him, but before he let himself drift off into a nap he resolved to get well as soon as he could. Barry's Patricia would be coming home, and he'd want time off to see her. He could only have that if O'Reilly could carry his load, as Barry was carrying it this morning downstairs.

6

All the World's a Stage, and All the Men and Women Merely Players

After five months in Ballybucklebo, Barry had learned how to keep his amusement hidden and his sense of decorum in place. He resisted the temptation to ask Santa Claus if Donner, Blitzen, Prancer, and the rest of the reindeer were parked outside. Instead he walked the man to the front door and showed him out. He was better known as Billy Brennan, a usually out-of-work labourer, who had been making a few extra Christmas pounds working as Saint Nick for Robinson and Cleaver's department store in Belfast.

His periorbital haematoma—the classic black eye—was the direct result of having told a rambunctious six-year-old sitting on his lap that Santa might not be able to deliver a real motor car. "By Jesus, Doc," he'd said, "I never thought a wee lad like that had such a punch in him."

Barry had examined the eye, satisfied himself that there was no damage to the eyeball itself or the bones of the eye socket, and reassured the man. That had been easy. The tricky bit, for which Barry had no answer, was trying to decide whether the injury might be considered an occupational hazard and so eligible for disability benefit. Barry had given a palpably grateful Billy the necessary certificate. He'd let the bureaucrats at the ministry make the final decision, but as far as Barry was concerned, with a shiner like that, Billy would hardly be an acceptable Santa.

Barry did allow himself a little chuckle as he walked back to the waiting room. Most of the worried well had been seen and dealt with, and he felt satisfied that he was coping. He opened the door. Two patients left to see. He did his mental sums. Two plus the others already seen made fourteen . . . no, sixteen. He was pretty sure that was fewer patients than usual for a Monday morning. In some ways that was just as well because he knew he was getting through the caseload more slowly than O'Reilly would have. It was nearly lunchtime, and he still had to see Mrs. Brown and her six-year-old son Colin.

Colin wore shorts, his school blazer, and school cap—a peaked piece of headgear made of contrasting rings of red and blue cloth. Barry himself had worn something similar as a schoolboy, and as far as he knew the peculiar fashion had started in Victorian times. In its own way it was another symbol of the unchanging nature of rural Ulster.

"Morning," Barry said. "You know your way, Colin.

Take your mum on down to the surgery." The lad had been in to have a cut hand stitched a few months ago. Barry wondered what would be wrong with the little chap this time. He followed the pair along the corridor. He hoped Colin's complaint wouldn't be, like those of many of the earlier patients, another upper respiratory infection.

Barry had clapped his stethoscope on several wheezy chests and written enough prescriptions for the "black bottle"—a mixture of morphine and ipecacuanha, *mist. morph. and ipecac.* in Latin shorthand—to repaper the waiting room walls and cover the god-awful roses. The locals had great faith in the mixture. The morphine certainly was a cough suppressant, but the ipecacuanha had only one purpose. It tasted appallingly bitter, and among the countryfolk it stood to reason that the fouler the taste, the more potent the nostrum.

O'Reilly had been right when he'd said it was sniffle-and-cough season. Those were not conditions seen in a busy teaching hospital, but to the victims they were every bit as annoying as the exotic complaints Barry had been exposed to during his training.

Once in the surgery Barry sat himself on the swivel chair and waited for mother and child to be seated. There was no obvious clue to what might ail the boy, assuming he was the patient today. No coughing, no snotty nose, no sweating.

"How's your paw, Colin?" Barry asked.

The boy whipped off his cap, held it in one hand, and silently offered the other for inspection. Barry could see the scar across the palm. It had been a nasty cut, inflicted by a chisel, and had required several stitches. It had healed well.

"Looks good." He turned to the mother and smiled. "And so what can I do for you today?"

"It's Colin, so it is."

"I see. And what seems to be the trouble." The child looked perfectly healthy.

"He doesn't want to go to school, so he doesn't."

"Does he not?" Barry's immediate thought was, neither did I at his age. For the second time that morning his ability to keep a straight face was called upon. In all of his medical training years there had been no attention paid by his teachers to the emotions of childhood. "Hmmm . . . ," Barry said, leaning forward, putting one elbow on his knee, and resting his chin on one hand. He squinted at Colin and, hoping for the best, asked, "And why would that be, Colin?"

"Dunno."

That was a great help. Think, Barry told himself. Why didn't you want to go when you were his age? "Is it one of the teachers?"

Colin hung his head and shook it.

"Maybe the work's too hard? I wasn't very good at sums."

More head shaking.

"Is one of the big boys picking on you?"

"No."

Barry, who in local parlance didn't know where to go next for corn, sat back and asked the mother, "Can you think of why, Mrs. Brown?"

She leaned forward and shook Colin's shoulder. "You tell the nice doctor about the Nativity play."

"Don't wanna."

"Maybe," Mrs. Brown enquired, the solicitude in her tones belying her words, "maybe you'd rather get a good clip round the ears?"

"No." Colin pursed his lips, frowned, and narrowed his eyes at his mother.

One thing about kids' emotions, Barry thought, they don't wrap them up behind bland expressions.

"I'm warning you, so I am."

Barry had to intervene. "Is there something the matter at the play?" he asked, looking Colin straight in the eye and turning his back on Mrs. Brown. Funny, that was the second time the event had been mentioned this morning, and O'Reilly had said something about a Christmas pageant last night.

Colin nodded.

Barry waited. Colin remained silent.

"Would you like to tell me about it?" He cocked his head to one side. "Would you?"

"It's that wee gurrier Micky Corry," Colin sniffed. "He's going to be Joseph. It's not fair, so it's not." A tear ran down one cheek. "Teacher said I could be Joseph again." He prodded himself on the chest. "I have the robes and the Arab headdress and everything from last year."

"You see, Doctor Laverty, Colin was Joseph last year. Everybody said he done the part very well," Mrs. Brown added.

"That's right. But now Miss Nolan's changed her

mind and says it's somebody else's turn. It's not fair." Colin stamped his foot, and his knee-length sock slid down his calf like the skin falling off a shedding snake. "I don't wanna be the innkeeper. He only has three lines. 'Who's there? Mary and Joseph?' and 'Well, you can go into the stable.' "

Nations, Barry knew, had gone to war over less, and he was blowed if he could see an acceptable solution. Should he offer to go and see Miss Nolan and try to intercede? No, because if she changed her mind again, he'd probably have Micky Corry and his mother in here tomorrow. "Um," he said, knitting his brow and regretting that he didn't have a pair of half-moon glasses to perch on his nose the way O'Reilly did when faced with a tough problem. He also regretted that unlike O'Reilly he did not possess the kind of wisdom King Solomon was reputed to own. O'Reilly would find a way to cheer up the little lad.

"Have you a half-notion you might like to be an actor when you grow up?" Barry asked.

"Mebbe." The little lad brightened a bit. "I'd not mind being like your man Joseph Tomelty."

Barry knew of the Belfast actor with the great shock of grey hair who had moved from regional theatre and portraying Bobby Greer on the BBC series *The McCooeys* to more important roles in the British cinema. "Perhaps you will be one day."

"I'm not fussed about 'one day.' I want to be Joseph this year, so I do."

Barry turned to the mother, shrugged, and shook his head.

"Aye," she said. "Me too." And he knew she meant she was as at a loss for an answer as he was.

He cleared his throat, looked seriously at Colin—and had a flash of inspiration. "Tell me, Colin, isn't the play all about the birth of Baby Jesus?"

"Aye."

"And when he grew up, didn't Jesus teach us to forgive our enemies?" He mentally blessed the boring Sunday afternoons that he, like every Protestant child of his generation, had spent at Sunday school. "So what do you think Jesus would have done about . . . what's his name?"

"Micky Corry."

"Right. Micky."

"I think Jesus would have done a miracle . . . and turned the wee gobshite into a pile of horseshite, so I do."

"*Colin!*" Mrs. Brown delivered the promised clip. Colin howled.

This time, Barry had to work very hard to stifle a grin; then he held an admonitory finger to Mrs. Brown. He had hoped the respect of the countryfolks for physicians would have been instilled in wee Colin Brown and would have given those words of wisdom the weight he sought. Clearly, though, Colin was not a turn-the-other-cheek kind of fellow. "Well, Colin, you might be right, but if you want my opinion, I'd try to forget about it, go back to school, and just get on with the play."

"Thank you, Doctor." Mrs. Brown rose and made

a little bow to Barry. "See, Colin, isn't that what I told you he'd say?"

"Aye." Colin scowled at Barry. "Youse grown-ups all stick together, so you do."

Mrs. Brown lifted her hand again, and Colin quickly said, "All right. I'll go back to school."

"Excellent," Barry said, rising. "Will that be all?" He moved to the door. As he showed the two out through the front door, he said to Colin, "And I'm sure you'll be a great innkeeper." Barry caught the glint in the little boy's eyes. God, Barry thought, he'd seen gleams like that in the eyes of demons in mediaeval illustrations. He wondered for a moment what it might presage.

His thoughts were interrupted by the sight of a lugubrious, middle-aged man standing on the front doorstep. He looked to be six feet tall and sported a black bowler hat and grey doeskin gloves. A pair of narrow, muddy, patent-leather shoes escaped from the pinstriped trouser legs that emerged from under a mid-calf–length raincoat. Barry could see a polka-dotted bow tie nesting between the white starched triangles of a wingtip collar. And above that was the largest, most angular Adam's apple Barry had ever seen. He watched it bob up and down as the man swallowed. "I'm sorry," Barry began, "but patients have to use the waiting room door—"

The stranger interrupted in a harsh, high-pitched voice, "I'm not a patient, sonny. I'm Doctor Fitzpatrick, and I'm here to see Doctor Fingal Flahertie O'Reilly."

"Oh. In that case—"

It was as far as Barry got. Doctor Fitzpatrick forced his way into the hall. Barry pulled the front door shut, turned, and regarded the new arrival removing his hat and gloves. He had turned to face Barry, who saw a thin-lipped mouth, turned down at twenty past eight, set between a clean-shaven receding chin and a narrow, high-bridged Roman nose. A gold-rimmed pince-nez with thick lenses clung to it, distorting Barry's view of what seemed to be grey, lustreless eyes. If I'd had to guess this man's occupation, he thought, I'd swear he was an undertaker's assistant.

"Take these." Doctor Fitzpatrick tossed his gloves into his hat and handed them to Barry like a condescending master to his valet. Barry set them on the table of the hall clothes stand. The stranger unbuttoned his coat and was slipping the sleeves down his arms when Barry spotted Mrs. Kincaid heading down the hall from her kitchen. She took in the scene before her and halted at the foot of the stairs, arms folded across her bosom, chins thrust out, agate eyes flashing.

"My coat." Doctor Fitzpatrick handed Barry his raincoat.

Barry hung the garment on a hook on the stand above the man's hat and gloves.

"You must be Laverty," Doctor Fitzpatrick remarked.

"Yes," Barry said levelly. "I am Doctor Laverty."

The man's gaze swept over Barry from head to toe.

His thin lip curled. "You look to me as if you should still be at school." He sniffed. "I'm not here to waste my time with minions. I've come to see the principal of the practice. Where is O'Reilly?"

Barry's eyes narrowed. He kept his voice level as he said, "*Doctor* O'Reilly is a bit under the weather today. He's upstairs." Barry glanced above his head. "He's not receiving visitors."

He heard a strange, dry, braying noise and realized that the man was laughing. "From what I hear, I suppose you mean he's hungover."

"I do not." Barry's hands, which had been hanging loosely at his sides, curled into fists. He hesitated before continuing, but he decided that as the man in front of him was medically qualified, it would not be breaching a confidence. "My senior colleague has tracheobronchitis."

"Smoker too?"

"Yes. Doctor O'Reilly smokes a pipe."

"Filthy habit. Bronchitis, is it? Serves him right."

"Now listen—"

But Doctor Fitzpatrick was already striding to the foot of the staircase, head turned back as he remarked over his shoulder, "I'm not a visitor. I am a medical man with every right to visit a sick colleague."

"Is that a fact, sir?" Barry heard the tone in Kinky's voice. It was the same kind of understated growl that Lady Macbeth would give—seconds before she sank her fangs into the nearest piece of yielding flesh. He saw the man's head turn. He slammed to a halt and took two steps backward. To Barry it seemed as if Fitzpatrick, who had been proceeding like a square-rigger under full sail, had run up on the reef of Kinky Kincaid, where she still stood at the foot of the staircase, arms folded, feet apart, legs braced to withstand any shock.

Fitzpatrick shuddered, as would the masts and yards of the grounded vessel, collected himself, and then demanded, "And who might you be?"

"I," said Kinky very civilly, "am Mrs. Kincaid, housekeeper to Doctor Fingal Flahertie O'Reilly."

Barry thought of how O'Reilly had described Kinky when he had first introduced her: his Cerberus, the three-headed dog who guarded the entrance to Hades. Except Kinky was such an effective guard she probably merited a fourth head.

Yet her effectiveness seemed to be lost on Doctor Fitzpatrick. As a grounded ship might try to force its way over an obstruction and might succeed with soft, yielding coral, he bore on. "Well, Mrs Kincaid, I am here to visit my colleague. If you would kindly show me the way . . ."

"I'll not, sir." Barry saw Kinky's shoulders rise. The good ship Fitzpatrick had hit granite, and jagged rocks at that. "When you phoned this morning, I told you himself was not receiving."

"Rubbish. I'm a medical man."

"That's as may be. Doctor O'Reilly told me he wasn't up to having visitors today."

As if to give emphasis to her words Barry heard a

hoarse voice from upstairs call, "What in the hell's going on down there, Kinky?"

Before she could answer, Barry saw Doctor Fitzpatrick tilt his head back and look up to the landing. He took one step and said, "My good woman, step aside." He was beginning to raise his voice.

Barry's fists unclenched. He started to grin. He had to admire Doctor Fitzpatrick's persistence, but the man clearly had not got the measure of Kinky Kincaid. This was shaping up as the classic irresistible force meets the immovable object—and Barry knew *exactly* where he'd put his money. He saw Kinky's eyes narrow to the merest of slits.

"Your good woman, is it? I am not one of your chattels, *sir.* My virtue, with all due respect, is none of your business, *sir,* and I will not step aside, so. Himself is ill. Himself needs his rest. Himself will not be disturbed by the likes of you, *sir.*"

"I don't think you know who I am." The man's Adam's apple bobbed furiously. His voice grew louder.

Kinky chuckled but didn't budge an inch. "Don't know, is it? Don't know who you are, is it, *sir*?"

"That's right, my good woman. I am *Doctor* Fitzpatrick. *Doctor*, d'ye hear? I'll not be spoken to like that by a mere servant. Let me by." He was shouting.

"Aye, so. I hear well enough." Kinky's voice remained calm, measured. "*Mere*, is it? *Your good woman*, is it? *Doctor*, is it? And here I thought you doctors were all meant to have very good memories."

"What on earth are you going on about?"

"Aye so. Sure it's only one wag of a wagtail's tail since I told you I am *not* your woman, good or otherwise. And I told you Doctor O'Reilly's not to be disturbed. Maybe you've forgotten that too, so I'll not step aside." She took such a deep breath that, as her bosom swelled, her crossed arms rose like a lift ascending from the depths of a coal mine. "Ah, sure," she said, "it'll be the poor memory you have indeed, so." She moved forward, grabbed him by the elbow, and steered him back along the hall. She stopped at the clothes stand, handed Doctor Fitzpatrick his hat and gloves, and helped him into his raincoat. She looked at Barry and jerked her head to the door, which Barry instantly opened. A cold blast swept into the hall, its force only slightly blocked by Doctor Fitzpatrick's body as Kinky pushed him out onto the step. "And it'll be the same poor memory that led you to ask me if I know who you are. Sure only a fellow with a *very* poor memory could forget who he is. I'd wonder if you are really a doctor at all?"

And with that she shut the door and turned to Barry. Kinky took a very deep breath, expelling it in a long sighing exhalation. Rather than show pleasure in her victory, however, it seemed to Barry that she actually deflated. She shook her head. "I hope himself upstairs won't be cross with me."

"Why on earth should he be, Kinky?"

"I wasn't altogether polite to that gentleman, and he *is* a doctor, so. If he goes away cross, he might try to take it out on Doctor O'Reilly."

Barry heard real concern in her voice and hastened

to reassure her. "I think, Kinky, that Doctor O'Reilly, once he's better, will be able to look after himself, and because he can't right now, and you did, he'll be proud of you. I certainly am."

"Honest to God, sir?" She managed a small smile.

Barry nodded.

"Well, I don't normally rear up on my hind legs, but that new doctor wanted to go up there"—she tossed her head upward—"and disturb himself."

"And we couldn't be having that, could we?"

"No, sir." She hesitated, then asked, "And you don't think Doctor Fitzpatrick could harm our practice, do you?"

Barry heard the possessive "our" and understood how protective Kinky felt. If things ever came to a fight, he'd not want to be trapped facing Mrs Kinky Kincaid on the one flank and Doctor Fingal Flahertie O'Reilly on the other. He laughed, in part because having just met the lugubrious Doctor Fitzpatrick, Barry had great difficulty believing the man could be much competition. But mostly he was laughing at the way Kinky had dealt with the obnoxious fellow. "I'd not worry about that," he said, keeping to himself the tiny nagging thought that Fitzpatrick *was* competition. "You did very well, Kinky. I mean it."

"Och, it was only a shmall little thing, so." She wiped her hands on her apron and smiled at Barry, but her smile fled as a hoarse, stentorian voice from upstairs yelled, "What's all the shouting about down there, and when the hell am I going to get my lunch?"

7

I'm Sickly but Sassy

Those raised voices from below had roused O'Reilly, and he forced himself to sit straighter in his armchair. While he'd been napping, Kinky had lit the lounge fire and covered him with a blanket. He rubbed a hand under his chin and along the front of his neck. His throat hadn't been made any better by shouting down to ask what was going on, but damn it all, he'd wanted to know. Not that anyone had bothered to answer him. He imagined his bellow had simply sent Kinky scurrying to the kitchen and caused Barry to smile and confirm his suspicions that his employer was an ill-tempered old curmudgeon.

O'Reilly felt an uncomfortable burning with each in-drawing of breath, but in his opinion he wasn't any worse than he had been earlier, and perhaps his nap had even brought about a little improvement.

Now he was hungry and he was curious, and he was irritated and not just in his throat. Kinky had promised chicken soup for lunch, and it was past lunchtime. Presumably she'd been held up by whoever had been down in the hall yelling at her, and that delay made his curiosity more intense, and in no small part was the cause of his irritation.

Still, it took a certain talent to remain irritated

when you had a little white cat purring on your lap. Lady Macbeth was curled up on top of his stomach, and he could feel the pleasant warmth of her through the blanket. He smiled down at her, stroked her, then looked up when Barry came in.

"How are you, Fingal?" he asked, as he moved across the room and stood beside the chair.

"I've been worse." O'Reilly felt the back of Barry's cool hand pause on his forehead, then drop to hold his wrist.

"You don't feel as if you've a fever, and your pulse is normal."

"So the odds are I'll live and you won't inherit the practice just yet?" O'Reilly growled, as he felt a cough rise again in his throat.

Barry laughed, clearly unabashed by O'Reilly's tone, took the armchair opposite, and said, "They'll have to shoot you, Fingal, and even then you'd not lie down."

O'Reilly recognized that he was being unfair venting his spleen on Barry. He softened. "I heard a bit of argy-bargy down there. What was it all about?"

"You were going to have a visitor. He tried to insist on coming up here. He wanted to surge past Kinky with all sails set full and by, but he ran onto a reef."

"A reef?"

"Kinky."

O'Reilly chuckled and said, "Nice analogy, Barry. The RMS *Titanic* tried to insist on forcing her way through an iceberg, and she came to a sticky end too."

"Fifteenth of April. Nineteen twelve. She was built

here in Belfast. The marine architect was Thomas Andrews, a Comber man."

The boy knew his history, O'Reilly thought, as he wriggled to make himself more comfortable. He felt a needling in his left thigh as Lady Macbeth registered her disapproval. He idly petted her head and asked Barry, "So if Kinky was the reef, who ran afoul of her?"

"A Doctor Fitzpatrick."

"Fitzpatrick?" O'Reilly abruptly stopped stroking the cat. "The fellah who took over from Doctor Bowman in the Kinnegar?"

Barry nodded.

"The one that phoned this morning and wanted to see me, and she told him, 'Not today.' "

"Right."

"But he came anyway." O'Reilly frowned. That was simply ill-mannered, and he disapproved of bad manners—at least in others. "He's got the quare brass neck on him."

He watched as Barry smiled, presumably at the Ulsterism, which meant someone with arrogant persistence. It seemed to fit the scene he'd heard playing out downstairs.

"Aye, and an Adam's apple like the blade tip of a ploughshare."

That certainly sounded familiar. He had a half-notion he knew the man. "And did he wear a gold pince-nez and a wingtip collar?"

Barry nodded. "And he had a hooter that would have made Julius Caesar's nose look snub."

"Begod," said O'Reilly, remembering sharing a dissection station with four other students, a formalin-reeking cadaver, and Fitzpatrick. There'd been more *craic* to be had from the stiff. "He was a classmate of mine at Trinity."

"Oh?"

"Aye, Ronald Hercules Fitzpatrick. Why in the hell his parents called him that is beyond me." Actually, O'Reilly thought, if he is the man I remember, they might have done better to strangle him at birth.

"Hercules?" Barry shook his head. "He hardly suits that moniker."

O'Reilly grunted. "But he suits his Fitz. He *really* suits it."

Barry frowned. "I'm not sure I understand."

"Way in the past, the Irish gave their newborn boys surnames derived from the first names of relatives. Back then, if my grandpa had been Reilly, I would certainly have been O'Reilly, grandson of Reilly. My father was Connan, God rest him." For a moment O'Reilly fondly remembered the big Dublin professor in classics at Trinity College who had died of leukaemia three weeks after he'd proudly watched his son graduate from the medical faculty of his own university. "If they'd decided to call me for him, I'd have been MacConnan, Connan's son. But of course the old ways changed, and the Irish took on the English way of the son simply assuming the father's surname. It made keeping records easier. We've been O'Reillys since one of our lot was killed with Brian Boru at the Battle of Clontarf against the Danes in 1014."

"That explains O and Mac. What about Fitz?" Barry asked.

Before O'Reilly could answer, Kinky came in and set a tray on the sideboard. He sniffed, and despite his stuffy nose he felt his mouth start to water at the aroma of Kinky's chicken soup.

"It's chicken soup and wheaten bread and butter," she said.

Grub at last. Great. He sat up and dislodged Lady Macbeth.

"Fitz, is it?" she remarked, handing him a bowl and a spoon. "That won't need any salt," she said.

O'Reilly ignored her and drank a spoonful. The soup was hot, rich, and felt like healing balm on his scratchy throat. He took another spoonful and nodded at Kinky. She was right. It didn't need salt. It tasted just right.

She handed Barry his bowl and spoon.

"Go on, Kinky," he said, "explain Fitz, please."

"Fitz," she said, "is Norman. It means 'son of,' a very special kind of son." She glanced at O'Reilly. "Very special."

O'Reilly saw the twinkle in her agate eyes and kept a straight face. He knew she was leading Barry down the garden path to set him up for her punch line.

"A special kind of son?"

"Yes, Doctor Laverty. Special . . . a bastard son."

"Bastard son. Honestly?" Barry laughed and choked on a mouthful of soup. "Honestly?"

Before O'Reilly or Kinky could answer, O'Reilly heard the doorbell ring.

"I'll see who it is," Kinky said, "and unless they're bleeding to death, I'll ask them to wait until you gentlemen have finished." She left.

"And that's why you said he suited his name, Fingal?"

"It is. He was a gobshite of the first magnitude then, and I doubt very much if he's changed."

"So does that mean you don't think he'll be much competition?"

O'Reilly shook his head. Barry was so transparent, so worried about his future here. Should he reassure him or be completely honest? "Did you ever hear of a fellah called Rasputin?"

"The Siberian monk?"

"Aye. He claimed to be able to use hypnosis to cure Tsar Nicholas's son of haemophilia."

"But that's a load of rubbish."

"*I* know that and *you* know that, but the tsarina and a lot of her court believed him because they wanted to believe him. He'd quite the following for a while."

"And you think Fitzpatrick might be able to do the same here?" O'Reilly could see how Barry was frowning, how he'd stopped eating his soup.

"He might, for a while." O'Reilly knew that he himself harboured a small concern, but as senior man it was his job to keep it to himself and keep Barry's spirits up. "But old Rasputin ended up poisoned, stabbed, and chucked into the Neva River."

"So you're saying we should just sit tight?" Barry said. "See what happens?"

"Do you have a better idea?"

"Not unless you want me to stab him and chuck him in the Bucklebo River." Barry was smiling.

"Good lad." One thing about Laverty, his sense of humour never deserted him for long. "I reckon—" O'Reilly couldn't finish the sentence. A harsh, barking cough overcame him.

Kinky came in, followed by the Marquis of Ballybucklebo, a tall man in his mid-sixties with unruly iron-grey hair and a neatly clipped military moustache. He wore a tweed Norfolk jacket over an open-necked shirt, where a silk cravat in the colours of the Irish Guards took the place of a neatly knotted tie. "Good day, Fingal. I hope I'm not intruding."

Barry set his soup aside and stood.

"Please be seated, Doctor Laverty," the marquis said. "And both of you, please, finish your lunch."

"I know we decided, sir, no visitors," Kinky said, "but after his honour had hung up his coat below, and we'd had a bit of a chat, and His Lordship promised he'd only stay for a toty, wee minute and not tire you out . . . well, I relented, so." She fixed the peer of the realm, whose rank O'Reilly knew lay between that of a duke and an earl, with a momentarily stony look, wagged a plump finger, and said, "Remember, you promised." Then her face softened, and she said almost to herself, "Perhaps I was a bit harsh on that other gentleman."

How couldn't you love a woman like Kinky? O'Reilly thought, seeing her confusion over whether or not she had done the right thing. She had a heart of corn. "Nonsense, Kinky," he said. "You were right on both occasions." He was gratified to see her smile.

"I'll be running along then, Doctor O'Reilly," she said. Then she turned to the marquis and asked, "Is there anything I could be bringing for your honour?"

"Not a thing, thank you. I'll not be staying long."

O'Reilly could tell by the look on her face that Kinky would be back making not-too-gentle hints if she thought the marquis had overstayed his welcome. She left, but not before remarking, "And, sir, you'll be the last I let in here today, so." She closed the door behind her with what O'Reilly knew was just a little more force than usual. *Non passerà.* Kinky had nailed her colours to the mast.

He smiled, shook his head, and turned to the marquis. "Would you mind bringing over that chair so you can have a pew, John?" O'Reilly indicated a small chair in the corner of the room. While he would afford the marquis his due deference in public, just as His Lordship in turn would always refer to him as Doctor O'Reilly, the two old friends were much less formal in private. O'Reilly had discovered from Sonny, the font of all knowledge of local history, that the present marquis was descended from the original Irish aristocracy, not the later invaders who had usurped many of the Irish titles.

As the marquis crossed the room and brought back a small chair with a cane back and carved arms, O'Reilly recalled what Sonny had told him.

John, 27th Marquis of Ballybucklebo, was the latest of a long line of Irish lords who were descended from both Conn of the Hundred Battles and Niall of the Nine Hostages. The family, like their more famous O'Neill cousins, had kept their estates here in Ulster, while many of the other Irish lords had lost theirs to the Normans, the Plantagenets, and the Tudors. John was every inch a nobleman, and yet in the words of one of O'Reilly's favourite poems by Kipling, he could "walk with Kings—nor lose the common touch," just as he was doing now. O'Reilly watched him set his chair with its back to the fire and sit so he could face both O'Reilly and Barry. He seemed not one whit disconcerted to chat away while the two doctors got on with eating their lunch.

"I ran into Cissie Sloan on Main Street," he said. "That woman could talk the hind leg off a donkey, but she told me you were not altogether up to scratch, Fingal. Just happened to be passing. Thought I'd drop in. Nothing serious, I hope?"

O'Reilly shook his head. "Bit of bronchitis. There's a lot of it about at this time of the year." He coughed.

"With a cough like that you shouldn't be going out of doors," the marquis said.

"I agree, sir," Barry said.

"So I'll not be able to get to the Rugby Club executive meeting tonight, will I?" O'Reilly said, not altogether disappointed. He could find committee meetings a little boring, even if he was the secretary/treasurer. "Will you handle the matter of the rise in the annual subscription for next year?"

"I don't see—"

The door flew open, and O'Reilly found himself

staring at a rotund figure in the doorway. Mother of God, it was the Great Panjandrum, Grand Master of the Ballybucklebo Orange Lodge, Councillor Bertie Bishop himself. He was wearing his overcoat and bowler hat and looking rather pleased with himself. "How the hell did you get in here, Bertie?"

"I came in the back door and sweet-talked Kinky. I'd been pricing a job in the village, and that new doctor fellah came in. He was spitting blood because Kinky had chucked him out." Bishop smiled. "And we all know what Kinky's like when she gets her dander up."

O'Reilly heard Barry make a strangled, spluttering noise.

"You sweet-talked her?" O'Reilly wondered if his tracheitis had affected his hearing too. Councillor Bishop was known for his bull-in-a-china-shop approach, not for sweet-talking anyone, and certainly not Kinky in full Cerberus mode.

"I told Kinky I'd a couple of wee things for you. She said she couldn't leave something she had in the oven, and I was to bring them up at once and then skedaddle." He held out two brown paper bags and started to cross the room. "Good afternoon, my lord . . . Doctor Laverty."

O'Reilly heard the two men return the greeting.

"My missus, Flo, ran into Cissie Sloan," the councillor began. "So Flo says, 'Bertie, run you round to the shops and get some grapes and a bottle of Lucozade and take them round to the doctor.' I did, so I did. Here." He thrust the bags at O'Reilly, who grabbed them and thought, good old Bertie's starting his "Peace on earth, goodwill to all men" a bit early this year. He decided to be grateful for small mercies. "Thank you, Bertie," he said.

"Right. I'm off, and I hope you get better soon, so I do." The councillor headed for the door.

"Thank you, Bertie," O'Reilly said again, "and thank Flo for me."

Bishop grunted and scowled. "Flo? You know what she's like. Thick as two short planks. She's already probably forgotten she sent me." The door was closed.

O'Reilly heard footsteps going downstairs. "That last crack's more like the old Bertie . . . but Good Lord, grapes and Lucozade? Will Christmas wonders never cease?"

Barry and the marquis were both shaking their heads.

"I hope," said the marquis, "he'll be in such generous form tonight when it comes to setting next year's dues." He rose. "Don't trouble yourselves, Doctors. I've stayed long enough. I'd not want to have Mrs. Kincaid after me."

O'Reilly stood, pleased to find the act had cost him a lot less effort than he had anticipated. He must be on the mend. "Thanks for coming, John."

"My pleasure, Fingal." The marquis crossed the floor and opened the door, turned, and said, "Do hurry up and get better. The club's playing Glengormley on Saturday."

"I'd not miss it," O'Reilly said. "It's the biggest

needle match of the season." He settled back into his chair, and by the time he was comfortable, Kinky had reappeared, set a tray on the sideboard, and was fussing around him, twitching the edges of his blanket straight. When she was finished, she stood up and pulled a sheet of paper from her apron pocket. "Here you are, Doctor Laverty. Two calls for this afternoon."

O'Reilly was happy enough that Barry could manage, so he didn't ask who the patients were. Instead he snuggled down under the blanket, and on the grounds that this morning's nap seemed to have done him a power of good, he announced, "Off you trot, Barry. I'm going to have a nap."

"Indeed you are, sir," said Mrs. Kinkaid, "but not until after you've had another go at the friar's balsam."

O'Reilly rolled his eyes. "Och . . . Jesus, Kinky."

"There will," she said, "be no 'ochs' about it. I've the makings there on the tray."

O'Reilly muttered as Kinky turned to Barry. "You'll want to be running along to see your patients, Doctor Laverty, while I see to himself here . . . ," she said.

Barry nodded and started to leave.

"And by the way," she said, "that nice young Miss Spence phoned from Cambridge and said she'd be in her residence at six o'clock and could you please phone her?"

O'Reilly saw Barry's face light up the way a lough will sparkle when the sun comes out from behind the clouds. He envied the young man and thought, well, damn it, if he's going to phone Patricia, I might just get on the blower myself and have a bit of a *craic* with Kitty. I will, he resolved, as soon as Kinky's finished making me inhale those bloody awful balsam vapours.

8

Blow, Blow, Thou Winter Wind

Doctor O'Reilly, sir. Have you no wit at all, at all?" Kinky stood in the hall, fists on hips, a lock of her silver hair hanging down over her forehead and dancing in the force of her words. "Go you back up to the comfortable, warm sitting room this instant before you take your death standing there in that draught."

O'Reilly suspected that the sight of her employer, standing in the hall with the telephone receiver pressed to his ear, was a shock to poor Kinky, who seemed convinced he was as sick as a poisoned pup. Yet the idea of talking to Kitty had so lifted his spirits that he felt quite transformed. And nothing was going to stop him. "Hang on a minute," he said to Kitty; then he covered the phone with one hand and addressed his housekeeper, a slight edge to his voice. "I'm on the phone, Mrs. Kincaid."

"And if you catch the pneumonia you'll soon be on a cold slab, so. Is it not my job to take calls from the patients?"

"It is," O'Reilly said, "but this is not a patient. It's—"

"I don't care if it's the Archangel Gabriel himself. You've no business being down here—"

"Kinky." He continued to let that steel edge of control creep into his voice. He was unaccustomed to *anyone* interrupting him. "I'll thank you to wait until I've finished, and I'll only be a minute. Are you still there, Kitty?"

He heard her say she was, and again he asked her to wait.

Mrs. Kincaid was now standing, both hands clasped before her thighs, her head tucked down between her inwardly rolled shoulders. She pursed her lips, frowned, and snorted down her nostrils, much, as O'Reilly imagined, a small dragon might warm up before giving an impression of a flamethrower.

"Are you there, Fingal?" he heard. "I'm tying up the ward telephone. I should ring off."

"I've said it before, and I'll say it again. Doctors who treat themselves are *amadáns*."

"Kinky, I'm nearly done." Poor Kinky, O'Reilly thought. I shouldn't have snapped at her. It's been a confusing morning for the woman, with her not altogether successful campaign to protect me.

"Look, Kinky, I'm having a chat with Miss O'Hallorhan, and I'll only be a minute, I promise." Kinky did not look mollified, O'Reilly thought. She won the battle with Fitzpatrick, capitulated to the marquis, and was outflanked by Councillor Bishop, and now I'm being an unyielding bastion—or perhaps that should be "bastard." He softened his voice and smiled at her.

"Fingal, I'm warning you," he heard Kitty say. "I'm going in a minute."

"Kinky, Kitty's on duty at the hospital and can't talk for long." He saw Kinky's stance soften. "I'd like to ask her down for supper tonight after her work. Would you be able to manage for one more?" He cocked an interrogative head at Kinky. She harrumphed, then said, "I don't think yourself is well enough for guests, sir."

"Well, I say I am. Would you like a second opinion?" O'Reilly roared. He thrust the receiver into Kinky's hand so forcibly she almost dropped the phone. She tutted, then spoke into the mouthpiece. "Did you hear all that, Miss O'Hallorhan?"

O'Reilly couldn't hear what Kitty was saying, but he saw Kinky's grin widen as she made affirmative noises. Then he was gratified to see her smile and nod.

"She says, Doctor O'Reilly, sir, she could have heard the roars of you all the way to Belfast . . . without the telephone, but she'll come if you promise to behave. And if you don't, she'll pack you off to bed and leave."

"Tell her I'm sorry and I'll be good . . . but I'd really like to see her."

Kinky relayed the message, then said, "Grand, so. I'll just throw an extra spud in the pot."

Some women would be disconcerted at having to feed an extra mouth at short notice, O'Reilly thought, but he knew it was Kinky Kincaid's delight to meet the challenge.

"And here now," she continued, "I'll give you back to himself."

O'Reilly took the receiver. "I hear the giggles and laughs of you, Kitty. Heaven help a poor man when the likes of you two gang up on him, but I'll forgive you if you come for about six." He looked at Kinky and raised a questioning set of eyebrows. He was pleased to see her smile and nod. "Wonderful. That means we'll eat at about six thirty." He saw Kinky shake her head. "Sorry, Kitty. *Exactly* six thirty." Kinky nodded briskly.

"Good," he said. "So we can expect you at six? Splendid," he said. "Ah, duty calls. I quite understand. Off you go. Bye." He replaced the receiver.

Funny, he was fifty-six, had only ever loved one woman, and yet he was sure his pulse was going a bit faster than it should at the thought of seeing Kitty O'Hallorhan in only a few hours.

"Now, Kinky," he said, turning for the stairs. "I'll do as I'm bid and go back up." He hesitated with one hand on the newel post; he ran the other hand over his chin. "But I'm going up to the bathroom first. I could really use a shave. You won't mind that, will you?"

"I'll not," she said, "but I still will mind you, sir, standing in this draughty hall. Will you please, for the love of the wee man, get yourself along?"

O'Reilly started to climb. By the time he reached

the landing he was only a bit wheezy. He was definitely improving. As his breathing rapidly eased, he was aware that Kinky was hovering around in the hall like a mother duck around her ducklings.

"Now," she said, "go you on up the next flight to the bathroom, and I'll go back to my kitchen to see to my mince pies."

"I will, Kinky. I'll be all right on my own."

"Aye, so," she said, "but you'd not be if you didn't have that nice young Doctor Laverty to share the load."

"True on you, Kinky," he said. As he climbed the next flight, he wondered how the young man was getting on with the home visits.

Barry had parked Brunhilde by the kerb of Comber Gardens in the housing estate. He'd found an empty space between other parked, older-model cars. One he reckoned had to be twenty years old if it was a day.

He grabbed his medical bag, got out, closed the car door, and turned up his coat collar to the bitter blast. The wind behind him whipped the tails of his raincoat past his legs, and the material was chilly against the backs of his calves. He was outside Number 19, and with the system of odd-numbered houses on one side of the narrow street, even numbers on the other, there were only five narrow terrace houses between Numbers 19 and 31, his next port of call.

He strode rapidly but not rapidly enough. He was overtaken by dead leaves and fish-and-chip wrappers being bustled across the footpath's badly laid paving stones. He almost tripped where one concrete slab had ridden up like some urban tectonic plate over its neighbour. Typical, he thought, of the shoddy workmanship of Councillor Bertie Bishop, whose work crews had built the estate.

Barry stopped in front of Number 19, where Kieran and Ethel O'Hagan lived. He lifted the cast iron knocker and let it fall. One sharp knock was all it took to get Ethel to the door. The couple would have been waiting for his arrival, and although she was more than eighty, Ethel had the quick, bustling movements of a much younger woman. "Come on in, Doctor, out of that. It would founder you, so it would."

"Thanks, Ethel." Barry stepped into a narrow hall, and as the front door was closed behind him he shivered. It wasn't much warmer in here than it was on the street. That would account for why Ethel O'Hagan was wearing a heavy sweater, a knitted bonnet, and woolen gloves with the fingers cut off. Not only did Bishop's workmen lay bloody awful footpaths, they hadn't a clue about proper insulation of brick walls or such niceties as double glazing. Finding central heating in a Bishop-built house would be as likely as finding an orangutan perched on top of the Ballybucklebo maypole.

"Kieran's in the kitchen."

Barry followed Ethel. The last time he'd been in this house, poor old Kieran, who was suffering from benign prostatic hypertrophy, had been experiencing an episode of acute urinary retention. He'd had his surgery in September and had made a complete recovery. Kinky had said today's call was something to do with the man's finger, and Ethel didn't want to take her elderly husband out in the gale.

The kitchen was small and snugly heated by a wall-mounted gas fire that popped and spluttered and threw out a cheering warmth. Kieran sat on a simple wooden chair beside a cleanly scrubbed pine table. A saucepan simmered on the stove. The window in the back wall was covered with chintz curtains.

Ethel loosened the strings of her bonnet, took off her gloves, and filled a kettle from a single tap over the porcelain sink. "Would you like a wee cup of tea in your hand, Doctor?"

Barry smiled. The cup of tea. It had to be offered, but no offence would be taken if it were to be declined. God, if he accepted a cuppa in every house where he called, his tonsils would be as well afloat as Noah's ark. "No thanks, Ethel, but you go right ahead." Barry took off his raincoat and folded it over a chair back. Then he asked, "So Kieran, how're the waterworks?"

The man's old, lined face split into a huge grin. "You know the waterfall at the head of the Bucklebo River, sir?"

Barry nodded. "I hear there's big trout in the pool under it," he said with a grin.

Kieran chuckled. "Ever since my operation, Doctor, I'll give that pool a run for its money. I'm pissing like a stallion. I could fill a lake for a whale."

"I'm delighted," Barry said, now openly laughing. "Now, what's the bother today? Kinky said it was your finger."

"My thumb." Kieran held out the offending digit. "Herself wanted a hook driven for to hang some Christmas decorations. Would you look at that?" He stuck his left thumb under Barry's nose.

Barry could see purple discolouration of at least half of the nail bed.

"I hit it a right dunder with the hammer, so I did."

"I can see that." Barry held the thumb gently and inspected it. The joints were knobby with the arthritis of age, but they did not seem to be displaced. "Can you bend it, Kieran?" He did without great difficulty. "I don't think any bones are broken," Barry said.

"That's a mercy . . . but it's throbbing away like a Lambeg drum, so it is."

"It's the blood under the nail. It's a huge bruise, Kieran. I'll let it out for you, and it'll feel much better." He turned to Ethel. "Have you a soup plate?"

"Aye." She left the kettle on the stove and went to a cupboard.

While Ethel was fetching the plate, Barry opened his bag and took out a bottle of Dettol disinfectant, some cotton swabs, a prepacked sterile scalpel, and a roll of Sellotape.

"Can I wash my hands in the sink?"

"Aye, certainly," Kieran said, eyeing the scalpel blade, which was clearly visible through the transparent packaging.

Barry washed his hands and shook most of the water off. He didn't bother drying them. He didn't need dry hands, and he didn't want to waste the prewrapped sterile towel in the bag.

"Can you give me a wee hand, Ethel?"

"Yes, sir, and here's your nice clean soup plate," she said, crossing the linoleum-covered floor.

"Just set it on the table beside Kieran." Barry noticed how the plate's glaze glistened in the rays from the single overhead sixty-watt bulb. When Ethel said "clean," she meant thoroughly scrubbed. Her housing might be verging on being a slum, but it would not stop Ethel O'Hagan being a tidy housekeeper. "Kieran, hold your hand over the bowl, and Ethel, unscrew the top of that bottle . . ." He nodded to indicate the Dettol. "Now pour some over Kieran's thumb."

She did, and Barry's eyes were stung by the strong fumes of the disinfectant. "Right, Ethel, one last job. Can you open the package the scalpel's in?"

She looked puzzled.

"Take each side between your one finger and thumb, and pull."

She followed his instructions, and Barry had no difficulty removing the surgical knife. "Now, Kieran," he said, "I'm going to cut a wee window in the nail." Before Kieran could object, Barry seized the thumb in the ring of his own left thumb and index finger and used the pointed scalpel blade to cut a small rectangle in the nail over the bruise. In a second the piece of now free nail was lifted and dropped in the bowl, and the dark old blood beneath welled up and dripped over the side of Kieran's thumb.

Kieran whistled, then said, "Boys-a-boys, that's powerful. The throbbing's stopped already."

"It's because the pressure's been relieved."

"Just like a safety valve on an engine," Kieran said wide-eyed, and whistled on the intake of breath. "Modern science is a wonderful . . . a wonderful . . . thing."

"Hold your thumb there." Barry wrapped it in a cotton swab and used the adhesive Sellotape to bind the swab in place. "A week or so and it'll be good as gold . . . but you'll probably eventually lose the nail, and it'll be a while before a new one grows back."

"Och, well," said Kieran, "sure I'll just ask Santa for a new one for Christmas." And he laughed.

"I'll wash the soup plate," Ethel said, as the kettle started to whistle on the stove. "Are you sure, Doctor, you'll not have a wee cup?"

Barry shook his head. "I'll just wash my hands again and be running along. I've another call to make."

"No rest for the wicked, eh, Doc?" Kieran asked.

"None," Barry said, drying his hands on the towel Ethel offered. Then he shrugged into his coat. "Can you bring him in tomorrow, Ethel, if the weather's warmer, and I'll change the dressing?"

"Aye."

"Good. Now you two enjoy your tea. I'll see myself out." And so saying, Barry left the cosy kitchen and walked down the chill hall and out through the front door into the teeth of a blast that must have started its life somewhere north of Spitsbergen.

His next call was six doors down, and on a warmer day he would have enjoyed the chance to stretch his legs and take in the atmosphere of the neighbourhood. Today, though, he hurried, the wind pushing at his back. The narrow street usually echoed with the high-pitched cries of children at play: boys in short pants swinging on ropes tied to the lamppost; boys noisily trundling old, tyreless bicycle wheels along the road, guiding them with bent pieces of wire and rolling along with roller skates clamped to the soles of their boots; girls skipping rope, chanting, "One potato, two potato, three potato, four . . ."; others hopping over the hopscotch squares that were chalked on the paving stones. But not today. It was far too cold.

Barry stopped at Number 31, knocked, and waited, stamping his feet, his shoulders turned to the wind.

O'Reilly had made the first call here ten days ago to see the tenant's nine-year-old son. The little lad had been one of the many cases of upper respiratory infection in the village. Barry had visited four days ago, and young Sammy had seemed to be well on the mend. But today Kinky said the mother felt he'd had some kind of relapse.

The door was eventually opened by a woman he knew to be twenty-eight. But the dark rings under her eyes, her complete lack of any makeup, and her barely combed, lank brown hair made her look at least forty. It was a shame, because Eileen Lindsay was usually a pretty young woman, and, O'Reilly had told Barry, she had shown courage and independence when her husband scarpered to England two years ago. "Come in, Doctor Laverty." Her voice was listless, and she stifled a yawn, brushing back a few strands of hair with the same hand she'd used to cover her mouth.

Barry followed Eileen into the hall, where his nostrils were assailed by the smell of boiled cabbage.

"Thanks for coming, Doctor Laverty." She stepped aside to let him into a hall that was an identical twin of the one he had just left—and equally chilly. "Sorry to drag you out on a day like today." She closed the front door. "Sammy's upstairs. I don't like this rash he took last night."

Barry looked at the bags under her eyes. "And were you up with him all night, Eileen?"

She nodded.

"Why didn't you send for me?"

"Och, sure, but it was only a wee rash. No need for the pair of us to lose a night's sleep, and you might have had something important to do, like delivering a baby or something."

Barry shook his head. Countryfolk. "That was considerate of you, Eileen, but if you are worried about anything you should call."

"Go on, Doctor, sure I told you it's only a wee rash."

It was the wrong time of the year for most of the

diseases of childhood that were usually accompanied by rashes, but with the history of an earlier chest infection Barry was already halfway to formulating a diagnosis.

"Let's go and have a look at him," he said, "but next time call. Please."

"I will," she said, but he knew by the tone of her voice that she would not.

Barry followed her up a narrow uncarpeted staircase onto a landing and into a small bedroom where there was barely room to move between a single bed and a set of bunk beds. "The tribe usually all sleep in here, but I've Mary and Willy in with me while Sammy's sick," she said.

Barry knew that Eileen had three children, and that she did a remarkable job rearing her little family on her pay as a shifter at the Belfast linen mills. It was hard physical work, running up and down between the thundering looms replacing empty bobbins with full ones. A lot of millworkers developed hearing loss from the constant assault of the thunder of the machinery on their unprotected ears.

Sammy lay in the single bed. He was a tousled-haired boy, and Barry could see at first glance how his head lay on the pillow, hardly moving, and how the lad's blue eyes were dull. "How are you, Sammy?"

His voice was soft and slow. "My knees and ankles is achy, Doctor, and I've bumps all over me like a seed potato."

"Is that so?" Barry smiled at the image. "Seedy

spuddy knees? Is that what I've to call you? Like your other fella, 'Skinnymalink melodeon legs, big banana feet'?" Barry tossed his head from side to side as he chanted the words of a favourite children's taunt for someone with long thin legs.

"Away on, Doctor Laverty. Away on and feel your head." Sammy managed a weak smile. "My legs isn't that skinny."

"I'm only pulling your leg," Barry said, admiring the child's spunk. He sat on the edge of the bed and took the boy's pulse, noting also that the skin was cool and dry and that the pulse rate was normal. He turned to Eileen. "How's Sammy's chest been, Eileen?"

"Grand for the last two or three days, so it has. I was going to let him go back to school, but . . ." He saw her shrug and the way her lips pursed.

It didn't take a genius to know what she was thinking. She had had to stay at home to nurse him. The effect on the family finances would be noticeable. At the first visit O'Reilly had given her a certificate, which Barry had renewed and would again renew today, but the pittance paid by the state was a great deal less than her wages would have been. Barry sighed. It was frustrating; maybe, after he'd got on with the technical doctoring, he could try to think of a way to help out a bit. That's what O'Reilly would do. "Let's have a listen. Sit up, Sam," he said.

The boy sat, with a bit of help from Barry supporting his shoulders. Barry lifted his pyjama jacket. There was no sign of a rash on the boy's skin. Another clue. The chest was moving easily; the respiratory rate was normal. "Deep breaths." Barry listened through his stethoscope, moving it from lung base to lung base. No rustling, no cracklings, just the gentle sounds of air moving in and out of the lungs. Good. "Now," said Barry, "lie down, Sammy, and roll over onto your tummy."

The boy did as he was told. He smiled at Eileen and nodded his head toward the door. Little lads could get embarrassed when their pants were pulled down, even in front of their own mothers.

Her eyes widened but she withdrew.

Barry eased the pants of the boy's pyjamas down, and as he expected saw the hives of what his textbook referred to as an "urticarial rash" on the buttocks and backs of the thighs and calves. In a day or two, if his diagnosis was right, the hives would have been replaced by dark, flat purplish areas, the classical "petechial rash."

It came as no surprise to note that both knees and both ankles were slightly swollen. That, taken in conjunction with the nature of the rash, pretty well nailed things down.

Sammy had a condition that often followed upper respiratory infection in children, Henoch-Schönlein purpura. In most cases it was self-limiting and cleared up without treatment, although it could take several weeks or even months before the signs and symptoms disappeared completely. Barry pulled up the lad's pyjama bottoms. "You can roll over, Sammy.

"Now, young Sam, you're going to have to stay in bed for a while."

"No school?"

Barry shook his head. "Not until after the Christmas holidays."

"Wheeker. Christmas Day's seventeen days away, and school doesn't start until after New Year. I'm going to get a brave long holiday, so I am." Sammy's smile was very wide, but it faded. "Does that mean I'm ferocious sick, like?"

Barry saw the concern in the little boy's eyes. It was strange that during his training it had never occurred to him that children could worry as much as adults. He looked for simple words to explain to the boy what ailed him and realized that he'd have enough difficulty trying to explain it to an adult. Henoch-Schönlein purpura was an autoimmune disease, an ill-understood group of conditions like rheumatoid arthritis, dermatomyositis, and lupus erythematosus in which the body mysteriously began to attack itself.

Barry hoped he could get away with confidently expressed reassurance. "You'll be fine," he said. "Do you play soccer?"

"Aye. I do that. I'm a right-winger, so I am."

"Well," said Barry, "you'll be out there scoring goals again in no time. Just like Stanley Matthews." The Blackpool player was the most famous soccer player of his day. Barry wasn't much of a sports fan, but he did understand the power of the familiar when someone needed reassurance. Somehow his being able to trot out the player's name would persuade Sammy that

Barry was also an initiate into the soccer fans' world and hence to be trusted.

"Wheeker," Sammy said with a grin. "Just like Stan the man."

"But you'll have to do exactly what your mammy says for a while."

The lad's face fell.

It was going to be a boring few weeks for the child, and that could make things hard on his mother. And God knows, Eileen didn't need any more grief than she already had. He hesitated but then decided to reinforce the message. "And if you don't obey your mam, Sammy, maybe Santa won't come."

"Huh," said Sammy, "it won't make a wheen of difference this year anyhow."

"Oh?"

"Nah. Mammy says poor oul' Santa's a bit short of the do-re-mi this year, so me and my brother and sister've to go easy on what we ask him for."

Barry could understand why Santa might be a bit hard up. With the lad needing to stay in bed longer, Santa's budget was going to be cut even closer to the bone if Eileen couldn't go back to work. Barry had been proud of his ability to make a confident medical diagnosis of what ailed the lad, but now he wished O'Reilly was here. He would be bound to have a solution to Eileen's financial woes.

Barry stood. "You listen to your mammy, Sam, like a good lad, and I'll be back to see you in a day or so."

He was rewarded with a big smile.

"And don't you worry about Santa; I'm sure he'll come."

"Too true he will." Barry was struck by the absolute confidence in the boy's voice. "Me and Mary and Willy have a way to help him out."

"Good for you." Barry moved to the door. "I'll see you in a day or two, Sammy."

As Barry went downstairs, he heard the boy call, "Bye-bye, Doctor Laverty."

"In here, Doctor."

He heard Eileen's voice coming from a room across the hall. She would be waiting for him in the front parlour. He went into her best room. It was carpeted. Eileen stood beside the mantelpiece. Two bamboo-framed armchairs faced a small grate. He noticed in one glance that the coal fire was set, but not lit, and one of Eileen's nylons was laddered.

She must have seen where his gaze had gone. She blushed, looked down, and said, "Wouldn't you know it, a new pair, right out of the package, so they were, and one of Sonny Houston's dogs jumped on me in the village yesterday. Poor Sonny felt awful. Was halfway to insisting he buy me a new pair, but, well . . ." Barry could see the pride and resolve lift her chin a little higher. "Anyway, I'm sorry the fire's not lit, Doctor, on such a cold day as this . . ."

Barry understood why. Stockings and coal cost money.

"I'm saving the fire up for the week before Christmas when the kiddies send their letters to Santa."

Barry could vividly remember being a child and laboriously writing a letter of wishes to Santa to be burnt in the living room fire so the charred paper, with the words still readable, would be wafted up the flue and directly, at least according to his parents, to Santa's workshop at the North Pole. Which reminded him, it was about time he dropped his folks a note. "I hear Saint Nick's a bit hard up this year, Eileen," he said.

"He is, but look, sir." She lifted a tea caddy from the mantel and handed it to him. He noticed it bore a picture of the 1947 wedding of Princess Elizabeth to a lesser Greek prince, Philip. "Open it."

To his surprise Barry found it full of ten-shilling notes.

"See," she said with a shy pride, holding out her hand so he could return the caddy. "I've been putting away ten bob as often as I can from my wages so the kiddies won't go short on Christmas Day. I've nearly fifteen pounds in there."

"Good for you, Eileen."

She used the back of her wrist to shove a few strands of hair off her forehead. "It's not much between the three of them, but I will be able to get them some wee things. Just to unwrap on Christmas Day, like."

Barry coughed. He felt a tightness in his throat. It was humbling to see how she was exerting herself for her family. Dear God, but he had to admire the woman. Putting some small savings away for little luxuries for her children, but neglecting her own needs. He glanced at the laddered stocking again. Unbidden, his hand went into his pants pocket looking for a pound note. Then he pictured the scene if he tried to give it to her. She'd stand ramrod stiff, scowl at him, and say haughtily, "The Lindsays don't accept charity." Damn it, just like the meanness of her State allowance, it was something he was powerless to do anything about. Still, he could explain to her what was wrong with her son, perhaps give her some small comfort. He smiled, hoping she would find that reassuring.

"About Sammy . . ."

"Yes, Doctor?"

"He's got a condition that we often see after coughs and colds. It's got a German name as long as your arm—"

"Och, sure, don't you bother your head telling me it, Doctor. I'd only forget."

"It's a miracle I remember it myself sometimes. But never mind the name, Sammy's going to be alright."

"Thank God for that," she said. "I've enough on my plate without a really sick one to nurse." There was a tear at the corner of one eye. "He's a very good wee lad, so he is."

"He'll be right as rain," Barry said, "and there're usually no lasting problems once the patient gets better." He saw no reason to worry her that occasionally a child would bleed from the bowel or develop kidney failure. Such complications were extremely rare. "But if he complains of a sore tummy or if you notice any blood in his urine, call me at once."

"I will, Doctor."

"And Eileen?" His gaze held hers. "I mean *at once*."

"Yes, sir."

"And I'll pop in and see him in a day or two."

"Thank you, Doctor." She replaced the caddy on the mantelpiece and turned back. Barry realized she wanted to ask him something else. He could sense her worry and wondered if he'd not explained Sammy's condition well enough.

Finally she asked, "How long is he likely to be in bed?"

She hadn't wanted to ask. Most mothers in Ballybucklebo were able to stay home with their children. But Eileen would be worried sick about how she was to make her living and remain home with her sick son. It could be a month, even more, before the little fellow was recovered. He took a deep breath. "It can be a few weeks, Eileen."

Barry heard her sharp intake of breath. "How long's a few?' "

"Two or three maybe." Barry knew he was being optimistic. "But it could be quicker."

She must have seen through his prevarication. "Or more like six or seven?"

He couldn't meet her eye. "It's hard to say, Eileen, but it might be a while."

She lifted the caddy from the mantel. Her cheeks were tear-streaked when she turned back to him, but she held herself erectly, and he heard the touch of pride in her voice when she said, "If I have to dip into the kiddies' Christmas fund to make ends meet, I will."

Perhaps . . . perhaps . . . a germ of an idea began to take shape . . . the kind of thing O'Reilly would have come up with, but Barry didn't want to hold out false hopes. "I know it's going to be tricky for you to get to your work, Eileen."

"Tricky?" Her voice was raw-edged. "Hard? It's going to be bloody well impossible, Doctor."

"I do understand, Eileen."

"How could you, you a doctor and all? You'll never be short a few bob." Her eyes flashed for a split second, but then her shoulders slumped and she said, "I'm sorry, sir. I shouldn't have lost my temper like that."

Barry wanted to hug her and tell her he understood, but instead he said, "I may have a suggestion." He saw her eyes widen.

"Honest? Honest?" There was hope in her voice.

"I . . . I'll pop in tomorrow and let you know."

"Will you, Doctor? That would be wonderful, so it would."

"Now, Eileen, I'm not making any promises, but I'll do what I can."

"Me and the kiddies would be very grateful," she said, "and I'm sorry I snapped at you, sir."

"Don't worry about it, Eileen. Now I have to get home, but I will come round tomorrow. I promise." He rummaged in his bag and fished out a pad of Ministry forms, filled one out, and handed it to Eileen. "That'll do you for six weeks if you need it."

She flinched at the words "six weeks" but took a deep breath and said, "I'll let you out." She accompanied him to the door. "Cheerio, Doctor Laverty, and thanks."

He bade her good night and hunched his shoulder to the gale for the walk back to Brunhilde. He glanced at his watch. It was time he went back to Number 1 Main Street and discussed with O'Reilly his bright idea for helping Eileen.

He was to phone Patricia at six. He had the irrational idea that often afflicts people waiting for something important to happen, that if they arrive early whatever they desire will happen sooner. He started to trot.

If nothing else, the knowledge he'd be talking to Patricia very soon made the evening seem less bitter.

9

A Mighty Maze! But Not Without a Plan

When Arthur Guinness came bounding out of his doghouse, eyes fixed on Barry's trouser legs, Barry was too tired from his day and too eager to talk to Patricia to suffer much nonsense. He stood his ground. *"Sit, you!"* he yelled, and to his amazement the big dog did. Then Barry said, "Go home."

Barry waited until the dog was back in his kennel before he crossed the backyard, wondering as he did why Arthur had been amenable to being ordered about. Was Barry gaining a bit more confidence, a bit more authority? He hoped so.

"Evening, Kinky," he said, as he opened the kitchen door.

Mrs. Kincaid was standing at the counter with her back to him. She turned and handed him a small metal basin. "Would you look at that, sir?" Her voice was hushed, as if she had just witnessed a miracle.

He took the basin and turned it over. There was a jagged hole in the bottom, about one inch across. "It looks as if it's been hit by a shell," he said. "What happened?"

She pointed to a round, dark brown, fruit-studded Christmas pudding, one of a pair, that sat on a plate. Its shape was exactly that of the basin.

"I think something ate the bowl," she said. Her eyes were wide. "Or else it was the little people."

"I beg your pardon, Kinky?" Barry smiled. "*Ate* the bowl? Little people?"

"Do you see, Doctor Laverty, I always make this year's Christmas puddings the year before, keep them in basins in my pantry, and bring them out once a month to season them with a taste of brandy. Then a week or two before the big day, I get two out of their bowls and wrap them in greaseproof paper so they're ready to boil on Christmas Day."

"I see." Of course, being absolutely ignorant of matters culinary, he didn't understand a thing Kinky had said, but he thought it best to humour her in her distressed state.

"Well . . . ," she sighed, "when I got those two out, the bowl you have in your hands, sir, had that hole." She made the sign to ward off the evil eye. "My cooking never hurt nobody, sir. Not ever, but something must have done it. Maybe the leprechauns. Maybe Old Nick himself." There was a tiny tremble in her voice.

It would be useless to tell her not to worry. Only a rational explanation would calm her. Barry frowned and tried to remember some of his organic chemistry classes. Something about sugars in fruits and alcohol. "Kinky, you put fruit and brandy in your puddings, right?"

"Bless you, sir, I do, so. Raisins, sultanas, currants, glacé cherries, mixed peel, and then that nip of brandy each month."

Fruit, brandy? Sugar plus alcohol? Then he remembered. The combination could produce a powerful acid. One powerful enough to eat through . . . he looked at the metal bowl. "What's this made of, Kinky?"

"Stainless steel, sir. Himself gave it to me out of the surgery last year when I'd the pudding mixture made but broke one of my regular ones. Like that one." She pointed to a grey ceramic bowl on the counter.

Barry smiled. "I don't think you need worry about the little people or the devil, Kinky."

"And why not?"

"I'm pretty sure the fruit and the brandy combined to make an acid that attacks stainless steel but not pottery."

She looked from one bowl to the other, then back again. "Now there's a thing, so." But she did not look entirely convinced. Still she said, "I suppose I'll have to take your word for it, sir, seeing as you're a learned man and understand all that science."

"You don't have to take my word for it, Kinky; ask Doctor O'Reilly."

"Och, no, Doctor Laverty. I believe yourself. Sure aren't you a gentleman and a scholar?"

Barry laughed. "And the last line of that toast, as you very well know, Kinky Kincaid, is 'And if the truth be known, sir, probably a fine judge of Irish whiskey'—which I am not."

They both laughed but then her face fell. "But if there's acid, would that not make anybody who ate it sick?" She looked sadly at her puddings. "I'd hate to have to throw them out."

"You used lemon juice in Doctor O'Reilly's hot Irish, didn't you?"

"Yes."

"Lemon juice is full of citric acid and it doesn't hurt anybody, does it?"

"No."

"Then don't worry about your puddings. They'll be fine."

"You're sure, sir?"

"Positive."

"That's all right then. I'll get on with wrapping them, and you get on with making your phone calls."

"Calls? I thought I'd only one to make."

"Your pal Doctor Mills rang. He wants you to try to get hold of him."

"I will. Thanks, Kinky."

Barry headed for the hall, shedding his coat as he went. He'd been chilled when he came in, but standing round chatting with Kinky in the hot kitchen had made him uncomfortably warm. He hung the coat in the hall, picked up the phone, dialed the Royal's number from memory, and asked the operator to page Jack Mills.

"Hello, Barry?" Barry recognized the strong Cullybackey accent. "How the hell are you?"

"Fine. You?"

"Grand. We'd one of your customers in last night and whipped out his ruptured spleen. Good thing you got him here as quickly as you did."

"You can thank O'Reilly for that."

Barry heard a chuckle. "Nah. You thank him. Your patient's doing fine, but he's sore from his incision and a couple of bust ribs."

"Will you get him home for Christmas?"

"Don't see why not."

"Good. I'll let his wife know."

"No need. Sir Donald phoned the wife immediately post-op. She knows."

"Thanks, Jack."

"All part of the service. How're things at your end of the universe?"

"Busy. O'Reilly has bronchitis so I'm running the shop on my own."

"And if I know you, Laverty, you're loving it."

"Well, I—"

"Might as well because the love of your life is miles away."

"Yes, but I'm going to phone her tonight."

"Daft. There's a million gorgeous birds out there, and most of them are up for a bit of slap-and-tickle. I'd imagine it's a bit tricky over the phone."

Barry shook his head. Typical Jack Mills. "Are you still seeing Helen Hewitt?" he asked.

"The redhead with the green eyes?"

"Yes."

"Oh, aye, when I'm not seeing your old friend Mandy, the brunette ward clerk with the great legs."

Barry laughed. "You're incorrigible, Mills."

"I probably would be if I could spell it. Any chance the pair of us could get together for a jar?"

"Not until O'Reilly's back on his feet, unless you want to take a run-race down here."

"I maybe could at the weekend, but this time of the year there's a brave wheen of Christmas parties. The nurses' Christmas dance is on at the Nurses Home. Why don't you try to get up here to Belfast? It would do you a power of good to get out."

Barry shook his head. That wouldn't be fair to Patricia. "You try to get down here, mate. You've already had a go at Kinky's cooking."

"I have that, by God, and it beats hospital grub by

a country mile. Tell you what. I'm off on Saturday. I'll give you a bell on Friday night."

"Fair enough."

"And Barry?"

"What?"

"I'll let you know if there's any change in the splenectomy."

"Thanks, Jack."

"Right," said Jack Mills. "If I fall through the mattress, I'll see you in the spring."

Barry chuckled, hung up, and headed up the stairs.

"You're home," said O'Reilly from his armchair when he saw Barry at the sitting room door.

"From the wilds of the Ballybucklebo housing estate."

"Well," said O'Reilly, nodding toward the sideboard, "that surely calls for a drink."

"Whiskey?"

"Indeed," said O'Reilly, "and purely for medicinal purposes." He coughed and winked at Barry.

Barry shook his head. "You're getting better, aren't you, Fingal?" He poured a small measure. "Aren't you?"

"Jesus," said O'Reilly, "I'm on the mend. The chest's not as tight, and I'm not coughing as much." Barry could see O'Reilly frowning at the glass. "But the dose you've poured there is the kind of thing a homeopath would prescribe, or a vet treating a flea."

"It's all you're getting." Barry poured himself a small one and carried O'Reilly's drink over to him.

"Jesus," O'Reilly repeated, accepting the glass and

draining half of it in one swallow. "It's only enough to give a gnat an eyewash."

"Hogwash," said Barry. "We all want you back on your feet."

"Have you not heard . . . ," said O'Reilly, emptying the glass and holding it out to Barry, "have you not heard that alcohol is an antiseptic? It kills bacteria."

Barry thought O'Reilly looked like a penitent supplicant. "Oh, very well." He set his glass on the coffee table and topped up O'Reilly's with a more generous measure. "Here," he said, handing it back.

"*Sláinte,*" said O'Reilly.

"*Sláinte mHath.*" Barry sipped his whiskey.

"So," said O'Reilly, "how was your afternoon?"

Barry shoved Lady Macbeth out of the other armchair and sat. "Pretty light. Two patients on the estate. Kieran O'Hagan had a subungual haematoma. I drained it." Barry was pleased to see O'Reilly quietly nodding. "Then I'd to see wee Sammy Lindsay."

"Chest bad again?" O'Reilly sipped his Irish.

"No. I'm pretty sure he has purpura."

"Henoch-Schönlein?"

"Yes. I'll be keeping an eye to him."

"Good lad. He could get kidney damage."

"Jesus, Fingal, he could die."

O'Reilly frowned. "That's what the textbook says. I've never seen it happen, and Lord knows I've seen enough cases over the years."

"I know, but I'll be watching him."

"We will, son. Once I'm up and doing. We'll watch him. He'll be sick for a while."

"I know." Barry took a big swallow of his whiskey. "That's what worries me."

"It shouldn't. He'll be right as rain in no time."

"Not him, Fingal. His mum. Eileen's the only support of the family, and she'll have to stay at home. The other two children, Mary and Willy, can go to school, but Sammy's too young to leave on his own."

O'Reilly scratched his stubbly jaw. "I hadn't thought of that. And at Christmas too. Bad time to be a bit short of the ready."

Barry thought of the tea caddy and its little hoard of ten-shilling notes.

O'Reilly frowned. "Have you any ideas?"

Barry set his now empty glass on the table. "I did have one half-baked notion, but I wanted your opinion."

"And?"

"You remember when Sonny had to go into hospital in August and Maggie looked after his dogs?"

"Yes."

"What do you think Maggie would say if we asked her to be a sort of honorary granny for Eileen's brood?"

O'Reilly guffawed. He leant across the gap between the two chairs and patted Barry's shoulder. "That, my boy, is a stroke of genius. Pure bloody genius. Sonny and Maggie have been married for four months now, and he'd probably not be sorry to have an excuse to get her out from under his feet for a while each day. She's very good with chisellers. It's a pity she never had kids of her own. I'm sure she'd love to look after Eileen's. And Eileen could get back to work." He finished his glass. "Brilliant."

Barry grinned. He'd thought it wasn't a bad idea, but he had not expected such a powerful endorsement from the senior man. "I'll run out now and see Maggie." Barry started to rise.

"Take, as they say locally, your hurry in your hand." O'Reilly held out a restraining hand. "If you don't mind braving the bleak midwinter, you could go after supper."

"Why not now and get it over with?"

"Because," said O'Reilly, "I seem to remember Kinky saying you were to telephone a Miss Spence at eighteen hundred hours—that's six to you—and it's ten to six now." Barry looked at his watch; O'Reilly managed a small cough. "Now by the time you've done that, and blethered to her, it will almost be suppertime, and you're a better man than me if you're willing to be late for one of Kinky's specials."

"Why special tonight, Fingal?"

"Because we're having a dinner guest. Kitty O'Hallorhan. She'll be here at six."

Barry looked at O'Reilly. The big man was striving quite heroically to keep a bland expression on his face, but the lines at the corners of his eyes were a tiny bit deeper, and the twinkle in his eyes had some cause other than Jameson's Irish whiskey.

"You are getting better, Fingal. A dinner guest indeed." And inwardly Barry was delighted both that his senior colleague was recovering his health and that he was seeing Kitty again. He wondered if that relationship might just develop into something more than simply a regular reunion of old friends. He hoped so.

"Fine, Fingal," Barry said. "I'll phone in a few minutes, then join you and Kitty for supper, but I will go out immediately after and have a word with Maggie."

"Now there," said O'Reilly, as Lady Macbeth leapt up on his blanket-covered lap, "is a young man with a sense of occasion, to say nothing of tact." He stroked the cat's head as she settled herself. Then he said to the paws-tucked-under loaf of cat, "Shall we keep him on in the practice, puss?"

Lady Macbeth yawned so widely, and stuck her pink tongue out so far, that Barry thought she had dislocated her jaw.

10

La Donna è Mobile, or Women Change Their Minds

"Who? Patricia Spence? Never heard of her." The unknown woman's voice had a plummy accent.

Barry growled in his throat, then said. "This *is* the Girton College common room phone?"

"Mmmm." That vague, guttural noise, beloved by

the English upper classes and meant to sound affirmative without making a complete commitment.

"My girlfriend was supposed to be there to take a phone call from Ireland."

"Really? Do they have telephones in Ireland? My word."

"No," said Barry, if only to keep the wretched girl talking until Patricia got there, "we usually send messages in cleft sticks carried by teams of trained runners. That's why some of the English call us bog trotters."

"Bog trotters?" He heard an in-drawing of breath and a giggle. "I say. Cleft sticks. That's awfully good." More tittering then. "Hang on. Would this Patricia of yours be a dark-haired girl with a limp?"

Barry's heart gave a little hiccup. "Yes." Dark eyes and ebony hair, like the words of the song, "My Lagan Love." *The twilight's gleam is in her eye, the night is on her hair.*

"Barry?" Patricia sounded rather short of breath, but he'd recognize her County Down contralto anywhere.

"Patricia? I thought I'd missed you."

"Sorry about that," she said. "The traffic was really heavy."

"Traffic? In Cambridge? I thought Cambridge was pretty rural."

He heard her laugh. "It is, silly, but everyone here gets around on bicycles, and when all the classes get out at once it's bedlam. Trumpington Street looks like something in Shanghai or Dublin."

"Oh."

"I had to pedal like mad to get here."

For a moment Barry had an incongruous mental image of Patricia as the Wicked Witch in *The Wizard of Oz* frantically charging along a Kansas dirt road with Dorothy's dog, Toto, in the basket of her bike. "I'm glad you made it." His voice softened. "I've missed you." It had been a week since he had spoken to her last.

"And I've missed you, Barry."

He glanced around to make sure no one could overhear him, chided himself because the only one who might was Kinky, and she certainly knew what he was going to say next, yet his Ulster reticence was difficult to override. "I love you, Patricia," he said softly, and hoped she could hear the yearning in his voice.

"Me too," she said, "but it's very public in here . . . listen." She held the receiver away from her ear, and Barry heard a babble of female voices. "I wish it wasn't," she said, "so I could tell you properly."

"So do I," but for the time being he knew he must make do with that crumb. "Anyway, you'll be able to tell me soon, won't you?"

"Mmmm."

God, was she already being infected with English habits? What did "mmmm" mean? "You will, won't you?"

"Well, I . . . I . . ."

"But you promised you'd be home for Christmas." He felt his grip tighten on the plastic. "You will, won't you?"

"Barry, please try to understand. It costs a lot to fly back to Ulster from here, and my folks aren't made of money."

She wasn't coming? But back when she told him she had won the scholarship to Cambridge, she said she'd be home for the holidays. Barry took a deep breath. He wasn't going to plead, but damn it, she'd promised. "I see. So where will you spend Christmas? In your rooms?" He knew the earlier warmth in his voice had fled.

It was some time before Patricia said, "I'm not sure yet. I'd like to come back to Ulster, Barry. I really would."

Barry bit back his immediate response, which would have been a sarcastic "Decent of you," and instead said, "It's up to you, but you know how much I want to see you. I just told you I love you."

"I know you do." She lowered her voice, and he had to strain to hear her next few words. "And I love you, Barry. I really do, but this term was more expensive than we'd budgeted. The bursary didn't cover everything, and I had to ask my folks for money."

"But where would you go if you don't come home?"

"I've made some friends since I came here in September."

"That's nice," he said. He hoped to God they weren't men friends. He had thrown himself into his work and avoided the company of women since she left in October for what Cambridge University referred to as the Michaelmas term.

"Yes, it is nice. You didn't expect me to sit all alone for three months, did you?"

"No," he said, although in truth his answer really was yes.

"Jenny Compton's another engineering student. She's an amateur ornithologist like me. Her parents live in the village of Bourn. It's only eight miles from Cambridge, and she's invited me to spend the holidays there. Actually I'm going home with her tomorrow now that term's over. We can go bird-watching on the Norfolk Broads."

He sighed. "Like the day I took you to Strangford Lough, to Gransha Point?" He could see her when a sudden summer squall had broken, standing, reveling in the gale, the driving rain plastering her wet blouse to her braless breasts.

"Yes." He heard the enthusiasm in her voice. "And I really want to see the Slimbridge Wildfowl Trust place on the River Severn. It's not far to drive, and Jenny has a little car."

"Slimbridge? Is that the place Peter Scott opened in . . ."—he had to think, but he'd seen the naturalist, son of Robert Falcon Scott of the Antarctic, on television—"nineteen forty-six?"

"That's right. He's made it a mecca for people interested in waterfowl, and I certainly am."

So is O'Reilly, Barry thought, but Fingal would want to shoot them, and as Barry was now becoming convinced he would be playing second fiddle to birdlife, he thought it served them right. And, dear Christ, she'd just said term was over. She could be here in Ulster already if she'd kept her promise. He knew now he wasn't going to talk Patricia into coming home unless she really wanted to. Better, he thought, to seem to accept defeat graciously. "I suppose," he said, "if you must, you must."

"Barry, you are wonderful," she said. "I really *do* love you . . ." He noticed that this time she had not lowered her voice. "And I didn't say I wasn't coming home. I just said I wasn't sure yet."

Barry sighed. He'd have to lie content with a half promise. "When will you know?"

"Not for another week. That still gives me nine days until Christmas Eve. Lots of time to get a flight. It all depends on how big Dad's Christmas bonus is."

"Patricia, you'll only need a lot of money if you fly." He had a sudden thought about an alternative solution. "What about taking the ferry?"

"Ferry?"

"Yes, the one from Holyhead in Wales to Dun Laoghaire in the Irish Republic." The more he thought about the idea, the more he liked it. "If you could get to Holyhead and catch the boat, I could drive down—It's only about ninety miles from Belfast—pick you up, and we could have a night in Dublin before we drove back up north."

"Welll . . ." She didn't sound very enthusiastic.

"Come on, Patricia, you know it's an option."

"All right, Barry," she said. "I will go to Jenny's now for a few days, but I will look into it . . . promise."

"Great—"

In the background he heard another female voice saying, "Come on, Patricia. You've been on for bloody ever. It's my turn." Then Patricia said, "Barry, I'm sorry. I have to go. I love you, and I'll call again as soon as I've found out about the ferry. I promise." The line went dead.

"Bugger. Bugger." He replaced the receiver. He'd been banking on her coming home. Damn it, she'd promised him she'd come home, never mind phoning again as soon as she could. He wanted all of her, not just a bloody phone call. He shook his head. Well, at least she was willing to try to find a solution. That had to prove something, didn't it? Didn't it?

The only comfort he could take was that there didn't seem to be another man in the picture. One thing about Patricia, she would never prevaricate, never beat about the bush. She'd have come right out and told him. Mind you, he thought, as he heard the front doorbell ringing, it was small consolation.

If he'd been in her shoes, he'd have been finding out about the next ferry. Forget about going to any friends like this Jenny. He'd be getting himself home as quickly as possible. Patricia may not have recognized what she'd done to the man she was supposed to love. She had, although not in so many words, told him that for a few days anyway he was going to be runner-up to a bunch of flaming ducks.

He crossed the hall and opened the front door.

"Hello, Barry." Kitty O'Hallorhan came into the hall, and he closed the front door behind her. "Nippy out," she said, "but at least the wind's dropped, and the skies are clear again. The stars were lovely tonight driving down from Belfast." She shrugged out of a cream raincoat, took off a pair of kidskin gloves and a head scarf, shook her head, and used her hand to rearrange her hair.

He'd thought her a handsome woman when he'd first met her on duty as a ward sister in the Royal, and he saw no reason to change his opinion tonight with the hall lamp highlighting her silver hair. Her title might be "Sister," denoting her seniority over staff and student nurses, but it was a throwback to the days when most nurses were nuns. Kitty O'Hallorhan would have been wasted in a convent. "Come on upstairs, Kitty. Fingal's expecting you, and the fire's lit in the lounge."

"Lovely," she said. "How is the old rapscallion anyway?" Her Dublin tones were obvious to Barry's ear. She smiled broadly. "I'll bet he's as cantankerous as all get out. I'd not want to have him for a patient."

Barry chuckled. "Come and see for yourself." With that he stepped aside to let her precede him upstairs. As she climbed, he admired the rounded contours of her buttocks under her tightly fitting knee-length black skirt and the flex and relax of her calves beneath its hem, their shapeliness accentuated by a pair of suede stiletto-heeled pumps. She paused on the landing and stood staring at a framed photo of a battleship. "That's HMS *Warspite*, isn't it?"

"That's right." Barry was surprised that a woman

would know the name of the old vessel. "Fingal and my dad served in her."

"I didn't know about your dad, but Fingal was on the *Warspite* when his wife was killed in 1941." Barry heard a catch in her voice. Had she perhaps harboured some hope back then? "The last time I heard from him was in 1939 when he joined up. He sent me a picture taken on his ship." She turned and grinned at Barry. "He looked quite the salty sailor man in his uniform."

"I'll bet." Barry opened the door to the upstairs lounge. "He's in there. Go on in." He followed her into the big comfortable room, knowing that it was crisply icy outside, yet in here the lighting was softly warm and the heat from the coal fire made the room welcoming.

"Kitty." O'Reilly stood. Barry was surprised to see he was freshly shaven and dressed in a sweater, shirt, and tweed pants, looking just a bit outdoorsy for the large, tartan carpet slippers on his feet. "Kitty." O'Reilly stood and hugged her. "Glad you could come. Have a pew." He waited until she took one armchair, then sat again in his own. Barry took the plain wooden chair the marquis had occupied that morning.

"So," she remarked, peering at O'Reilly, "how are you, Fingal?"

He grinned. "On the mend, and all the better for seeing you, Caitlin O'Hallorhan. You're looking lovely tonight."

"Go on with you, Fingal Flahertie O'Reilly, you great eejit! You always were full of the blarney," she said, shaking her head. Yet Barry heard the smile in her voice, saw the tiny heightening of colour in her cheeks.

"And," said O'Reilly, "you'd look even better with a glass in your hand. What'll it be? The usual?"

"Please."

"Barry, will you do the honours? And help yourself."

Barry rose. "Certainly." He knew exactly what O'Reilly wanted, but he had no idea what the "usual" was. Lots of women drank gin and tonic, vodka and orange, or a pear champagne, Babycham. He looked at Kitty.

"Jameson please, Barry," she said.

"Right." He stood at the sideboard and poured three Irish whiskeys. He handed one to Kitty and one to O'Reilly before returning to the sideboard and picking up his own glass.

"*Sláinte,*" O'Reilly said, but he coughed before he could take a drink.

"Indeed," said Kitty, "I'll be happy to drink to your health, Fingal, as long as you promise me you'll look after it."

Barry hid his smile. Poor old O'Reilly. Beset not only by Kinky but by Kitty O'Hallorhan as well. If concern was a medicine, he thought, O'Reilly would arise like Lazarus in no time flat.

"*Sláinte mHath*," Barry said. He sipped the peaty spirits, the *uisce beatha*, the water of life, and relished its warmth. He now preferred it to the sherry he had favoured when he first came to Ballybucklebo.

Barry sensed movement behind him, and turned to see Kinky in the doorway. Her chignon was freshly coiffed, and she wore a hint of lipstick and rouge. Her calico apron was obviously fresh from the laundry, and she wore her best low-heeled brogues. "Miss O'Hallorhan," she said, "nice to see you."

"Hello, Kinky. How are you?"

"Grand, so." Kinky smiled. "Now I want you all to enjoy your drinks but . . ." Barry heard the edge in her voice. "Doctor O'Reilly asked you to be ready to sit down and eat at six-thirty, Miss O'Hallorhan. If you need a little time to finish your drinks"—she looked straight at O'Reilly—"there's honeydew melon balls ready in the dining room. They'll not spoil for waiting a few more minutes, but the main course will be ready at six forty-five. I'd not want for it to be overcooked."

"Fair enough, Kinky," O'Reilly said. "We'll be on time."

"I'll have the pork fillet ready in fifteen minutes, so," Kinky said. Then, glancing at the clock on the mantel, she said, "No, I tell a lie. Fourteen."

11

The Stars in Their Courses

Dinner was over. O'Reilly pushed his chair back, dumped his linen napkin on the dining room table, and stifled a satisfied belch. Kinky, as usual when a guest was coming, had done him proud. Mind you, he thought, it wasn't as if she'd skimped in all the years he'd dined alone.

He knew he'd been content with his solitary life. The customers gave him more than enough contact with the human race, but he had to admit it had been pleasantly companionable since July to have Barry here, even if the pair of them were a bit like the two bachelors, Ratty and Mole, in Kenneth Grahame's classic *The Wind in the Willows*.

O'Reilly looked at Kitty and he smiled to himself. Tonight he'd thoroughly enjoyed having a woman at his table. Kitty added a sparkle to the evening.

And he'd enjoyed the meal. Melon balls sprinkled with ginger to start, stuffed roast pork fillet, roast potatoes, cauliflower in a cheese sauce, baby carrots, and for dessert Kinky's lemon meringue pie.

The whole had been finished off with coffee, and for O'Reilly another Jameson, and for Kitty a small Cockburn's port. Barry, who would shortly be popping out to see Sonny and Maggie, had elected to make this drink his last. Good lad, O'Reilly thought.

Barry and Kitty were deep in conversation. O'Reilly was happy simply to listen to what Barry was saying and keep his thoughts on the subject to himself.

"Actually, the three stars in the Summer Triangle are Vega, Altair, and Deneb." O'Reilly knew Barry had learned a fair bit of astronomy from his dad, who had been the navigating officer on the old *Warspite.*

O'Reilly hadn't known that Kitty would be keen to know the names of the stars and constellations, but then she always had been interested in the world beyond the confines of her chosen profession. He watched her face, animated one minute, serious the next, frowning when Barry was unclear.

"So Altair's the brightest star in Orion's belt?"

"No. It's the brightest star in a line of three stars in the constellation of the Eagle, which are often *mistaken* for Orion's belt. Do you remember the names of the belt stars?"

"Alnilam, Alnitak . . . I can't remember the third."

"Sure you can. Give yourself a minute."

She smiled.

It was a handsome smile on a handsome face framed by her well-cut silver hair. Her eyebrows were firm and arched above her deep-set, amber-flecked grey eyes. O'Reilly had seen many women's eyes in his years of practice but could not recall a pair as striking as Kitty's. They sometimes seemed more feline than human, as he well remembered Kitty herself could be.

He sighed. They'd both been so young then. The thirties were not a time when unmarried men and women fell into bed together, but he could remember summer nights when he was a student, still an overgrown boy, taking her to his digs, kissing her, holding her, caressing her, and how intensely she had responded. Perhaps, he thought wistfully, if they had made love even once, his life might have taken an entirely different path.

O'Reilly grunted to himself. Water under the bridge.

She interrupted his reverie by saying excitedly, "I've got it. Mintaka. Mintaka." Her laughter brought him back to the conversation.

"Well done, Kitty," he said.

"Such lovely, musical names."

"They're Arabic. Mintaka means 'belt,' and Alnilam means 'string of pearls,' " Barry said.

"Really?" Her smile broadened. "Glen Miller could have called his dance tune 'Alnilam.' " She chuckled deep in her throat before asking Barry the names of the stars in Orion's body.

"Rigel, Betelgeuse, Meissa . . . ," he began.

O'Reilly let his mind wander. She has young Barry eating out of the palm of her hand, he thought, and he was surprised to find a stirring within him, he who had refused to become involved with any woman since Deidre had been killed. Not that he'd been entirely celibate—he left that up to the Catholic priests. He'd just had neither the time nor the desire to fall in love again. And, he smiled, not much opportunity either. As every woman in the village was one of his patients, the chances of his meeting anyone during his working days were pretty remote.

His occasional overnight trips to Belfast, or to Dublin to watch Ireland play rugby football, were times when in naval gunnery parlance he might be able to find a "target of opportunity" in the hotel lounge or in the bar after the game for a mutually satisfying night. But he rarely saw the same woman more than two or three times. He'd never had any interest in anything permanent.

So why, he wondered, had he been seeing Kitty on a more or less weekly basis since he'd taken her to Sonny and Maggie's wedding back in August? Well, she was an old friend and she seemed to enjoy his company and reminiscing about the old days as much as he did. That was it. Nothing more.

He looked at her more closely. She was more than a handsome woman. In his opinion she was strikingly beautiful. It didn't matter that her nose was too large, her lips perhaps overly full. She had taken off her jacket when they sat down to dine, and he could see the top of her cleavage in the open neck of her cerise blouse, the silky material of which accentuated the curve of her full breasts.

He smiled to himself. In the country she'd be referred to as a "powerful woman." "Powerful altogether," he said, realizing too late that he had spoken aloud.

"I beg your pardon, Fingal," Kitty said with a chuckle. "They taught us in nursing school that talking to yourself can be a sign of insanity."

"Divil the bit," said O'Reilly. "I was just thinking aloud." He was looking straight at her, was surprised to realize he was seeing her in a different light. It was the kind of change he might notice on the seashore when he and Arthur were pursuing ducks and the morning sun suddenly transformed ill-defined shapes into cleanly etched rocks and clumps of seaweed. It was almost as if he'd not been paying attention on the other evenings he'd spent with Kitty.

Perhaps, he thought, it was the musky perfume she was wearing, perhaps all the stars she and Barry had been discussing had lined up in a row, but whatever the reason, he was going to enjoy being alone with her later tonight.

He turned to Barry. "Now young fellow, far be it from me to chase you but . . ."

Barry rose. "I know. I promised to go see Sonny and Maggie about Eileen Lindsay's Sammy."

"Good man ma da," O'Reilly said. "And Barry, while you're at it, would you do me a wee favour?"

"Certainly."

"Arthur hasn't had a walk today." O'Reilly saw Barry glance to heaven. He couldn't blame the lad. The big Labrador still seemed obsessed with a desire to mate with Barry's trouser leg at the slightest provocation. "He'd really appreciate it, and I can't have him getting fat. I'm going to take him to Strangford for a day at the ducks soon."

To O'Reilly's surprise, Barry said. "All right, Fingal, just this once. When I came home earlier tonight, I seemed to be able to persuade him to do as he was bid." He turned to Kitty. "I'll say good-night, Kitty. You may be gone by the time I get back."

"Good-night, Barry. I hope to see you soon."

You will, O'Reilly thought. This isn't the last dinner you'll be eating in this house.

"I want to hear more about the constellations."

"My pleasure," Barry said. "Perhaps I'll see you later, Fingal?" It was his last remark as he closed the dining room door behind him.

"Right," said O'Reilly, rising and standing behind Kitty's chair, ready to pull it back when she rose. "Let's take our coffee and drinks back upstairs. It's warmer up there. Would you like a little more port?"

"No thanks, Fingal." She stood. "Let's go on up."

O'Reilly refreshed his whiskey and settled into his chair. He watched Kitty standing at the fireplace. She had her back turned to him and was looking at a row of Christmas cards on the mantel. "Pretty early for cards," she said.

"For local ones, they usually start showing up in Christmas week, but those ones are all from overseas. Classmates who emigrated. Shipmates from the navy. There's one there from Barry's folks in Australia. That one"—he indicated a hand-drawn card with a caricature of a doctor on the front—"is from an old patient of mine. Read it."

She picked up the card, half turned, and read, *Old doctors never die. They just lose their patients. Merry Christmas and a Happy New Year from Seamus, Mau-*

reen, and Barry Fingal Galvin. We're all doing very well here, and Barry Fingal is growing like a weed . . .
"There's more but it'll be personal." She put the card back on the mantel and turned to face him.

"They're in California. They went in August," he said. "Seamus Galvin was the greatest skiver unhung. His wife, Maureen, sent the card."

"Still, it's nice they'd remember you."

O'Reilly laughed. "Never mind them not forgetting me. *I'll* not forget Seamus Galvin in a hurry. But he's in California and we're here." He looked at her face again. God, she *was* a handsome woman. "There are more interesting things to talk about," he said. "What have you been up to since I saw you last?"

"Since when? Ten days ago? Not a whole hell of a lot."

"Come and sit down and tell me about it anyway." He watched her cross the floor as he imagined a Celtic princess might have glided. Why the woman had never married was beyond him. He waited until she was comfortably settled, legs crossed, thigh over thigh, shapely calves leaning to one side.

"So what *have* you been up to?" O'Reilly asked.

"Do you really want to hear about the doings of a ward sister on duty, keeping my unit running smoothly?"

He shook his head. "I didn't mean that. What did you get up to last week when you were off duty?" And have you been seeing any other men? he thought, although he realized it was none of his business.

She chuckled. "Enjoying a life of wild hedonism, if

you consider it's living dangerously doing the housework in my flat, cooking for myself, shopping, getting my hair done, a trip to the dentist, my Monday night painting class, and an evening at the cinema with my friend Mairead to see *My Fair Lady*. I don't think Audrey Hepburn did as good a job as Julie Andrews in the stage production."

"I haven't seen either," he said, "but I saw *Pygmalion*. I took . . ." He could visualize Dublin's Abbey Theatre on Lower Abbey Street and a young Fingal O'Reilly escorting a young Kitty O'Hallorhan. "I took you to see it." There was the suspicion of a catch in his voice. "We were awfully young then."

When she replied he heard wistfulness in her voice. Then she looked into O'Reilly's eyes. "I remember you when you were young, Fingal. I remember a lot about you." He felt her hand brush against the back of his.

O'Reilly coughed and not because his throat tickled. It gave him a split second to collect his thoughts. If his pipe had been handy to fiddle with, he could easily have stretched the second to a minute. He'd been looking forward to time alone with Kitty, but now that it had arrived he realized he wasn't entirely comfortable with the way the conversation was going. And if Kinky walked in just then and saw them practically holding hands, he knew he'd be embarrassed.

"There's another reason I need to get back in harness," he said, hoping to deflect her. "There's a niggling question about how a new doctor in the area, a

Doctor Fitzpatrick, might compete with us for patients. They'll be less likely to shift allegiance if their regular doctor, me, is there. I owe that to Barry. I should meet Fitzpatrick. I'll maybe get Kinky to arrange for him to come round here tomorrow."

"Fitzpatrick?" She frowned. "Not the great Ronald Hercules? He was a student with you, wasn't he?" she said. She did not remove her hand.

"None other than." It was pleasant, the warmth of her. He turned his wrist and enveloped her delicate fingers in his paw.

"He was the ugliest young man I have ever seen," she said.

O'Reilly guffawed, then said, "I'll bet he hasn't improved with age." He tightened his fingers around Kitty's, careful not to exert the kind of pressure he usually put into a handshake.

"But *you* have, Fingal," she said. Her voice was lower, huskier. He felt her hand squeeze his. "You're . . ." She hesitated. "You're distinguished."

He wanted to laugh, make some disparaging comment, but he looked into her eyes and was silenced. He saw a softness there. Somehow they were the same soft young eyes that had first attracted him in the springtime of his years. And Doctor Fingal Flahertie O'Reilly, he who never let anyone, never mind his patients, get the upper hand, that same Doctor F. F. O'Reilly found himself completely at a loss for words.

Kitty solved his problem by leaning across the gap between them and softly brushing her lips on his.

He opened his mouth and savoured the port-wine

taste of her. He wasn't such a confirmed old widower that he had forgotten the pleasures of the flesh, but inside something else was stirring, something that had lain dormant for a very long time.

He moved his head back. He was a little short of breath and very confused. He looked into her eyes again. "Kitty," he finally managed to say.

She gave him no chance to say more. She still held his hand. "Fingal, I was in love with you thirty-odd years ago. I've never quite forgotten you."

He stared down at the carpet.

"I could care for you again, if you'd let me." Her voice was level but still low and husky.

He didn't know what to say, but he saw the compassion, the understanding, in her expression. "I . . . Kitty . . . that is . . . well . . ."

She chuckled. "I've floored you, haven't I, Fingal Flahertie O'Reilly?"

He nodded, not trusting himself to speak.

"It's a big chunk for you to swallow all at once. I understand. It might take you a while to get used to the idea."

"It will." The words slipped out.

"So," she let his hand go, "pour me another port. We'll say no more tonight, but I've told you how I feel, Fingal, and I can wait for you to decide how *you* feel."

He rose and walked to the sideboard to pour her drink and refresh his own. Ordinarily he despised people who needed a drink in times of stress, but at the moment he needed one. If he followed where his heart seemed to be leading, it would be disloyal to Deidre's memory. And yet . . .

He carried Kitty's drink back to her. The smile lines at the corners of her eyes and at her upturned lips lit up her face. What had he called her before? A powerful woman. She was that, all right, and a beautiful one too. He handed her the glass of port.

She took it, and once more looking him directly in the eye, she said, "I *will* wait, Fingal, but I'll not wait forever."

12

You Can't Have Your Cake and Eat It

Get in, lummox." Barry held the back door of Brunhilde open and waited for Arthur Guinness to jump in. The little car lurched under the weight of the big dog. Barry was bundled up in his navy blue duffle coat and his old, six-foot-long, black, red, white, and yellow, vertically striped Belfast Medical Students Association scarf, a reminder of his recent undergraduate days.

As he went to get into the driver's seat, the mud of the back lane crunched under his Wellington boots.

He noticed the puddles were filmed with an icy rime that shone with a silver sparkle in the light of the half-moon that was setting in a cloudless sky.

His breath hung in a small cloud. The gale had died with the coming of the night. It was cold, but it was crisp—Christmassy, not the bone-chilling rawness of earlier in the day when it had been so damp.

He put the car in gear.

Arthur stood and draped his front paws around Barry's neck. Barry braked before the lane opened onto the main Bangor-Belfast Road. Let's see, he thought, if Arthur remembers doing as he was told earlier today. Barry turned in his seat and lifted each paw in turn. "Let's you and me get one thing straight, dog . . ." He shoved Arthur away. "*You*, dog. *Me,* boss. Now . . . *lie down, sir*." He was gratified to hear Arthur sigh as only a Labrador can, and as far as Barry could tell in the dim light, the dog subsided into the rear-seat well. "Right," he said, and turned right on the road to Sonny and Maggie's place. "And stay there, d'ye hear?"

The traffic was light and the road clear of snow. The drive to where Sonny's house stood on a hill was uneventful. In the daytime, Barry knew there was a splendid view overlooking the fields, down across the waters of Belfast Lough to the Antrim Hills of the far shore.

He parked on the road outside the fenced front garden and told Arthur to stay. Then he got out and let himself in through the cast-iron gate. Not four months ago he'd walked this path, crushing black horehound underfoot where it was growing through the cracks in the paving stones; he remembered how unpleasant it had smelled. That was the time Councillor Bishop, true to a promise O'Reilly had wrung out of him, had a crew at work replacing Sonny's roof, the necessary condition for the celebration of the long-delayed marriage of Sonny Houston to Maggie MacCorkle, spinster of this parish.

While he was still a few yards from the front door, Barry heard the clamour of barking dogs. Sonny had five and he doted on them. Before he and Maggie married and moved into this house, Sonny had lived in his car and housed his dogs in an old caravan. Now they must all be living in the house together. Oh, well, Barry thought, being greeted by animals was an integral part of visiting houses and farms in Ulster.

He climbed the two front steps. The barking from inside was deafening. In many houses without telephones, and as far as Barry knew the Houstons didn't have one, excited yapping was the first indication that someone was coming to call. It was the Ulster equivalent of an early warning system.

Before he could rap on the front door, it was opened by a tall, older man with an erect posture, bright eyes, and cheeks that were slightly dusky, which Barry knew was a sign of controlled congestive heart failure. The man held a pair of horn-rimmed glasses in one hand. Dogs, yipping and barking joyously, tumbled through the open door and out along the path created by the hall light's rays.

"Doctor Laverty." Sonny extended his hand. "What a pleasant surprise."

"Good evening, Sonny." Barry removed his right glove before shaking hands. It would have been impolite not to do so. "May I come in?"

"Please." He stepped aside and as Barry passed him, Sonny stuck two fingers in his mouth and produced a whistle that Barry thought would have done justice to a steam-driven locomotive.

Barry was surrounded by a tide of dogs as they jostled with each other to obey their master's summons home. "Kitchen," Sonny commanded, and the dogs disappeared along the hall. He heard Sonny close the door.

"Let me take your coat, Doctor."

As Barry took off his coat and scarf, he noticed framed black-and-white photographs hanging on the hall wall. He could see porticos and pillars and house fronts carved into cliff faces. "Where's that, Sonny?"

"Petra. In Jordan. I took those snaps thirty years ago. I was on an archaelogical dig. It's quite spectacular in colour."

Barry remembered that Sonny Houston, Ph.D., was an expert on, among other things, Nabataean civilization. "Petra." Barry struggled to remember the obscure quotation. "Something to do with roses?" he said.

"Petra, 'a rose-red city, half as old as time . . .'" Sonny said and smiled. "That's what Dean Burgon called it after a Swiss chap, Johann Ludwig Burckhardt, discovered it. Fascinating place. I must say I'd rather like to go back, but it would be much too hot for Maggie. Much too hot." He smiled fondly. "She's in the front room. Do come in, Doctor." He opened a door and held it for Barry.

His immediate thought was that Sonny was preparing Maggie for a trip to Jordan by getting her acclimatized to the heat to be expected there. A turf fire roared up a wide chimney, and the temperature in the room was probably close to that usually experienced in the boiler room of a coal-fired ship.

"Doctor dear," said Maggie from her seat in a high-backed rocking chair, "come on, on, in." She grinned her toothless-as-an-oyster grin at him and turned to an overstuffed armchair where a large one-eyed, one-eared cat lay curled in a ball. "And you get to hell out of that, General Montgomery." Then she pulled a ball of wool from a knitting bag on her lap and chucked it with unerring accuracy at the cat, who awoke, yowled, and leapt down from the chair. "Sit down, Doctor dear."

Barry sat. He knew better than to argue with Maggie.

Sonny moved to a second rocker beside his wife and lifted a book in his gnarled hands. Barry noticed the title, *The Decline and Fall of the Roman Empire*. As Sonny, a little creakily, lowered himself into the chair, he slipped his glasses onto his nose and smiled at Barry.

"Now," Maggie said, putting her knitting aside, "you'll take a wee cup of tea in your hand and a slice of my plum cake?"

It was less of a question than an order. Barry, who had tried Maggie's culinary delights before, had his excuse ready. "I'd love to, but I've another call to make so I can only stay for a few minutes." Maggie's tea was brewed strong enough to trot a mouse on.

"Not even a slice of cake?" She sounded disappointed.

He shook his head. "Sorry." It was an old country custom at a wedding to throw a slice of the wedding cake onto the ground. If, as was usual, the cake shattered, the couple would be assured of many children. If it remained intact, infertility might ensue. But in the case of Maggie's cakes, the concern was for whether or not the ground would fracture.

"Oh, well, I'll cut you a slice to take home." She leant over and pinched his cheek. "Young men always have a sweet tooth."

"That would be wonderful, Maggie." Barry made himself more comfortable. "So how's married life suiting you?" he asked. He saw how she took Sonny's hand and gazed at him. No words were needed. Hoping he'd not embarrassed Maggie, Barry cleared his throat and changed the subject. "Maggie, I have a favour to ask."

"A favour?" Her dark eyes twinkled. "From me? Dead on. What do you want?"

"Do you know Eileen Lindsay?"

"Aye. Lives on the estate? Her with the three kiddies and the useless layabout of a husband that done a bunk a couple of years back?"

"That's her."

"What can I do for her?"

He leant forward and spoke seriously. "Her Sammy is a bit sick and needs looking after so Eileen can still go to her work, and I was wondering . . . that is, Doctor O'Reilly and I were wondering . . ."

"God bless you, Doctor Laverty dear. Of course. Sonny and me'd be delighted, so we would. Wouldn't we?" She smiled across to Sonny, who nodded and smiled back. "When would you like us to start?"

Barry was now regretting that he had not accepted Maggie's offer of a cup of tea. He knew that would have pleased her. "How about the day after tomorrow? I'll need to have a word with her first."

"That would be grand, so it would. She still lives at 31 Comber Gardens?"

"Yes, she does."

"You'll run me there, won't you, Sonny?"

"Of course, my dear." Sonny whipped off his glasses, squinted at her, and asked, "Are you sure you're warm enough, Maggie?" Without letting her answer, he let go of her hand, rose, went to the hearth, lifted a sod of peat from a wicker basket, and tossed it on the fire. Sparks burst forth like a flock of overexcited fireflies to whirl and dance and cavort up the wide chimney mouth. "She feels the cold, you know, Doctor Laverty."

Barry heard the concern in the man's voice. Sonny had waited thirty-odd years to marry the woman he loved, and it certainly appeared to Barry that for Sonny the wait had been worth it. At the rate he himself was going with Patricia, he wondered if he'd have to wait thirty bloody years. It certainly was beginning to feel like it. And there wasn't a damn thing he could do about it.

Barry stood. "I must be running, but I'll speak to Eileen tomorrow."

"And you won't need to come all the way out here, Doctor, to tell us what she says," Sonny said, opening the lounge door. "We've had a phone installed. I'll give you the number."

Maggie bustled past him. "Thanks, Sonny," Barry said, returning his pen and notebook to an inside pocket.

Maggie reappeared and handed him a small parcel. "Here you are, Doctor dear. A wee slice of cake to have with your tea. There's enough in there for himself too."

Barry accepted the gift. "Thanks, Maggie."

Sonny stood beside Maggie, his arm draped around her shoulder. He inclined his head to the parcel and winked at Barry. Clearly, Barry thought, Sonny shared his opinion of Maggie's cake, but perhaps that was part of the definition of true love—Sonny would eat it without complaint just to please her.

"Good-night," he said, letting himself out.

The parcel seemed heavier than its size would suggest. He smiled. Arthur was in for a treat.

As Barry walked down the path, he realized he was feeling a little smug, perhaps justifiably so. He was well on the way to solving Eileen's problem, which although hardly a medical matter was as much a concern to him as it would have been to his senior colleague. And he had dealt with it as O'Reilly would have.

He opened the car door and hopped in. Arthur was snoring in the backseat, and already Brunhilde held aroma of dog. Well, having a smelly car was a small price to pay for the opportunity to work here in Ballybucklebo. So different from impersonal Belfast. Here people knew each other, were ready to help out, and didn't throw older folks on the scrap heap. He remembered with great pleasure how the whole village had pulled together in August to get Sonny's house ready for the newlyweds.

He started the engine and turned on the headlights. The beams didn't penetrate the darkness very far, but it didn't matter. He'd be driving slowly, and he knew where this road went. Perhaps that's exactly why he was enjoying living in this rural village. Life was busy but the pace was still slow, and he knew where he wanted to be: right here in Ballybucklebo.

Brunhilde bounced and rattled over a large pothole. Barry hoped his personal road would be less of an obstacle course. Still, there were some potholes to negotiate: the vague threat of Doctor Fitzpatrick and the nagging worry that Patricia's not coming home for Christmas might be an omen for the future. Civil engineers had nasty habits of heading off to distant parts. Wasn't his own father in Australia?

He stopped at a crossroads to let a tractor go past, and in the distance he could see the lights of the village sparkling in welcome.

Bugger it! he told himself, driving on. He wasn't

going to worry tonight. He was going to take Arthur for his promised walk and reward him with a lump of Maggie's cake. Then, to give O'Reilly a bit more time on his own with Kitty, Barry would drop in at the Mucky Duck for a nightcap. Then he'd head back to Number 1 Main Street, the big house that was not only a large part of his working life but was well on the way to becoming his home.

Barry and Arthur Guinness had enjoyed a brisk walk along Station Road, under the railway bridge, through the sand dunes, and out onto the firm shingle. The tide was out and he couldn't make out the edge of the water, but he could hear the waves as each caressed the shore and made the pebbles rustle and rattle.

The noise of the surf grew louder when one of the big freighters going to or leaving the port of Belfast at the head of the Lough sent its wake to crash ashore. It was then he was sure the salty scent of the sea was at its most pungent.

Now all he could hear was the gentle surf, the scuffling of Arthur's paws, and his panting as he raced to and fro. The burbling noise of the diesel engine of the Belfast-to-Bangor train, the train on which he'd first met Patricia, had faded, and there'd not be another for at least an hour.

He relished the quiet, the serenity, and the darkness. The beams of the few street lamps in Ballybucklebo did not have the strength to reach out here. Across the Lough, the lights from Greencastle, past Greenisland,

and onto Carrickfergus looked as if flickering candle flames were being reflected from a silver mirror. With measured regularity, the beams from the lighthouses at Blackhead on the Antrim side and from the Copeland Island light further down the Lough thrust questing fingers into the night.

Barry looked up to a cold sky of polished, black obsidian. The moon had set early to the west of the Ballybucklebo Hills. The stars blazed in the clear frigid air, and he saw them as cleanly and as distinctly as he imagined Ernest Shackleton, another Irishman, would have seen them shining in the crystal skies of Antarctica. There in the northeast, low to the horizon, was Ursa Major, the Great Bear. The Plough, what the Americans called the Big Dipper, had all but slipped beneath the horizon.

In August, when he'd walked Patricia from the station to her flat in Kinnegar, the whole of the Plough—the blade and the handle—had been high in the soft black velvet of a northwest sky, with the great stars of the handle—Alkaid, Mizar, and Alioth—blazing free.

Tonight only Alioth, the one nearest the blade, could be seen. It was as if the Plough were sinking, and for a moment he hoped to God his love for Patricia wasn't going to be sunk if she didn't come home for Christmas.

Then he told himself to get a grip and whistled for Arthur, making the big dog come to him. "Sit."

Arthur sat.

Barry unwrapped the two large slabs of Maggie's

plum cake, shoved the paper in his coat pocket, and set the slices in front of Arthur.

In the dim light he saw the Labrador's square head move forward. He heard Arthur sniffing, scenting the offering. "Aaarf," said Arthur, as if to say, "You've got to be joking." Then he stood and wandered away.

Barry chuckled and dug a hole in the shingle with the toe of his boot, shoved the cake in, and spread the shingle over it. As he did he muttered a line he remembered from *The Burial of Sir John Moore after Corunna:* "We buried him darkly by dead of night."

Satisfied that the evidence was well concealed, he called Arthur to heel, and together they strode for the Mucky Duck. He'd have a quick one there, waste a bit more time, and by then he'd have done his tactful duty, and more, by leaving Number 1 Main Street to O'Reilly.

13

Will Someone Take Me to a Pub?

The batwing doors of the Duck swung closed behind Barry and Arthur. After the quiet, crisp cold outside, this single low-beamed room with its noisy conversation and fug of pipe tobacco and damp undervest was a bright warm haven. The place was packed. Men leant elbows on the marble top along the bar. The tables were all taken by patrons in trousers, collarless shirts, and waistcoats, rust black jackets, and flat tweed dunchers, most smoking cheap cigarettes or stubby clay dudeens. Straight pint glasses of black Guinness and short ones of amber whiskey stood on the tables.

Mary Dunleavy, the proprietor's daughter, waved to Barry from behind the long bar. He smiled back and waited until two men standing with their backs to him turned, saw him, and moved sideways to give him room to get up to the bar. Barry recognized Fergus Finnegan, the bowlegged jockey, all four feet ten of him, dressed in jodhpurs and a tweed hacking jacket.

Barry felt Arthur collapse in a heap beside his leg. Mary was moving along the bar to where he stood.

"Evening, Doc," Fergus said. "It's a bit nippy out the night, so it is."

"Evening, Fergus." Barry took off his gloves. "Chilly enough. It must be the lack of heat out there."

They laughed together; then Barry asked, "How's your brother?"

"Declan? He's a brave bit less shaky since he'd that operation, so he is."

"I'm glad to hear that." Declan Finnegan suffered from Parkinson's disease.

"And my eye's never been better, Doc."

"Good." Fergus had suffered from acute conjunctivitis.

"Do you fancy a pint, sir?"

"Thanks, Fergus, but I'm on call. I'll buy my own tonight, and I've to get one for Arthur too." The effects of the whiskey he'd had at dinnertime should be pretty well gone by now, he thought, but he did not want to get involved in the "I'll buy you one—you buy me one" convention of drinking in an Ulster pub.

"Hello, Doctor Laverty." Mary, a plump twenty-two-year-old with a tawny mane, freckles, and a snub nose, stood across the bar. "What would you like, sir?"

"Pint, please, and a Smithwick's for Arthur."

"Right." She busied herself at the pumps.

"Glad to see you're drinking stout, Doc," Fergus said. He nodded to a table where four younger men were drinking paler beers.

Probably Tennants lager or Harp lager made by Guinness and Company, Barry thought. Lager, particularly lager cut with a measure of concentrated Rose's lime juice, was becoming popular with the younger folks.

"Did you ever try one of them lagers, sir?"

"Once in a while. On a hot day."

Fergus shook his head and took a healthy swallow from his own Guinness, then said very seriously, "I had one once. Do you know, sir, there's more hops in a dead frog." He finished his pint and said to Mary, "When you've a wee minute, I'll have a half-un."

Barry laughed. "More hops in a dead frog." He'd remember that one.

"Take your hurry in your hand, Fergus," he heard

Mary say. "And here, earn your keep and give that to Arthur." She handed Fergus a bowl of Smithwick's. "Sorry, Doctor, but you know it takes a wee while to build a decent pint." She pointed at the two-thirds full glass on the countertop.

"Of course. It has to settle." He watched the mysterious cascades in the glass and couldn't decide if the white bubbles were moving up or the black stout was moving down. "And so do I. Settle up, that is." He put a note on the counter and waited until she rang it into the till and quickly made change.

"You'll not mind if I pour Fergus his whiskey while I'm waiting?" Her smile was impish. "I hear the estate of a fellah like him might sue the establishment if he died of thirst in a public house."

"I might," said Fergus, straightening up from giving Arthur his bowl. "But sure wouldn't I forgive you for one wee kiss now, Mary?"

"Kiss is it, Fergus Finnegan? Kiss?" She handed him his whiskey. "That'll be two and sixpence."

He took the glass and put the coins on the bar top. "Just one wee kiss?"

She laughed. "I'd rather kiss a billy goat with bad breath."

"Och, Jesus, Mary, you've cut me to the onion," he said, clutching the left side of his chest. "You've my heart broken in me, so you have."

"You don't have a heart." She grinned and gave Barry his pint. "There's nothing in your chest, Fergus, but a big hard swinging brick. And it stunted your growth too."

"Well," he said with a pretend leer, "you know what they say about short men."

"Away off and chase yourself." Mary tossed her mane, stuck out her tongue at Fergus, and headed off down the bar to where another customer was beckoning to her.

Fergus laughed and shook his head. "That's a right sharp one there, so it is. She can give as good as she gets."

"She can that, Fergus. Mind you, she'd need to, working in a place like this."

"Not at all, Doc," Fergus said, and Barry could see that the little man was suddenly serious. "A bit of *craic* with her's all right, but God help the fellah that stepped over the line. The lads would murder him."

It might not be quite the mediaeval code of chivalry toward women, Barry thought, but the Ulster folk did have their own clearly defined standards.

There was a sudden burst of laughter from further along the bar. Barry turned to see Mary standing, one hand on her hip, eyes bright, grinning fit to burst, and the men she'd been serving pointing at an obviously discomfited member of their number. All but him were laughing.

"I see what you mean," he said. The transformation in Mary Dunleavy since she'd quit her position as the henpecked assistant to Miss Moloney, the dress-shop lady Barry suspected of having anaemia, was quite amazing. He took a pull on his stout and ignored Arthur, who was making small "I'd go another pint" noises in the back of his throat.

"Fair play to her," Fergus said. "Her dad's very lucky to have her as a full-time barmaid."

"Indeed he is," said Barry. "In more ways than one." Not so long ago, Councillor Bishop had been planning to take the Black Swan's lease away from Willy Dunleavy. And he would have if Doctor O'Reilly hadn't enlisted the help of Sonny and the marquis to put a stop to Bishop's schemes and make sure Willy's lease was renewed for another ninety-nine years. Once secure, Willy'd been able to give his daughter Mary a full-time job, and she'd quit her position at the hat shop, got away from Miss Moloney and her critical, domineering ways. Her transformation from a timid retiring girl to the self-assured one who now stood before him had been miraculous. Here she was, gaily asking if he'd like another pint and remarking to Fergus, "Tell me again what they say about short men, or are you the exception that proves the rule?"

Fergus glanced down at the front of his trousers. Barry knew they were implying that there was an inverse relationship between a man's height and the size of his organ. Now what would Mary say?

Nothing, but her scalding laugh was a masterpiece of sarcasm.

Barry and Fergus both laughed. "All right, Mary. You win." Fergus finished all but the last sip of his whiskey. "Anyhow, it's time I was for home."

Barry finished his pint. "Me, too," he said. He set

the glass on the bar top just as Fergus put his whiskey glass down.

"I'm off, Doc," he said. "By the way, will you be at the Rugby Club Christmas party?"

"I hope so."

"Great. Then I'll see you there. I'm captain of the fifteen."

"Are you not a bit short, Fergus?"

"Bless you, not at all, sir. I play scrum half, so I do." Barry heard the pride in the little man's voice.

"Scrum half? Good for you, Fergus." Traditionally the player in that position was a small man. The scrum half was the rugby equivalent of the American quarterback. Barry had learned about American football in one of the old Francis the Talking Mule movies, which had revolved around a championship game of the American sport.

"And I'll be seeing Doctor O'Reilly there too, so I'll wish the both of youse a Merry Christmas then. It's early for that tonight with more than two weeks to go 'til the big day."

"Fair enough, Fergus." Barry spoke to Arthur. "Come on, Arthur." The big dog stood and followed Barry as he and Fergus walked to the doors.

"Night, Doc," Fergus said, as he turned to walk away. "By the way, how is Doctor O'Reilly? I hear he has a touch of the wheezles."

"He has but he's on the mend."

"Good. Do you know if he'll be at the club committee meeting?"

"I doubt it."

"I'm sure we'll manage without him, but tell him I was asking for him."

"I will, Fergus." Barry sensed Arthur nudging his leg. "I've to get the dog home," he said. "Good-night, Fergus."

"Good-night, Doc." Fergus walked away, and Barry with Arthur at his heels headed for Brunhilde and home.

With Arthur back in his doghouse, Barry let himself in through the kitchen door.

"Evening, Doctor," Kinky greeted him. She was wearing a pink felt dressing gown and fluffy slippers. Her hair was done up in paper curlers under a hairnet. She stood at the stove waiting for a kettle to boil. "Is there anything you'd like before I head off to my bed?"

"No thanks, Kinky. Away you go."

"I'll just be a little minute, sir. I'm going to fill myself a hot water bottle."

"Go right ahead, Kinky. I take it there were no calls?"

"Not a one, praise be."

"Is Doctor O'Reilly still up?"

"Huh. Up and right back to his old self." She sniffed. "Not ten minutes after that nice Miss O'Hallorhan left, didn't I tell him it was time for some more friar's balsam?"

"And?"

"A good Christian woman wouldn't repeat what he said to me."

For a moment Barry worried. Could Fingal have overstepped the mark?

The kettle whistled, and Kinky turned off the gas. "You doctors talk a great deal about symptoms, don't you?" She started to pour the water into a cloth-covered rubber bag. "Well, there's a symptom with himself I look out for. When he's as carniptious as a wet hen"—she screwed the stopper in the neck of the hot water bottle—"he's back to his old normal self." She dried the place where the stopper was. "Sure it's a great relief to me to have him better, so." There was a small smile at the corners of her eyes.

"And to me, Kinky."

"Well," she said, "I'm for my bed, but run you up the stairs and see how he's doing. He's still in the lounge."

"I will," Barry said, taking off his coat.

"Doctor Laverty, would you do me one wee favour?"

"Certainly."

"Don't encourage him to have any more whiskey tonight."

He heard the concern again. "I promise." He said. "Not a drop."

"Thank you, Doctor Laverty. Now be on with you."

"Good-night, Kinky." Barry headed for the hall, and as he climbed the stairs he heard the massive sounds of the majestic final movement of Beethoven's Ninth Symphony.

It was dim in the upstairs lounge. O'Reilly stood

with his back to Barry, looking into the grate where the fire had died to embers. He had switched off the lights and was enjoying the music in the glow of the dying fire. He was singing along with the choir in his deep baritone, *"Such' ihn ber'm Sternenzelt! ber Sternen mu er wohnen."*

Barry waited quietly until the symphony ended and O'Reilly had turned off the Phillips Black Box. Then he coughed and said, "I'm back, Fingal."

For a moment he thought O'Reilly hadn't heard him, but the big man turned slowly. Even in the dim light, Barry could see O'Reilly's eyes were brighter than normal, and when he spoke there was a hint of a catch in his voice. "Do you know that work?"

"I do."

"It used to be a favourite of an old friend of mine." He pulled out a handkerchief, blew his nose, and dabbed his eyes. "Bloody head cold. Makes your nose and eyes run."

So can some memories, Barry thought, but he kept his counsel. "Kinky said she reckoned you were on the mend."

"Much better, my boy." O'Reilly parked himself in his armchair. "Do you fancy a jar?"

"Not for me, thanks, Fingal."

"Nor me," said O'Reilly, much to Barry's surprise. "Come and sit down. We've a bit of catching up to do."

Barry sat in the other armchair.

"Now," said O'Reilly. He coughed once. "I'm much better, but I'm not *altogether* at myself yet, so

I'll not be back at work tomorrow, but I expect to be ready to go on Thursday. In the surgery anyway, if you don't mind still doing the home visits and taking call for the next couple of nights?"

"Aye, certainly."

"Good," said O'Reilly. "Now, about the practice. I know you've not been too busy, but tell me about the patients you're going to have to follow up."

Barry thought for a minute. "Nothing very serious," he said. Then he began to list them by ticking them off with his right index finger against the palm of his left hand. "Cissie Sloan, pharyngitis. She'll be back if she's not better in a few days."

Even in the dim light Barry could see O'Reilly roll his eyes. "It's a good thing we've chairs in the surgery, not stools."

"Because she could talk the leg off a stool? The marquis said she'd talk the hind leg off a donkey."

"I think Cissie inhabits a world populated by three-leggèd donkeys and biped stools." O'Reilly laughed and coughed one short, sharp cough. "Who else is there?"

"Liam Gillespie should be home for Christmas."

"Good."

"Colin Brown won't be back—"

"What was wrong with Colin?"

Barry laughed. "A bad attack of 'I don't want to go to schoolitis.' His nose was out of joint because he wasn't going to be allowed to play Joseph in the Christmas pageant."

"Sounds like Colin. If I were his teacher, I'd keep an eye on him."

Barry remembered the evil look he'd seen in the little boy's eyes as he was leaving just as Doctor Fitzpatrick had shown up at the door. He was glad his responsibilities were for his patients' ailments only. "And then there's Jeannie Jingles's lad with pneumonia. I've forgotten to phone the hospital to find out about him, but I'll do it tomorrow."

O'Reilly nodded.

"Miss Moloney's back, and I'm pretty sure she has iron-deficiency anaemia. I'll see her when her results are in."

"Begod," said O'Reilly, "I wonder if she's a vegetarian."

"I hadn't thought of that."

"Might be worth finding out."

"Thanks, Fingal." Barry shifted in his chair. "Miss Moloney and young Sammy Lindsay's purpura are the most interesting cases. I'd a bit of luck there. Maggie says she's happy to take care of him so Eileen can get to work. I'll go see him tomorrow and let Eileen know."

"That was a good idea of yours about Maggie. Eileen'll be relieved."

"I hope so. It would be a shame if she had to dip into her Christmas savings. She works hard enough as it is."

"Och," said O'Reilly, "'the world is ill-divided. Them that works the hardest are the least provided.'"

"True and poetically put."

"It should be. I pinched the words from a Scottish folk song." O'Reilly leant forward and patted Barry's knee. "It could apply to junior assistants and to country GPs."

"Come on, Fingal. You pay me a fair wage."

"Perhaps, but I have been sweating you a bit in the last few days."

"I don't mind. Honestly."

O'Reilly sat back. "I'm grateful, Barry." He cocked his head to one side. "It's important that one of us is here all the time now there's a new man in the Kinnegar."

Barry had almost forgotten about Doctor Fitzpatrick.

"Anyway," said O'Reilly, "Kinky phoned him this evening. He's going to come over tomorrow to pay his 'courtesy call.' "

"Indeed? Well, I suppose we should get to know him. Professional ethics and that sort of stuff."

"Ethics, my arse," said O'Reilly with a snort. "Better the divil you know than the one you don't. I want to find out more about the man, and if it looks like he could be a threat, we'll have a better notion how to counter him."

"True." Kinky was right. O'Reilly was back in form.

"So that's for tomorrow, and the next day I will be back at work."

"If you're up to it."

O'Reilly grunted. "And I'll work this weekend. You deserve a break."

"*If* you're up to it, Fingal."

"I bloody well will be. Count on it."

"All right, all right. Actually I'd not mind being off on Saturday. I'm hoping to see my friend Jack Mills."

"Good, because I want the next Saturday off. The tides are right at Strangford Lough, and I'm going to take Arthur out for a day's wildfowling."

"Fine. It'll be my turn to work anyway."

"Thanks, Barry," O'Reilly said, rising. "And we both have busy days tomorrow." He yawned. "So I'm for my bed."

"Good-night, Fingal," Barry said, as O'Reilly left. He hoped they both would get a good night's sleep, so that he could face the practice tomorrow and Fingal could have his meeting with Doctor Ronald Hercules Fitzpatrick.

14

What's in a Name?

Doctor O'Reilly stood at the window of the lounge, looking down. The pedestrians on the footpaths beneath him were bundled up, and they scurried along, too eager to get in out of the cold to stand around chatting. The shadow cast by the church steeple was twice as long as it would have been in

June. Judging by the crystal rime on the verges of the gravel path through the churchyard, it was a crackling, frosty morning.

He gazed over the church roof. The sun hung low in a crisp, blue, cloudless sky, and so clear was the day, O'Reilly could almost have been persuaded that it was summertime. He watched two herring gulls glide lazily by, one with the brown-speckled feathers of an immature bird, the other with adult plumage as smooth as a well-pressed, dove-grey morning coat set off with a new white waistcoat. He heard the raucous bickering of the gulls, harsh against the occasional muttering of traffic on Main Street.

In the distance, over the Lough a vee of geese, purposeful as a sortie of light bombers, thrust its way east toward Ballyholme and the stubble fields of the Ards Peninsula. He smiled. Next Saturday he might get a shot at a goose.

"Excuse me, Doctor O'Reilly." He turned to see Kinky standing inside the doorway. "Will I take away your coffee tray?"

"Please."

Instead of lifting it, she stared at him and frowned. "Tch. Tch. Would you look at your jacket, sir?"

He glanced down. He'd been at particular pains this morning to dress properly so he'd look smart to greet Doctor Fitzpatrick. His brown boots shone—he'd polished them himself—the tweed pants of his suit were pressed, his white shirt was fresh, and he wore the tie of the Royal Navy Association. And yet Kinky was right. There was a large stain above the left jacket pocket. Damn it. He must have spilled some coffee. "Sorry, Kinky."

"Give it here," she said, "and I'll take it and sponge it, so."

O'Reilly shrugged it off and handed it to her.

"I'll bring it back in a little minute," she assured him, and so saying, she left.

O'Reilly sat down in his armchair. Kinky wouldn't let him meet a guest in a stained jacket, but as far as he was concerned there was not a damn thing wrong with being in a shirt with the sleeves rolled up and letting the guest see that your pants were held up with a pair of red braces. He thought that whoever had said, "Clothes don't make the man," had said it all.

He smiled. Kinky, who had reappeared, would not have shared his opinion. "Put this on you now, sir." She handed him the coat, waited until O'Reilly put it on, and then straightened his tie, clucking as she did so. Then she bent and lifted the coffee tray. "I'll be off now. Your guest should be here in ten minutes. I'll show him up when he comes."

O'Reilly thought of Barry's description of how Kinky had dealt with the man the last time he was here. "You'll not fire a shot across his bows first, will you, Kinky?"

"Not if he minds his p's and q's and treats me properly," Kinky said.

"I'm sure he will."

He watched her step aside, tray in hands, to let Barry come in. "So," said O'Reilly, "you've finished the surgery a bit early today?"

"Yes. It wasn't too bad this morning. A few of the regulars, four for tonics," Barry smiled. "I saw the tonics one at a time, and made them take their pants down."

He's remembering the day I lined up six patients in a row, O'Reilly thought, and gave them their injections right through their clothes. It didn't do them one bit of harm, and getting rid of six at once let me get through the work so I could see some really sick folks that bit sooner. But Barry had his own ways, and it was right that he be allowed to do what he reckoned to be correct, at least until he discovered the error of his ways.

"Kieran O'Hagan was in to have his dressing changed," Barry said. "His thumb's fine."

"Good." O'Reilly waved to the plain chair. "Have a pew there. You'll not be in the direct line of sight of our esteemed colleague, Doctor Ronald Hercules Fitzpatrick, when he sits in the armchair. You can keep an eye on him and he'll not be aware you're watching. He should be here any minute now." He coughed once.

"How's the chest today, Fingal?"

"Almost a hundred percent. I'll be in the surgery tomorrow."

"Good." Barry peered at his senior colleague's face. "Your colour's a damn sight better today."

If you like the colour of plums, O'Reilly laughed to himself. He was under no illusions about the hue of his cheeks made ruddy by years of braving the Ulster elements by day and by night. Ulster farmers weren't the only ones with weather-beaten complexions. He looked at his watch. Fitzpatrick was supposed to be here at noon. Five minutes to go and . . . He cocked his head and listened. Front doorbell's jangle. Pause. Kinky's tread in the hall. Voices. Door closing. Footsteps approaching.

"He's early," O'Reilly said.

"Punctuality is the politeness of kings," said Barry.

"I thought it was the virtue of princes," O'Reilly said.

Barry shook his head. "Not if your source is Louis the Eighteenth."

O'Reilly chuckled. "I stand, or rather sit, corrected."

Doctor Fitzpatrick came in, followed by Kinky. He was an older version of the student O'Reilly remembered. If he'd been asked to pick out three of the man's salient features, they would have been his massive Adam's apple, the wing-tip collar, and the pince-nez.

Kinky bustled past Doctor Fitzpatrick. "This would be the gentleman you were expecting, sir?" Something in the inflection of her voice told O'Reilly that as far as Kinky was concerned, "gentleman" was something of an overstatement.

Fitzpatrick glowered at Kinky over his pince-nez. "Thank you, my good woman. You may go now."

Barry half rose. "Good morning, Doctor Fitzpatrick. We've already met."

O'Reilly remained seated and ignored them as they exchanged pleasantries. "My good woman" Fitzpatrick had called Kinky, summarily dismissing her. O'Reilly had a suddenly vivid mental image of a café in Dublin, thirty-odd years earlier, where Fitzpatrick, then a student at Trinity College, had called a waitress "my good woman." She had told him in no uncertain terms to go and do something anatomically impossible.

He wondered if Kinky would say anything more, but she contented herself with one enormous sniff, a stiff about-turn that would have put a sergeant major to shame, and a departure worthy of the queen of Sheba, so rigidly did she hold herself. O'Reilly chuckled.

Barry had returned to his chair. O'Reilly saw Fitzpatrick take a seat and realized he was being addressed.

"I trust you are feeling better, Fingal."

"Oh, indeed, Hercules." Obsequious bastard.

Fitzpatrick's larynx bobbed up and down. The wattles on his neck quivered.

Good Lord, O'Reilly thought, if he was a turkey he'd gobble.

"I believe I told you, O'Reilly, when we were students together that I prefer to be addressed as Ronald."

"Aye. People are funny about what they like to be called, *Ronald.*" Before Fitzpatrick could reply, O'Reilly continued, "Take Kinky, for example. She responds well to 'Mrs. Kincaid.' Some other things don't please her very much." He winked at Barry and said, "I think they gave up dragging the Lough after three days." O'Reilly saw the great grin on Barry's face. O'Reilly wondered, has he worked out what I'm hoping he'll say when Fitzpatrick rises to the bait?

"I'm afraid I don't understand. 'Dragging the Lough'?" Fitzpatrick scratched his cheek.

Up like a trout to a fly. O'Reilly glanced at Barry and raised one eyebrow. He was delighted when Barry, who clearly had followed O'Reilly's train of thought, said with a smile, "They were looking for the body of the last man who called Mrs. Kincaid 'my good woman.' "

O'Reilly heard a dry cackling noise. Fitzpatrick's narrow shoulders were shaking. Gracious. The man was laughing. He pulled off his pince-nez and polished them with a handkerchief. I'll often fiddle with my pipe to give myself time to think, O'Reilly thought. Does he use the same trick but with his glasses?

Finally Fitzpatrick said, "Heh, heh. Droll. Very droll. Looking for a body. Heh."

Barry spoke and this time there was just a hint of an edge to his voice. "Mrs. Kincaid did tell you, the last time you were here, she wasn't keen on being called that." Then his words were softer. The olive branch. "You must have forgotten."

Fitzpatrick sat more erectly, with his knees together like a prim dowager afraid some lecher might try to look up her skirt. "I will remember for the future. It's Mrs. Kinsale."

"No," said O'Reilly. "Kincaid. Mrs. Kincaid."

"It seems to me you're making an extraordinary fuss over a mere servant."

O'Reilly saw Barry stiffen and shake his head. Then Barry relaxed and said nothing. Fitzpatrick had, on the surface, come to establish professional diplomatic relations. If by his attitude he chose to make himself persona non grata, he might well end up regretting it. He'd already made an enemy of Kinky, and she was certainly one of the most important arbiters of public opinion in the townland. O'Reilly was quite happy to let the man dig his own grave. "You could be right," O'Reilly said in his most placatory voice, "and I'm sure you didn't come merely to discuss our domestic arrangements here. Actually Doctor Laverty and I have been remiss. As the established practice, we should have visited you to welcome you to the district."

"I'm glad you recognize that, Fingal." Fitzpatrick looked down his nose at O'Reilly. "Very glad."

God, Fitzpatrick, you were a prissy bastard at Trinity, and you're a prissy bastard now, O'Reilly thought. But he said. "We'll let bygones be bygones, won't we, Ronald?"

"That would be the Christian thing to do."

The man had belonged, and almost certainly still did, to one of the ultraconservative fundamentalist sects that abounded in the north of Ireland. "A bit of other-cheek turning, you mean?"

"Precisely."

"Och," said O'Reilly, standing to give himself the physical equivalent of the moral high ground. "Consider mine turned." He offered his hand to the seated

Fitzpatrick, who accepted the handshake with a grip O'Reilly found soft, clammy, and about as welcoming as touching the scales of a recently boated flounder. "How's business in the Kinnegar, anyway?" He released the hand and foreswore the temptation to wipe his own on the leg of his pants. O'Reilly decided he would remain standing.

"Very promising. It *was* a bit slow at the start. I suspect some of my predecessor's patients started consulting this practice." He looked over the top of his pince-nez at O'Reilly and smiled his grim smile. "I'm very pleased to say that in the last month the tide seems to have been reversed. Quite a few of yours are now coming my way."

"Is that a fact?" O'Reilly glanced at Barry to see that he was sitting on the edge of his chair, forehead creased in a frown. He took a deep breath as if he was about to speak, so O'Reilly said, "Doctor Laverty and I haven't noticed any reduction of our load." He fixed Barry with a glare. "Have we, Barry?"

"None at all."

Good lad. Give nothing away. It's our business, not his. O'Reilly wandered over and leant on the mantelpiece.

"Well, I think you soon will. They seem to like my more traditional approach."

"And what would that be?" O'Reilly enquired. "Eye of newt, and toe of frog?" He laughed.

Fitzpatrick's larynx bobbed once.

"Or maybe wool of bat, and tongue of dog?" said Barry.

O'Reilly laughed more loudly. Barry could never resist playing their quotations game. Fitzpatrick wasn't the only one who would rise if offered the right fly.

"You may jest, Fingal, but I have had some quite spectacular successes with old country remedies."

"Have you, Ronald? Would you like to give us a for instance?" O'Reilly made sure he wore an expression of rapt interest. "I'm always up for learning something new." It was annoying, he thought, that just at that moment his throat tickled and he was forced to cough.

Fitzpatrick pointed his bony index finger at O'Reilly. "You yourself are a case in point."

O'Reilly coughed once more, then said, "And how would that be?"

"You have tracheobronchitis. How are you treating it? No, I can guess. Antibiotics. Modern medicine is hopelessly wedded to them."

"Actually, I'm not—"

"Don't interrupt." The finger wagging increased. "*I* have very little use for them, but *I* find a home-prepared tincture very effective."

O'Reilly found the man's stressing of "I" irritating. "Would you like to tell us about it?"

"It would be my pleasure. Take primrose roots, crush them up, and put them in the whey of goat's milk."

"Interesting," said Barry. "And are primrose roots easy to come by in December?"

O'Reilly couldn't tell whether Barry was genuinely interested or was having Fitzpatrick on.

"The plant doesn't flower, but its roots are still in the ground."

"Oh," said Barry. "Thank you."

"Primrose roots in the whey of goat's milk?" O'Reilly frowned. "Sounds simple enough. And does the patient drink the mixture?"

Fitzpatrick leant forward. In his eyes, O'Reilly saw an evangelical gleam. "No. The next step is the clever one because it gets right to the root of the disease." He tittered. "That's rather good, using roots to get to the root."

"Go on," said O'Reilly, thinking that once in a while the old adage "Laugh and the world laughs with you" could be wrong. "I'm all agog."

"You stick the mixture up the patient's nose." Fitzpatrick smiled smugly. "What do you think of that?"

O'Reilly guffawed. For a while he couldn't stop. When he finally gained control, he said, "Sorry, Ronald, but I just got what you said earlier: 'Using roots to get to the root.' Very good. Very good."

"Well, that's all right then. For a moment, I thought you were mocking my therapy. Worse, that you were laughing at me. I hate it when people laugh at me. I always did. *I hate it*." He actually stamped one foot.

"Me?" said O'Reilly, all injured innocence. "Laugh at you, Ronald?" He glanced at Barry, who was also struggling to keep a straight face. "I'd never do such a thing. I remember how it used to upset you."

"Thank you." Fitzpatrick seemed to be mollified.

"It's not every day I hear such an *incredible* approach," O'Reilly said.

"Well, thank you, Fingal." The man actually simpered.

O'Reilly looked at Barry, who inaudibly mouthed, "Incredible," and grinned broadly. *Oxford English Dictionary,* O'Reilly thought. More people should read it. If they did, they would find "*incredible*: that cannot be believed." But if it made old Fitzpatrick happy, who was O'Reilly to spoil his morning? O'Reilly's stomach grumbled. He realized he was hungry. Barry must be too. It would be close to lunchtime, and that meant it was time to get rid of their colleague.

"I'm pleased you're settling in so well, Ronald." O'Reilly moved toward the door. "And Doctor Laverty and I wouldn't want to keep you from your work for too long, would we, Barry?"

Barry rose. "Certainly not."

Fitzpatrick stood, made a half bow to Barry, and said, "Young Laverty." Then he strode to O'Reilly, paused, offered his hand, accepted the handshake, and said, "I've enjoyed our little meeting, Fingal. I do hope we can do it again."

I'd rather sit through a two-hour sermon by the Presbyterian minister, O'Reilly thought. But he said, "I don't see why we can't. Perhaps we can do a bit of catching up on what the pair of us have been up to since medical school?" And I'll bet your story, Hercules, will be as fascinating as the manual that came with the washing machine I bought for Kinky last year.

"I might quite enjoy that, Fingal, but for the moment I'd prefer to keep things on a professional basis." He cleared his throat. "I think we might find we're going to be in competition."

"Suits me," said O'Reilly, standing clear of the mantel and adopting his old familiar boxer's attacking stance, with one foot in advance of the other. He hadn't boxed since he'd left the navy, but old habits died hard.

"I hesitate to be the ghost at the feast," Fitzpatrick continued, looking particularly cheerful, "especially at this festive season, but I have wondered if the region is big enough to keep three doctors busy."

O'Reilly saw Barry flinch. The lad would be worried. O'Reilly shared his concern, but if Fitzpatrick was throwing down a professional gauntlet, Fingal O'Reilly was the man to accept the challenge. "Probably not, Ronald," he said blandly. "I'm sure Doctor Laverty and I will miss you when you leave." He moved across the room and opened the door. "Now let me show you out." He glanced at Barry. "Doctor Laverty and I are on our way down to our lunch. Sorry we can't invite you to stay and join us."

15

A Primrose by a River's Brim

O'Reilly knocked the dottle out of his briar into a huge ashtray that Kinky had this Thursday morning, under some protest, placed in its habitual spot on the dining room table. It was beyond him why she'd been under the impression he'd given up smoking forever, just because he'd not picked up his pipe for the few days his chest had been afflicted. He'd missed his tobacco as a man might miss an old and dear friend.

He crammed the pipe into his jacket pocket, finished his tea, and rose. Time for him to be in the trenches. He'd promised Barry he'd take care of the surgery this morning, and by God, he would, and he'd be well enough by Saturday to cover the weekend too.

O'Reilly shoved his chair away from the table, rose, glanced up, and hoped Barry was still asleep. The lad had worked hard for the last few days. O'Reilly had not heard Barry leave this morning, but he had heard him return just after dawn had broken. Let him sleep. He'd earned it.

O'Reilly passed the big table, went into the hall, and opened the waiting room door. Jesus Murphy, he thought. It was like Paddy's market in there, standing room only. Barry would be pleased to hear the place was packed. O'Reilly ignored the chorus of "Good morning, Doctor," and roared, "Right, who's first?"

Cissie Sloan, blue beret on her untidy mop of hair, woolly scarf wrapped around her neck, the rest of her bundled up in an army surplus great coat that O'Reilly knew would have been purchased at the Army and Navy Store in Belfast, lumbered to her Wellington-booted feet. "Right, Cissie," he said, "you know your way."

As he followed her to the surgery he remembered yesterday's lunch when, try as he might, O'Reilly did not seem to be able to reassure Barry that Doctor Fitzpatrick probably did not present a real threat. Once his novelty had worn off, the Ballybucklebo patients would be quite happy to return to Number 1 Main Street. Some of them, he thought, watching Cissie process along the hall and into the surgery, didn't even seem to have any notion of leaving at all. He heard the chair creak as Cissie settled herself. Passing her, he parked himself in his swivel chair.

"Doctor Laverty not in the day?"

"My turn, Cissie. He was up half the night."

"Right enough? He works very hard, so he does." She made a sympathetic clucking noise and leant forward. "And I hear you've been a bit under the weather yourself, sir."

"Och, sure it was only a slight touch of the bubonic plague and leprosy, and I shook them both off in no time." He looked at her over his half-moon glasses. "I've the constitution of a Clydesdale horse."

Cissie's laugh was throaty, though whether from

her earlier thyroid deficiency or her recent sore throat he couldn't be sure.

"You're the terrible man, Doctor dear, so you are, teasing a poor countrywoman like me. Leprosy, my aunt Fanny Jane. You only get that in darkest Africa. Wasn't I just telling my cousin Aggie, you know the one with the six toes, her and me was working in the parish hall getting it ready for the pageant, we'd just hung up another red paper chain, and Aggie says—"

"Cissie," O'Reilly said forcibly, "what ails *you* today? Doctor Laverty told me you'd a sore throat."

"Would you like to have a wee look? It's not better. I think maybe you should look at it. My cousin—"

"Right." He grabbed a tongue depressor from a jar that stood on his desk and pulled a clip-on pencil torch from the inside pocket of his jacket. "Open big and stick out your tongue." If nothing else, that would stem the verbal torrent. The back of her throat was red, but it looked to him pretty much as he would anticipate pharyngitis to appear after a couple of days of treatment. "Doesn't look too bad—" he started to say, as he removed the wooden spatula.

"Aggie says that maybe the Saint Brigid's cotton isn't working, that maybe the penicillin the young doctor, no harm to him . . ." She hesitated and looked at O'Reilly, who knew very well that "no harm to him" inevitably presaged a criticism. "Well, maybe what he prescribed me isn't the right thing, she says—"

"What?" O'Reilly pulled off his half-moons and dangled them by one leg from between his finger and thumb, resisting the temptation to enquire which of the five Irish medical schools was Aggie's alma mater.

"She says what I need is to buck them pills down the sink and get goat's milk whey and stick a wheen of ground-up primrose roots—"

O'Reilly dropped his glasses, silencing Cissie for a moment, and sat bolt upright. "And does she recommend shoving the mixture up your nose?"

Cissie beamed. "Aren't you the quare smart one, Doctor O'Reilly? That's exactly, *exactly,* what she said. And do *you* think I should?" She frowned. "I'm never quite sure about our Aggie . . ."

O'Reilly bent, retrieved his spectacles, took out his pipe, and filled it, quite happy to let Cissie prattle on while he thought rapidly. For starters, either because she had a sore throat herself or on behalf of her cousin Cissie, Aggie had almost certainly consulted Fitzpatrick. Until yesterday, in all his years here, O'Reilly had never heard of that particular nostrum being popular among the local citizens, and he was sure he was familiar with all the local folk remedies.

"I always think she needs an anenema."

O'Reilly ignored the mispronunciation. He was more worried that the suggested cure, which he was certain had come from Fitzpatrick and which was blatant quackery, could harm one of Barry's patients. As far as O'Reilly was concerned, Fitzpatrick could prescribe boiled water to those he treated. But when his advice started to affect the customers of Number 1 Main Street, it was time to start paying attention. In

O'Reilly's opinion, Cissie needed the penicillin Barry had prescribed.

"Aggie needs an anenema because I think she's usually full of shite, but I thought I'd come and get a second opinion just to be sure."

O'Reilly stifled his irritation at being considered a backup to cousin Aggie. The main thing was to make sure Cissie kept on taking her tablets.

He stuck his filled pipe in a side pocket, leant forward, and said, "I made a mistake about you in July, didn't I, Cissie?"

"Aye. You didn't know I'd the thyroid thingy." She smiled. "But sure a bishop can be wrong too sometimes. Only your man in Rome's infallybubble."

"True, Cissie, I'm not infallible, but who found out your thyroid was out of whack?"

"Doctor Laverty."

"And now did he suggest crushed primrose roots or penicillin for your throat?"

"Penicillin." She looked puzzled, then said, "Aye, and he told me to go on using the Saint Brigid's cotton too."

"Powerful stuff, the cotton," O'Reilly said. "Now, Cissie, if you'd to bet money on it, where would you put your cash? Penicillin or primrose roots?"

"Doctor Laverty—and I'd give him odds on, so I would."

"Good for you, Cissie." O'Reilly rose and helped her to her feet. "Doctor Laverty wouldn't see you wrong, you know that. So you keep taking that penicillin as

Doctor Laverty prescribed, and you'll be right as rain in another few days."

"Thank you, Doctor," she said. "I'd not fancy sticking that stuff up my nose," she giggled. "Maybe Aggie could use it for her anenema. I think I'll tell her—"

"I'm sure you will, Cissie." He manoeuvered her toward the door, opened it, and guided her out. "And come in anytime you're worried."

"Thank you, Doctor. And I'll—"

She was still talking as he closed the surgery door, and through it he could hear her chuntering on in the hall. He fished out his pipe, lit up, and relished a few good puffs until he heard the front door close. Then satisfied that she had left, he wandered back to the waiting room. He opened the door a crack and listened. He could overhear the tail end of a conversation between two of his regulars, two older folks who regarded their weekly trip to their medical advisor more as a social outing than a therapeutic endeavour.

"I didn't see you here last week, Bertha."

"I wasn't in, Jimmy."

"Oh. Why not?"

"You know bloody well there's only one thing would keep *me* away. I was *sick*, so I was."

O'Reilly chuckled. He was just a tiny bit humbled when she said, in tones so serious as to underline the absolute truth of her sentiments, "And I didn't want to trouble the doctors. Not when I was poorly."

He opened the door wide. "Who's the next—"

The door to the outside was opened, and the

marquis came in. Everyone rose, the men knuckling their foreheads, the women dropping small curtsies. All stood aside so the presence could go first. Rank has its privileges, O'Reilly thought, as he often did when he pulled it to get to the head of a queue. "Morning, my lord," he said.

"Good morning, Doctor, and everyone, please be seated." The man exuded a natural graciousness. "I'll only keep Doctor O'Reilly for a very few minutes."

O'Reilly stood aside, then followed the marquis to the surgery and closed the door. He waited as with familiar ease the man took off his camel hair overcoat with the black velvet lapels and his blazer with the crest of the Irish Guards on the breast pocket, rolled up his shirtsleeve, and climbed up to lie on the examining couch.

"You've not noticed any changes since you were in a couple of months ago?" O'Reilly asked, as he wrapped the blood pressure cuff around the upper arm and inflated it.

"Not a thing, except those ruddy pills make me pee too much." He grinned. "Small price to pay, I suppose."

"Very small. At your age, untreated high blood pressure can cause a stroke." O'Reilly stuck his stethoscope in his ears and put the bell into the front of the elbow beneath the cuff. Then he slowly deflated the cuff and watched as the column of mercury fell, noting the pressure of 150 when the first sounds of the blood coursing in the radial artery could be heard and noting the pressure of 85 when they disappeared. Not much above the normal 120 and 80 for a younger man. "Same as before," he said, removing the cuff. "Sit up, please."

The marquis swung his legs over the edge of the couch and sat up.

O'Reilly lifted an ophthalmoscope from the instrument table and turned on its light. "Just stare at the wall over my shoulder, please." He shone the light into the lens of the left eye. All he could see was a red blur until he had fiddled with the focusing wheel. The optic disc, the bright red retina, swam into view. There was a small light-coloured circular area in the middle of this field. That was the macula, the place where the optic nerve left the back of the eyeball; running from it were the tiny arteries and veins that supplied and drained the retina. There were no blurring of the macular margins, no constrictions in any of the blood vessels, nor any signs of those small areas of bleeding described graphically as "flame haemorrhages." The presence of any or all would be evidence that the hypertension was worsening. "Good, that disc's fine," he said, turning his attention to the right eye. "Now as our record-playing friends would say, let's have a look at the flip side." In a few moments he confirmed that the right retina too was healthy. "You'll do for another couple of months."

O'Reilly went to his desk and sat in his swivel chair, as the marquis put his clothes back on. "Here you are." O'Reilly half turned and handed his patient a prescription for chlorothiazide, five hundred milligrams, to be taken daily. "That'll keep you right, John."

"Thank you, Fingal. Now I'll just keep you for another minute. I'm pleased to see you are better."

"I'm grand."

"Good, because the executive of the Rugby Club would like you to attend an extraordinary meeting on Saturday evening after the game."

O'Reilly spun to face the marquis. "Did the daft buggers vote down the one-pound rise in dues on Wednesday night?"

"Not at all. They passed it with barely a murmur. I hinted when I came to visit you on Tuesday morning that I thought Councillor Bishop would object. He did, but we all know he'd wrestle a bear for a halfpenny, so we soon shut him up. No, Fingal, they want to make the final arrangements for this year's Christmas party, and if you're up to it they'd quite like you to be in attendance."

"Saturday?" O'Reilly frowned, then said, "I should be able to make that. I'll be on call, but I'm sure I'll be able to work round it."

"Good," said the marquis, heading for the door. He held one finger beside his nose. "I think they may be preparing a little surprise for you, but I'd appreciate it if you don't say anything."

"Surprise?" O'Reilly's frown deepened. "What sort?"

"A wink is as good as a nod to a blind horse," said the marquis, letting himself out. "We'll say no more."

"Thanks for the tip-off, sir." O'Reilly followed the marquis to the front door. "I'm not a big fan of sudden surprises, even if they are well meant."

"I do know that, Fingal. It's why I told you." And without waiting for an answer, he left.

Kinky removed the ashtray and fixed O'Reilly with a glare. "This'll be for after lunch, Doctor, sir. You'll not be needing your pipe until then. You'd agree, Doctor Laverty?"

"Oh, indeed, Kinky." Barry, now clean-shaven and dressed, sat at his usual spot at the other end of the table.

"You two ganging up on me?" O'Reilly asked, but then he nodded and smiled. He'd had a couple of pipefuls of his favourite Murray's Erinmore Flake during the surgery. He could wait for another half hour or so. "What's for lunch, Kinky?" His stomach gurgled.

"I've a nice potato soup ready," she said, "and when the pair of you has got that into you, there's a bacon-and-egg pie to follow." She walked to the door. "And you'll get none of it if you don't let me get back to my kitchen."

O'Reilly wanted to find out what Barry had been up to in the small hours. "I heard you coming back early this morning. Bad night?"

Barry yawned. "You know Jeremy Dunne?"

"Farmer," O'Reilly said. "Forty acres mixed farm, beef cattle, and grain. His land marches with the Gillespies' place to the west and the marquis's estate to the east. Grown son lives with him. Jeremy's a widower. Excitable type. He has trouble with a duodenal ulcer."

"He had real trouble with it this morning. It perforated. It wasn't a difficult diagnosis once his son was able to tell me about the ulcer. The poor devil was in shock . . . severe abdominal pain and all the signs of peritonitis. All I could do was call an ambulance and get him up to the Royal P.D.Q. I phoned my mate Jack Mills when I got up today. Jack and your mate Cromie operated, closed the hole, and cleaned all the intestinal contents out of his belly. They expect he'll be home for Christmas."

"Aye," said O'Reilly, "he should be better in a week, that would be . . ."

"The seventeenth," Barry said. "Lots of time to spare."

"Right." O'Reilly was pleased. He didn't like to think of anybody being in hospital on the day, and he was pleased that Barry's diagnosis had been correct. The boy was learning to keep a watchful eye on their customers, even if they were under a specialist's care in hospital. "You did well, Barry."

Barry grinned. "Thanks, Fingal, but it was hardly a difficult diagnosis given the man's history."

Barry was possessed of an inherent modesty. Some people might see it as a lack of confidence, but O'Reilly was sure he knew better. "You did well, son," he said, "very well, and maybe with a bit of luck you'll not be too busy this afternoon. Have you many calls to make?"

"I'm going to pop in at Eileen Lindsay's and see how Sammy and Maggie are getting on; then I'll stick my nose in at Kieran's, change his dressing. They only live a few doors away. It'll save him a trip, and I think that's about it for today, unless Kinky has more for me or some other calls come in later." Barry toyed with his soupspoon. "How was the surgery?"

O'Reilly stretched in his chair. "Pretty routine. And busy as hell. Not everybody's scarpered up to the Kinnegar."

That news brought a smile to Barry's face.

O'Reilly continued. "Cissie was in. She's not sure your penicillin is working fast enough."

Barry laughed. "Typical Cissie. What did you tell her?"

O'Reilly was pleased to see the laugh. Four months ago Barry would have bridled because he would have felt insecure. The boy was learning. "I told her not to pay any heed to her cousin Aggie's helpful advice." He decided not to bother Barry by telling him where he thought the advice had come from. "She'll be fine."

O'Reilly wrinkled his nose and detected the scent of onions and leeks mingled with potatoes wafting through the door. Old Arthur might be a good gun dog, but by God when it came to sniffing our grub, O'Reilly reckoned he himself had no match.

Kinky came in carrying a steaming tureen, set it on the table, and handed O'Reilly a ladle. He started filling his own soup plate.

"Any calls this morning, Kinky?" Barry passed his soup plate along the table.

She stood beside O'Reilly, hands linked in front of her apron, clearly awaiting his verdict on the soup. "None from patients, Doctor Laverty," she said, "but your young lady called when you were still asleep—"

Barry half rose. "When I was asleep? I missed her? Bloody hell." Barry saw Kinky purse her lips. "Sorry, Kinky."

"I've heard worse," she said.

Good old Kinky, O'Reilly thought, our unflappable Rock of Ages.

"Miss Spence said she was rushing off somewhere, not to disturb you, and to tell you she'd call—"

"When?"

"First thing Saturday morning."

Barry subsided into his chair. He sighed. "Saturday?"

"Come on, Barry," O'Reilly said, handing along a full plate of soup and starting to fill his own. "It'll be here in no time."

"I suppose." Barry took his first mouthful of soup.

"And there'll be plenty for us to do in the meanwhile to keep your mind occupied."

"And that's a good thing, sir," Kinky said seriously. "The divil finds work for idle hands, so."

"Well, by God, Kinky, he's not found much for yours. This soup is magnificent." O'Reilly made a point of smacking his lips noisily and was gratified to see her smile.

"Delicious," said Barry, even though he still looked pretty crestfallen. The boy was missing his girl, and O'Reilly thought of some lines of A. E. Housman's.

"The heart out of the bosom . . . is sold for endless rue."

Kinky bobbed her head. "It's my mother's recipe, so." She ladled the last of the soup into O'Reilly's plate. "Now enjoy you that, sir, and I'll go and get the bacon-and-egg pie."

O'Reilly finished his soup and looked out the window. The sky over the church steeple was that metallic blue that only comes on crisp, frosty days. He decided he needed to get some fresh air. He'd been cooped up too long, and Barry wasn't going to be very busy this afternoon. "You know," he said, looking straight at Barry, "Kinky's right about the devil and idle hands so I've a notion."

"About what?"

"I'd like to come with you on your visits this afternoon, then pop into the parish hall and see how the preparations for the pageant are coming on, give Arthur his run and—"

"Pop into the Duck on our way home." Barry laughed.

"How did you know that?" O'Reilly didn't really need an answer. He knew Barry was beginning to understand his habits, just as he was beginning to understand Barry's.

"And if you'll be doing all that gallivanting about," said Kinky, setting on the table a large bacon-and-egg pie, the pastry crust glazed and brown, "you'll be needing your strength, Doctors dear, so eat up."

16

My Poor Fool Is Hanged

It had been some time since Barry had been chauffeured by O'Reilly in his long-bonnetted Rover, but even blindfolded he'd know he was in the old car by its unique attar of pipe tobacco smoke and tincture of damp dog. Arthur was fast asleep in the back.

O'Reilly, while driving through the village, had been stopped at the traffic light and had not been able to accelerate before the turn-off to the housing estate. He had been forced to keep his speed down to a reasonable thirty miles per hour. Barry was not one bit heartbroken that their progress had been stately this afternoon as opposed to O'Reilly's usual motorized version of the Charge of the Light Brigade.

They parked in Comber Gardens outside Eileen's house.

Maggie MacCorkle answered the door. She smiled her toothless smile. "Hello there, Doctors dear. You're better, Doctor O'Reilly, I see."

"Much better, thanks, Maggie."

"Come in. I've the wee lad teed up on the sofa in the front parlour. There's a fire lit for him, so there is."

Barry noticed she was wearing a brown knitted toque with a sprig of holly stuck into the weave. Maggie wouldn't be Maggie if she wasn't wearing a hat with some floral adornment. He thought it looked like an unlit Christmas pudding. "How is he, Maggie?" he asked, as she closed the front door behind the two doctors.

"Sammy? He's a bit better, I think. He ate up his lunch all right." She frowned. "But he didn't finish a piece of my plum cake."

Barry hid his smile. "What ails him does cut down the appetite. He's probably a bit bored too."

"I've been keeping him amused, so I have, Doctor, but he's still a wee bit peely-wally, if you know what I mean."

Barry did. It was an expression borrowed from the Scots that meant "under the weather." "It's to be expected," he said. He followed Maggie along the hall and was himself followed by O'Reilly. After all, Sammy was Barry's patient, and the medical niceties should be observed, with O'Reilly staying well in the background—unless his opinion was asked for.

Maggie waited in the hall, as Barry knew she would. She wasn't direct family, and convention excluded her from the examination even if she was acting in loco parentis.

The front parlour was toasty warm, and coals burnt merrily in the grate. Barry surmised that as Eileen was now working again, the restrictions on lighting the fire had been removed. Sammy lay on a sofa underneath a tartan rug, his head supported on two pillows. He looked up from a comic book he was reading. "Hello, Doctor Laverty," he said, before returning to the comics.

"Is that the *Beano*?" Barry asked. "Does it still have Dennis the Menace and Lord Snooty in it?"

"Aye," said Sammy, showing a little more interest. "How do you know that?"

"I used to get it every week when I was your age."

"Right enough?" From the look on the boy's face, his doctor's knowledge of comic-book characters had made an impression. He offered the comic to Barry and pointed at an open page. "This fellah Billy Whiz's new this year."

Barry took the comic, smiled at the colourfully drawn character, and returned the thin magazine to its owner. "Thanks, Sammy. How are you today?"

"Them bumps is different looking, so they are, and my knees and ankles are a bit better."

"No tummy pains?" Barry was pretty sure he already knew the answer, but he wanted to be certain. Patients with Henoch-Schönlein purpura could develop abdominal pain accompanied by passing blood in their faeces. The pain was usually violent, and in Sammy's case it would have certainly forced his mother or Maggie to summon the doctor at once.

"Nah." He shook his head. "I've to be better for Christmas, so I have."

Barry sat on the side of the settee. "Can I take a wee gander at your rash?"

"Aye, certainly." He threw back the blanket and, remembering Barry's last visit, pulled his pyjama pants down and rolled over onto his tummy. "I'm not like a seed potato no more."

Barry saw at once that the swelling of Sammy's

knees and ankles was subsiding and the raised urticarial blemishes, now flush with the skin, had taken on the classical purplish colour. "Pull up your pants, son," he said. Barry glanced at O'Reilly, who was standing quietly beside them. "What do you reckon, Fingal?"

"You're spot on, Barry. That's *porphura* all right."

"Pardon?"

"It's the Greek root for 'purple.' Purpura to you."

"I'm glad you agree." And in truth Barry was. He'd been pretty confident in his diagnosis, but it was nice to have it confirmed by his senior colleague. He turned back to the child. "You're on the mend, Sammy."

"Great." He smiled shyly. "I think it's Mrs. Houston is doing it."

Mrs. Houston? It took Barry a moment to remember that Maggie, who had been Miss MacCorkle when he'd come here, was now Mrs. Sonny Houston. Silly of him. He told Maggie to come in, and then he asked Sammy, "And how's she doing that?"

"Go on, Mrs. Houston," Sammy urged, "show the doctors."

Barry saw Maggie blush. "I will not, so I won't."

"Och, go on," Sammy insisted.

"Youse doctors don't mind?"

Barry, who hadn't the faintest idea what they were talking about, shook his head. "Pay me no heed," he said.

O'Reilly shrugged and winked at Barry. Perhaps, Barry thought, O'Reilly had seen before whatever it was Maggie was going to do.

"Wait 'til you see this, Doctor Laverty," Sammy said, grinning widely.

Maggie went and stood in the doorway, raised her hands, grasped the edge of the upper door frame, grunted mightily, and somehow managed to hoist her body through one hundred and eighty degrees.

Barry stared, openmouthed. He heard Sammy clapping his hands and O'Reilly muttering, "Sweet mother of Jesus."

Maggie, now fully inverted, locked the heels of her shoes on the door frame and removed her hands so she hung by her heels alone. Her voluminous black skirt hung down over her head so she looked to Barry like a huge, oddly shaped bat, a bat wearing ankle-length white bloomers that must have been handed down from Maggie's granny.

"Maggie, come down out of that at once. You'll kill yourself," O'Reilly bellowed.

Maggie executed a forward somersault, landed nimbly on her feet, bent her knees for a moment, and then stood as erectly as a dismounting gymnast.

"Yay, Maggie," an excited Sammy called. "That was cracker, so it was."

Barry shook his head and smiled.

"Begod," O'Reilly remarked, "will wonders never cease? Where in the name of the wee man did you learn to do that, Maggie?"

She smoothed her skirt and said, a little breathlessly, "You mind at the wedding Sonny let it out I was a springboard diver when I was a girl?"

"Yes," Barry said, "I do."

"Well, our trainer was very progressive for his day. He made us do gymnastics to keep us supple. Would youse like to see me do the splits?"

"I think," said O'Reilly, "we've had enough excitement for one day." He turned to Barry and winked slowly. "Doctor Laverty, do you think this could account for Maggie's headaches?"

Barry vividly remembered his first consultation with Maggie, when she had complained of headaches, headaches two inches *above* the crown of her head. Now he did his best to keep a straight face. "No question of it, Doctor O'Reilly."

"Away off and chase yourselves, Doctors," Maggie said. "Doing that there never done me one pick of harm in my entire life."

Sammy chipped in eagerly, "And she's going to teach me how to do it as soon as I'm better."

"Is she?" said Barry with a sigh, wondering how easy it would be to set a broken neck when Sammy fell, as he almost certainly would. "It'll be something to look forward to. Anyway," he said, as he stood up. "I think you're on the mend, Sammy. You might even be better for Christmas Day." He turned to Fingal. "What do you think, Doctor O'Reilly?"

"You'll be at the Rugby Club Christmas party, I'd bet on it, and you'll see Santa there."

Sammy grinned a big grin. "Aye. And he'll be coming here too. I fixed it. You remember I told you I would, Doctor Laverty?"

Barry vaguely recollected that Sammy had proudly told him he and his brother and sister had a scheme to help out Santa this year. Probably now that Eileen was back at work, she was adding more to her Christmas savings. The tea caddy with the ten-shilling notes was still in its place on the mantel.

He tousled Sammy's hair. "Good lad," he said, then turned to Maggie. "We'll be off. We've to call with Kieran and Ethel."

"You run along, Doctors," Maggie said, "but if you need me . . . I'll be hanging around in here." She threw back her head, opened her toothless mouth, and cackled. Her eyes screwed shut, her shoulders shook, and finally she managed to say, "Hanging around. Oh, dear. Boys-a-boys, that's a good one, so it is. Wait 'til I tell Sonny. He'll crack himself, so he will."

She was still chuckling as Barry followed O'Reilly out onto the street for the short walk to the O'Hagans' house. They were almost there when they met Eileen Lindsay hurrying in the opposite direction.

She stopped when she saw them. "Good afternoon," she said. "Is Sammy all right?" Barry heard the concern in her voice.

"Much better," Barry said. "Much better."

"Thank God for that."

"You're home early," O'Reilly said.

"Aye. The managers shut the mill down for the day to do some maintenance to the looms. I'll not be sorry to get home early. Then Mrs. Houston can get home to her husband." Barry had to strain to hear her mutter under her breath, "We should all be lucky enough to have one." She raised her voice and continued, "She's been a godsend, so she has. Thank you, Doctor Laverty. Thank you very much."

"You thank Maggie, not me," Barry said, warmed inside even though the day was chilly. "Go on home now, Eileen."

He watched Eileen continue along the street at the same quick pace, a woman who always seemed to be short of time. It was an understandable condition for a single woman with three children, and Barry felt a pang of sympathy. "Come on, Fingal. Let's get that last call made."

It only took a short while to reach the O'Hagans' home, where Barry changed Kieran's dressing. The old nail was beginning to separate and would soon fall off. Barry reassured Kieran and Ethel, asked Kieran to drop into the surgery early the next week, and then nodded to O'Reilly to indicate they should leave.

They walked in companionable silence along the narrow street to where the Rover waited. Barry was looking forward to a leisurely drive to the parish hall, a walk on the dunes with Arthur, and then a pint at the Mucky Duck.

The sight of Maggie, coatless in the frigid air, running down the street toward them, didn't make sense at first. She was waving her arms and yelling, "Doctors! Doctors! Come quick! For God's sake, come quick."

Her cries could only mean one thing. Sammy. The Henoch-Schönlein purpura must be showing its sinister side. Barry broke into a run with O'Reilly hard on his heels. Damn. The little fellow had looked so well only half an hour ago. If he was bleeding into his gut, he'd need a subcutaneous injection of adrenaline and oral antihistamines while an ambulance was summoned to take him to the Children's Hospital. "Is Sammy okay? Is he in pain?" he yelled, as he came up on Maggie. She now stood bent double with her hands on her knees.

"No . . . no," she gasped and hauled in a deep breath. "It's not Sammy. It's Eileen."

17

There's No Smoke without Fire

Barry charged in through the open front door, vaguely aware of O'Reilly following. The scene before him seemed to be frozen in time. Eileen stood beside the fire half turned, so he saw her in profile. Her head drooped. Tears streaked her cheeks. She held a ten-shilling note in one hand; the other clutched the Princess Elizabeth tea caddy. Its lid hung open, and Barry could see that it was empty.

Sammy was sitting up on his sofa. His arms were wrapped around his bent knees, and he stared wide-eyed at the caddy held in his mother's hand. His comic lay on the floor along with the tartan rug.

At least Eileen wasn't lying on the floor with the comic and the rug, Barry thought with a great sense of relief.

O'Reilly arrived. "What's up?" he asked.

"Dunno yet," Barry said.

Eileen moved nearer to Barry and handed him the caddy. "It's gone," she said, her voice tiny and cracking. "All of it. I was going to put this ten bob in, but look . . ."

Barry wished he could miraculously make the money reappear.

"Fifteen pounds. All I could save since last Christmas."

He earned thirty-five pounds a week, and that wasn't a lot of money. Barry looked at Eileen, saw how her shoulders shook, noticed that one of her nylons was laddered again, and knew that she neglected her own little luxuries to put money aside to buy her children something, and not a very big something, on Christmas Day. He felt a lump in his throat. No wonder she'd told her children that Santa was hard up this year.

Where the hell could the money have gone? Was there any way to get it back? *Something* must be done to help her. But what? Before Barry could decide, O'Reilly took charge.

He moved past Barry, put a fatherly arm round Eileen's shoulder. "When was the last time you saw the money, Eileen?"

She sniffled and rubbed her eyes with the heel of her

hand. "This morning after I'd lit the fire for Sammy and brought him down here." She forced a little smile in Sammy's direction. "He gets terrible bored in his bedroom, so he does."

"So," O'Reilly said, "the money went missing since then."

"Yes, Doctor. It must've."

"So who's been in the room since you lit the fire—other than Sammy and Maggie?" His bushy eyebrows met almost in the middle of his forehead.

Despite the seriousness of the situation, Barry had to hide a smile as he pictured Fingal Flahertie O'Reilly as Sherlock Holmes, deerstalker cap on his head, meerschaum pipe in his mouth. That of course would cast Barry in the role of Doctor Watson.

Eileen sobbed, and O'Reilly produced a large handkerchief and gave it to her. "Take your time," he said.

Eileen blew her nose and returned the hanky. "Sammy, and Mary and Willy. They were by themselves for a wee while after I'd gone to work. His brother and sister mind Sammy until Mrs. Houston gets here; then they go to school."

Something stirred in Barry's memory. What had Sammy said about having a notion for helping Santa out of financial difficulty?

"And I got here at half past eight." Maggie, still out of breath, was standing in the doorway. "And I've been here since."

"And there were no visitors?" O'Reilly asked.

"No," she said.

"No tradesmen came to call?"

"Nobody," Maggie said, "except yourself and Doctor Laverty."

"And Sammy's been in the room all the time?"

"Aye." She scratched her cheek. "No," she said, "I tell a lie. He'd to go for a pee."

"Hmmm," O'Reilly's eyebrows met. "Hmmm."

His dilemma was obvious to Barry. If no one had come to the house, the only possible suspects were Eileen's children and now Maggie, who had been alone in the room while her charge was in the bathroom.

Getting to the truth of the matter was going to take a great deal of tact. Barry opened his coat. With four adults, a child, and a coal fire, the little parlour was getting stuffy.

O'Reilly took his arm from Eileen's shoulder, turned, and looked at Sammy.

The child looked back.

"Now, Sammy," O'Reilly asked very quietly, "did you or Mary or Willy steal Mammy's money?"

Tact, Barry knew, was not O'Reilly's strong suit.

Sammy jerked back. "Steal? No. We *never* did, so we didn't."

And that "never did, so we didn't" was the most emphatic denial in the Ulster vocabulary. Barry waited to see if O'Reilly would accept the child's word, or ask again, or challenge Maggie. Just for the moment, the big man seemed to be lost for words.

There was a rattling noise, and Barry looked around in time to see the coals settling in the grate. The fire. What was it about the fire? Barry glanced at Sammy, who was looking from the tin in his mother's hand to the fireplace and back to the caddy. Barry remembered. Eileen had not been going to light the fire until it was time for the kiddies to send their letters to Santa. Sammy couldn't have. Could he? Christ. Barry saw something in the boy's eyes and was suddenly certain he knew exactly what had happened. And if he was right—he glanced at Eileen—it was going to be very difficult to help her. The lad couldn't have, could he? Barry felt a chill in his stomach.

"Doctor O'Reilly," Barry asked, "could I ask Sammy a question?"

"Go right ahead."

Barry hesitated. He didn't want to give Sammy the impression that the grown-ups were ganging up on him. Barry smiled, then said, "Sammy, I know you didn't steal the money."

"See?" Sammy looked at O'Reilly.

Barry glanced over his shoulder at Maggie. From the way she was frowning, she had worked out for herself that she was now the prime suspect. "And I know you didn't, Maggie." She nodded to him.

Barry moved across the room, picked up a poker, got down on his hunkers, stirred the fire, and then looked Sammy right in the eye. "But you wanted to help Santa out, didn't you?"

Sammy looked up at his mother and at the caddy in her hand. "Aye," he said in a very small voice, "and I wanted to help my mammy." He looked down and fidgeted with the material of his pyjama jacket. "You mind my mammy said Santa was a bit hard up this year and when we sent our letters to him up the chimney we weren't to ask for too much?"

"I do, Sammy."

"She was awful unhappy about it, so she was." Sammy's voice started to crack. "Me and Mary and Willy, we thought if Santa had a bit more money, Mammy would cheer up . . . and I was going to tell Mammy today what we done, but I never got the chance." He started to cry. "She opened the caddy and she stared in, then took on something fierce, and . . . and . . ."—his sobs strangled his words—"and I think we've done a bad thing, so we have."

"So, Sammy, the three of you sent the money up the chimney to Santa?"

Eileen's hand flew to her open mouth.

"Yes," Sammy managed to say. Then, as if having made a clean breast of things had in part restored his spirits, he continued, "So now Santa'll have pots and pots of money, won't he, Doctor?"

But Eileen won't, Barry thought.

"Won't he, Doctor?" Sammy started to cry again.

Eileen went to him, wrapped her arms around him, and said. "It's all right, Sammy. It's all right. Don't cry. It's all right."

O'Reilly put a hand on her shoulder and said, "And it will be all right, Eileen. Don't you worry about the money. It will all work out, you'll see." He fixed Barry with a stare.

"Yes, Fingal," Barry said. He knew full well that he hadn't the faintest idea what O'Reilly was talking about, but the man had spoken with such authority that if he had told Barry to levitate as far as the ceiling, Barry would have replied, "Yes, Fingal." And then he would have risen accordingly.

"Honest, Doctor O'Reilly? Honest to God?" Eileen smiled at O'Reilly through her tears.

"Honest to God, Eileen," he said.

Barry inwardly shuddered. There was no more binding Ulster promise.

"That's grand then, so it is," Maggie chipped in. "I'm very glad it's all sorted out. Do you know, I think we all need a nice wee cup of tea, and I've a few slices of my plum cake out in the kitchen."

Before Barry could speak, O'Reilly said, "You make it for Eileen and yourself, Maggie. Doctor Laverty and I have another call to make."

Neither man spoke until the Rover was halfway up one of the backroads into the Ballybucklebo Hills above the village. "Fingal," Barry finally said, "you told Eileen not to worry, so I presume you have a plan?"

O'Reilly hurled the Rover round a bend. Its inside wheels jolted over the verge until he straightened out the car's progress, slowed, turned into the entrance to a field, and braked viciously. "Open the gate."

Barry did as he was told and waited for O'Reilly to drive through. Then he followed on foot and closed the gate. They were standing in a field that had been left fallow and that lay as its own patch in the wider quilt of little fields. Some were in pasture, with small flocks of cotton-wool sheep or suede-brown cattle. Others were freshly ploughed, and their black loam furrows waited for the spring sowing of barley or oats or wheat. In the spring, the crops would sprout and dress the land in fine green muslin. In the late summer, there would be fields of gold, where soft winds made the grain ripple as the evening breeze ruffles a calm sea. He paused, thinking of the slow turning of the farmers' seasons, pleased that already he had had his first summer and autumn and was now in his first winter here.

It wouldn't be much longer until the partnership he was now sure he wanted was in reach. Perhaps he wasn't dealing with the challenging cases he'd seen in the teaching hospital, but being involved in the life of the village, and not just the locals' medical problems, had its compensations. The whole episode just past was another example of how a GP like O'Reilly could make a difference in people's lives, and Barry had no doubt that O'Reilly would have a solution to Eileen's worries. Working here was what appealed to him all right, unless that wretched Fitzpatrick . . .

Barry left the thought unfinished and started to walk to where O'Reilly had parked, about twenty yards away. The field, like all Ulster fields, was small and irregular in its borders of drystone walls, the grey stones flecked with brown lichen. Even in mid-afternoon, the grass was rimed with a sugar icing of frost.

In the middle of the grass rose a hummock, crowned

by a single blackthorn tree and surrounded by blooming gorse bushes. Barry knew it was a fairy hill; when the field was under cultivation, no plough would touch the hillock for fear that the little people who lived there might curdle the cows' milk or blight the crop.

He inhaled a mixture of the almond scent of the yellow whin flowers and the pungency of cow clap. A herd had been pastured here recently. A hazy wisp of smoke, which rose from the next little valley, hung in the still air. He could smell the burning wood. Someone who had been cutting back a hedge and cleaning out a ditch must have been disposing of the cuttings.

Barry saw O'Reilly leave his side of the car and open the back door for Arthur Guinness. The big dog piled out, sniffing the air, his tail wagging. He headed off at a gallop, only to be called back by O'Reilly's "Here, sir. Come."

To Barry's surprise the usually unruly beast obeyed at once.

"Come on, Barry," O'Reilly yelled, as he started to walk toward the fairy ring. "Heel, you." And the big dog stayed at O'Reilly's side, his muzzle not one inch in front of his master's leg.

Barry ran to catch up, his breath puffing in the still air. He wanted to know how O'Reilly planned to help Eileen Lindsay restore her fortunes.

From overhead came a plaintive *pee-wit, pee-wit*. Looking up, he saw a flock of green plover, their head crests obvious, against an eggshell blue sky, flapping their langorous way home with the peculiar wing beat that gave them their Ulster name, lapwing.

O'Reilly and Arthur had reached the edge of the fairy ring. O'Reilly stood legs astraddle and commanded, "Sit."

Arthur obeyed, his nose twitching, scenting, questing. He made little excited mutterings somewhere in his throat, and his tail swept from side to side, clearing a pie-wedge shape of clear grass in the frost.

Barry caught up with them. "Fingal," he said, "I asked you what your plan for Eileen was."

O'Reilly frowned, seemed not to have heard the question. "Those whins are full of rabbits. Watch this." He pointed to the gorse bushes. "Hi lost, Arthur," he said quietly.

The big dog took off, nose to the ground. He quartered back and forth, and Barry knew he was attempting to cut across a scent trail. Arthur stopped dead, spun, and took a straight line to the edge of the bushes. Then he stopped and looked back at O'Reilly.

"Push 'em out, boy. Push 'em out."

The bushes crackled and swayed as Arthur thrust his way in beneath, belly close to the ground. He disappeared, and for a few moments all Barry could hear was a crashing in the undergrowth; then the crashing was replaced by a hurried rustling. Three rabbits, brown-and-beige furred, ears flattened to the backs of their heads, tore from the cover and bolted across the field.

O'Reilly grinned. "If I'd had my shotgun, we'd be having rabbit pie tomorrow night."

Barry felt a moment of sympathy for the rabbits but realized that he'd not have objected, not one bit, to tucking into one of Kinky's game pies. He stared at the bushes, expecting Arthur to appear, but instead he heard a renewed crashing heading deep into the thicket. He rubbed his hands. They were getting chilly. So was the tip of his nose. He'd like to go back to the car and head off to the warmth of the Parish Hall as O'Reilly had suggested at lunchtime. And he'd like an answer to the question that was still niggling at him. "Fingal, about Eileen's money. How are we going to get it back for her?"

O'Reilly shrugged. "To tell you the truth, Barry, just at the moment I haven't the foggiest notion."

"But you sounded so sure back at the house and—"

With the suddenness of the explosion of a landmine underfoot, the whins rustled, and a staccato clattering of stubby wings was accompanied by a hoarse cry of *kek, kek, kek*. A cock pheasant hurled himself into the sky above the bushes, his emerald head iridescent in the sun, his long striped tail feathers streaming behind as he clawed for height. Barry flinched, then collected himself.

O'Reilly yelled, "Come in, Arthur!" Then he turned to Barry. "Did you see that big fellah?"

"Hard to miss him."

"It's unusual for a pheasant to be so far from the marquis's estate," O'Reilly remarked, "but once in a while the unexpected happens."

Arthur reappeared, and O'Reilly called him to heel. "Come on, Barry. Let's head on to the Duck. We'll look in on the pageant some other day." He started back toward the car, and Barry followed, wondering if the exertion and the cold had tired his usually indefatigable older colleague. "You feeling all right?"

"Couldn't be better," he said, but he shivered. "I just fancy a pint. I haven't had one since Monday."

It would kill the big man to admit to any weakness, Barry thought. "Fair enough and . . . Fingal?"

"What?"

"You really don't have a plan for Eileen, do you?"

"Not a clue, but remember the pheasant. The unexpected has a habit of happening."

"So you are going to reassure everybody and simply hope that something turns up?"

"No." O'Reilly opened the car's back door and waited for Arthur to jump in. "I leave those nonspecific upturning aspirations to Mr. Micawber."

"Dickens."

"I know that. *David Copperfield.*" He slammed the rear door. "No, I said I'd think of something, and I bloody well will." He opened the driver's door. "But I'll think a damn sight better with a pint in my hand. So trot off and open the gate like a good lad."

And Barry, vaguely reassured, did just that.

18

Matters of Fact . . . Are Very Stubborn Things

The weather had held until Saturday, and when Barry came down for breakfast, sunlight was dancing in the facets of the cut-glass decanters on the sideboard and bouncing from the silver-domed cover of a chafing dish. The aroma of fresh coffee was being overpowered by the smell of poached kippers.

O'Reilly, sitting at the head of the table, waved his fish fork in the general direction of the dresser. "Morning, Barry. Help yourself. I've left you a brace." He shoved in a mouthful and added, "Not like certain dumplings I *could* allude to."

"Morning, Fingal." Barry yawned, ignoring the jibe coming from the man who not so very long ago had consumed a whole roast duck meant for both of them. He opened the chafing dish and stepped back to let a cloud of fish-scented steam dissipate.

He was pleased that Fingal was on call today. Yesterday had been hectic after lunch. He'd dropped in on Sammy and Maggie, and he'd visited Jeannie Jingles and arranged follow-up visits for her Eddie who, his pneumonia on the mend, had been discharged that day from Sick Kids. Then he made three other home visits.

Now that the steam cloud had vanished, he used a wide-bladed fish server to put the golden-hued, oak shaving–smoked herrings on his plate. He took the plate to his place and returned to pour himself a cup of coffee. Patricia should be phoning at any minute. Maybe by now she'd be able to tell him she'd be coming home. Maybe she'd caved in and would accept his offer to pay for the ferry ticket. He bloody well hoped so.

"Pour me one while you're on your feet." O'Reilly handed Barry his cup and pushed his plate, laden with kipper skeletons, away.

As he poured two cups of coffee, Barry counted four backbones. O'Reilly had not stinted himself. Kinky reckoned the return of O'Reilly's irascibility was a sign of his recovery. So was the return of his appetite. Barry handed O'Reilly his coffee. "Here."

O'Reilly accepted the cup and saucer. "Thanks, Barry. How was your night?"

Barry returned to his place and took a big swallow. "Busy."

"Oh?"

"Aye. I'd to go out at two. Judge Egan was having chest pains."

"He's got angina," O'Reilly said. "Was he having a coronary?"

"I don't know, but his nitroglycerine tablets weren't stopping the pain, so I gave him a quarter grain of morphine and sent for the ambulance. I'd to wait until they got there."

"Good lad," said O'Reilly, buttering his third slice of toast. "Eoin's a decent man. He'll be seventy-three next Thursday."

Barry shook his head. He could swear O'Reilly carried around every scrap of useful information about every one of his patients in his big, craggy-faced, shaggy-haired head. Barry set to work to separate the filet from the bones but stopped when O'Reilly said, "He suits his name."

"Eoin? Why? It's just archaic Irish for John. Most folks today use Sean."

O'Reilly shook his head. "I'm not talking about Eoin. I'm talking about his surname, Egan. It's derived from *MacAodhagáin*. The family were the *brehons,* the hereditary lawyers and judges, to the chieftains of Roscommon."

"I'll be damned." Barry chuckled and returned to filleting his fish. "That would make him Judge Judge . . . just like that bloke Major Major Major in *Catch*-22."

"Joseph Heller. Bloody funny book." O'Reilly, who had finished his toast, eyed the toast rack.

Barry slid the slice of fish, now bone-free, to the side of his plate. "We had a research registrar who was working with urinary incontinence. Poor chap's name was Leakey. It suited him. He was a real drip."

O'Reilly guffawed long and hard, and that was why Barry didn't realize that the phone was ringing in the hall until Kinky came in and said, "Your Miss Spence is on the line."

Barry came out of his chair like a greyhound from

the starting gate, jostled past Kinky, grabbed the receiver, and said, "Hello, Patricia?"

"Barry, how are you?"

"Fine. How are you . . ."—he lowered his voice—"darling?" The dining room doorway was open.

"You'll have to speak up," she said.

He turned his back to the open door, cupped his hand around the mouthpiece, and said a little more loudly, "I love you."

He heard her chuckle. "I love you too, Barry. I really do."

That was a relief. He wanted to ask her if she was coming back to Ulster, but instead he said, "Where are you? The Residency?"

"No. I'm in Bourn. I'm spending the weekend with Jenny."

"Jenny who?" He wished to hell she were spending the weekend with him.

"Jenny. Jenny Compton. I told you about her."

"Right." The girl Patricia would go to for Christmas if she didn't come back to Northern Ireland.

"Her folks have pots of money. Her dad's a stockbroker and says I can chat as long as I like on his phone, and hang the cost. He can write phone calls off as part of his business expenses."

"Must be nice," Barry said. "Still, being able to have a decent blether makes a change from a quick two minutes on the phone or the odd letter."

"I'm sorry, Barry," she said, "but my study load is very heavy. I just don't have time to write epistles every night."

"I understand that," he said, thinking that he *still* owed his folks a letter. "I'm as guilty as you are. But I do miss you, Patricia."

"And I miss you . . . particularly in my little room at night. It's quite chilly at this time of the year." There was a husky edge in her voice.

Christ, he longed to hold her. He was about to tell her how much he'd like to be there to keep her warm, but she ploughed ahead.

"My bedroom's lovely and cosy here. Jenny and her folks live in a cottage. Thatched roof, old oak beams. It was built in sixteen forty-three."

"Sounds very rustic." How could she do that to him? Make a sexy remark, then change the subject. He wished she would stop prattling and tell him what he wanted to know.

"It is. It's just a wee ways from the local manor house, Bourn Hall, and that's a fascinating place."

"I'm sure it is." So was her mouth and her breasts, and he ached for her.

"It was owned by the De La Warr family . . . the one the American state Delaware is named for."

"Patricia . . ." He smiled at Kinky as she headed back to the kitchen. Barry's smile faded. Patricia wasn't usually the garrulous type. She was rabbitting on because she had something unpleasant to tell him. He could sense it.

"The same family own property with a big wood, and that was the very spot A. A. Milne called the Hundred Acre Wood in the Pooh stories."

"Really?" He started to let his tone show his disinterest. He was certain she was using all this trivial chitchat as a smoke screen to avoid having to tell him she wasn't coming home. "That's interesting."

He heard her chuckle. "Speaking of Pooh, darling, you sound a bit like Eeyore."

Barry took a deep breath. "Look, Patricia, it's great to chat, but I need to know so I can work out on-call schedules with Fingal . . . are you coming home?"

He heard the edge of irritation creep into her voice. "I still don't know."

Barry tried not to let his own disappointment show. "If you still don't know, why did you call?"

"Because, Barry, I like to hear your voice"—her tones were measured—"and I knew Jenny's dad wouldn't mind. I miss you, and I was happy we would be able to talk."

"Christ. I like to talk to you too, but I'd rather be doing it face to face."

"So would I."

"Did you find out about the ferry?" He waited to see how she would respond. Nothing. "Patricia, are you still there? Did you find out about the ferry?"

"Not yet. I've been busy."

"Too busy to make a phone call? Damn it, Patricia, I'll pay for the ticket; it can't be that much."

There was a long pause before she said flatly, "I'm not sure I'd like that, Barry."

"Why the hell not? I'm working. Making money. You're a student. I love you. I want to see you. I presume you want to see me?"

"Don't be silly."

He pursed his lips. "Why is offering to pay for your ticket silly?"

"I meant of course I want to see you, and if you think I don't, you're being silly."

"Then let me pay for your ticket." He waited.

"Barry . . ." Her voice was level. "I do love you . . . but . . ."

"But? But? But what?"

"But it seems like an awful lot of money for an underpaid medical assistant . . ."

He sensed she was trying to let him down gently. "It's my money."

"And you work very hard for it."

He recognized he was fighting a losing battle. "I don't think it's that at all. It's your damn pride. Somehow you think it would threaten your independence to accept money from me."

He heard her clear her throat, then say levelly, "I do believe women shouldn't be financially dependent on men."

"Oh, come on, Patricia. I'm not asking you to. I'm not asking you to compromise your principles. All I want to do is see you. I'm missing you like crazy."

"And I'm missing you, Barry. But I won't accept your money."

"That's not principles. That's being stubborn. You told me not to be silly. Don't *you* be stupid." His hand was squeezing the receiver.

"Barry, I love you, but this conversation's going nowhere."

The words slipped out. "Neither are we, not with you over there refusing to come home."

Her words were clipped. "I am not refusing to come, but I am refusing to take your money."

"And that's final?" He waited. Could he hear a catch in her voice when she said yes?

He held the receiver in front of his face and stared at it. Absence makes the heart grow fonder? The hell it does. He put it back to his ear and mouth.

"Are you still there, Barry? . . . Barry?"

"Yes."

The silence hung and stretched. He'd be damned if he'd be the first to speak.

"Barry? I love you."

"Then let me buy your ticket."

"No."

He screwed his eyes shut, took a deep breath, and said, "I'm going to ring off now, Patricia. You know where to find me if you change your mind." There was a prickling behind his eyelids.

"Good-bye, Barry." He heard the click and the line went dead. Bugger it. Why couldn't the bloody woman see reason? He replaced the receiver. "Enjoy your stupid ducks," he said to no one in particular. Barry cleared his throat, rubbed the back of his hand across his eyes, smoothed down the tuft that he knew would be sticking up from the crown of his head, and went back into the dining room.

O'Reilly was chewing, and the plate of two kippers that should have been waiting in Barry's place had miraculously moved in front of O'Reilly, who was finishing the last scrap. He smiled guiltily, Barry thought. "They were getting cold," O'Reilly said. "It would have been a shame to waste them. Kinky's gone to boil you a couple of eggs."

"Jesus, Fingal . . ." But Barry found he couldn't be bothered to start another fight. Not immediately after the last one. "Never mind. Eggs will be fine." He picked up his half-full coffee cup and went to the sideboard to fill it with fresh brew from the coffeepot.

O'Reilly burped. "Excuse me," he said, and went to look out the bow window. "It's a lovely day out there, Barry. What are you going to get up to now you're free?"

Barry shrugged. "I'm not sure. Put my feet up for a while."

O'Reilly laughed. "You yust vant to be ahloan?"

Barry couldn't help smiling. "Fingal, that's the worst imitation of Marlene Dietrich I've ever heard."

"But it's true, isn't it? I wasn't eavesdropping, but I couldn't help hearing the tone of your voice."

Barry shrugged. "She's being stubborn, that's all."

O'Reilly moved closer to Barry, laid a hand on his shoulder, and said gently, "She'll come round, son. You'll see."

Barry would have laughed at anyone else who said that, but O'Reilly was an astute judge of people. Barry found his advice comforting, if not altogether believable. "Thanks, Fingal."

"And in the meantime," O'Reilly continued, "you can relax this morning and do your cryptic crosswords, but this afternoon you're coming with me and Kitty."

"And Kitty? Where to?"

"I phoned her last night. She's coming down, and we—Kitty, me, and Arthur . . . and that includes you now—are going to watch a battle of the Titans. A rugby match between the Ballybucklebo Bonnaughts and the Glengormley Gallowglasses."

Barry laughed. The Bonnaughts were named for fourteenth-century Irish mercenary soldiers, and the Gallowglasses for professional Scottish fighting men who had first come over to Ireland in 1258. And the way the two teams carried on every time they met, it was very apt that each was named for a group of warriors. Some of their encounters were legend in Ulster rugby football circles. "Should be quite the tussle," Barry said. "You're on, Fingal, but—"

"But what?"

"Would you not prefer to be by yourself with Kitty?"

O'Reilly guffawed mightily. "At a rugby match? Alone? Don't be daft. I'm taking her to the Crawfordsburn for dinner, and I could use your help there."

"You need my help eating?"

"No. Eejit. I have to go to some mysterious committee meeting after the game. I'd like you to amuse her until it's over."

"Fair enough."

"But, Barry, I'd not take it amiss if you disappeared when the meeting's over."

Given O'Reilly's naturally high colour, it was

impossible to tell if the big man was blushing. "I can do that, Fingal," Barry said. He remembered he was meant to contact Jack Mills and either have him down for a bite of Kinky's cooking or—now that was a thought—join Jack at the dance at the Nurses Home. "I'll just need to go and make a phone call."

19

The Muddied Oafs at the Goals

O'Reilly parked the Rover in a graveled parking lot beside a row of ancient beeches that grew in front of a grassy berm. He reckoned they were all at least a hundred feet tall. He leant over, pecked Kitty's cheek, and said, "We're here."

He got out and opened the back door for Arthur. The dog immediately ran to the nearest tree and cocked a leg. O'Reilly glanced back to the road. No sign of Barry's car. He was bringing Brunhilde so he could drive Kitty back to Number 1 Main Street after the match, when O'Reilly would be at his committee meeting.

O'Reilly looked up through the skeletal fingers of the trees' bare branches to where cirrus clouds seemed to be white crayon smudges on a toweringly high, pale blue, cartridge-paper sky. The clouds barely moved, there was little wind, and it wasn't bitterly cold. Kitty wouldn't freeze standing on the touchline to watch the game. Good.

He walked toward her side of the car. The beech mast crunched underfoot. He looked at her where she stood. None of this "waiting for the gentleman to open the door for a lady" about Kitty. She was a very self-possessed woman. He'd suspected that all along. But since she'd taken the initiative Tuesday night, kissed him, and hinted that she was still in love with him, he had been in no doubt that Kitty O'Hallorhan was her own woman. And he admired that in her.

She was wearing a three-quarter-length bottle-green coat over black stirrup pants, and small flat-heeled shoes. The coat's fur collar was turned up against her lower face, and her remarkable grey-flecked-with-amber eyes sparkled from under a silk headscarf with a racehorse motif. Begod, he thought with a smile, *she's* a thoroughbred is Kitty. Face it, Fingal, he told himself as he saw the soft look for him in those eyes—a look he well remembered from many years ago—she does care for you very much.

And he recognized that since Tuesday she'd given him a great deal to think over, but here on the way to a rugby match wasn't the right time to talk to her about it. Perhaps tonight at dinner. If he could just sort out *exactly* how he was feeling.

He stood beside her. "Here comes Barry," he said, as he watched the Volkswagen come along the drive and pull up beside the Rover. Barry got out and came over.

"What kept you?"

"Jesus, Fingal," Barry said, "I'd need afterburners on my car to keep up with you. Do you know you put another cyclist in the ditch?"

"Did I hit him?" O'Reilly grinned. "It doesn't count if I don't give them a nudge."

"You very nearly did, Fingal," Kitty said. "You had me terrified."

O'Reilly's grin vanished. "I'm sorry," he said contritely.

"Honestly," she said, shaking her head. She linked her arm with his. "I'll forgive you this time, but I will expect you to drive more carefully in future." She started striding to the pitch. "Come on. Let's go and see the game."

"Hang on a minute." O'Reilly reached into the back of the Rover and brought out a canvas gamebag. "Sustenance," he said, slinging the strap over his shoulder. "Kinky's given us a couple of thermoses of her tomato soup and"—he produced a silver flask from an inside pocket—"I've brought the snake antivenin . . . just in case."

Kitty's laugh was deep and melodious. "I thought Saint Patrick chased all the snakes out of Ireland."

"Och," said O'Reilly, popping the flask back into his overcoat pocket, "you never can be too careful. One or two might have slipped back." He was about to head off when a black Sunbeam-Talbot arrived, and none other than Doctor Ronald Hercules Fitzpatrick emerged. O'Reilly waited until the man had approached, greeted him civilly, and then introduced Kitty.

The man obviously recognized her. "Charmed to meet you again, Miss O'Hallorhan. It's been a very long time since Dublin and our student days," he said, rubbing his gloved hands with the kind of delight an undertaker might show over a recently dead corpse. "So, Fingal," he continued, "do you think your lot have a chance?"

O'Reilly grunted. Silly question.

"I'm here to offer my support to the opposition. I've supported the Glengormley Gallowglasses for years." Fitzpatrick sniffed.

"Have you now?" said O'Reilly. "Well, I'd not give much for their chances today. The Bonnaughts have two Ulster players on their side."

"My good man . . ."

He's bloody quick off the mark with the "my goods," the condescending bugger, O'Reilly thought.

"*We* have a chap—he plays fullback—who shall be nameless, on loan from North. He's played for Ireland three times, you know. We're simply going to eat you alive. Devour you."

"Are you now?" O'Reilly folded his arms across his chest. Having a player from the North of Ireland Football Club, one of the clubs in the Senior League, a player who was not a regular member of the Gallowglasses, was almost like cheating, but O'Reilly wasn't going to object. Instead he said, "Ronald, I know you take your church seriously, but would you like to back up that remark with a few quid?"

Fitzpatrick frowned, then put a crooked index finger against his lower lip. "I really shouldn't."

He just needs a little nudge, O'Reilly thought. "In my opinion, Hercules, your lot couldn't beat the skin off a rice pudding . . . with the wind at their backs."

Fitzgerald gobbled, his wattles swung, and his Adam's apple bobbed. "Very well, Doctor O'Reilly, I will accept a small wager. Say . . . say, a pound."

O'Reilly smiled broadly. "Och, come on. You might as well be hung for a sheep as a lamb." His eyes narrowed and his voice hardened. "Make it ten pounds and I'm your man."

There was one massive excursion of Fitzgerald's larynx as he swallowed; then he extended his hand. "It's a bet."

O'Reilly shook the offered hand, noticing that the man lacked the courtesy to remove his glove. "You," he said, "are on. I'll see you at the clubhouse after the match. Now if you'll excuse us, we don't want to miss the kickoff."

He took the lead over the top of the berm toward the edge of the pitch, exchanging greetings with other supporters of the local team who had taken their stance on the near touchline. The visitors' cheering section had occupied the far side of the pitch. Already good-natured abuse was being exchanged across the field.

"See your Ballybucklebo scrum half?"

"What about our Fergus Finnegan?"

"His legs is so bandy you could drive a pony-and-trap between them." Cheering and catcalls from the far touchline.

Not to be outdone, Archie Auchinleck yelled back. "See *your* scrum half? Last time he was here, never mind passing to your outhalf, he tried to throw the ball to the ground . . . and he missed." Roars of support and laughter went up from this side.

"See you? Your mother wears army boots."

"Now *that's* what I'd call really quick on the repartee." Gales of laughter followed. "You're so bloody sharp, you'll cut yourself, so you will."

O'Reilly joined in the laughter as he stopped at the centreline. "Lie down, sir," he said to Arthur, then waited for the locals to make room for him and his party. He stood foursquare, surveying the scene.

The pitch's springy, close-cropped turf and lime-marked touchlines, centreline, twenty-five-yard lines, and goal lines were pretty much standard right up to the H-shaped goalposts at each end. The pitch had been carved out of raw farmland.

He knew because he'd helped with the carving back in 1947.

Originally it had been a piece of farmer's waste-land: rough; covered in whins, brambles, and bracken; stony; and not well drained. It was of no use as arable land. O'Reilly and a group of similar-minded villagers had raised the money to buy the plot for a song, and by dint of their own efforts they had cleared and drained it. Admittedly, it lay halfway up one of the famous County Down drumlins, small rounded hills left over from the last Ice Age, and hence was canted at a ten-degree angle from one goal line to the other, but this was regarded merely as a local eccentricity.

What made the place truly unique, a constant source of pride to O'Reilly, was that both the Rugby Union Club *and* the Gaelic Athletic Association had participated in the land reclamation and so had equal claim on the facilities. The predominantly Protestant rugby players used it on Saturdays. The totally Catholic GAA football team and hurling team used it on alternative Sundays after mass. Both the Protestant and Catholic groups would come together for important functions like the upcoming annual Christmas party.

The opposing tribes were often at each other's throats in other parts of the North or else were in a permanent state of what O'Reilly thought of as "armed neutrality." So the sporting cooperation here spoke volumes for the peace that ruled the two communities in Ballybucklebo.

But there was no olive branch to be exchanged between today's two teams, rivals since the ground had been opened. Glengormley, from the Irish *Gleann gorm liath,* the blue-grey glenn, was a suburb of Belfast City. Ballybucklebo was definitely rural.

In addition to preparing the field, the founding fathers had built a small one-storey clubhouse that stood at the far side set back some distance from the touchlines. He'd be going there after the game for the committee meeting. But that was after the game.

The cheering started from the far touchline as the opposing fifteen, the Glengormley Gallowglasses, wearing their blue-and-yellow vertically striped shirts and black shorts, ran out from the clubhouse. Two of the bigger men, forwards, wore leather scrum caps.

They were pursued by the Ballybucklebo Bonnaughts in their black-and-white-chequed shirts and white pants. O'Reilly joined in the roars of approval from the Ballybucklebo supporters. He had a fierce loyalty to his club and wanted a win for them today, never mind his bet with Fitzpatrick. That simply added piquancy.

A tall, iron-grey–haired, solitary figure trotted onto the pitch. He sported the green jersey of Ireland with its white cloth shield surmounted by a sprig of three shamrocks fixed to the left breast. O'Reilly felt a stab of nostalgia when he remembered his own opportunity to represent his country before the war. The marquis had won his caps a few years before O'Reilly.

Capping was a custom that dated back to the school caps boys had worn in the mid-nineteenth century. A tradition had sprung up of presenting athletes at various levels, including international, with ornamental caps. It was akin, O'Reilly had been informed, to the custom of awarding letters to American college athletes.

O'Reilly reckoned that Ballybucklebo was the only rugby club anywhere with a peer of the realm acting as referee. When the marquis reached the centre of the pitch, he blew his whistle, and the two team captains joined him. A coin was tossed. The Bonnaughts won and elected to play the first half uphill, which would give them the advantage in the second half. Then, flagging from their earlier exertions, they would have gravity on their side. Their choice gave the opposition the right to kick off.

As the Bonnaughts lined up across the field ten yards from the halfway line, the opposition kicker, their imported fullback, set the oval ball on one of its pointed ends in the middle of the centreline. He then took exactly eight paces back and turned quickly to both flanks to make sure his team was standing behind him and thus onside. When the marquis blew his whistle, the kicker charged forward and fetched the ball an almighty boot. His team, as if suddenly galvanized, tore after it in hot pursuit.

O'Reilly watched the ball climb into the sky, hesitate, and then plummet to earth to be caught by the home team's fullback. Almost simultaneously the fullback collected a bellyful of the shoulders of an opposing forward.

O'Reilly heard the thump and the sudden explosive expulsion of the fullback's breath. He'd have given his chance for immortality to still have been playing but, he shrugged, *anno domini* had taken their toll and he had to accept it. He reached out and took Kitty's hand, and smiled at her and Barry. At least, he could settle down now and watch eighty minutes of orchestrated mayhem.

20

The Nearest Run Thing You Ever Saw

It had been a hard-fought campaign. Two Bonnaughts and three Gallowglasses had gone off hurt. None required more than first aid, but black eyes, bloody noses, and staved ribs did take their toll. Only one from each team had returned. The game bag was lighter on O'Reilly's shoulder now the three of them had finished Kinky's comfortably warming soup. Arthur was snoring gently, having presumably decided that the thirty figures charging about weren't worth chasing. O'Reilly was starting to feel a bit chilly. He looked at Kitty. "You warm enough?"

"I'm fine, Fingal."

She moved closer to him and he noticed her faint perfume. Her cheeks were rosy red, and a tiny drip hung from the end of her nose. She *was* cold, but she was tholing it so as not to spoil his fun. He put his arm around her shoulder and gave her a squeeze. "Good lass." He produced the hip flask. "Fancy a nip?"

She shook her head.

"Barry?"

Barry stamped his feet. He looked chilled. "Why not? It's been a while since I've been to a rugby match. I'd forgotten how much fun they can be. I went to the Schools Cup with Jack Mills last Saint Patrick's Day."

"Who won?" O'Reilly handed the flask and cup to Barry.

"Belfast Royal Academy shared it with my old school, Campbell College." Barry accepted the flask and poured a measure into its small silver cup. "It was a cold day that day too. A wee warmer wouldn't have hurt then."

"So you do enjoy watching? You are enjoying yourself?" O'Reilly said. "Good. You've been working very hard, and as this is your first day off since I took ill I'd hate you to waste it."

"I'd much rather be here than hanging about Number One waiting for Jack to phone." Barry sipped his whiskey, and Fingal, much as he wanted to have his turn, was perfectly happy to wait until Barry had finished. He was glad he'd brought Barry along. The boy really was disappointed that his girl wouldn't promise to come for Christmas. Better to keep him occupied.

O'Reilly looked at his watch. With only three minutes of the regulation eighty minutes left, Ballybucklebo were ahead by two points. His ten pounds seemed secure. "So Kitty," he asked, "do you think our local gladiators can do it?"

She hesitated, then stared across the field to where the Bonnaughts were attacking close to the Gallowglasses' goal line. "Glengormley will either have to kick a penalty goal or score a touchdown." She frowned. "And if they can get in range, their fullback is a bloody fine kicker. But they've a long way to go . . . and it's uphill."

"I agree, Kitty." Turning to Barry, he said, "She always knew her stuff about this game."

She chuckled. "I had to. I spent enough Saturday afternoons on bloody freezing pitches watching you and your young friends romping in the mud."

O'Reilly squeezed her shoulder more tightly and said, "And if memory serves, you enjoyed the hooleys in the clubhouse after the games." He felt her respond by moving closer, holding his arm, and smiling up at him. "You were a pretty dab hand at the dancing, Fingal."

O'Reilly looked into her eyes and laughed.

The marquis whistled loudly for an infringement of some kind.

O'Reilly had not seen the foul. "What happened?" he asked.

"A Bonnaught was offside," Barry said. "The ref'll have to give a set scrum. Advantage to the Gallowglasses."

O'Reilly agreed. If Ballybucklebo could win the ball, they would have a very good chance of scoring and putting the game—and his bet—to bed. He grinned.

The forwards, the "packs" of each side, prepared. Three men of one team put their arms around each other's shoulders. This was the front row. The one in the middle, the hooker, would be the one to try to capture the ball. Two more big men, also with their arms around shoulders, thrust their heads between the hips of the hooker and the men to either side, his props. The two rested their shoulders on the props' and hooker's backsides. This was the second row, and O'Reilly felt a twinge of envy. That had been his position. He could close his eyes and smell the fresh sweat, feel the tight muscles of the other second-row man.

A single chap, the lock forward, put his head between their hips. On each side of both halves of the scrum, a man waited. These four men were the opposing wing forwards.

Ballybucklebo had been the offending party, so Glengormley had the advantage of initially controlling the ball. Their scrum-half, a small man, stood to the side of the opposing ranks, the ball held in his hands. Fergus Finnegan stood close by on his side of the action.

The marquis blew his whistle. The opposing front rows, propelled by the thrust of the second rows and lock forwards, bent at the hips and charged each other, interlocking head to head. The wing forwards shoved with all their might at the sides of their respective packs. The sixteen men, looking O'Reilly thought like some huge cetaceous turtle, heaved and groaned and strove against each other.

There was a tunnel between the opposing two front rows, and into it the scrum-half fired the ball. More great heaving and shoving, a communal groan from the Ballybucklebo supporters, and a cheer from the far touchline followed.

Glengormley had won possession of the ball, and the second it appeared behind the legs of their lock forward, their scrum-half grabbed it.

"Give it to the fullback!" a Glengormley supporter yelled.

That was the classic defensive tactic, O'Reilly thought. The fullback could send a towering kick as far down the field as possible, thus moving the play away from his side's vulnerable goal line.

But with only a couple of minutes left, the Gallowglasses had decided to gamble. The enemy's whole three-quarter line was in motion, tearing uphill in echelon covering most of the width of the pitch. Wild cheering from their supporters egged them on.

"Watch out for their fullback!" O'Reilly roared. He'd spotted their fullback, the ringer from North, joining the end of the line as an extra attacker. This could be dangerous.

He could feel Kitty at his side making excited minijumps, and he heard her muttering, "Tackle that man."

The moment before a Glengormley player was tackled, he passed the ball sideways to the next man. Then the moves unfolded like some sweaty chess game, as the ball moved down the line. Player after player was tackled until finally the ball reached the hands of their fullback. Only one Ballybucklebo player stood between him and an inevitable score.

O'Reilly found he was holding his breath as the man, ball clutched under his arm, thundered past so close that he wakened the sleeping Arthur Guinness.

"Arf," Arthur said.

O'Reilly ignored the dog.

"Arrf, arf," said Arthur, ignoring O'Reilly.

"Watch out for a kick!" O'Reilly yelled. If their man could get the ball past the only Ballybucklebo player now in his path, he might be able to run around the defender, recover the ball, and carry it over for a touchdown.

The Glengormley player dropped the ball onto his boot and made a delicate chip shot of a kick over the Bonnaught player and into the open ground behind him. O'Reilly flinched and muttered, "Oh, shite."

Across the pitch, the supporters were waving their coloured team scarves and cheering mightily.

"There," said O'Reilly with resignation. "There goes my ten quid." It should have been an easy score. It should have been.

Arthur gave a ferocious yodel and started to charge up the field.

"Call him in, Fingal!" Barry yelled.

Kitty burst into peals of helpless laughter.

The Ballybucklebo crowd started to chant as with one voice, "Go, Arthur!"

Two Gallowglasses hurled themselves at the dog as he raced past, but he easily avoided them.

"Go, Arthur! Go, Arthur!" The roaring of the crowd rose to a crescendo, and encouraged by the cheers, Arthur grabbed the ball, slithered to a racing turn, and headed back to his master as if he were proudly retrieving a fallen bird.

The marquis didn't so much whistle as play a long solo on his instrument. O'Reilly thought it sounded like a train announcing that it was going into a siding.

A chorus of boos rose from the opposite touchline only to be drowned by the deafening cheers from O'Reilly's side.

O'Reilly, desperately trying to hide an enormous grin, took the slaver-damp ball from Arthur's mouth. "We'll get you a Bonnaught jersey next week," he said. "Here, Barry. Hang onto his collar."

Holding Arthur by the collar, Barry said, "Sit, sir."

Arthur grinned and panted, pink tongue lolling, tail wagging. He paid not a blind bit of attention to Barry's command.

O'Reilly stepped onto the pitch and carried the ball to the marquis. "Here you are, John." He gave him the ball. "Sorry about that."

"Can't be helped, Fingal. I'll have to give them a penalty kick."

"I'm sure you're right, sir," O'Reilly said; then he walked off the pitch to the cheers of his side's supporters. Only a minute left now.

The teams arranged themselves, with the Bonnaughts lined up behind their goal line.

"Do you think he can kick it, Kitty?" O'Reilly asked, as soon as he was by her side again.

"They'll win if they do." She stared at the Gallowglasses' kicker, who was setting the oval ball on one narrow end in a shallow pit he'd hacked in the turf with the heel of his boot. Then she narrowed her eyes and looked across to the H-shaped goalposts. "He's almost on the touchline, so it's a very narrow angle and it's a fair distance."

"And," said Barry, "the breeze is against him."

"He'll miss. Bound to," O'Reilly said, with a confidence he didn't quite feel. If the ball was booted through the uprights, it was worth three points. He could afford the ten pounds but did not relish the satisfaction its loss would give to Doctor Ronald Hercules Fitzpatrick.

The kicker walked seven paces back from the upright ball, turned, and stood rigidly, arms by his sides, feet together.

The supporters of both sides fell silent. It was considered extremely unsporting to make a noise and possibly spoil the kicker's concentration.

The man ran at the ball, head down, swung his right leg, and kicked the ball with an almighty wallop. The thump of leather on leather echoed over the field.

O'Reilly watched the ball soar into the sky. It was at a good height and would have the range. It was heading to one side of the space between the uprights but should get through. Bugger, he thought, there goes my ten quid, but he felt the breeze against his cheek. A sudden stronger gust. He saw it catch the ball and give it a nudge that was just enough to alter its trajectory and push it wide of the left-hand goalpost.

He clenched his fists and thrust both arms into the air, yelling, "Bloody marvelous!" Then, oblivious to the frenzied cheering and the referee's whistle signalling the end of the game, he grabbed Kitty in an enormous bear hug, lifted her off the ground, swung her around in a great circle, and kissed her firmly.

"Put me down, Fingal," she said through her laughter. "Put me down."

He did, but he took her hand and held onto it as he said, "Well done, our side."

"Well done, indeed," Kitty said, bending and patting Arthur's head. "And well done, Arthur."

"Daft dog," he said fondly.

"Aarf," said Arthur.

"And," said O'Reilly, "it's time you were back in your kennel, sir. I've got a committee meeting to go to now."

Barry, who still had hold of Arthur's collar, said, "If you're ready, Kitty, I'll run you back to Number One."

"Please."

O'Reilly, still holding Kitty's hand, discovered he was loath to let go. He gave it a squeeze, released it, and said, "I'll not be long. Just a bit of business with Fitzpatrick, and it should be a short meeting; then I'll be home in no time."

"And you drive carefully, Fingal," Kitty said. "Do you hear me?"

He almost said, "Yes, dear," but managed to strangle the words. "Go on," he said, "run along." And as Barry, Arthur, and Kitty walked away toward the car park, O'Reilly lingered for a moment longer, noticed Kitty's head scarf, and remembered what he had thought earlier. She was a thoroughbred, Kitty O'Hallorhan. A real thoroughbred.

21

You Can Never Plan the Future by the Past

O'Reilly stood outside the clubhouse and watched the last of the victorious Bonnaughts go inside for their well-deserved showers. The light was fading and the temperature falling as evening crept on. His attention was caught by the sounds of a flock of bickering jackdaws on their way to their roosts in the big beech trees. He looked up as the birds tumbled across the pale grey-blue sky's gloaming. Their feathers were as glossy as the freshly currycombed coat of a black mare.

He stamped his booted feet and briskly flapped his arms across his chest. There was no sign of Fitzpatrick. He owed O'Reilly ten pounds and was meant to be here to settle his debt of honour. If he had any.

O'Reilly had known since long-ago medical-school days that Ronald Hercules Fitzpatrick was a miserable worm. But a man who had shaken hands on a bet—a contract in Ireland more binding than one drawn up on vellum by the chief justice, witnessed by two high court judges, and sealed in blood—well, such a man was beneath contempt.

At a minimum Fitzpatrick owed O'Reilly a face-to-face explanation. O'Reilly might even concede that the bet was off, courtesy of Arthur Guinness. But to simply not show up was more than discourteous. It was cowardly.

He decided he'd wait five more minutes. After all, it was possible that Fitzpatrick had been legitimately delayed. But after five minutes O'Reilly would go inside and get warm.

O'Reilly's thoughts were interrupted by the marquis, who appeared in the doorway. "Are you coming in, Fingal?" His hair was sleek and damp from his postgame shower, and his cheeks glowed. "We'd rather like to get the business settled and get home."

"Right. Coming."

O'Reilly climbed the three shallow steps and passed through the door the marquis held open. Then he headed down a hallway, where framed photographs of every rugby fifteen since the club had been founded hung on one wall and similarly framed photos of Gaelic football and hurling teams adorned the other.

He was so deep in thought that he was hardly aware of the marquis walking next to him.

Bloody Fitzpatrick. Some of his self-described medical practices left a certain amount to be desired, but O'Reilly was enough of a realist to recognize that a great deal of the received wisdom of his own brand of medicine was probably suspect. Much of what he and Barry practised was merely based on the authoritative statements of their professors, who had in turn learnt it from their predecessors. Mind you, last year when surgeons in Leeds had successfully transplanted a kidney from a cadaver to a living patient, you had to be impressed.

Was Fitzpatrick's quackery a real threat? It might be to his patients, in which case something would have to be done. But was he likely to attract enough customers to make things tricky in Ballybucklebo? O'Reilly doubted it, but he'd seen how worried Barry was, even if the boy tried to hide his concerns.

Those might be reasons enough to hasten Fitzpatrick's departure to parts unknown. His welshing on their bet, while being an irritant, was not a reason for O'Reilly to mount a vendetta, but it did not endear Ronald Hercules Fitzpatrick one bit.

O'Reilly wasn't certain how to help Eileen Lindsay, but he knew he must try. While he was scheming about her future, he might as well see if he could come up with a plan to discomfort Fitzpatrick too. If the man proved to be as medically dangerous as O'Reilly suspected he was, then as sure as the tides ebbed and flowed O'Reilly would see to him. A bit of thinking about how to achieve that end wouldn't hurt.

But now he had to deal with the business at hand.

He opened the boardroom door and held it open for the marquis, who went straight through. O'Reilly followed him into a comfortable, oak-panelled room. Conversation was stilled when the peer entered.

A paraffin stove served to take the chill off the air, and O'Reilly could smell its fumes. Through the fug of tobacco smoke, he could make out the photographs of past presidents, various officials, the chairwomen of the ladies' committee, and head-and-shoulder snaps of players who had represented Ulster over the years.

He smiled to see pictures of himself and the marquis, the two club members who had been capped for their country.

He looked away from the old pictures to the group, the executive committee, surrounding a long mahogany table in the centre of the room. The lone female, Flo Bishop, had remained seated. A large woman, she wore an expensive hat and a fashionable dress meant for a woman half her age. O'Reilly hid his smile. Kinky would say she was "mutton dressed up as lamb."

The five men, all well known to O'Reilly, had stood for the marquis. Fergus Finnegan as team captain; Reverend Robinson, the Presbyterian minister in his white dog collar; the parish priest, Father O'Toole, in his cassock; the captain of the hurling team, Dermot Kennedy, whose daughter Jeannie had had an appendix abscess in August; and Councillor Bertie Bishop, the member at large—very large, O'Reilly thought. Bishop's dark three-piece suit was crumpled. O'Reilly could see, looped across the waistcoat, a gold watch chain with the Masonic Order's set square emblem dangling from one end.

"Please do sit down," the marquis said, taking his place as club patron and honorary president at the head of the table. In front of him were a gavel and the leather-bound minutes book.

The men sat and O'Reilly, after hanging his overcoat, cap, and scarf on a clothes stand, joined them, sitting at the marquis's right hand. He was after all the secretary-treasurer and had been for more years than he liked to remember. "Evening, all," O'Reilly said. "Evening, Mrs. Bishop." He nodded to Flo Bishop, this year's ladies' committee secretary.

"Evening, Doctor." The chorus in unison could have come from his waiting room, but here for once the deference was from respect for his past skill as a rugby football player.

The men looked expectantly at the marquis.

O'Reilly smiled and leant over to Flo Bishop, who was sitting on his right. He asked quietly, "How are you, Flo?"

"I'm grand, so I am, Doctor. Thank you. Them wee pills Doctor Laverty give me is dead on, so they are. I'm not tired all the time anymore. I'm running round like a liltie."

"Good." In August, Barry had made an astute diagnosis of her myasthenia gravis, a rare disease that interfered with the transmission of nerve impulses to the skeletal muscles. Sufferers were perpetually lethargic, but the neostigmine bromide Barry had prescribed was obviously doing the trick, and she was full of energy.

"I'm delighted," O'Reilly said.

She leant closer and whispered, "And I've lost a whole stone."

"Impressive, Flo," he said, looking at her again. He reckoned that even at fourteen pounds less than her old fighting weight, she could probably afford to lose a fair bit more.

He heard the marquis cough, rap once with his gavel, and say, "I'd like to call the meeting to order.

As you all know, this is an extraordinary meeting of the executive, so we can dispense with approving the minutes of the last plenary meeting." He pushed the minute book aside, unopened.

Councillor Bertie Bishop lifted his hand as if to strike the tabletop. He heaved himself forward in his chair at the opposite side of the table. He had to sit some distance back to accommodate his ample belly. "I'm still not happy with that rise of one pound in the dues, so I'm not."

"Houl' . . . your . . . wheest . . . Bertie." His wife, Flo, enunciated each word clearly and fixed him with a glare that O'Reilly reckoned would have given the fabled basilisk a run for the beast's money; its look could turn a man to stone. "That's old business, so it is," she growled.

"Yes, dear." He lowered his hand and subsided muttering.

The marquis, a wry smile on his lips, said, "You are a *tad* out of order, Bertie."

"It's daylight robbery, so it is."

"Bertie." Flo leant across the table. "That'll do."

The marquis nodded. "We've two items on our agenda for this afternoon, and I'd like to move along as quickly as possible in dealing with them. First is the Christmas party. Will you bring us up to date on that, Flo?"

"I can, sir." She produced a handbag that O'Reilly thought could have done duty as a steamer trunk, put it on the tabletop, rummaged inside, and hauled out a notebook with a spiral wire running along the spine. "We'll be having it as usual on the twenty-third, that's a Wednesday, eleven days away. It'll start at five so the youngest kiddies can come for a wee while before their bedtimes, and . . ."—she smiled at O'Reilly—"at six Santa will arrive, if that's all right with you, Doctor O'Reilly."

"Ho, ho, ho," said O'Reilly, who had enjoyed his annual role for many years.

Flo bobbed her head, reached into her handbag, and produced a tape measure. "If you'd not mind standing up, sir?"

O'Reilly stood and waited while Flo also rose and ran the tape measure round his waist. She pinched to mark the measurement, removed it, rolled it up, and made a note in her notebook. She shook her head at O'Reilly. "I'll have to get one of the ladies to let the pants out an inch at the waist, sir. If you don't mind me saying, you're getting a bit tall around."

O'Reilly laughed, not one bit offended. "Doctor Laverty told me that Miss Moloney's back from her sister's. She's a grand seamstress. You might want to have a word with her." If nothing else, he thought it might be a way to start Miss M on the road back to acceptance in the village.

"Is she? I'll pop in the dress shop and have a wee word. Now"—she consulted her notes—"my ladies will take care of the catering." She smiled at O'Reilly. "Do you think your Mrs. Kincaid would like to help out?"

"I'll certainly ask her, but I'm sure she will."

"Good, and when we've finished decorating the

Parish Hall for the pageant"—she nodded at Father O'Toole, who smiled back—"we'll do the clubhouse here."

"Thank you, Mrs. Bishop," O'Toole said.

"And," she continued, "Fergus, can you get the tree?"

"You can cut one on the estate," the marquis offered.

"Thank you, sir. I'll see to it."

"Mister Chairman," Bertie Bishop interrupted. He stood as he always did, with his thumbs hooked behind the lapels of his suit jacket. "Will it be the same arrangement for the kiddies' presents this year?"

The marquis frowned. "I think the ladies' secretary still has the floor."

Flo stared at her husband. Perhaps, O'Reilly thought, he had been hasty in likening her to the basilisk. If she had a few serpents for hair, she'd have made a first-class Medusa. "You go ahead, Bertie, dear . . ." Her expression gave the lie to her honeyed tones.

"Like I said, will it be the same for the kiddies' presents?"

"Aye, Councillor." The priest spoke softly, his Cork brogue musical like Kinky's to O'Reilly's ear. "We'll tell the parents to bring a wrapped present for each of their own children. They'll mark the child's name clearly on a label and give the parcels to me to put in Santa's sack." He smiled at O'Reilly. "Just before Santa arrives, I'll pop the sack under the tree; then when Father Christmas pulls out a present, he can read the tag, call the child's name, and the wee one can come forward for its gift, so."

O'Reilly nodded. It was a good plan and had worked for many years. It should bloody well work; it had been his idea. Bertie Bishop was rabbitting on about something else, but O'Reilly was not paying attention. The image of himself pulling presents out of a sack had given him the germ of an idea, a brilliant idea if he did think so himself. With a bit of luck, he might well be able to solve Eileen Lindsay's Christmas fund difficulties. "By God," he said aloud, "it'll be just the ticket . . . literally."

"I beg your pardon, Fingal?" O'Reilly saw the marquis looking puzzled and realized that he himself had just voiced his thoughts.

He coughed. "I'm sorry. Just thinking aloud. I didn't mean to interrupt."

"It's perfectly all right. You had finished, hadn't you, Bertie?"

"Aye." The councillor sat down.

"Thank you. Now does anyone have anything more to say about the party arrangements?" He waited. No one spoke. "Very well. That brings me to the last item. It was on the agenda on Tuesday, but unfortunately Doctor O'Reilly was a bit under the weather and couldn't be with us. Fingal, will you please stand up?"

O'Reilly frowned. This must be the surprise the marquis had warned him about when he had visited on Tuesday. O'Reilly stood.

The marquis picked up a small parcel, wrapped in

brown paper, from the tabletop. O'Reilly hadn't noticed it before.

"Doctor O'Reilly," the marquis said, "after due consideration for your efforts on behalf of the Ballybucklebo Bonnaughts for fifteen years, ever since we started working on making the pitch, the committee has decided to recognize your contribution by making a small presentation." He handed the parcel to O'Reilly to the accompaniment of applause from the other members.

"Open it, Doctor," Flo said.

Completely at a loss for words, O'Reilly, not least because of a considerable lump in his throat, started to remove the wrapping slowly and carefully. He frittered with a bit of Sellotape that stuck the paper closed. He was always embarrassed by public displays of gratitude, and indeed when the occasional patient said thank you, he found that recompense enough.

Once the paper was removed, he found a small velvet-covered box and opened it. Nestled in its recesses were a matching Parker fountain pen and mechanical pencil. Still feeling embarrassed, he managed to say, "Thank you all; thank you very much."

"Read what the inscription says," Bertie Bishop called. "Read it out loud."

There was a small brass plate on the inside of the box's lid. It read: *To Doctor Fingal Flahertie O'Reilly in recognition for many services rendered to the Ballybucklebo Bonnaughts Rugby Club.*

There was a chorus of "Hear! hear!" and applause, and then Bertie Bishop, never the shrinking violet, said, "It was me made them write 'many,' so it was."

"Wheest, Bertie," his wife said, and her chiding was greeted by chuckles from around the table.

O'Reilly was grateful that those interjections had given him time to collect his thoughts. "Look," he said, holding the open box toward his audience so every one could see. "I've never had a Parker pen, never mind a pen *and* pencil. I've always wanted a set like this, and considering the circumstances of how I got it"—he closed the box and slipped it into his pocket—"I'll treasure it. I really will. Thank you. Thank you all."

There was another, longer round of applause.

Good God, he thought, the gift was in recognition of the fifteen years he'd spent with the Rugby Club, almost as many years as he had spent here in Ballybucklebo. Good years, very good years, and it was humbling yet gratifying to be singled out as someone who had contributed to the little community. He'd not realized how truly moved he was until he became aware of a prickling behind his eyelids.

When the applause died, everyone was still looking expectantly at him.

O'Reilly swallowed. He wasn't used to this sort of public recognition, wasn't entirely sure if he approved, and yet he sensed he must say something more. He cleared his throat.

"It's like Eeyore in *Winnie-the-Pooh* said, 'It's nice to be noticed.' But I have to say, there's many a one's done just as much, aye, and more for the club as I—"

"We thought," said the marquis with a broad grin, "it was more a gift from the committee given in self-preservation."

O'Reilly frowned.

The marquis offered the open minute book to O'Reilly. "We felt that if our esteemed secretary-treasurer had the right implements, we might finally have a fighting chance of reading the minutes."

Everyone laughed.

"Och," said O'Reilly, relieved. Obviously, the marquis had sensed his friend's embarrassment and was making everyone laugh to divert their attention for the moments it had taken O'Reilly to collect himself. "Do you not know that writing an illegible scrawl is the hallmark of every first-class doctor?"

"In that case, Doctor," the priest said softly, "if the last prescription you wrote for me is anything to go by, you should be soon up for a Nobel Prize, so." There was more laughter.

O'Reilly smiled and shook his head. "I am very touched, and all I can say is thank you very much. Thank you very much indeed. I will treasure this gift . . . and . . . seeing as how I am apparently in favour at the moment, I'd like to ask for an indulgence. I know I should have given advance notice of a small item I'd like the committee to discuss, but when I said a minute ago, 'By God, it'll be just the ticket,' the notion had just occurred to me."

The marquis looked from face to face, then said, "Please go ahead, Fingal."

"I'm going to ask you to take this on trust for a

week or two because I have to keep it a secret. I want to run a raffle for a very good cause. I can't tell you what at this moment, but I know all of you"—he let his gaze linger on the faces of each man of the cloth in turn—"will approve." He made a rapid mental calculation. "And I want the club to agree to take only twenty-five percent of the proceeds."

"'Scuse me, Doctor." Bertie Bishop spoke from where he was sitting. "I don't see what any of this has to do with the club. Why don't you just run the raffle yourself?"

"I'm asking, Bertie, because the club has the legal right to sponsor a raffle. I don't—"

"Right enough. I never thought of that."

"And," O'Reilly ploughed on, "the party would be a great place to have the draw." Because, he thought, when Eileen gets the money, and I know how to arrange that, she can go shopping for presents the next day and Santa would come to her house on Christmas Eve after all. "I would like to ask for the executive's approval." He looked around the table and hoped mightily. Ordinarily he would have first done his political homework, a bit of quiet lobbying of the members, often lubricated with a jar or two.

"Do you want to make that a formal motion, Fingal?" the marquis asked.

"Not if everybody agrees." He waited.

"Does anybody object?"

"I don't like the percentage split," Bishop said. "How about fifty-fifty?"

"Councillor," Father O'Toole said, "I believe Doctor O'Reilly said it was for a good cause."

"A very good cause," O'Reilly added. "And it's Christmas, Bertie."

Bishop had the grace to blush. "In that case I withdraw my objection."

"Good man, Bertie." The marquis looked around the table and waited before finally saying, "I hear no other dissent." He smiled at O'Reilly. "Looks like you have the go-ahead, Fingal, and the split you've asked for. I presume you will look after the details?"

"I will. Thank you, everybody," O'Reilly said. All right, problem one was almost solved and off O'Reilly's agenda. Fitzpatrick might have to wait, but although he was out of sight, he was not out of O'Reilly's mind but merely tabled.

"Very well," the marquis said, "if there is no further business, I'll entertain a motion for adjournment."

With the motion duly proposed and seconded, the meeting broke up. O'Reilly had to wait for the other members to collect their hats and coats before he could get his own. He stayed at the table, wishing they would get a move on. He took out his gift. It was a truly handsome set. He *would* treasure it.

The little crowd thinned out quickly, each member bidding O'Reilly a good evening as they departed. Only the Presbyterian minister remained when O'Reilly came forward to get his coat, scarf, and cap. "Doctor O'Reilly," he said, "I'm willing to take your idea at face value, that it's for a good cause. Can I help you with it?"

"That's very civil of you, Reverend; if you'll forgive me, very Christian . . ."

The minister chuckled.

"But I'm on my way home now to discuss it with Doctor Laverty, and I already have a man in mind to run the raffle for me."

"Oh?"

"Indeed," said O'Reilly, "Donal Donnelly will be back from his honeymoon on Monday, and I've no doubt, no doubt whatsoever, that he's the man for the job."

22

Thou Art a Hard Man

Barry drove carefully home to Number 1 Main Street. He and Kitty greeted Kinky and and then started to head upstairs, but the smell of brandy from the kitchen was overpowering. Kinky was about to start icing the Christmas cake she had baked in August and which she had liberally seasoned with spirits on a regular basis ever since.

"Can I watch, Kinky?" Kitty asked. "I never seem to be able to get the icing quite right on mine."

"Bless you, Miss O'Hallorhan, of course you can."

Barry kept his counsel and watched too.

The cake stood on a pastry board on the countertop, and as she worked, Kinky explained her methods step-by-step to Kitty.

"The marzipan needs to be half an inch thick, so, and you stick it on with apricot jam," Kinky said. "You put it on four days before you do the icing; otherwise the almond paste leaks through the icing."

"That's what I've been doing wrong. Thank you, Kinky," Kitty said.

"Most folks do make the same mistake," Kinky said. "You have to leave it for four days before you put on the royal icing." She lifted a ceramic bowl covered with a piece of damp gauze. Pulling the gauze away, she revealed a pure white paste that Barry could see was soft enough to be spread with a knife over the marzipan. As she worked, Kinky hummed to herself. She used the knife to transform the initially smooth surface into a series of irregular ridges like the sastrugi found on Antarctic ice sheets. "There. Now that looks more like a snow scene, so." She rummaged in a tin caddy and produced a miniature snowman, two circus clowns, and a ballerina wearing a short gauze tutu and carrying a star-tipped wand. All of the figurines were two inches tall and stood on circular flat bases. Kinky set them in a group at one corner of the cake's top by pressing their bases into the already setting icing.

"I'll put a sprig of holly at the other corner on the big day," she said. "The decorations please the kiddies, so"—she looked knowingly at Kitty—"and the big fellah likes them too."

Kitty chuckled.

Barry smiled with the two women, yet watching Kinky at work had made him a little sad. Her cake had unexpectedly reminded him of times from his own childhood Christmases, with his own mother—now in Australia and to whom he really must write—decorating their cake. He'd not be surprised if even O'Reilly felt nostalgic when some sights at this season brought back memories. "It's beautiful, Kinky," he said.

She gave a little start. "Lord Jesus, Doctor Laverty. I'd forgotten you were there," she said. "Don't creep up on a body. You could give a poor Cork woman the rickets, so."

"I'm sorry," he said.

"No real harm done. I'll forgive you—but thousands wouldn't." She was smiling as she lifted the cake to put it into a cake tin. "Will you take Miss O'Hallorhan upstairs now, sir? I've a bit more to do here."

"Certainly," Barry said. "Doctor O'Reilly should be home soon, Kinky. We left him at the Rugby Club." Then he spoke to Kitty. "Come on. We'll go up and wait for Fingal."

"Thank you for the lesson, Kinky. I'll remember the trick with the marzipan," Kitty said.

"Och, sure, it's what my own mother taught me," Kinky said, her grin wide. "Go on with you now."

"Right." Kitty walked to the hall door. "I know my way. I'll leave my coat in the hall."

Barry had started to follow when Kinky said, "It's himself that's on call today, is it not?"

"It is," Barry said, hesitating. "Have there been any calls for him?"

"Nary the one, but your friend Doctor Mills rang and said he was sorry he'd not called last night and then missed your call today. But he said he'd ring back later."

Barry had expected to hear from Jack, but he had guessed, as was often the case in the lives of junior doctors in training, that things medical had come up. "Thanks, Kinky."

He headed for the staircase and on the way past the hall telephone thought about some of the conversations he'd had on it recently.

A few days earlier he'd suggested Jack come here for one of Kinky's dinners. Now, given Patricia's stubbornness about allowing Barry to pay for her ticket home, Barry wasn't so sure. Perhaps, he would go with Jack to one of the nurses' parties or to the dance he'd mentioned. The dance might be a bit of fun. He'd almost certainly see some of his old classmates and be able to catch up with their doings. Why not? he asked himself, as he resumed his climb. Why not indeed?

Kitty was standing in front of the fireplace in the lounge, her back to the fire, her black stirrup pants complemented by a cream, heavy knit, rollneck wool sweater that Barry couldn't help noticing she filled rather well.

"Would you like something, Kitty?" Barry nodded at the cut-glass decanters on the sideboard.

"No, thanks, Barry. I'll wait for Fingal." She held her hands behind her to the fire for a moment before rubbing them together and blowing on them. "It got nippy enough out there. I'm not sorry to be here in the warm," she said, moving to sit in one of the armchairs.

Suddenly Barry saw Lady Macbeth spring lightly into Kitty's lap, to be greeted with a stroke as the little cat made herself comfortable. Kitty smiled at Barry. "It's a law, you know."

"What is?"

"Whatever the colour of the cat, they'll be attracted to clothes of the opposite shade. My black pants will be covered in white hairs." She chuckled. "I don't mind and she's a pretty wee crayture. Aren't you?" She tickled Lady Macbeth under the chin and was rewarded with a low purring. "I'd never have thought Fingal was a cat man," she said. "He's more like that bull-in-a-china-shop dog of his."

Barry nodded. "I don't think he ever had any notion of getting a cat, but someone abandoned her here and he just took her in. It seemed a natural thing for him to do."

Kitty looked up into Barry's eyes. "He's always been like that, you know, ever since I've known him. Always on the side of the waifs and strays. I think," she said, "he's a big softie inside, and all the bluster and bravado is a cover for that." Barry thought he heard a touch of wistfulness in her voice.

"You could be right, Kitty."

"It can make him a hard man to get to know well. Very hard."

He was in no doubt now. And it was less the tone of her voice than the way she was looking at him that made Barry decide she was somehow seeking reassurance. "It's difficult for me to know. I've only been here for a few months, but I think I am getting to understand him a bit." Lord, he thought, she could be my own mother. I'm hardly in a position to advise her. "Maybe it just takes time."

She sighed. "You could be right."

Barry had an unexpected desire to go give the woman a hug and mutter, "There, there. It'll be fine." He'd not expected Kitty O'Hallorhan to be so open with him, a relative stranger. When next she spoke, his eyes widened, and he wondered if she had been able to read his mind.

"It's not for myself I'm asking you this," she said. "I'm very fond of the big eejit, Barry, but he's only had Mrs. Kincaid to keep an eye to him and now there's yourself. Will you do me a favour?"

He saw something deep in those amazing grey-flecked-with-amber eyes that would have had him saying yes, even if she'd asked him to pluck out a couple of his own fingernails. "Of course," he said.

"Take the time to get to know him, and in time,

and don't ask me how long that will take, try to be his friend. Please?"

Barry wasn't quite sure how to respond, so he simply said, "I'll do my best, Kitty."

"Thank you, Barry." She looked away and stared to somewhere in the middle distance. Her eyes were very shiny as she said, "I'd appreciate that very much."

Barry was trying to frame a suitable answer when the subject of the conversation arrived.

"It's as cold out there as a stepmother's breath," said O'Reilly, barging in past Barry and heading for the sideboard. "I think," he remarked, pouring himself a stiff Jameson, "a little internal antifreeze is indicated. Anyone else?"

Kitty, with her back still turned to him, said cheerfully, "Could I have a gin and tonic, please, Fingal?"

O'Reilly smiled at her. "We don't normally stock the stuff, but I remembered you used to like it as well as Jameson so I did get a bottle." He bent, opened a door in the sideboard, and produced a bottle of Gilbey's gin and a bottle of Schweppes tonic water. "Barry?" O'Reilly straightened and started to mix Kitty's drink.

Barry shook his head. "I'll be driving up to Belfast later, Fingal, and the roads are a bit icy."

"I didn't notice," O'Reilly said, "but then I was in a hurry to get home." And when that happens, Barry thought, not even an ice age would have the temerity to hinder your progress, Fingal, never mind the odd patch of black ice.

O'Reilly handed Kitty her drink, plonked himself

down in the other armchair, grinned at her, raised his glass, and said, "*Sláinte*."

She faced him and clinked her glass against his, smiling openly. "Cheers, Fingal. Nice to have you back. It really is."

Barry wondered if there was a deeper subtext to her comment. "How did it go at the Rugby Club?" he asked.

"Short, sharp, and to the point," O'Reilly said. "We've all the arrangements made for the Christmas party. I'll be Santa."

"And any idea you have of me being an elf—"

"You're far too tall," O'Reilly said, "and anyway I've another job for you."

"Not tonight you haven't. I'm going up to Belfast as soon as my friend Jack phones."

"Good," said O'Reilly. "Enjoy yourself and sleep late tomorrow. My job'll keep until Monday, until Donal Donnelly and Julie get back from their honeymoon."

Barry sensed the ringing of distant alarm bells at the merest mention of Donal's name.

"Yes," O'Reilly charged on, "I've the answer to Eileen Lindsay's financial woes."

"Oh? What is it?" Barry frowned. He was all for helping Eileen, but if O'Reilly wanted to involve Donal, the plan probably involved robbing the Ballybucklebo branch of the Bank of Ireland, and Barry did not fancy being cast as the driver of the getaway car. Before O'Reilly could offer an explanation, Barry heard the telephone ringing below.

"That'll be your friend Mills," O'Reilly said. "Nip down and see like a good lad. Save Kinky having to climb up here."

Barry remembered that O'Reilly, who planned to take Kitty to the Crawsfordsburn Inn for dinner, had said he'd not take it amiss if Barry disappeared at about this time in the evening. "All right, Fingal." Barry started for the door, half turned, and said, "If I don't see you again, have a pleasant evening, Kitty." Without waiting for a reply, he trotted down the stairs, picked up the receiver, and said, "Hello?"

"How the hell are you, Barry?" Jack's Cullybackey accent was as thick as ever. "Sorry we've been missing each other, but you know what it's like when a ward's busy."

"I'm grand, Jack," Barry said, "and never worry about missing a few phone calls. It can't be helped." He took a deep breath, thought about Patricia, realized he was still feeling somewhere between disappointed and angry, and decided what the eye didn't see, the heart wouldn't grieve over. "Are you still on for some kind of do tonight?"

"Is the pope Catholic? There's a dance at the nurses' home."

"Let's go to it. Do you want to come down here for supper first? Kinky's made a steak-and-kidney pie."

"No, thanks. I've to pick up Mandy, and she lives away out the Antrim Road. It'll take me a while to get to her place and back before seven. The dance is at eight in the nurses' home, Bostock House, just across the road in the grounds of the Royal."

"Jesus, Jack, don't try to teach your granny to suck eggs. I know where Bostock House is. Didn't we both use to pick up nurses there?"

"Indeed, Effendi. What a silly man I am, but then I am coming from a silly people. Let us meet in the oasis of O'Kane at sevenish. It is of my father's people, the Beni-sadr, not of the Howitat tribe, and the drinks are ours for the taking." Jack's accent was a perfect imitation of Omar Sharif's in *Lawrence of Arabia,* which Barry and Jack had seen together a couple of years earlier.

Barry laughed. "You and your imitations. Bugger off, Mills . . . I'll see you and Mandy in the Oak at seven." Barry replaced the receiver.

He glanced at his watch. Good, he'd have time enough to get cleaned up and then eat Kinky's steak-and-kidney pie. He knew she would be very hurt if he left it uneaten. She knew O'Reilly was not dining at home tonight, and it would have been very inconsiderate of Barry to let her prepare supper for him alone rather than tell her well in advance that she'd not need to. He had some understanding of how hard Kinky worked to keep her charges properly fed. She never minded if her doctors had to miss a meal if they were called out for medical reasons, but she could get sniffy if they knew in advance they'd be out and neglected to inform her. And rightly so, Barry thought. Keeping her apprised of his plans was the least courtesy he could pay her.

He climbed the stairs on the way to his attic bedroom. As he passed the closed door to the upstairs lounge, he heard O'Reilly say, ". . . and Donal Donnelly's the man for the job," followed by O'Reilly's booming laugh and Kitty's higher-pitched chuckle.

Barry smiled. He realized that whatever the job for Donal was, it would be revealed in the fullness of time. Tonight he was going to see his friend and forget about medicine, the citizens of Ballybucklebo, and the stubbornness of the love of his life.

23

A Feast of Wine on the Lees

O'Reilly stood back and held Kitty's coat for her. He noticed how delicately the fine hairs curled from the nape of her neck, her subtle perfume.

"I think, Fingal," she said, "as I've only had a small gin and tonic and you had your snake antivenin at the game *and* a large John Jameson just now, I should drive."

"Drive my Rover? It's a big heavy brute."

"My Mini is parked in the lane beside Barry's Volkswagen." She linked her arm in his and began to walk toward the kitchen. "I'll drive to the Crawfordsburn, and I'll bring us back here afterward so you can have a drink there and not worry about driving home."

The kitchen was empty. Kinky must have disappeared up to her quarters to watch her small television set. The comedy *Steptoe and Son*, about a couple of English rag-and-bone men and their horse, Hercules, was one of her favourites, and O'Reilly knew she had also enjoyed the late-night political satire *That Was the Week That Was* before it was taken off the air the year before.

"I'd not worry. It wouldn't be the first time Constable Mulligan, Ballybucklebo's finest, has driven me home. He says it's less trouble than arresting me. But I'll only have the one or two more tonight. I *am* on call." He opened the back door for her. He frowned. He wasn't sure he'd be comfortable being driven by a woman.

"I'll hold you to only a couple," Kitty said, "and we *are* taking my car. It's not just yourself you could put in the ditch. I like being in one piece."

And I like you that way too, he thought, as he followed her through the back door and closed it behind him.

"You're beginning to sound like a wife, Caitlin O'Hallorhan," he said without thinking. He was glad they were out in the darkness of the back garden and she couldn't see his face. He knew he was probably grinning like an idiot because as the words slipped out, it had struck him that he could do worse—if ever he married again. Aye, and that would be when cherries grew on his apple trees, the bare limbs of which he could just make out limned against a dark sky. The stars were shining like chrome-plated rivets in a black knight's ebony cuirass. "But . . . all right. You drive."

"Aaarf?" Arthur asked sleepily, as they passed his kennel.

"*Next* Saturday," O'Reilly said to the dog, who snorted and stayed in his doghouse.

As O'Reilly let Kitty out through the back gate, he explained, "The pair of us are going to Strangford Lough next weekend for a day's wildfowling. Arthur really enjoys that."

"I'm happy for Arthur," she said, "but I'm sorry for the poor ducks. I can't see them enjoying it very much."

O'Reilly shivered. That was exactly how Deidre had felt.

"Here we are," Kitty announced. "Hop in."

He opened the car door, scrunched himself into the front seat of the Morris Mini, and immediately felt great empathy for those undergraduates who from time to time tried to see how many men they could cram into a telephone box. By dint of expelling his breath and tucking his arms tightly against his sides, he was able to get his door to close. Just. "Neat little car," he said, inwardly cursing its designer, Sir Alec Issigonis.

Kitty swung out onto the Belfast-to-Bangor road. O'Reilly thought it better to let Kitty concentrate on her driving, so he sat quietly even though the traffic was light. The inside of the little car was lit, then plunged into darkness, as it moved between the pools of light cast by the few streetlights.

They left Ballybucklebo and drove through the countryside.

He sat in the darkness and let his mind roam freely. O'Reilly considered his plan to help Eileen. It seemed pretty foolproof. He smiled. Good. He wondered idly how the Irish rugby team would fare in the international series this season. France, Wales, England, and Scotland all would be fielding powerful teams.

The inside of the car was illuminated by the headlights of an oncoming vehicle. He turned and studied Kitty's profile. She'd been a pretty girl as a student nurse. She was a handsome, mature woman now.

Why, he asked himself, as he had done several times since Tuesday, why had she not married? She'd surprised him on Tuesday, telling him she had never forgotten him, could still care for him if he'd let her. She couldn't have been carrying a torch for him, not for twenty-five years or so. Could she?

Why not? He rubbed his forehead with the heel of his gloved hand. He had carried one for Deidre for twenty-three years, The light from the first streetlamp in the village of Crawfordsburn was reflected in Kitty's eyes; then the car was in darkness again. Maybe, just maybe, he thought, he should let his torch's flame gutter. Not go out, oh no, but flare a little less brightly.

He remembered the touch of Kitty's hand on his after dinner at Number 1 Main Street, the brush of her lips on his own, and for a moment he had an almost overwhelming urge to lean across and kiss her cheek. But she was indicating for a left turn into the Inn's car park, and he didn't want to distract her.

After she parked, they stepped into the Inn and

hung their coats in the hall cloakroom; then he held her elbow as he steered her to the front desk. The entrance to the Inn was decorated for Christmas with sprigs of holly placed on top of the gilt frames of Irish landscapes. Two multicoloured paper chains looped diagonally from corner to corner under the ceiling beams. A mirror on one wall was half sprayed with artificial frost.

O'Reilly paused at the desk. "Evening, John. This is Miss O'Hallorhan."

"Evening, Doctor O'Reilly. Pleased to meet you, miss."

Kitty smiled at him. "John."

"Will you do me a wee favour?" O'Reilly asked.

"Same as always, Doctor?"

"Aye. Miss O'Hallorhan and I will be in your dining room. If Mrs. Kincaid phones, will you come and get me?"

"Like at the wedding?"

O'Reilly nodded.

"My pleasure, sir, but I hope I won't have to."

"So do I," O'Reilly said. He looked at the grandfather clock against one wall. "We're a bit early so we'll wait in the bar until our table's ready." Still holding Kitty by the elbow, he guided her to the Parlour Bar where the turf fire burned beneath a mantel hung with a holly wreath. Patrons, many of them the same men who'd been in on Monday, the regulars, occupied the same booths. He'd no need to come here very often, but the Duck had no restaurant, and if he were honest, taking Kitty there would set tongues wagging in Ballybucklebo.

Colette was behind the bar. She greeted them with a huge grin, moved along the bar, and said, "How's about ye, Doctor O'Reilly? You're in for your dinner, I hear. Table for two? It'll be ready in a wee minute, so it will. Would you both like a wee drink while you're waiting?" She was already picking up a bottle of Jameson. She'd been serving O'Reilly on his infrequent visits for as long as he could remember, and Colette, he knew, was a superb barmaid with an encyclopaedic memory for what her customers favoured. She knew her wines too. She had to in a place that was too small to have a sommelier. He smiled and nodded his assent.

"No, thanks," Kitty said firmly. "We'll be having a bottle of wine with our dinner, and I'm driving, and Fingal's on call."

Colette's eyes widened, but she kept her counsel and replaced the bottle. "You have a wee seat then and I'll get you the menus, so I will." She headed off along the bar.

O'Reilly glanced at Kitty, shrugged, and reminded himself that he had promised to have only one or two more drinks. He waited for Kitty to sit at a small table, fished out his briar, and asked, "Mind if I smoke?"

"Not at all. My father used to smoke a pipe. The smell of the tobacco reminds me of him." When O'Reilly had the pipe well lit, she leant across the table, put both hands palm down on top, and looked into his eyes. "Thank you for taking me to the game today, Fingal. I really enjoyed it. It took me back."

O'Reilly smiled at her, and he knew she was alluding to the times she'd come to watch him play. Hearing her words, he too remembered those days, and the memories were bittersweet. His hand covered one of hers. "Me too," he said.

He heard a cough. Colette had returned. "Here youse are," she said, handing each a menu. "And here's the wine list." She offered it to O'Reilly, but he shook his head. "Give it to the lady, Colette." He saw the barmaid's eyes widen for the second time in as many minutes. Men always selected the wines. "Kitty's the wine expert. I'd not know a merlot from a marron glacé."

Colette shrugged and handed the list to Kitty. "I'll give youse both a couple of wee minutes." She left.

O'Reilly opened the menu, scanned it quickly, and made up his mind. Scampi for a starter and then the lobster thermidor. He was particularly fond of the way the chef here prepared the scampi, deep-frying Dublin Bay prawns in a delicious batter. His tummy gurgled in anticipation. "Pardon me," he said, putting the menu on the table.

Kitty ignored him as she read. He watched her shaking her head over many of the offerings, nodding at others. Finally she gave one emphatic nod and closed the menu.

"What would you like?" he asked.

"Escargots," she said, "and then . . . do they do the filet steaks well here, Fingal?"

He nodded.

"Fine," she said. "I'll have mine medium rare."

O'Reilly sat back in his chair and took his pipe from his mouth. He shook his head rapidly, then blinked twice, but the vivid mental image remained. A small restaurant in Dublin, low lights, a candle guttering on the table, a medical student wondering if he would be able to afford the meal they had just ordered to celebrate his date's having qualified as a nurse. "That's exactly what you had the very first time I took you out for dinner," he said softly. "I remember because I'd never seen anybody eat snails before. We thought only the French did that."

"The restaurant was owned by a Frenchman." She smiled, and he saw her colour heighten, her smile widen. She covered the back of his hand with her palm. "I didn't think you'd remember," she said, and there was huskiness in her voice.

"I do, Kitty," he said, "and you wore a green dress, and I leant over to tell you I thought you looked stunning . . . and I spilled a glass of red wine over your lap." He felt her hand squeeze his and heard her throaty chuckles.

"You've a very good memory, Fingal," she said.

"For some things. Important things." He looked into her eyes and said, "Before you order the wine, so I can't possibly spill it tonight, I'm going to lean over"—he leant so close that he was practically whispering in her ear—"and tell you you still look stunning." He turned his hand and took hers in his. "Positively stunning."

"Thank you, Fingal."

He saw Colette approaching, guiltily released Kitty's hand, leant back, stuck his pipe back in his mouth, and released a cloud of smoke that might have hidden the old *Warspite* from enemy eyes.

"Ready?" Colette asked, pencil and notebook poised.

O'Reilly gave the food order.

Colette turned to Kitty. "And for the wine?"

"I think we'd like the Bâtard-Montrachet," Kitty said. "But is that all right, Fingal? It's a bit pricey."

Typical Kitty, he thought. Great taste but a good eye for economics too. "For you, Kitty, on a day the Bonnaughts won, I think the O'Reilly exchequer can stand it."

"Thank you," she said, smiling. "The Montrachet's worth a few extra pounds, and it's not hugely expensive, not like a Lafite Rothschild '61."

Colette's eyebrows shot up, and there was a tone of respect in her voice when she said, "We've a . . . we've a '52 Montrachet; I know that for a fact, so I do."

"That would be lovely," Kitty said. "Perhaps we could have a glass now?"

"I'll bring it right away." Colette left.

O'Reilly laughed. "And I suppose you like your martinis shaken not stirred, and you carry a Beretta 418 automatic or a Walther PPK?"

"What ever do you mean, Fingal?" Her brows knit.

"I mean like your man James Bond . . . he sure as hell knows his wines."

"I see." She laughed. "Have you seen the films?"

"No," O'Reilly said, "but I've read every one of Ian Fleming's books."

"Do you not go to the movies?"

"I haven't had the time," he said, "but now I've Barry to share the load . . ."—he remembered kissing her in the back row of a cinema in Dublin—"we could go together."

"I'd like that very much."

"And I hope you'll like this, miss," Colette said, setting two glasses on the table and showing Kitty the bottle's label.

Their table in the Crawfordsburn dining room was in a small horseshoe-shaped alcove tucked in a corner. There was a semicircular banquette instead of chairs, and O'Reilly sat comfortably close on Kitty's left side, with his back to the red velvet curtains he'd noticed as they were being shown to the table. He knew they were drawn over windows in the outside wall.

Cotton-wool snow was stuck to the top of the half partitions separating the niche from other booths. The room was full of other diners and hummed with their conversations. O'Reilly was pleased that there was none of the tinny piped music now becoming a fixture in most Ulster restaurants.

The lighting provided by two massive antique chandeliers was pleasantly dim. Dinner-suited waiters circulated silently, bringing full plates or retrieving empty dishes.

On an immaculately white tablecloth, secure in its cut-glass candleholder, a single red candle burned in the centre of O'Reilly and Kitty's table. O'Reilly saw its flame reflected in Kitty's eyes. He smiled at her and raised his glass.

He wasn't much of a wine drinker, but the Montrachet she had chosen was crisp and dry. "Nice," he said, "very nice."

"I thought you'd enjoy it," she said with a chuckle. "At least you will until you see the bill."

"I've already told you, and thank you for asking. Tonight," said O'Reilly, sliding a little closer to her, "the sky's the limit. Here's to your bright eyes." He drank.

As she nodded in response, their waiter came to the table. "For madam," he said, placing a plate of escargots in front of Kitty. The garlicky smell tickled O'Reilly's palate. "And for you, Doctor, the scampi. *Bon appetit*," he said, with a thick Belfast overlay, as he withdrew.

O'Reilly watched Kitty pop the first snail into her mouth and the corners of her eyes crinkle. She swallowed. "That," she said, "is very good."

"Good." O'Reilly speared three scampi at once, shoved them in his mouth, and chewed with gusto. The batter was crisp and done to perfection, the flesh of the little crustaceans firm and delicate of flavour. As he speared three more, Kitty asked, "Do you like garlic, Fingal?"

He nodded, his loaded fork halfway to his mouth.

"Try this," she said, holding an escargot on a fork.

Before he could speak, she popped it into his mouth as a mother bird would feed a hungry chick.

He chewed.

Leaning closer to him, she said, "It's the only trouble with garlic. If you haven't eaten some yourself, it's not very pleasant being kissed by someone who has."

O'Reilly stopped in mid-chew. His mouth opened a trifle. By God, if that was an invitation to kiss her, he'd take her up on it at the earliest opportunity. That thought pleased him, and yet just as the wine had a slight aftertaste of apricots, so did her confident statement have an undertone. Kitty's remark was one of a woman not unused to being kissed, and that, quite irrationally, made him jealous.

He swallowed, grinned at her, and said, "You'll not have to worry about that tonight, Kitty." Let her decide if he meant he wasn't going to kiss her or if he was now well prepared to do just that.

Her smile was inviting and he moved a little closer, aware again of the musky perfume she wore. Bugger the other diners, he thought, and he inclined his head and kissed her cheek. As he straightened up, he saw John, the desk clerk, standing at the table. "Yes, John?"

"I'm sorry to intrude, Doctor O'Reilly, but your Mrs. Kincaid's on the phone and says it's urgent."

"Right." O'Reilly stood and shoved the table aside. He was oblivious to everything because he knew Kinky, who was a dab hand at fending off trivial calls, wouldn't phone him unless it really was an emergency.

He left the dining room and charged along the hall, not bothering to apologise to a guest he jostled on the way past.

The receiver lay on the desk. He grabbed it. "Hello? Kinky?"

"Doctor O'Reilly. I've just had Miss Hagerty, the midwife, on the phone. She's with a patient, Gertie Gorman, at Twenty-seven Shore Road."

Gorman? O'Reilly didn't recognize the name.

"The woman's in labour, Miss Hagerty doesn't think it's going smoothly, and she can't reach the woman's doctor. Doctor Laverty's in Belfast, so she wants to know would you go and help, sir?"

"Of course. Kinky, call Miss Hagerty, tell her I'm on my way, and then bring the maternity bags through to the kitchen. I'll be there in half an hour." He handed the receiver to John. "Hang that up for me."

O'Reilly trotted back to the dining room and explained the situation to Kitty and to the headwaiter, who agreed to sort out the bill the next time O'Reilly came in.

"Come on, Kitty," he said. "Drive me home."

As he hustled her along the hall, he said, "I'm sorry about this. When we get home I'll take the Rover, and you head home yourself—"

"The hell I will, Fingal," she said, grabbing her coat from the cloakroom. "I'm a nurse, remember? I'm coming with you."

24

On with the Dance! Let Joy Be Unconfined

It was a short way from O'Kane's pub, the Oak Inn, to Bostock House, the nurses' home. Barry, Jack, and Mandy walked companionably side by side, Mandy's stiletto heels clicking on the pavement.

Barry felt the chill December air on his cheeks and nose, heard the descant of the siren of a rapidly approaching ambulance as the *nee-naw, nee-naw* rose above the constant basso rumble of the traffic.

He inhaled the brassy city smells of exhaust fumes and chimney smoke. The noise and stink were so different from the quiet and the clean air of Ballybucklebo. He remembered with affection his recent years of training here in Belfast but knew now he could never live here.

As they approached the nurses' home he heard, faintly at first but louder as they neared the redbrick building, the sounds of a traditional jazz band.

The three friends climbed the stone steps to the entrance of the home. Joe, the doorman and general factotum, a retired boxer, and jealous guardian of his young charges, sat at a table taking tickets. Jack handed over three. It had been decent of him to buy them and refuse Barry's offer to repay him.

"Doctor Mills?" Joe took the tickets. He was bald

as a billiard ball. His battered face with its squashed nose broke into a wide, gap-toothed grin that spread from one cauliflower ear to the other. "How's the world abusing you?"

"Can't complain, Joe," Jack said. "Nice to be back at Bostock."

"It's great to see you, so it is, and you too, Doctor Laverty, sir."

"And you, Joe." Funny, Barry thought, a couple of years ago he and Jack had been chased across the lawns by an enraged Joe. They had brought two student nurses back after their curfew. It had been Jack's idea to taunt Joe so that he lost his temper, chased his tormentors, and left the door unguarded long enough for the two young women to nip inside undetected, thus avoiding being reported to the matron.

By the way Joe was greeting them, perhaps he had forgotten that particular episode. Then again, it had been widely believed among the medical students that Joe had taken one too many punches to the head, leaving him at least one stook short of a stack.

Barry went into the noisy, crowded foyer. Cut-out Santas and snowmen were stuck to the hospital-green walls. A fir tree stood in the far corner. Coloured glass baubles dangled from every tinsel-draped branch. A gold star at the tree's very top drooped sideways, acting as a pointer to a sign reading *Merry Christmas*.

The place was very warm. Barry waited in the queue behind Jack and Mandy, took off his overcoat, and then left it in the cloakroom. He reflexively smoothed down his blond tuft and straightened his Old Campbellian tie.

Couples and single men and women came and went through a set of open double doors leading to the home's main hall. It was used for assemblies, amateur theatricals, and tonight it was doing duty as a dance hall.

Barry recognized the strains of "Muskrat Ramble" being played inside the hall. He tried to hum along, cursed his tone deafness, and smiled at himself. If Patricia were here, she could have sung along in her deep contralto. His smile faded. If she were here? He ached for her to be here, wondered about making an excuse and heading back for home. Damn her intransigence.

"See you inside, Barry." Jack, holding tightly to Mandy's hand, led her to the dance floor. Barry watched them go, Mandy's buttocks mincing saucily under her tight red knee-length skirt, the curve of her calves accented by her sheer black stockings and her heels. Barry smiled. She really did have great legs. He felt a little stirring inside his pants. God, it had been a long time since he'd been near a girl.

"Nyeh, how are you, Barry?" He turned to see an old friend, Harry Sloan, a budding pathologist who prefaced many of his remarks with that peculiar braying noise. He was the one who had speeded up the microscopic examination of slides of heart tissue—from a patient of Barry's who had died in August—when Barry had needed the results urgently. He still was in Harry's debt.

"Fine thanks, Harry."

"I thought you had a steady bird. In the cloakroom is she?"

Barry took a deep breath, shook his head, and exhaled forcibly. "No, I'm on my own." And despite thinking of Patricia only a few moments ago, he didn't want to be reminded of her again. Not just now. Not when merely thinking of her refusal to accept his offer made his anger rise.

"Nyeh. Blew you out, did she?" Harry shook his prematurely white-haired head and tutted gently.

Barry pursed his lips. "Not exactly, but she won a scholarship to Cambridge and she's not home for the holidays yet." If she's even going to come at all, he thought.

Harry's grin was wide. "Aye. So when the cat's away, the mice'll play, is that it?"

Barry shrugged. "Something like that," he said. He realized he was here in part to try to punish Patricia, although how his going to a dance would affect her in the slightest, unless he told her, wasn't entirely clear. And there was some truth in what Harry said. Barry had been faithful to Patricia since she left for England in September, but he *had* felt that frisson just looking at Mandy's legs. And the room next door was full of attractive, single young women.

"Come on then," Harry said, moving toward the double doors. "Let's go and have a look at the talent."

Inside the hall the lighting had been dimmed, and Barry blinked as he waited for his eyes to get used to the low light and the prickly feeling caused by the tobacco smoke. The band, playing on a stage at the far end of the room, was well into "When the Saints Go Marching In." He could now read the letters painted on the bass drum. The White Eagles. He'd often danced to this well-known Belfast-based group at medical student affairs.

A large ball suspended from the ceiling spun so that the light reflected from the myriad small mirrors on its surface threw constantly moving bright patches against the walls, the floor, and the dancers. The patterns could have been made by a monochrome kaleidoscope. The dance floor was packed. Some couples maneuvered around, dancing a quickstep. Most happily jived, the men twisting and twirling their partners in flashing heels, with pirouetting legs giving glimpses of thigh above stocking tops, as skirts whirled merrily like the canopies of a multitude of carousels.

The trumpeter held a high note and the drummer whaled away happily as the music shuddered to its climax. Some couples stayed together as they left the floor; others thanked their partners and returned to their own side of the hall, men to the right, ladies to the left. The lights brightened. Barry felt Harry nudge him.

"Do you see that wee blonde?" He nodded to a girl talking to a petite brunette. "Her name's Jane Duggan. I took her out a few times last year. She's a bit of a flyer, so she is."

"Oh?"

"I'm going to ask her for the next dance. Will you ask her friend?"

Barry hesitated. Would Patricia be hurt if she found out? Damn it, if she was here in Ulster he wouldn't be at the dance in the first place—or if he was, she'd be with him, gammy leg and all. And it wasn't as if he was going to take the brunette to bed. It was only a dance. "Sure," he said.

Together they crossed the floor. For a moment, Barry thought of a story of the young man who had asked a girl from the Gallaghers' tobacco factory for a dance, only to be told, "Nah. Ask my sister. I'm sweating something fierce."

"So anyway," the brunette was saying, "Sister nearly went harpic . . ." Barry smiled. Harpic was a toilet cleaner with the slogan Cleans Round the Bend. He heard Harry ask the blonde to dance. Then he saw him take her by the hand and lead her out onto the floor.

Barry smiled at the brunette. "May I have the next dance?" He saw her dark eyes wrinkle at the corners, her full lips curve into a smile. Her dark hair—it was impossible to make out its true colour in the hall's light—hung to her shoulders, then curled in at the bottom to frame her face, the way Diana Rigg wore hers in the TV show *The Avengers*. He guessed she was about twenty or twenty-one.

"My pleasure." She offered a hand. He took it.

"Barry Laverty," he said, "from Ballybucklebo." Her hand was pleasantly cool in his. She wore a lime green V-necked sweater that showed a hint of cleavage, and a wide black patent-leather belt. Her knee-length pleated skirt was dark green.

"Peggy Duff. I'm living in Knock. We're nearly neighbours."

Barry was usually shy around girls, finding himself as often as not stuck with some inane opening gambit like "Do you come here often?" or a remark about the weather. But he suddenly remembered what he had overheard her saying. "Why did Sister go bananas?"

She laughed, a deep throaty chuckle that ended in a snort. "When I was a first-year student nurse, she sent me to clean all the old men's false teeth. I wasn't thinking, and I collected them all in one basin and washed them . . ."

"I'll bet you had hell's delight finding out what teeth belonged to which patient." Barry laughed.

"It took me two days of trial and error." She laughed again. "Sister was *not* happy with me."

He liked her easy ability to laugh at herself. "I'm sure she got over it," he said.

The lights dimmed. The band swung into a slow number, "Saint James Infirmary." He took Peggy to the floor, put his right arm round her waist, and held her right hand with his left, their arms outstretched. This was the position he had learnt at the dancing classes at his boys' boarding school. His partner there had been a wooden chair, and it certainly had not been as soft as the girl he was now holding close. Nor did it wear a perfume like Peggy's. He recognized it as Je Reviens because, it seemed like an aeon ago, he'd once bought a bottle as a birthday present for a certain student nurse. One he'd known before Patricia.

He worked them jerkily around the floor. Barry's tone deafness was complemented by his inability to keep on the beat. He knew film stars like Glenn Ford and Henry Fonda would have whirled this girl around and wooed her with their expertise. Barry Laverty, however, pushed her around the floor with a step somewhere between a waltz and the shuffling of a patient with some neurological disorder. At least he managed to avoid stepping on her feet.

They didn't speak during the dance, but she did allow him to hold her more closely and put his cheek against hers. He could feel the softness of her breasts, and he let his hand slip down below the small of her back. She did not pull it back up but rather pushed a little harder against him. He felt again the arousal he had when he had watched Mandy's retreating backside. Sorry, Patricia, he thought, as he gently brushed his lips on Peggy's cheek, but you should be here with me. You really should.

He was a little breathless when the music stopped, and it was not from the exertion of dancing. They stood apart, but he held on to her hand and she didn't object.

"You're no Fred Astaire," she said with a smile. "Do you really want to dance some more, or would you like to buy me a drink?"

"I thought you'd never ask," he said, relieved that he would not have to stumble clumsily about anymore. "The bar's out in the foyer." Still holding her hand, he guided her around the edge of the dance floor. He didn't see Harry and his blond partner anywhere, but did wave to Jack and Mandy as they spun past. Barry took Peggy through the double doors and into the foyer. "What would you like?"

"Vodka and orange, please."

He found a chair for her, left her sitting, and joined the line in front of the little bar. He turned and looked at her. Peggy really was a most attractive girl. Not as beautiful as Patricia, he reminded himself—no one was—but Jack Mills would describe Peggy Duff as "restful on the eye." Very restful.

He ordered her drink and an orange juice for himself. He'd be driving home soon; he hadn't really intended to stay for very long, but it had been pleasant to see Jack and Mandy, and Harry. Barry paid for the drinks and carried them over to Peggy. "Here you are," he said, handing her the vodka and sitting opposite.

"Thank you. You're a vodka drinker too?"

He shook his head. "Just orange. I'm driving."

She patted his free hand. "That's smart, Barry. When I was working in Casualty, I saw enough youngsters smashed to tatters because some eejit thought he could take a lot of drink and still drive."

"I've seen a few myself."

"How?"

"I'm a GP, assistant to a Doctor O'Reilly in Ballybucklebo, but I did three months in emergency at the Royal when I was a houseman last year."

She took a pull from her drink. "I must have just missed you. I was there this June, just before I got my R.N." She looked more closely at him and frowned a little. "Barry Laverty? Laverty? Are you the chap who used to date Brid McCormack?"

"That's me," Barry said, remembering Brid's green eyes and auburn hair, a remembrance made more real by Peggy's perfume.

"And she married Roger Grant, the surgeon, this September."

Brid had told him about that in January last year when she'd calmly announced she was going to marry someone else. Now it was December, and it looked as though Patricia was losing interest. There must be something jinxed about women, himself, and the wintertime. He sighed and was surprised to feel Peggy's hand covering his.

"She's a very pretty girl. She was a class ahead of me at nursing school." He looked into her eyes and saw sympathy.

"Och," he said, shrugging. "'That was in another country; and besides, the wench is dead,'" he said, quoting Christopher Marlowe's *The Jew of Malta*.

Peggy looked at him quizzically. "Brid's not dead, as far as I know."

"I know. It just means I'm over her." The next question would probably be "Are you seeing anybody else?" he thought. He didn't know how he was going to answer her, being warmed as he was by the increasing pressure of her hand on his.

"It's not nice to get dumped," she said. "My boyfriend and I split up six months ago." She sighed. "You get used to it, but it stings."

"Do you?" he said, wondering if Patricia dumped him would he ever get over it. He knew O'Reilly still grieved for his lost wife, but at least he was seeing Kitty now.

"Yes," she said, "you have to. Life has to go on."

Barry noticed that her glass was empty. "Would you like another?"

She shook her head and glanced at her watch. "I live in Knock, and I have to get up early tomorrow. My friend drove me here, but she seems to have vanished with your white-haired pal. I don't suppose you'd like to give me a lift home? It's on your way to Ballybucklebo."

Barry finished his orange juice and stood. "I'd be delighted," he said without hesitation. "Let's get our coats and I'll walk you to my car."

She waited to kiss him until they were far enough away from Bostock to be in the dark shadows, away from prying eyes. She kissed him softly at first, then harder, and Barry didn't mind. He didn't mind one tiny bit.

25

The Absent Are Always in the Wrong

"This is the house." O'Reilly parked the Rover outside 27 Shore Road. "Out," he said to Kitty, then piled out himself and opened the back door. He grabbed the two heavy maternity bags that minutes earlier he had taken from the kitchen at Number 1. "Can you close this door, Kitty?"

She came around from her side of the car and slammed the door.

"Open the garden gate."

Above the rhythmic crashing of surf on the nearby beach he heard the squeak of rusty hinges. The low cast-iron gate stood in a three-foot-high brick wall. Kitty hurried to the house, and he followed, leaving the gate open.

All the detached houses along this part of the Shore Road were identical, and although O'Reilly had not visited this one before, several of his patients lived nearby. He moved quickly after Kitty and had no difficulty finding his way along the short path, even though the night was black as pitch.

The door opened to Kitty's knock, and Miss Hagerty, the district midwife, smart as ever in her blue uniform and starched white apron, was backlit by the hall lights. "I'm very glad you could come, Doctor

O'Reilly," she said. Then she turned and started walking quickly. "The patient's in the main bedroom upstairs," she called over her shoulder. "I don't want to leave her alone for long. Follow me." He guessed that the husband, like any sensible Ulsterman with a wife in labour, was at the pub, and that was why Miss Hagerty had answered the door.

"This is Sister O'Hallorhan," he called by way of introduction, as he lugged the heavy bags along a well-carpeted hall and up a broad staircase. Oil paintings of fishermen and landscapes that he recognized as painted by James Humbert Craig hung in ascending order to keep company with anybody climbing the stairs. Craig, a Bangor man, had often painted scenes of Belfast Lough.

O'Reilly could hear a woman moaning, and he saw Miss Hagerty disappear through an open door on the right side of the landing.

He followed, set the bags on the carpet, straightened up, tore off his overcoat and jacket, and flung them into a corner of the room. Rolling up his shirtsleeves, he moved across to stand beside a large double bed. Miss Hagerty stood at the far side. Kitty came in and waited unobtrusively beside the door.

Gertie Gorman, a woman he guessed was in her late twenties, lay on top of a rubber sheet that Miss Hagerty would have placed there to protect the mattress. The bedclothes lay in a heap beside a dressing table. Gertie's nightie was rucked up just below her breasts. "Hello, Mrs. Gorman," he said. "I'm Doctor O'Reilly."

She managed a weak smile. "Thanks for . . ." Her face creased. She gritted her teeth and moaned. O'Reilly glanced at Miss Hagerty and raised one bushy eyebrow.

"She says the pains started about ten hours ago and are coming every three minutes and lasting for a minute. She's well along."

He nodded. "How many's this for her?"

"Number three. The other two were short labours, eight and six hours. And she has small babies, six pounds eight ounces and seven pounds one."

Be thankful for small mercies, he thought. Second, third, and fourth were the easiest deliveries, the least likely to be complicated. On the other hand, the time of labour usually grew shorter with each successive pregnancy. This time it was longer, and that was worrying, but she was probably close to being ready to deliver. It was time to start to ascertain exactly what was happening and mobilize his forces. "Kitty, could you clear a space on the dressing table and get all the sterile packs out of the bags?"

Kitty went to the dressing table and started removing things from the top.

"Miss Hagerty, I'll need you to bring me up to date. Is she at term?"

"Thirty-eight weeks," Miss Hagerty said, "and the pregnancy's been uncomplicated as far as I know."

O'Reilly frowned. As far as I know? Usually most of the antenatal care of a woman with an uncomplicated pregnancy was the duty of her midwife.

"When did you see her last?"

"A month ago."

He heard his voice rise. "A month? In the third trimester?"

Miss Hagerty sucked in her thin cheeks. "Doctor Fitzpatrick was most insistent that he be almost solely responsible for her care."

O'Reilly shook his head. Stupid. Stupid. An experienced midwife like Miss Hagerty was one of the most sensitive diagnostic tools available. It was the height of arrogance for Fitzpatrick to ignore her expertise.

"But as far as you know there haven't been any problems?"

"As far as I know. I asked Gertie as soon as I got here, and she said Doctor Fitzpatrick kept telling her everything was fine. No high blood pressure. Good weight gain. The baby was growing and its heart rate was normal." He heard a disdainful tone in her words. "So as far as I know there were no difficulties before labour . . . at least none that were noticed."

He frowned. What did that mean? O'Reilly disliked discussing a patient in so impersonal a manner in front of her, but he needed the critical information, and during a contraction she was in no position to hold a conversation anyway. He tried to reassure Gertie by squeezing her hand for a moment, and he was gratified to see her manage a weak smile as the contraction waned. It was time to examine her. He'd pursue Miss Hagerty's implications later.

"I'm going to examine your tummy," he said,

looking questioningly at Miss Hagerty. He had no difficulty lip-reading the midwife's silent, "I think it's a breech."

A breech? Christ Almighty. The risks of serious injury to the mother and of damage, asphyxia, and even death to the child were much greater when a baby came bottom first.

That would certainly explain the "at least none that were noticed" remark. It was a major responsibility of the attending midwife or physician to identify any abnormal presentations and to arrange for the patient to be transferred to a properly equipped maternity unit. A specialist obstetrician, who could if necessary call on the services of a team, ought to manage the delivery and if necessary do a caesarean section.

O'Reilly hadn't had to deliver a breech since before the war. His palms started to sweat. Miss Hagerty might be wrong, and if she wasn't he hoped that labour would be insufficiently advanced so he could get Gertie up to the Royal Maternity Hospital.

He stood facing her and laid his hands on either side of her swollen belly. Through the abdominal wall and the temporarily relaxed uterus, he could make out the smooth, curved contour of the baby's back lying on its mother's right side. He followed it upward until he could no longer feel it. He placed one hand on either side of the fundus, the top of the uterus, and moved his hands from side to side. Something solid moved back and forth between his hands. It was, in medical terminology, ballottable. Heads usually were, buttocks less so. He used his right-hand fingers and thumb curled like a claw to grasp the hard round thing, and he was sure it was the baby's head. He met Miss Hagerty's gaze and nodded.

Using both hands, one on either side of the lowest part of her belly immediately above the pubic bones, he was able to make out a shape that was deep into the pelvis. It didn't feel like a head. It was narrower. He nodded at Miss Hagerty again. "Is the fetal heart rate okay?"

"It was one forty just before you arrived."

Good. That at least was normal.

Before he could carry out any further manoeuvers, he felt the beginning of another contraction. He'd be unable to feel anything but the iron-hard uterine muscles until this contraction passed. Time to get ready to examine the patient vaginally.

"Is the bathroom on the landing?"

"Two doors down along to the right."

Gertie's moans pursued him, but had died away by the time O'Reilly returned from scrubbing his hands. While Kitty handed him a sterile towel and opened a packet of rubber gloves as he dried his hands, the moans started again. Then Gertie cried, "I have to push! I have to push!" while Miss Hagerty responded, "Huff, Gertie. Huff." O'Reilly donned the gloves to the accompaniment of the patient's short, rapid, shallow breaths. He hoped to God the cervix was fully dilated.

If, as he was almost certain, the baby's buttocks were coming first, they were narrower than the head and could slip through a partially dilated cervix and descend into the pelvis. There the pressure the buttocks exerted on the muscles of the pelvic floor would give the woman an uncontrollable desire to push.

She might well push the narrower parts of the baby past the cervix and out into the open with no apparent difficulty, but once the neck had passed through the muscular cervical ring, the wider head would become irretrievably stuck. The consequences would be disastrous for both mother and child.

O'Reilly lifted a pair of sponge forceps that Kitty had placed on the dressing table, her makeshift instrument trolley. He chucked a handful of sterile cotton-wool balls into a bowl of dilute Savlon disinfectant and moved to the patient's side, accompanied by Kitty, who carried the bowl.

"Can you draw up your legs, Gertie?" He waited as Miss Hagerty helped the patient bend her knees and open her thighs. The labia were gaping, and in the opening he could see something smooth and dusky. It was a buttock. Its plum colour was caused by the blood being dammed back in its blood vessels due to the constriction of the pelvic canal. That answered two questions. It definitely was a breech, and there was no time to arrange a transfer. Bloody Fitzpatrick should have made the diagnosis weeks ago. O'Reilly knew Miss Hagerty would have—had she been given the chance.

No time to get tried about that now. He'd deal with it later. Gertie Gorman needed his undivided attention.

"I'm going to give you a wash," O'Reilly said, loading the forceps with sodden cotton-wool balls. "Sorry if it's a bit cold." She flinched when he started to paint her vulva, inner thighs, and her buttocks with the pale yellow Savlon solution, its fumes tickling his nose. He chucked the forceps back into the basin. "Now you'll feel me touching you."

"Here." Kitty offered him an opened pack of sterile towels.

"Thanks." He took one and draped it over the patient's pubis and lower belly. He put his left hand on the towel and slipped the first two fingers of his right hand inside her vagina, past the buttocks, and into the pelvis. Reaching as high as possible, he could make out the baby's thighs where the legs were flexed up against the belly. The toes would be inside the uterus close to the baby's head, so it was a frank breech, not a footling breech where the feet came first, or a complete breech where the baby's legs were crossed like those of a squatting tailor. Good. In the frank presentation, there was much less risk of the umbilical cord slipping out past the baby, being compressed and cutting off the oxygen supply, before the child was delivered.

His left hand felt a contraction starting. Gertie moaned and wriggled on the bed. Miss Hagerty's instructions to huff were falling on deaf ears. O'Reilly felt Gertie's belly muscles stiffen as she bore down and the baby's buttocks advanced lower into the pelvis. He managed to insert his fingers more deeply, and to his great relief he could find no evidence that the cervix was not fully dilated or that the cord had prolapsed.

O'Reilly, though not a religious man, offered up a small muttering of thanks.

"She's fully dilated," he said and then removed his fingers. Jesus, but he wished she was in hospital. For one thing, having her feet in obstetrical stirrups and her buttocks over the edge of the delivery table would greatly facilitate the manoeuvers he'd need to carry out to expedite the child's delivery. Of even greater importance, he would have an anaesthetist there who could knock Gertie out if any difficult procedures were required.

He'd have to make do, and it wouldn't be for the first time, with what was at hand. "Kitty, in the packs there's a kit for putting in local nerve blocks and also a bottle of Xylocaine. Get them." No time for the niceties of "please" and "thank you."

"Miss Hagerty, do everything you can to stop her pushing." He didn't need to tell such an experienced midwife to listen to the fetal heart between contractions. She would tell him if there were any abnormalities.

"The pudendal nerve block kit's open," Kitty said, stepping back from the dresser. "I've not seen one of those since I took my midwifery training during the war."

"I didn't know you had." O'Reilly began assembling the large syringe with its very long needle. In Ireland, state registered nurses who wanted to be midwives took two extra years of training after gaining their S.R.N. qualification.

Gertie moaned as another contraction hit.

"I thought I'd like midwifery," Kitty said, holding the bottle of the local anaesthetic Xylocaine so he could penetrate the rubber cap with the needle and fill the barrel of the syringe.

"Didn't you?" He drew back the plunger.

She shook her head. "I preferred general nursing."

To each her own, O'Reilly thought, but even if her knowledge was rusty, it was a great comfort to him to be assisted by not one but two trained midwives.

It had taken two more contractions before he'd been able to identify the nerves that supplied the lower vagina and the area between the anus and pubis. Once they were infiltrated with Xylocaine, he was more comfortable because no matter what he did now, he'd not hurt the patient.

He exhaled a very large breath, used the back of his arm to wipe perspiration from his forehead, and said, "Kitty, there's a rubber apron in the kit. Could you help me put it on?" As he spoke, he handed her the used syringe.

She slipped the straps over his head and tied the waist tie. The patient was washed and draped; the doctor was gowned and gloved. The labour was progressing, and now came the difficult part. Waiting. O'Reilly knew that more damage was done to breech babies by impetuous attendants who intervened too early.

"Get her pushing, Miss Hagerty. Open that pack, Kitty." He made a snipping action with the first two fingers of his right hand.

She nodded and opened the pack, which contained a pair of heavy bladed scissors.

He waited until another contraction had passed and one buttock and the cleft in the backside were visible at the vaginal opening.

"Now, Gertie," he said, "we're going to move you a bit. See if you can help."

Aided by both Kitty and Miss Hagerty, he managed to turn Gertie so that she lay across the bed, her head supported on pillows, her buttocks at the bed's edge. O'Reilly picked up the scissors and moved to stand between her flexed legs. Kitty and Miss Hagerty both knew what to do. Each took a leg and supported it, acting as human stirrups so O'Reilly had the best possible access to the operative field.

He waited for the next contraction, slipped a finger inside, and guided one blade of the scissors into the vagina. At the contraction's peak he sliced, cutting an episiotomy in the vaginal outlet to give the baby more room. He smelt the metallic blood smell and saw the drips falling on the carpet. Couldn't be helped. He dropped the scissors.

Now for more waiting. It took self-control not to start tugging and pulling at the baby's hips as soon as they appeared. "So why didn't you like midder, Kitty?" he asked, as Miss Hagerty encouraged Gertie to push.

"It wasn't so much I didn't like it. I'd spent some time on the neurology and neurosurgery wards, and I just found those subjects much more fascinating."

Interesting, O'Reilly thought, looking at her. He had always enjoyed obstetrics, might have specialized if the war hadn't intervened. He'd always been a bit intimidated by the diseases of the nervous system. Their study was a very intellectual discipline. He smiled to himself. He'd not like to admit it, he knew, but it was probable that in some ways Kitty was smarter than him. He turned back to look at the patient. He mustn't let his attention wander.

"Big push, Gertie," Miss Hagerty encouraged. "Puuuussh."

The baby's body, its back to the mother's right side, began to emerge and climb upward, forced by the uterine contractions and the configuration of the birth canal. He saw the lower buttock. He noted no evidence of a swollen scrotum, so he knew it was a girl, and then both buttocks were in the open followed by the hips, the lower belly, and finally the umbilicus and the cord.

Soon it would be time to act. He waited until Miss Hagerty told Gertie once more to push.

O'Reilly used a finger and thumb to pull a loop of cord down; then he hooked one index finger into each fold between the baby's thighs and belly, pulling gently until the hollows behind the knees appeared. He flexed the baby's legs each in turn, and by sweeping the lower limbs outward across the baby's trunk, he guided the legs into the open.

He took his hands away. The trunk rotated until the back faced upward. The rotation was a function of the uterine contractions forcing the widest parts of the little body into the widest parts of the birth canal. More and more of the baby's back slipped into view, and the trunk and legs hung down toward the carpet.

O'Reilly still kept his hands to himself, allowing gravity to help the uterus move the baby out.

He glanced at Miss Hagerty, who immediately put one hand on the patient's belly to feel for the start of a contraction and to exert pressure to prevent the child's arms extending.

He reached under the little trunk, slipped two fingers into the vagina, and found the arms crossed in front of the chest, like the stone limbs on top of the tomb of a medieval knight. In a moment he had flipped them out, and they dangled limply.

Gertie started grunting in her throat.

"Another one coming," Miss Hagerty said. "Puuush, Gertie."

The trickiest bit was to come. Delivery of the head. It was just about to enter the birth canal, and as soon as it did, it would compress the umbilical cord and interfere with the baby's oxygen supply. O'Reilly had four minutes to get the head out before the child asphyxiated itself. He knew that two of those minutes must be allowed to elapse to let the head descend slowly into the narrow bony pelvis, thus protecting the soft skull and the vulnerable brain within from compressing too rapidly.

O'Reilly knew that older obstetricians favoured using their hands—one above the pubis to push, and one with fingers in the baby's mouth and hooked around its shoulders to pull. This Wigand-Martin manoeuver was named for the two doctors who had first described it. But a Doctor Burns had suggested a simpler method while O'Reilly was still a student, and that was the one he had been taught.

He simply allowed the baby to hang, as the infant girl was doing now, and by its own weight pull the head into the pelvis. He saw the nape of the neck appear, and he turned so he was standing with his back to the patient's left leg. He grinned at Kitty, who was supporting the right one.

"Hard work," she said. He wasn't sure if she was referring to herself, to him, or to Gertie.

He concentrated on his work. Holding the child's ankles in his right hand, he pulled gently, then lifted the legs to a vertical position above the mother's pubis.

"Now, Doctor?" Miss Hagerty asked.

He nodded, and as the midwife started telling Gertie not to push if she could help it, O'Reilly used his left hand to put pressure on the perineum beneath the vaginal opening. The combination of that pressure and the cessation of pushes would allow him to deliver the head slowly, avoiding the risk of ripping the soft tissues of the mother.

He saw the face appear and the little mouth. He'd have sold his immortal soul for a second pair of hands. Someone should be using a suction apparatus to clear the child's mouth and throat of mucus.

Slowly, slowly, he allowed the head to appear until finally he was holding the baby girl aloft by her heels. He used the little finger of his left hand to clean some mucus from her mouth. She screwed up her eyes, pulled air into her lungs, and gave a long high quavering howl.

"It's a girl," he roared, so Gertie could hear over the newborn's noise. "A pretty wee girl."

Miss Hagerty and Kitty flexed Gertie's knees and set her feet on the bed.

"Phew," Kitty remarked. "She *was* getting heavy."

"Never mind that," he said. "Open the clamps kit."

In a trice, he'd clamped and cut the umbilical cord, bundled the child in a towel, and handed her off to Miss Hagerty, who in turn gave her to Gertie to hold.

O'Reilly smiled. To him there were few more satisfying sights than a mother with her healthy newborn.

He'd little time to enjoy the scene.

With a small gush of blood, the cord hanging from the vagina lengthened, and in no time the placenta was delivered, looking like a big lump of raw liver. "Give her the ergometrine, Miss Hagerty," he said, "and would one of you ladies open the suture pack, please?" He glanced at the open episiotomy wound. "I've a bit of embroidery to do."

He arched his back and pulled his shoulder blades toward each other to ease the kinks, screwed his eyes shut, and blinked. Once the suture pack was opened he removed the forceps, suture, and needle holders and began to stitch.

In what seemed like a surprisingly short time, the wound was repaired, Gertie was drinking a cup of tea Miss Hagerty had made, and Baby Gorman was wrapped up and sleeping soundly in her crib.

O'Reilly snipped the ends off the last suture, put

the instruments back in their towel, stripped off his rubber gloves, and asked Kitty to undo the ties of his apron. Then he headed for the bathroom to wash his hands and cleanse his forearms of blood and vernix, the cheese-like substance that coats a newborn's skin.

When he came back, Baby Gorman had woken and was demanding sustenance.

As Miss Hagerty carried the wee one to her mother, O'Reilly bent, retrieved his jacket, slipped it on, and moved to stand beside Kitty.

She smiled at him. "That was very well done, Fingal. I've seen specialist obstetricians not deliver a breech as well."

"That's perfectly true, Doctor O'Reilly," Miss Hagerty said.

Normally he would have brushed off any compliment like that with a gruff rejoinder, but coming from Kitty it pleased him. He felt a warmth in his cheeks. "Thanks, Kitty. It's a bloody good thing you both were here. I couldn't have managed without you or Miss Hagerty."

Kitty quickly kissed O'Reilly's cheek. "It was a great job and I was lucky to be here. I'd almost forgotten how moving a birth can be."

He saw her eyes glisten as she turned to gaze at Baby Gorman. O'Reilly's cheeks grew warmer, but fortunately Miss Hagerty was too busy supervising Gertie's attempts to breast-feed to have noticed.

"Even if it cost you your dinner?"

"I prefer having been here with you, Fingal. We can always have dinner some other time."

He would look forward to it. "I'll make up the missed dinner to you, I promise," he said, as his tummy growled. "How about next Sunday? Young Barry will be on call, so there'd be no chance we'd be interrupted like tonight."

Kitty shook her head. "I can't make that. I'm sorry," she said, and she sounded disappointed. "I've a week's holiday starting next Monday, the fourteenth, and I've promised to go down to see my mother. She's eighty-one. She lives in Tallaght, outside Dublin."

O'Reilly found that her not being available disappointed *him*, and he was going to be occupied or on call for the days after next Sunday. But he had an idea. "You'll be up north next Friday week for Christmas Day, won't you?"

"Yes."

"How would you like to come for dinner at Number One?"

Her eyes sparkled. "I'd love to."

O'Reilly's stomach rumbled more loudly.

She chuckled. "You must be starving. Take me back to Number One," she said, "and if Kinky won't mind me using her kitchen, I'll make us both a quick bite."

"By God, you're on. Give me just a minute." He went to the bedside.

He looked down on the feeding baby and her mother. Such serenity was on Gertie's homely face that O'Reilly immediately thought of *Madonna and Child* by Michelangelo. She smiled up at him. "Sorry we had to bother you, sir."

"Nonsense. Isn't it what I'm for?" He didn't wait for an answer. "What'll you call the wee one?"

"Well, sir, seeing it's the Christmas season, I can't decide between Carol or Noelle, but I think I like Noelle best."

"Good for you," said O'Reilly. "It's a lovely name, isn't it, Miss Hagerty?"

"It is indeed. It was my mother's." She straightened up and said, "Thanks for coming, Doctor O'Reilly. Don't you worry now. I'll tidy up. You and Sister run along."

"We will," said O'Reilly, crossing the room to pick up his overcoat. "And I'll arrange for Doctor Fitzpatrick to do the follow-up."

"Will you not want me to have a word with him, sir?" She hesitated before saying quietly, "It's not my place to criticize, sir, but he should have been here. He really should."

You're right about that, O'Reilly thought, *and* he should have made the diagnosis weeks ago and saved us all a lot of trouble. "I'm sure there's an explanation, and anyway, all's well that ends well. You go ahead and speak to him. You must, Miss Hagerty."

O'Reilly took Kitty by the elbow and began to steer her to the door. Then he said, "But so must I." And he caught a glimpse of his nose in a mirror hung on the wall. The tip almost as far back as the bridge was alabaster white. "So must I."

26

Woe unto Them That Rise Up

Barry helped Peggy into the car, went around to the driver's side, and got in. "Do up your seat belt," he said, fastening his own. He didn't always use it, but he knew it would please her. "You're the one who mentioned the carnage in casualty. I once saw a girl who'd put her face through the windscreen and bounced up and down on the broken glass. It took the plastic surgeons fifteen hours to try to give her back something that resembled a face."

"Yeugh," Peggy said.

"Seat belts aren't standard fixtures, but I had them fitted to Brunhilde." He started the engine.

"Brun who?"

"Brunhilde. My car." He drove out of the car park. "I thought she deserved a name. Volkswagens are made in Germany, and Brünhilde appears in a lot of Teutonic stories."

"Oh." Peggy paused while Barry signaled for a right turn onto the Grosvenor Road, then entered the city centre–bound traffic. "Who exactly was this Brun-thin-gummy-bob?"

"A Norse goddess. Wagner made her a heroine in some of his operas."

"You like opera?" Her voice rose in a surprised

question. "Good Lord." She giggled. "I prefer the Beatles and Buddy Holly. I cried when he was killed. Silly me." She giggled.

"February third, nineteen fifty-nine," Barry said, "along with the Big Bopper."

"And Richie Valens." She chatted on merrily about pop music and informed him proudly that the two best songs of 1964 were Jim Reeves's "I Won't Forget You" and Roy Orbison's "It's Over."

Barry was too busy concentrating on making his turns onto College Square, then onto Wellington Place.

Peggy seemed happy enough to prattle away. "I've never been to an opera. What's it like?"

"I'm just learning about it," he said, thinking of the first aria he'd heard—and who he'd heard it with. Damn you, Patricia. *Why* won't you come home?

"Tell me more about Brun-what's-her-face," she asked.

"Brunhilde. I'll tell you in a tic."

The traffic was slow-moving stop-and-go in Donegal Square. Barry had lots of time to notice the brightly lit storefronts to his left. A ski scene with hills of artificial snow and mannequins in gaily colored ski clothes filled most of the Athletic Store's window.

On the corner of Donegal Place the windows of Robinson and Cleaver's blazed with light. There was a crèche and . . . he was distracted by catching a whiff of Peggy's perfume. He glanced at her face in profile. She certainly had good cheekbones.

He stopped at the traffic lights at the junction of

Donegal Square with Donegal Place. He could hear "Oh, Little Town of Bethlehem" being piped through amplifiers.

He thought about her perfume, her open lips, the way she'd responded to his kisses in the car park. Peggy was a pretty—no, very—sexy girl. Barry wondered if she would invite him in when he got her home—and more importantly, he wondered how he would respond. He swallowed and looked to his right where the many-domed City Hall was festooned with fairy lights. Smack front and centre in the broad drive from the Square to City Hall's colonnaded portico stood a massive Christmas tree. Its lights flashed and sparkled.

"That tree's Norway's annual gift to Belfast," she said.

The traffic started to move. "I know," he said, "and Brunhilde was from Iceland. She was a princess and a mighty warrior. A bloke called Siegfried fell in love with her, but when he betrayed her with another woman, Gudrun, Brunhilde killed herself."

"Och," she said, "that's sad. Poor Brunhilde. I know exactly how she felt."

The traffic was on the move again, and Barry drove ahead. "How?" he asked.

"I found out my lad was seeing a girl who worked in the Civil Service, and when I asked him about it, he swore he wasn't. The two-timing bugger." He heard a catch in her voice.

"It must have been hard on you," he said, wondering who was speaking. Was it Barry Laverty, the ordinary young man who could be sympathetic to a young woman, or Barry Laverty, the doctor who was professionally interested in someone who was upset? Sometimes, he was discovering, it was difficult to disentangle the two sides of his life. Like O'Reilly, Barry's doctor self was never entirely off duty.

"I didn't mind so much that he'd taken her out, but he'd been lying to me about it. I couldn't stand that. A wee while ago there I think *I* might have done a Brunhilde. I honestly do."

Barry turned left onto Victoria Street and simultaneously ran through a mental checklist of what to do if someone threatened to commit suicide. He wondered how he should respond to Peggy's confession.

"But sure"—he heard a lightening in her voice, a gay light laugh—"life has to go on. It's just like my friend Diana says, men are like buses. There'll be another one along in a few minutes." He felt her hand squeeze his left thigh.

"There's lots of good fish in the sea," he said, not entirely sure he wanted to be regarded in such a light. But if that was what she was thinking, he could always invoke Jack's line, "Why buy a cow when you can get a bottle of milk anytime you want?" Do you want this Peggy as a bottle of milk? he asked himself. A quick bit of slap-and-tickle?

"I've heard that," she said and giggled. It was a harsh, grating sound. "Are you a good swimmer?" She'd let her voice drop, grow a little husky. Barry was a keen fly fisherman. He'd no difficulty recognizing a cast made to see if it would produce a rise. There was certainly a stirring in his pants.

If you let this go the way it seems to be going, will you be able to back out whenever you want? he asked himself. *Or will you want to see Peggy again, and if you do, will you be able to face Patricia—if, damn it, she does finally make up her stubborn bloody mind to get on the stupid bloody ferry and come home to Ulster? Patricia, I'd not be with this Peggy if you'd kept your promise.*

He decided to see how far this girl wanted to play the game. "Swimming? It was my best sport at school."

He was approaching the Albert Clock. In no time, he'd be across the Queen's Bridge and heading along the Newtownards Road to the suburb of Belmont.

She giggled again. It really was grating. "Ooh," she said, kneading his thigh harder. "I like swimmers."

And I'm starting to move out of the shallows, Barry thought. *I'd better tread water, slow things down a bit.* "That was at school. I didn't have much time for swimming at medical school. I'm a bit rusty."

The traffic sped up as he crossed the bridge, and he didn't dare risk a glance at her face to see if, in the illumination provided by the lights evenly spaced on the bridge's parapets, he could judge her response. By her silence and the stillness of her hand on his thigh, she was thinking about his last remark, deciding how to reply.

He passed Queen's Quay on his left. That was the terminus of the Belfast-to-Bangor railway line. That was where, in August, he'd waited for Patricia so together they could catch the last train of a summer night. That was the train ride where he had lost his heart, and at that time he'd been sure he'd lost it forever.

"Maybe," she said, "maybe you just need a bit of oiling?"

He'd often wondered what signals—perhaps the merest sensation of the sharp tip of the hook on its lip—made even the hungriest trout sip at a fly, then spit it out. "Maybe." He kept his voice noncommittal. "Maybe."

He sensed that Peggy drew away a little. "Suit yourself," she said. He heard a muted, "Huh."

Good. That had cooled things, given him time to think. She hadn't, in local parlance, been backward in coming forward, in taking the initiative. Girls usually didn't in Ulster. Barry had no doubt that if he really wanted to take things further with Peggy, it wouldn't be difficult to arouse her, but for the time being he was happy to drive.

"You'll need to turn off soon," she said and took her hand from his thigh.

He ignored the opportunity for a double entendre. "To get to where you live?"

"That's right. Take the Upper Newtownards Road to Ormiston Crescent. I live in a flat at Number Twelve."

"Right." Barry turned right at the fork at the Holywood Arches, where O'Reilly had arranged for the ambulance to collect Liam Gillespie the night he'd ruptured his spleen. Liam should be well on the mend by now. "And if I go on up Ormiston, I can get to the Belmont Road?"

"That's right."

"I thought so. I went to Campbell College, and it's just up the road." He had spent four years and met Jack Mills there. If it hadn't been for Jack, Barry wouldn't be here now.

"You're an Old Campbellian?" Peggy asked.

"That's right." The all-boys school had a reputation of being snooty. "The school for the sons of the cream of Ulster society."

"The cream?"

"Oh, yes," he said, turning left, "definitely the cream. Rich and *very* thick."

She laughed loudly at the old joke about the place. It didn't seem she was going to hold a grudge because he had cooled to her advances.

"It's here," she said, and he began to slow down. "Next house on the left."

Barry parked in front of a three-storey redbrick detached house, undid his seat belt, got out, went around the car, and opened Peggy's door.

Peggy got out. "Thanks for the lift." She rose on her tiptoes and kissed his cheek. "Would you like to come in? It's not very late . . ."

Barry hesitated. He inhaled her heavy perfume. His arms slipped around her waist, and she moved closer. He lowered his lips to hers, felt the warmth of her. He tasted her, felt her tongue probing. He held her more tightly, feeling through the layers of their clothing the firmness of her breasts against his chest. He broke the kiss and used his hand to guide her head to lie on his shoulder. She felt so natural in his arms, and it had been months since Patricia had left for Cambridge. His breathing quickened, and he bent to kiss her again, harder and more deeply.

"We really should go in," she said huskily, taking his hand and walking toward the gate.

Barry followed.

"My roommate Jane, the blonde with your white-haired friend, won't be back for ages if I know her." She said. The invitation was clear in her voice.

Barry took a very deep breath. Was it really true that what the eye didn't see, the heart couldn't grieve over?

"So you are coming in," she said. "I've some super Buddy Holly and Everly Brothers records." And then she giggled. The harshness of the sound broke the tenuous spell she had begun to weave around him.

Instead of her metallic braying in his ears, he heard in his mind Patricia's deep throaty contralto. Instead of Peggy's heavy, overly sweet perfume, he sensed the delicate musk Patricia sometimes wore. Instead of Buddy Holly, whose music Barry disliked, he imagined hearing the beautiful aria he had first heard in Patricia's flat. She'd said it was "Voi che sapete" from *The Marriage of Figaro*. He wanted Peggy now, but he didn't want her enough to jeopardize having Patricia for what he hoped would be forever.

Barry stopped walking and took his hand from hers. "Peggy . . ."

"What?"

"I'm not coming in."

"You're not? Jesus. Talk about leading a girl on."

"I'm sorry," he said, "I really am. But I have a girlfriend—she's in England at the moment—and it wouldn't be fair to her, and it wouldn't be fair to you."

She shook her head. "She's a lucky girl, whoever she is." She pecked his cheek. "And you're a decent man for telling me, not like some I could mention." She kissed him softly. "Good night, Barry Laverty," she said softly, turning to leave, "and if you get tired of your girl, you know where I live."

"Thanks, Peggy," Barry said, "but I don't intend to tire of her," even though, he thought, she seems to be tiring of me. "Good-night and merry Christmas."

"Merry Christmas, Barry, and safe home." She let herself through the gate, and he waited until he was satisfied that she was safely inside the big house.

Then Barry Laverty hopped into Brunhilde and pointed the car for the back road that climbed over the Craigantlet Hills before descending and meeting the road into Ballybucklebo and home.

He hoped O'Reilly hadn't been too busy taking calls to enjoy his evening with Kitty. That Kitty O'Hallorhan was a very special woman, and so, by God, was his Patricia Spence. And if he really wanted to know if she was coming home for Christmas, he'd ask Kinky. She was fey. He was convinced she was. He shouldn't be, not with his scientific training, but if Kinky didn't have the gift he'd eat his hat. Kinky would know. Of course she would.

27

It Is Best Not To Swap Horses While Crossing the River

Judging by his scowl, O'Reilly was in one of his bear-with-a-sore-head moods. He barely thanked Mrs. Kincaid when she set a serving plate bearing a large omelet in front of him and silently left. He helped himself to two-thirds and told Barry to pass his plate.

Barry accepted his one third, decided that discretion was the better part of valour, and kept his counsel. He poured himself a cup of coffee and sat at the breakfast table sipping it. He glanced out the bow window, past the church steeple, to a sky so bright blue that it looked as if God had fashioned it from enamel. He listened to the Sunday pealing of the chapel bells, loud in the clear and no doubt frosty air.

He tried the first mouthful of his omelet. It was light, fluffy, and filled with melted Cheddar cheese. He tasted a subtle hint of onion. The omelet was liberally studded with mushrooms and melted in his mouth. Delicious.

He tried to ignore O'Reilly where he sat in his customary place, hunched over his plate, filling his face. There was no doubt, thought Barry, the keen game fisherman, that in angling circles his mentor would be referred to as a coarse feeder. Still, if O'Reilly behaved in his usual fashion, the food should go directly from his stomach to whatever brain centre affected his mood and change it for the better.

"That was powerful," said O'Reilly, swallowing the last morsel of his lion's share. He grinned, then belched happily. "Good morning to you, young Barry." He stretched and picked up his coffee cup.

Barry smiled. The transit time from gut to brain had been very rapid this morning.

"Good morning, Fingal," he said.

"And how were things in your particular Glocca Morra last night, lad?"

Barry finished his mouthful before answering. "Well," he said, quite happy to play the quotations game, "the willow tree was certainly weeping there, and Finian's rainbow was as bright as ever. It was good to see Jack, and the nurses' dance was fun." He filled another forkful. "How was your night, Fingal? I got home early, and I heard you and Kitty in the dining room. But I didn't want to disturb you, so I went on up to bed." He'd wondered why they were in the dining room and not the upstairs lounge.

O'Reilly grunted and reached for the toast rack. "We were in the dining room because Kitty'd rustled up a bloody great fry. She's a grand hand with the pan." There was a dreamy look in O'Reilly's eyes.

If the way to a man's heart was through his stomach, Barry thought, Kitty O'Hallorhan must be well along the road. But it still didn't answer the question. Had O'Reilly still been hungry after a meal at the Crawfordsburn? "I thought you were taking her out for dinner," Barry said.

"Bloody Fitzpatrick. He damn nearly made me starve to death."

Barry hesitated, his fork halfway to his mouth. There were venial sins and mortal sins. Along with murder, adultery, and idolatry, keeping O'Reilly from his grub was definitely one of the latter. "How did he do that, Fingal?"

"Kitty and I were just getting going with our starters when Kinky sent for me to go and see one of Fitzpatrick's unfortunate customers. She was in labour, and your man might as well have been on the far side of the moon." He buttered a slice of toast.

"Was Miss Hagerty not able to cope on her own?" Barry had learnt that if the GP was not available, midwives were quite able to conduct normal deliveries. He popped the forkful into his mouth and chewed.

"Not this one," O'Reilly said, liberally spreading Kinky's homemade marmalade. "The Klutz from the Kinnegar had taken over all the antenatal care himself, told Miss Hagerty not to bother seeing the patient—"

Barry nearly choked as he swallowed. He coughed, then said, "Idiot."

"*Amadán*'s right. He missed a breech presentation. Miss Hagerty was pretty sure that's what it was—the husband sent for her because he couldn't find Fitzpatrick—but she didn't want to call for the ambulance until a doctor had examined the patient, a woman called Gertie Gorman. Miss Hagerty told me

Gertie's always been the kind who doesn't like to trouble people, so she waited until her labour was well along before she sent for help. She'd waited too bloody long this time."

"He missed a breech?" Breeches were always tricky, but any half-decent doctor should have made the diagnosis.

"By the time Miss Hagerty tried to find him and then sent for me, the patient was fully dilated and it was too late to get her to the hospital. I'd to deliver her there and then."

"And it went all right?"

"Och, aye," O'Reilly said. He devoured most of the triangular slice of toast in one bite, and his next words were difficult to make out as he spoke through a half-full mouth. "Nice wee baby girl. Her mum's going to call her Noelle." He swallowed and glanced at his watch. "It's nine forty-five. I'd half thought Fitzpatrick might have phoned here by now . . ."

"To thank you for looking after things?"

"Thank me?" O'Reilly shook his shaggy head. "I doubt if he knows the word. No. To get the medical details about how things went. He'll need them to take proper care of his patient." The remains of his toast disappeared.

"Perhaps she should transfer to our care now, Fingal," Barry said, feeling a glimmer of optimism that the flow in the tide of patients to Fitzpatrick might be starting to turn.

O'Reilly reached for the toast rack again and rapidly spread another slice with butter and marmalade.

He shook his head. "I've already told Gertie to stay with her own doctor." He looked Barry directly in the eye. "Fitzpatrick might be an unethical, parasitic, patient poacher. *We* don't do things like that in our practice. If she wants to come to us once all the necessary postnatal care and follow-up of the baby are finished, that's a different matter. It's not good for the patient to change doctors in mid-treatment."

Barry nodded. He was not surprised by what O'Reilly said. By now he'd have expected no less of his senior colleague. He was also gratified by the way O'Reilly had referred to the practice as "our." Barry finished his omelet and cast a hopeful eye at the toast rack's remaining slice. "Will we do anything about Doctor Fitzpatrick, Fingal?" he asked.

O'Reilly nodded ponderously and gobbled his toast before saying, "I gave the bugger the benefit of the doubt, but he *is* pinching our patients, he was bloody rude to Kinky, he's been handing out medical advice that borders on quackery, he welshed on a bet with me, and this, putting a patient and her baby in jeopardy, this is the final destructive piece of vegetable matter on the dorsum of the Bactrian."

"The straw that broke the camel's back?" Barry said with a smile.

"Right," said O'Reilly. "As far as I'm concerned, the man should collect one or two of the plagues of Egypt and then depart into the wilderness."

Barry had a mental image of O'Reilly as Moses, inflicting Pharaoh with lice, or a murrain on his cattle, or perish the thought, a rain of blood in the Kinnegar.

"Fingal, you weren't thinking of doing away with his firstborn, were you?"

O'Reilly laughed and it was a demonical noise, Barry thought, a laugh to match the fires deep in O'Reilly's brown eyes.

"No," he said, "but I do intend to meet with him and gently remind him of the error of his ways. Give him due warning."

"A kind of shot across his bows?"

"Yes," said O'Reilly, "and if a wink is not as good as a nod to that blind horse's arse . . ."—O'Reilly's nose tip paled—"I'll gut him, fillet him, and chuck the remains to the seagulls. I'll go round to the Kinnegar, and see him in the next day or two if I don't run into him sooner." O'Reilly munched his second piece of toast.

Barry rose, moved quickly around the table, and without a by-your-leave grabbed the last slice, nipped back to his place, and ignored the hurt look in O'Reilly's eyes. "Pass the butter and marmalade, will you, Fingal?"

"What's this?" O'Reilly said. "Mutiny in the ranks?"

"No, but after what you did to my kippers the other night, I began to understand, Fingal, that in the grub stakes with you, he who hesitates is lost."

O'Reilly laughed. "Well done, Barry, but it's actually 'The woman that deliberates is lost.' Thomas Addison said it."

"I stand, or rather sit, corrected, and I'd still like the butter . . ."

"And marmalade." O'Reilly passed them along.

He was looking wistfully at the toast rack when Kinky appeared in the doorway.

"Good morning, Doctor Laverty," she said. "And how was your breakfast?"

"Wonderful. Thanks, Kinky," Barry said. "The omelet was magnificent."

"Ah sure, and wasn't it only a shmall little thing?"

"No," said O'Reilly, "it was not. It was grand."

Barry saw her many chins wobble as she chuckled. He wondered if this would be a good time to ask her if Patricia would come home for Christmas, but he was forestalled when O'Reilly added, "The omelet really was grand but, Kinky . . . I think you were a bit, a bit . . ." He stared at the empty toast rack.

"Mean? I was not, so." Kinky put one hand on a substantial hip. "While you were sick there, sir, I wanted to get the nourishment into you, but now you're better"—she eyed O'Reilly's waistline—"I've already heard your Santa Claus suit needs letting out. I'll say no more."

O'Reilly took a deep breath, then sighed and absentmindedly patted his tummy.

Barry chewed the last slice of toast with gusto. It wasn't often he managed to put one over on Fingal. He intended to enjoy it, but his enjoyment was cut short by the ringing of the hall telephone.

"Excuse me," Kinky said and left.

Barry swallowed his last mouthful, turned to the door, waited, and then listened as Kinky returned and said, "It's Cissie Sloan, Doctor O'Reilly. Her wee lad Callum has swallowed sixpence. I told her to bring him to the surgery. To come to the front door. She'll be here in about fifteen minutes."

"Fine, Kinky," said O'Reilly. "You'll be busy in the kitchen, so I'll just wait here and let them in when they come."

Barry had been happy to pour them both second cups of coffee and to sit and chat with O'Reilly. He had planned to go upstairs to try to solve the *Sunday Times* cryptic crossword puzzle, but it could wait until after he'd examined Cissie. Barry wanted to see if her throat was better. If it was, it would save a follow-up visit later in the week. He also wondered how O'Reilly would deal with the missing sixpence.

The front doorbell jangled. O'Reilly stood and ambled out of the dining room. Barry followed. He felt the draught as the front door was opened. It was chilly, he thought, so the draught was a natural phenomenon and not the result of Cissie's nonstop blethering.

"Thank you so much for seeing us, Doctors . . . on a Sunday too . . . and me on my way to mass."

That, Barry thought, explained the gloves and flowerpot hat she wore to set off what must be her best coat and low-heeled brogues.

"And this rapscallion . . ." She thrust a boy of about eight or nine ahead of her. "This raparee goes and swallows a sixpence and—"

"Bring him into the surgery, Cissie." O'Reilly closed the front door.

"—And God knows if it'll get stuck in his wee tummy, and his daddy off to Belfast on the early train to see about buying a ferret. Nasty, smelly things, but he wants one for hunting rabbits . . ."

In the time it had taken Cissie to say this, O'Reilly had manoeuvered her and Callum into the surgery, got Callum to undo the waistband of his pants, pull out his shirttails and undervest, and hop up onto the examining couch.

Barry stood just inside the doorway watching and, Lord help him, listening. He had no doubt that Cissie's sore throat was better.

"I make a lovely rabbit pie, so I do, even if I say so myself. I got the recipe from your Mrs. Kincaid . . . she's a lovely woman . . . for one from the Republic . . ."

Barry heard the bred-from-the-cradle mistrust of many Ulster folk, even Catholics like Cissie, for their countrymen south of the border, even though here in Ballybucklebo there was no sectarian strife. He watched O'Reilly get Callum to lie flat. Then O'Reilly gently palpated the boy's stomach.

"You'd wonder if there'll ever be a united Ireland again," Cissie continued. That spoken thought must have set up deeper ones because Cissie frowned, rubbed her upper lip with the web of her right hand, unconsciously picked her nose, and said nothing for at least two seconds.

O'Reilly, like a rugby back running with the ball and seeing a hole in the defences, plunged into the gap. "He'll be fine, Cissie. No cause for concern. He'll pass it naturally in a day or two."

She stopped picking her nose. "Honest to God, Doctor?"

"Cross my heart. I'm so sure I'll not even ask you to get him to use a potty so you could go through his motions until you find it and prove it's out."

Cissie's nose wrinkled. "I'd not fancy that much, so I wouldn't. Still it's better than my cousin Aggie suggested . . . you know Aggie, the one with—"

"The six toes," Barry mouthed soundlessly, in time with Cissie's declaration. She rarely missed the opportunity to mention them. He saw O'Reilly nod and smile.

"Anyroads, Aggie said Callum would need a big operation with one of them surgeons up at the Royal, but then she wanted me to stick primrose roots up my nose." She turned to Barry. "Them pills you give me done the trick something smashing, so they did. That's two times now you've fixed me, Doctor Laverty . . ."

"You'll not need to come in to see me then, Cissie."

"Right enough," she said, allowing O'Reilly to steer her to the door. Callum was finishing tucking in his shirttails with one hand; the other was being held firmly by Cissie as she dragged him along in her wake.

"Off you trot, Cissie," O'Reilly said, starting to close the front door behind her. "And if you'll take my advice, Callum"—the little boy, still clinging to his mother's hand, turned to look at O'Reilly—"you'll not let your ma stop the sixpence out of your next week's pocket money. It'll be Christmas in another twelve days."

He was still laughing as he closed the door behind him. "Twelve more days. It'll be here in no time," he said. "It's no time at all since *last* Christmas. It seems to come round more quickly every bloody year." Barry thought he detected a wistful tone in the big man's voice.

"I haven't really noticed," Barry said, "but with only a few days left, the pair of us should each get a day off next week for a bit of Christmas shopping."

"Good idea."

"And I don't know what you're going to be up to this morning, Fingal, but seeing that wee lad and his mother reminded me of something I've been putting off for too long."

"Procrastination is, as Edward Young said in about sixteen ninety-five, the thief of time."

"You're right." Barry started to climb the stairs. "So this morning, crossword puzzles be damned, I'm going to write to my mum and dad."

"Give them my regards, Barry, but don't take too long writing. I want you to do me a favour later."

"Oh?"

"His Lordship's gardener always cuts a tree for me. It's to be ready today. Could you take a race out and pick it up?"

"Certainly, Fingal."

"Good lad. I'd like to get it done today because I have a funny feeling we might just be busy next week."

28

Plotting in the Dark, Toils Much to Earn a Monumental Pile

O'Reilly savored the ripe taste of the tobacco, a taste he had acquired as a second-year medical student. He'd no time for cigarettes. They were much too mild. He blew out a cloud of pungent smoke that swirled up to the ceiling of the lounge, and then he inhaled again. In his throat and chest it no longer felt like a sheet of rough sandpaper was being pulled over abraded tissue. He was completely recovered.

Last night he'd draped his coat over the back of an armchair. It now lay in a crumpled heap on the seat. Her Ladyship had dragged it down and was now curled up in the middle, her tail over her nose. She made gentle little whiffling noises as her limbs twitched spasmodically and her eyeballs rolled behind closed lids. "Sorry to disturb your dreams," he said, as he dislodged the cat and lifted his jacket.

Lady Macbeth gave him a look of scornful disdain, sprang to the floor, and crossed the carpet to the corner of the room. There a newly cut eight-foot-tall Norway spruce stood in an old butter box supported by wooden cross members nailed to either side of it. Lady Macbeth stretched her forelegs, put her front paws on the top of the box, arched her spine so that her back became concave, and yawned mightily. She eyed the tree, and for a moment O'Reilly wondered what would become of any dangling decorations that caught the little cat's attention.

He would let the tree remain undecorated for a while longer; then he'd marshall Kinky and Barry to help him trim it and to put presents underneath it as they arrived in the mail. He knew Barry had already received a parcel from Australia.

O'Reilly glanced at the mantel. It was filled with Christmas cards that had been sent to him and to Barry. They'd soon have to start putting new arrivals on the sideboard and downstairs in the dining room. He already left the morning post's quota of cards unopened on the sideboard: six addressed to him and three for Barry.

Barry was out visiting a child with asthma, a boy O'Reilly had seen the previous night. The boy, Billy Cadogan, was one of five children, the son of Phyllis and Eamon who ran the newsagent's. They lived in a thatched cottage beside the shop further along Main Street. Barry'd not known that Phyllis had psoriasis and Eamon a hernia, but the family had been members of the practice for years.

O'Reilly remembered delivering all but one of the children. Brid, who'd be six next September, had come very fast, and by the time he'd arrived Miss Hagerty was tidying up and the wee one was bathed and asleep in the drawer of a chest of drawers.

Last night O'Reilly had given Billy a subcutaneous injection of 0.3 millilitre of adrenaline 1/1000 solution, something he had done several times in the last three years.

The wheezing had improved, but his mother had phoned half an hour ago to say the child's condition had deteriorated. Barry would probably have to give him more adrenaline, as well as 10 milligrams of ephedrine by mouth.

Asthma was a most unpleasant condition. When O'Reilly'd arrived at the Cadogans', Billy was gasping, clutching his throat with one hand, and rolling his eyes at his doctor in a silent plea for help. Within minutes of the injection the wee lad had been able to gasp, "Thank you, Doctor." O'Reilly had silently blessed whoever had discovered that adrenaline, a hormone secreted by a gland that sat on top of the kidneys, could ease constriction of the bronchial tubes.

It was then that O'Reilly noticed his own breathing had improved, and praise be, since he'd got home and had a decent sleep, he was completely better. He inhaled the fresh piney scent of the spruce.

The aroma was, he thought, the most evocative of all the sights, sounds, tastes, and smells of Christmas. If he closed his eyes, he could let it take him back to 1940, to the one Christmas he'd spent with Deidre before the war had taken them both, him to sea and Deidre forever.

They'd been living in a little boardinghouse in Portsmouth. He had three weeks' shore leave. Their tree had been tiny but its piney perfume had filled their living room. Deidre had been as anxious as a kitten because she'd never cooked a turkey before, and he knew she wanted to make their first Christmas perfect.

He'd bought her a pearl necklace, and he could remember her cries of pleasure when she'd opened the box, and how she'd kissed him.

That the turkey had been undercooked hadn't mattered in the least.

He admired his gold cuff links, the ones she'd given him that Christmas. He wore them to this day. He sighed, put on his jacket, and headed back downstairs to the surgery.

He'd decided he must try to let that flame burn a little less fiercely, and now, now that Kitty had come back into his life, he was going to keep that promise he'd made to himself. Funny, he thought, how any wound to the flesh, unless it was lethal, would heal—not without scarring, true, and sometimes it might need help from stitches or an unguent—but heal it certainly would. Even wounds to the heart heal, he thought wryly.

But if he was going to let Kitty be the balm for his bruised heart, he'd have to let her in. He'd have to allow himself to be vulnerable if he were ever again going to feel the pleasure and contentment, the affection a good woman could bring.

It would not be the wild youthful joy he'd known with Deidre—that could never be—but there was something stirring within him for Kitty O'Hallorhan, the Kitty he remembered as a girl, the Kitty he now saw as a mature, self-possessed professional, and he admitted, as a beautiful and desirable woman.

Was it worth risking being hurt if she rejected him or if, after time had passed, they decided it was "just one of those things"? He smiled. He and Kitty used to dance to that 1935 Cole Porter tune.

By God, he decided, it was. It was worth taking the risk. And, he grinned, not only was Kitty a handsome woman, but she was also a superb cook. He recalled with relish the fry she'd made him last night. He wondered if she or her mother would be doing the cooking while she was in Tallaght.

Poor Deidre hadn't quite mastered the culinary arts, but with her he'd been pleased to dine on a bowl of Heinz tomato soup and bread from the bakery. He smiled—and he was pleased he could remember her with a smile.

O'Reilly's step lightened as he came down the last two stairs and along the corridor to open the surgery door. He noted that there was standing room only. "Right, who's first?" he bellowed.

"Us, sir."

O'Reilly immediately recognized Donal Donnelly's carroty thatch and buckteeth and Julie Donnelly neé MacAteer's cornsilk blond hair. "Come on then. You both know the way." He headed for the surgery knowing they would be following. This was a slice of luck. He needed Donal's help with the plan to raise money for Eileen Lindsay.

O'Reilly stood aside at the door, while Donal, holding tightly to Julie's hand, let her precede him into the surgery. Donal held one of the straight-back wooden chairs for her, waited until she was seated, and only then sat himself.

O'Reilly took his place on the swivel chair and put on his half-moon spectacles. "Well," he said, "nice to see the pair of you back. How was the honeymoon?"

Donal blushed as deeply red as his hair.

"London was marvelous," Julie said. Her green eyes sparkled. "And we'd a whole week there. We saw Buckingham Palace, and the Changing of the Guard, and the Tower of London . . ."

"Sounds like fun," O'Reilly said, "but I don't think the pair of you came in this morning to talk about London."

"Oh, no, Doctor," Julie said. "You remember I told you at the wedding I was in the family way again?"

O'Reilly nodded.

"You told me to come and see you or Doctor Laverty when we got home." She took Donal's hand again, looked at him for a long moment, and then continued. "You remember what happened the last time, Doctor O'Reilly?"

"I do." Indeed he did. She had miscarried in August. "It was a shame."

He saw a glistening in her eyes as she said firmly, "Donal says we're taking no chances with this one, so he made me come in the minute we were back."

"Very sensible of him." O'Reilly said, looking at Donal over his spectacles. "I'll need to ask you a few questions, examine you, and arrange some blood work, Julie. Do you mind if Donal stays?"

"Not at all." She shook her head, and her beautiful hair tossed and rippled. "Sure what he doesn't know about me now—after we've been courting for nine months, married for a week, and he's had me pregnant twice—you could write on the back of a postage stamp with a thick-nibbed pen."

"Fair enough." O'Reilly turned, bent forward, opened a drawer in the desk, and pulled out a chart for tracking a pregnancy. He scrawled Julie's name at the top and put in the name of the father. He asked her address ("Twelve Comber Gardens"), her age ("Twenty"), and her occupation ("Housewife").

He quickly filled in the details of Julie's previous medical and surgical history, her family history, and the dates and outcome of any previous pregnancies. "And your periods, Julie. Are they regular?"

"As clockwork."

"And what was the first day of your last one?"

"October the seventeenth, sir."

O'Reilly calculated rapidly. He used Naegele's rule. Add seven days and subtract three months. "That means you're due on the twenty-fourth of July next year."

"July, Doctor?" Donal asked. "So if it's a wee boy and he's born a bit early, there's a name just waiting for him. William," he said proudly.

"Victor of the Boyne, July Twelfth, sixteen ninety. King William of Orange of glorious and immortal memory," O'Reilly added.

"It'll be no such thing, Donal Donnelly," Julie said

firmly. "We'll call a wee boy Brendan . . . for my da, and a wee girl Minnie for your ma."

"Yes, dear," Donal said meekly.

Despite the fact that Donal was sporting his usual moleskin trousers and Julie was wearing a light blue skirt, O'Reilly had no doubt about who would wear the pants in the marriage. None at all. And a good thing too. Donal might have a heart of corn, but from time to time he needed someone to keep his feet from straying too far from the straight and narrow.

O'Reilly rose to go and wash his hands in the sink. "Go in behind the screens, please, Julie. You know what to take off, get up on the couch, and put the sheet over you."

In a short time, O'Reilly had completed his examination. He was pleased that her blood pressure was a normal 120/80 and that, after he'd donned a pair of latex rubber gloves and examined her internally, he could feel a firm uterus corresponding in size to the nine weeks that had elapsed since her last menstruation. "Get dressed now," he said, helping Julie down from the couch, "and when you're decent, come back and join us."

He stripped off his gloves, dropped them in a foot pedal–operated Sani Bin, washed his hands, and sat at his desk. In a matter of moments, he had completed the laboratory requisition form.

O'Reilly was sitting facing Donal when Julie came out from behind the screens and took her chair. "Take that to Bangor Hospital in the next day or two," he said, handing her the form. "It's routine stuff. Nothing to worry about."

"I know that, sir." She hesitated. "Sure didn't I have to do that . . . the last time?" Her lip trembled.

O'Reilly understood her natural concern. No amount of reassurance from him would stop a woman who has miscarried once from worrying the next time she conceived. But he'd try. "Don't worry too much, Julie. Miscarriages do happen, I grant you that, but it's not very often they happen twice in a row." He used his index finger to draw an imaginary cross over his left breast. "Cross my heart."

"Thank you, Doctor O'Reilly," Julie said. "You and Doctor Laverty always make me feel very comfortable. You really do."

"Och," said O'Reilly, "my pleasure. Everything does seem to be fine. Honestly."

Julie smiled and, clutching her pink requisition form, rose. "You're very busy, so we'll be running along. I'll go to Bangor today."

"Sit you down please, Julie," O'Reilly said. "Before you go I've a wee favor to ask of Donal."

Donal sat upright. "Me, sir?"

"Yes, you." O'Reilly laid one finger alongside his bent nose. "And I need you two to promise you'll keep this to yourselves. It's to be a surprise."

"We will, sir, so we will. Won't we, Julie?"

"Of course."

"The pair of you know Eileen Lindsay?"

"The wee lassie with three chisellers and no man?" Donal asked. "Shifter at the Belfast Mill?"

"That's her. She's a bit hard up this year."

"I'm sorry to hear that," Julie said.

Donal's grin ran from ear to ear. "And you want me to arrange a whip round with the lads at the pub, like? See if we can raise a bit of the old do-re-mi? Sure that would be easy as pie."

O'Reilly shook his head. "No, Donal. If we do that, Eileen'll know it's charity, and she's a proud woman. She'd not take the money."

Donal's brows came together. Vertical wrinkles appeared on his forehead. "Right enough," he said, "that's a bit tricky, like. I'm not sure what we can do then. I'd need to think on it a wee while."

O'Reilly smiled at Donal's obvious mental battle. He was a decent young man, a good-natured lad, but it was unlikely that he'd be off to Stockholm anytime soon to pick up a Nobel Prize.

"I'm sure Doctor O'Reilly has a plan," Julie said quietly.

Donal's frown vanished.

"I have," O'Reilly said. "I want to run a raffle."

"A raffle?" Donal's eyes narrowed. The vertical frown lines reappeared. "A raffle? I don't see why you need us for that, sir. Sure anybody can run a raffle. All you need is a prize, a wheen of folks to buy tickets, a draw, and a winner."

"And can anybody predict the winner in advance, Donal?"

"Not at all. You sell tickets with numbers on the ticket and the stub. The punter keeps the ticket; you keep the stub. You put all the stubs into a hat, mix them up, and get somebody honest to pull one out. Whoever has the ticket with the same numbers as the stub, that one's the winner. You can't fix . . ." As if a curtain had been lifted from behind Donal's eyes, they suddenly widened and brightened. His grin was so wide it exposed the gums above his buckteeth. "You can't fix the winner unless—"

"Donal," O'Reilly interrupted, "I honestly don't want to know."

"Oh." Donal's face fell.

O'Reilly lowered his voice. "I don't want to know *how* you could do it." He winked at Donal. "I want to know *if* you can do it."

"Is the pope Catholic?" Donal stood. "You just tell me the prize and how much for a ticket. Me and Julie'll get a roll of tickets and arrange the sales."

"Great," said O'Reilly.

"What's the prize?" Donal asked.

O'Reilly slipped a hand into a pocket of his tweeds and pulled out a ten-pound note. He handed it to Julie. "I want you to go to the poultry shop, pay for the biggest turkey you can, and get Johnny Jordan to agree to deliver it fresh to the Rugby Club on the twenty-third. We'll have the draw at the party."

"I'll do that."

"How much for a ticket, sir?" Donal asked.

"Pound a piece."

"Right. We'll collect the money and give it to you . . ." Donal must have seen O'Reilly's eyebrows shoot up. "It's alright, Doc. I mean *all* the money."

"You'd better," Julie said quietly. "It'll be going to Eileen, won't it, Doctor O'Reilly?"

"It will," O'Reilly said. "It'll be a seventy-five/twenty-five split, with the lion's share for Eileen and the rest for the club. I've already got the committee to agree to that."

"But will she accept it?"

O'Reilly nodded. "She will if she wins it."

"Wins it?" Donal frowned. "I thought the prize was a turkey."

"It is," said O'Reilly, "but we'll announce a bonus prize for anyone who . . ." O'Reilly clenched his fist. He hadn't thought this through as clearly as he might. "For anyone who . . . come on, Donal, this is your department."

"Has the winning ticket for the turkey. They'll get that for sure, but . . ."—his grin was vast—"but if that ticket also has all the same numbers in a row, like 111 . . ."

And if it was going to be yours, Donal, the numbers would be 666, O'Reilly thought with a smile.

"They collect the do-re-mi too."

"Brilliant," O'Reilly said and clapped Donal on the shoulder. Then a thought struck him. "But Donal, if you sell two hundred and fifty tickets, the winner could be 111 or 222 and that—"

Donal shook his head as a parent might at a rather dim child. "Doctor, sir, you stick to the doctoring of people. Leave the doctoring of raffles to me."

"I think," said O'Reilly, "that makes a great deal of sense. I've only one more question."

"Fire away, Doc."

"Are you absolutely certain you can arrange for Eileen to be the winner?"

Donal shook his head. "Not me. You, sir."

"Me?"

"Aye. If Eileen's as broke as you say, Doc, she'll not be able to afford a pound for a ticket . . . but you could give her one."

"On what pretext?" It was O'Reilly's turn to frown.

Donal scratched his chin, pursed his lips, and then said, "Tell her His Lordship bought a clatter for the club to give out for free. She'll accept that story. You know and I know the one you give her will have all the same numbers in a row."

And it will win. O'Reilly knew that. How Donal would arrange it was his business, but arrange it he would. "You, Donal," said O'Reilly, "are a genius." And perhaps Stockholm will be in your stars yet, he thought. "Right. Off the pair of you go." He escorted them to the door, then headed back to the waiting room. He'd spent quite some time with the Donnellys, so he would have to cut some corners with the rest of the patiently waiting mob, but Doctor Fingal Flahertie O'Reilly, M.B., B.Ch., B.A.O., was no stranger to cutting corners, not if the time saved was going to a good cause. And anyway, it was about three hours to lunchtime and already he was feeling a mite peckish. There was no reason why the customers should come between him and his lunch. None at all.

29

Till the Gunpowder Ran Out at the Heels of Their Boots

O'Reilly thought he knew everyone in Ballybucklebo, but this man, the last patient in the waiting room, was a stranger. "Come on then. Let's be having you," he said. "I'm Doctor O'Reilly." At first glance there were no obvious clues as to why the man was there.

He was lean-faced and looked to be in his early thirties. He wore a Dexter raincoat, a woolen muffler in the colors of the Glentoran Soccer Club, and a shapeless tweed duncher. He smiled weakly, rose from the bench, and followed O'Reilly to the surgery.

As he walked along the hall, O'Reilly noticed a most flavorful aroma wafting from the kitchen.

"Have a pew, Mr. . . . ?"

"Shanks, sir. Gerry Shanks." He sat and snatched off his flat cap.

"New here, are you?" O'Reilly asked.

"I just moved from the Kinnegar, so I did."

"Hang on," said O'Reilly. "I'll need to get a few details." He pulled out a patient record card and soon was filling in Shanks's address and phone number.

"That's a quare smart-looking pen, sir, so it is," Shanks remarked. "Parker, is it?"

"It is." O'Reilly regarded the new pen fondly. "It was a present. It certainly writes very smoothly." He held the pen poised over the card. "Would you like to tell me what brings you here, Gerry?"

"I will, sir. I come to see you special, like. My mate, Charlie, he lives here. He's lived here all his life. Him and me're platers on the Island. Charlie said he reckoned maybe youse could help me."

"So you and Charlie build ships on Queen's Island?" O'Reilly wanted to get this consultation over so he could find out what dish had wafted its scent into the hall. It irritated him that he hadn't a clue who Charlie might be, and he should if the man lived here. O'Reilly wanted to find out without asking directly. He certainly couldn't think of any Charlie in the village or in the practice who was a shipwright.

The new patient wore a Glentoran scarf. Knowing Charlie's soccer loyalties might be a useful clue, O'Reilly asked, "Does Charlie support Glentoran too?"

"Not at all, sir." Gerry grinned. "He's a bit thick. He's a Blues man. That lot couldn't fight their way out of a wet paper bag. Charlie thinks they're the bee's knees. But we're best mates anyway, like. Have been since we were wee lads together at Sullivan Upper School in Holywood."

To O'Reilly's knowledge there were no supporters of the Blues—more formally known as Linfield, serious rivals of Glentoran—in his practice either. His stomach rumbled. Hunger was about to trump pride when Gerry Shanks said, "You know Charlie, sir . . . Charlie Gorman . . . Gertie's husband."

O'Reilly grinned. No wonder he hadn't immediately known the Charlie in question. Presumably he was a patient of Fitzpatrick, like his wife whose breech delivery O'Reilly had supervised on Saturday night. "*That* Charlie. Right," said O'Reilly.

"Anyhow, sir, Charlie said you made a right good fist of his wife's delivery, and so he thought maybe you could help me a bit." He sat stiffly and glanced around as if making sure he couldn't be overheard. "Him and me was patients of good old Doc Bowman until he retired. Our parents used to go to him before you came here, sir. Now we go to Fitzpatrick because he took over the practice." Gerry lowered his voice. "To tell you the truth, sir, and maybe I shouldn't say it like, 'cos youse doctors stick together, but Charlie and me's not so sure your man's altogether at the match."

O'Reilly pulled his half-moons down to the very tip of his nose and stared at Gerry. He'd not comment to a patient on his opinion of Fitzpatrick's competence. That would be unethical. Instead, he said, "We're supposed to support each other, true enough, but"—he removed his glasses—"patients are fully entitled to ask for a second opinion." He sat back comfortably in his chair and let the hand holding the spectacles dangle over the side of the chair. "So what can I do for you, Gerry?"

Gerry visibly relaxed. "You'd not mind, sir?"

"Go ahead. I'm listening."

"It's a bit awkward, like."

O'Reilly's tummy rumbled, but he said, "Take your time."

Shanks took a deep breath. "It's me and the missus, so it is."

"Go on." Not all marriages were made in heaven, O'Reilly knew, but he hoped he wasn't in for a long rambling tale of woe.

"We'd like another baby, so we would."

"Mmm," said O'Reilly, wondering if Barry might be able to help. He was bound to be better acquainted with the use of the new fertility drugs like the recently introduced clomiphene and the powerful gonadotrophic hormone Pergonal. "And what advice have you had?"

Shanks shrugged. "It's weird, so it is. We have two kiddies. Angus is five and Siobhan's four, and the missus breast-fed her for eighteen months so we didn't start trying for another one until a couple of years ago." He frowned. "It used to be I'd just to hang my trousers on the end of the bed and Mairead was poulticed, but nothing happened this time." He blushed. "And it wasn't for want of trying, at first anyway."

"And did you go to see anybody about it?"

"Aye. Doctor Bowman, just before he retired. He was a right decent man, a sound man, so he was. He said straight off he didn't know nothing about fertility, so he had us go up to the clinic at the Royal with them specialist doctors."

"And?"

"They done every test and at the heels of the hunt said they could find nothing wrong."

O'Reilly frowned. "If you've seen the specialist doctors, Gerry, I doubt if there'll be much I can do. I'm a country GP." Confessing his lack of expertise in that particular field bothered Fingal Flahertie O'Reilly not one jot or tittle.

"Och, Doc, sure don't I know that?"

O'Reilly glanced surreptitiously at his watch.

"I'm taking up a lot of your time, so I am. I'd one wee question, that's all."

"Fire away."

"Seeing as how Fitzpatrick's new, the missus reckoned we'd nothing to lose if we asked his advice."

But you still might have lost something, O'Reilly thought. Infertile couples were some of the most vulnerable patients. They would often grasp at any straw, even if it were of no value, and indeed in some cases it might be harmful. God alone could guess what peculiar idea Fitzpatrick might have for the treatment of infertility. "And did he suggest crushed primrose roots in goat's milk?" O'Reilly asked.

Gerry shook his head.

"Or putting vegetable marrow jam in your left ear once a month by moonlight?" O'Reilly knew most patients, even the infertile ones, would laugh at such an idiotic suggestion. He had used the line many times in the past as a metaphor for a useless therapy asked for by a patient.

He was surprised when Gerry didn't laugh but said seriously, "I wish he had, so I do. He told Mairead something far worse."

"Oh?"

"Aye. I'm not kidding you, sir. He told her to stop putting sugar in my morning cup of tea."

"That's hardly a killing matter, Gerry."

"And to put in a teaspoonful, *a teaspoonful,* of black gunpowder instead."

O'Reilly's mouth opened wide. "Gunpowder? *Gunpowder?*" He struggled to keep a straight face as he resettled his spectacles on his nose.

"Aye. He told Mairead it would put lead in my pencil." Gerry started to squeeze his left knuckles with his right hand. He looked straight at O'Reilly. "It tastes bloody awful, sir, but I don't mind that. I'll take it if it helps. I have for the last four months"—there was a catch in his voice—"but I hate to see Mairead's face when her monthlies keep coming on."

O'Reilly leant forward. He put his big hand over Gerry's hands and stilled their wringing. "Gerry, I've never heard of such a treatment. I can't for the life of me think why it should work. Gunpowder's made of charcoal, and sulphur, and saltpetre. Sulphur can give you the skitters, but charcoal will bind you. You had any change in your motions?"

"No, sir."

"Saltpetre's a nitrate, like the stuff farmers use for fertilizer. If you get exposed to enough of it, it can cause skin rashes. Have you noticed any?"

"No, Doctor."

"There used to be a rumour in the navy that we doctors put saltpetre in the men's tea to stop them feeling randy. We didn't, but a lot of sailors believed we did."

Gerry smiled wryly. He lowered his voice. "Mebbe it's doing that to me. It's difficult to get interested, so it is. Fitzpatrick says I've to save myself except for the fourteenth day of the month." His face started to crumple. "Mairead's a pretty wee lass. It's not fair to her."

O'Reilly nodded and put as much sympathy into his next words as he could muster. "I don't think it's the gunpowder that's making you disinterested, Gerry, but only making love on the right night to make babies, whenever the hell that is, for I don't know. Sure, the fourteenth day of a woman's month *might* be a bit better, but some women don't ovulate on the fourteenth day. We know that for a fact. Having to perform to order could dampen anyone's enthusiasm."

"Too bloody true. It certainly sickened my happiness."

O'Reilly knew that the tip of his nose was becoming pallid. "You *know* I'm not infallible, but I think performing to order's a total bloody waste of time, and the gunpowder's worse than useless."

"Honest, sir?" Gerry managed a weak smile.

O'Reilly nodded. "Would you like me to have a wee word with Mairead? Let her hear it from the horse's mouth?" Instead of from the other end of the animal, he thought.

"Would you, sir? I'd like that a whole lot."

"Bring her in on Wednesday, but—I hate to advise you this—go on taking the gunpowder until I have the chance to tell her it's useless. If you stop now, it'll upset her. Once we've had our chat, you can chuck it out—or go and blow something up." Preferably that bloody menace of a charlatan Fitzpatrick, he thought. He scribbled a quick note in the chart.

"Fair enough, Doctor O'Reilly." Gerry rose. "We'll see you on Wednesday. Thank you, sir. Thank you very much. I'm most grateful, so I am, sir." He put on his duncher and headed for the door. O'Reilly followed. "Wednesday it is," he said, as Gerry left through the front door and O'Reilly headed for the dining room—and lunch.

30

A New and Original Plan

Finished in the surgery, Fingal?" Barry asked from where he sat at the dining-room table.

"Finished *and* I'm famished, a word incidentally derived from the same root as famine." O'Reilly sat, rubbed his hands, then picked up his knife and fork. He glanced from the table to the sideboard.

"And the Great Famine started in Ireland in eighteen forty-five when the potato crop failed . . . But there's no risk of being short of vittles here, not with Kinky in the kitchen."

O'Reilly wasn't so sure. The sideboard must have taken a lesson from Mother Hubbard's cupboard. It was completely bare. He frowned.

There was a plate in front of him. On it sat a solitary hard-boiled egg, three lettuce leaves, a tomato, six slices of cucumber, and a stick of celery. "Rabbit food," he growled. Then he softened. He knew, he absolutely knew, there was a second course to come. He'd known it since he'd smelled it cooking earlier that morning. He might as well eat up his salad with good grace. "Pass the mayonnaise," he said, and held out his hand.

He spread the rich creamy homemade dressing. "How was your morning, Barry?"

"Can't complain. The lad with the asthma, Billy Cadogan, wasn't doing so well, and he didn't respond to more adrenaline. It's frustrating. The poor mites always think they're going to suffocate to death." Barry ate some egg. "I could never have done pediatrics, Fingal. I hate to see the wee ones sick. I can remember being sick with the measles when I was a child. Wasn't much fun."

He had a very soft side, had Barry Laverty. O'Reilly approved. "We all have some part of medicine we don't like. Me? I hate cancer." Just before Barry had come to Ballybucklebo, O'Reilly had watched an old fisherman waste away to scraps from cancer of the pancreas. At the end not even morphine could control the pain.

"I'd love to be able to treat it effectively," he said, and he meant it, "but I could never have been a cancer specialist." O'Reilly felt himself shudder and saw Barry staring at him curiously.

"I'm surprised, Fingal. I really didn't think anything fazed you."

"Cancer does. All the treatments—radical surgery, radiation, and chemotherapy—are brutal, and I'm not convinced any of them work very well. It's a horrid disease. We do our best, but no matter how well intentioned, I could never have been the physician inflicting the treatments on some poor bastard."

It was Barry's turn to shudder. "Nor me."

"Maybe the treatments'll improve in the future," O'Reilly said. "I'm sure a lot of the causes are genetic, and now the laboratory boys have begun to understand DNA we should start to make progress." He certainly hoped so. "Maybe we'll even be able to prevent cancer one day. But now? We're pretty impotent." Just like Gerry Shanks, he thought.

"Come on, Fingal, it's not as bleak as that. The gynaecologists have the Papanicolaou smear for early detection of cervical cancer. The link between smoking and lung cancer is proven—"

"Aye, and everybody's suddenly stopped smoking, I suppose? And lung cancer's going to vanish overnight?" He grinned. "I'm not giving up my pipe."

"I'd not believe you if you said you would, but I quit, and other people eventually will." Barry pointed his fork at O'Reilly. "We *will* see the number of cases fall. And the work implicating asbestos as the cause of cancer of the pleural membrane was done right here in Belfast by Doctor Elwood. There'll be less of that too now we know what causes it."

Good for you, Barry, O'Reilly thought. Five months ago you'd not have pointed your fork at me, much less tease me and argue with me. "You're right," he said. "I remember Elwood studying shipyard workers exposed to the stuff in the building of ships." He sighed. "We *are* making headway but slowly," O'Reilly said. Then he added, "Wouldn't it be wonderful if we had an anticancer vaccine?" He chewed and swallowed. "It's a horrid disease. You feel so bloody useless."

"I suppose if you put it that way, sorting out a kiddie with asthma isn't so terrible. At least if we can't prevent it, we can treat it pretty well."

"I hear you, but I also know it's upsetting when a child's scared or in pain." He sighed. "You just have to try to get used to it if you're going to be able to help."

"I know. I am trying to."

"So what *did* you do for Billy?"

Barry shrugged. "The usual. Sent for the ambulance."

O'Reilly frowned. "I think that's eleven times this year's Billy's had to go to Sick Kids." He smiled. "His mum's sat with him so many times while he's been given intravenous bronchial dilators that she could probably tell the doctors what dose of aminophylline to give."

Barry laughed. "She certainly seemed pretty calm about the whole thing."

"Phyllis Cadogan's one of the most sensible women in Ballybucklebo," O'Reilly said. "Her husband *thinks* he runs the newsagent's shop, but it's Phyllis who's really in charge of the business. She has to be because her husband's on a waiting list to get his hernia fixed, and until it is, she has to do all the lifting."

"I'll remember that."

"Good." O'Reilly ate most of the egg in one bite. "And was that it for the morning?"

"No. I popped in to see Sammy and Maggie. He's really recovering fast. Maggie reckons he'll be well enough to come to the Rugby Club party next Wednesday, the twenty-third. I think she's right. He might even make the Christmas pageant on the twenty-first. Eileen doesn't want her kids to miss it, but they will if she has to stay at home with Sammy."

O'Reilly finished the egg and demolished the celery stick in a couple of crunches. "The kiddies really enjoy the pageant and the party; it would be a shame for them to miss them." He sliced the tomato in half. "And I want Eileen at both too."

"Why?"

O'Reilly bolted one tomato half. "I'd Donal and Julie in today, and before you ask, because I know you were worried that she'd got pregnant too soon after her miscarriage, she's nine weeks and doing fine."

"That's good, Fingal, but what have the Donnellys to do with Eileen being at a couple of functions?"

The rest of the tomato went. "What do you know about raffles?"

"Sir Thomas Stanford Raffles, 1781 to 1826. Founded Singapore."

"True." Barry was certainly well grounded in the history of the British Empire. It was a pity, O'Reilly thought, there wasn't more Irish history taught. "But I mean the other sort of raffle," O'Reilly said.

"The lottery kind? And Donal's involved?" Barry's eyes widened. He grinned. "Go on."

The cucumber was pierced and went straight into O'Reilly's mouth. "I had an idea for repairing Eileen's finances . . ."

"And Donal's helping?"

"Yes."

"What's he going to do? Raffle off a bunch of Irish thruppenny bits as Beatrix Potter medals because they have the image of a hare on them?"

O'Reilly laughed. "He'd not get away with that with the locals."

"He did in August when he persuaded that bloody awful Englishman Captain O'Brien-Kelly that half-crowns were medallions commemorating Arkle."

"There are," said O'Reilly, "no flies on the boul' Donal, but this time he has a better scheme. We're going to raffle a turkey at the Rugby Club party."

"I don't see how that will help Eileen, even if she does win it."

"Because a big turkey as a prize will persuade lots of folks to buy tickets. That brings the money in."

"And the club benefits."

"Not much," said O'Reilly, glad he'd been able to get the committee to agree. "They've agreed to split the take seventy-five/twenty-five with the winner, as long as the winner also holds a special ticket." He watched Barry's face go from a frown to a smile. Barry had come up with the answer as quickly as he solved clues in those cryptic crosswords, which O'Reilly hated to admit were completely beyond him.

"Eileen's going to win the turkey *and* the money. I'd bet on that if you and Donal are involved."

"Right, but we'll keep it hush-hush. If Eileen suspected for one minute it had been a put-up job, she'd not accept a penny."

"I agree. She struck me as a very proud woman." Barry scratched his chin. "How is Donal going to make sure she gets the winning ticket?"

O'Reilly laughed. "Don't ask me *how* Donal will fix things. I haven't the faintest idea, but he will. That's one tricky problem solved." O'Reilly allowed himself a tiny bit of smugness.

"I wish he could help us with our other one. Dear Doctor Fitzpatick."

So Barry was still worried about losing patients, was he? O'Reilly started on the first lettuce leaf. "I'd another of his customers in today. Secondary infertility. They've two kiddies, but number three is slow coming. The highheejins up at the Royal are flummoxed." The second lettuce leaf was next. As soon as it was finished, O'Reilly paused with knife and fork at "Present arms." "And I'll bet you'll not even begin to guess what the Kinnegar's answer to Hippocrates has suggested."

Barry shook his head. "Fingal, I'm not even going to try. Tell me."

"Gunpowder."

"What?" Barry sat bolt upright.

"You heard right. Gunpowder, one teaspoon every morning in the husband's tea."

"Good God. I don't know whether to laugh or to cry, it's so ridiculous. Gunpowder."

"I think," said O'Reilly slowly, "we need to pay Fitzpatrick a courtesy call of our own." He looked straight at Barry. "I really don't think he's a threat to us, son. He'll get away with handing out his weird nostrums for a while . . . you can fool all of the people some of the time—"

"So said Abraham Lincoln."

"But country folks are a damn sight cleverer than many people give them credit for. I reckon they'll start to see through him soon enough."

"Do you know, Fingal, ever since you told me about the breech he missed, I've thought about him?"

"And?"

"I still worry a bit about him pinching our patients, but I'm *really* getting concerned that he's going to kill somebody," Barry said.

"Aye. I know. Or make someone worse instead of better. You'd think nobody had told him that the most important rule in medicine is 'First, do no harm.'"

"So what are *we* going to do? Report him to the authorities? Try to talk to him?"

O'Reilly frowned. "I'm no great respecter of authority, and . . . get that grin off your face, Laverty. I know what you are thinking. I do pay respect where respect is due."

"Sorry, Fingal."

"I'd be in no rush to report a colleague, not even Fitzpatrick. You don't go round making reports just because you don't like somebody."

"He's not an easy man to like."

"Nobody much liked him when he was a student. Kitty will tell you that. He picked on student nurses like her. I had to tell him to leave her alone. I like him even less now. But I'm with you, Barry; I'm a damn sight more concerned that he's going to hurt somebody badly, and you know how slowly the powers that be react. If we wrote a report tomorrow, it could be months before anything happened." O'Reilly leant forward. "It's up to us to act. And soon."

"How?"

"I'm going to phone him today and set up that meeting." O'Reilly scratched his chin. "When we meet, the first item on the agenda will be to try to get him to see reason about his practices."

"And the other items?"

O'Reilly lifted his shoulders. "I'm not much for lost causes, but he wasn't a bad student. I didn't like him, but then you don't have to like everybody. Maybe, just maybe, he'll see the light and be a better doctor for it."

"And if he doesn't agree, is there anything else we can try?"

It would be a forlorn hope, O'Reilly knew, and he didn't want Barry to think that he, O'Reilly, was letting this become a personal matter. He looked at Barry and said, "You know that in Ireland they say you can rape your best friend's sister and he might forgive you, but if you informed to the British, or reneged on a wager, they'd still be talking about you in a hundred years."

"I don't see what that has to do with Fitzpatrick."

"He reneged on a bet with me," O'Reilly said.

"He what? Here in North County Down? He must be mad. If the folks knew that, his reputation would vanish overnight." Barry grinned. "You can blackmail the man, Fingal. Threaten to let the word out."

"You're absolutely spot on. Threaten. I'd never actually tell, but he'd not know that because, as far as I'm concerned, the whole thing's between him and me."

"But if he *thought* you might do it, he'd know he'd be an outcast," Barry said.

"He would, but then he always has been a bit of a one."

"And do you honestly think we can get him to see the light? Reason with him or threaten him, get him to change?"

O'Reilly shook his head. "Leopards and spots . . . but it won't cost anything to try."

"Good. Can I come too? I might be able to help."

"I'd like that, Barry." O'Reilly scowled at his empty plate. "And I'd like the second course of lunch too."

As if reading from a script, Kinky came bustling in carrying a tray for the empty plates. "There'll be no second course, sir. I'll not have the women of the village laughing because *my* doctor is starting to look like one of those zeppelins I saw in a documentary on television the other night."

"Zeppelin? Zeppelin? Who said that, Kinky?" O'Reilly bristled.

"No one yet, sir. I just said I wasn't going to let it happen. Just calm yourself."

O'Reilly swallowed. Damn it, he was still hungry. "But there's got to be a second course. I smelled it cooking not half an hour ago."

"Doctor dear," she said, lifting his plate, "that was no second course. That was sweet mincemeat I'm making for to fill Christmas mince pies, so. I've a lot to make, what with the ones for the party and the ones for this house."

"Oh." O'Reilly sighed. "Oh, well." He knew he'd have to content himself. Sweet mince pies wouldn't make much of a second course of lunch anyway, but perhaps he could get Kinky to serve some with an early afternoon tea.

"Now," she said, carrying her laden tray to the door, "you've no calls to make this afternoon, Doctor Laverty dear. No medical calls, that is, but there was one phone call."

"Patricia?" Barry spun in his chair, a great smile beaming.

Kinky shook her head and Barry's face fell. Poor Barry, O'Reilly thought.

"No. Not Miss Spence. Cissie Sloan."

"Cissie?" Barry frowned. "Has she had a relapse? Is something else wrong with her?"

"Perhaps," said O'Reilly with a grin, "she had to stop talking for half an hour and she bust her stays."

Barry laughed.

Kinky tutted. "That's not entirely fair, Doctor sir, but she does have the gift of the gab, I'll agree. Anyway she's not sick," Kinky said. "She was just wondering if you two gentlemen were going to pop into the parish hall to see how the preparations are coming on."

O'Reilly remembered he had promised to drop in last week but had been sidetracked by the drama of Eileen's missing money. "Why don't we do that this afternoon, Barry?"

Barry sighed. "Fair enough. I've nothing better to do."

"That's right," Kinky said, with a twinkle in her eye. O'Reilly knew he was the only one to notice it, along with the great softness in her voice, a softness like that of a mother comforting a disappointed child. "But you will have very soon . . . when your Miss Spence comes home."

31

Folks Who Live Beneath the Shadow of the Steeple

Barry's nape hairs were still standing on end when he went into the back garden with O'Reilly, and it wasn't the bitter wind that had made them so. It was eerie. Kinky had the gift. Barry had no doubt about that. But it was a pity that when he'd pressed her to be more precise about Patricia's arrival, Kinky had smiled, shaken her head, and said, "That's all I know, sir."

The tingling in the back of his neck had subsided by the time he passed Arthur's kennel. The Labrador lolloped out, tail going like a threshing machine with slipped gears, tucked his nose an inch behind O'Reilly's leg, and stayed perfectly "at heel" without having to be told.

"He always behaves himself in duck season," O'Reilly said. "I think he can read the calendar." He stopped to pat the big dog's head. "We're going on Saturday," he said. "Saturday. Five more days."

"Aaarghow," said Arthur. His tail drooped, and he heaved a massive sigh.

"But you can come for the ride," O'Reilly said, as he took the last step to the back gate and opened it.

Barry and Arthur piled into the Rover. Barry was glad to be out of the half gale. He loved Ulster, but at this time of the year he could almost be persuaded that practising somewhere with a lot more sunshine—Fiji or Tahiti, say—might have some merit. And, he sniffed, in a dry climate he'd not have to put up with the pong of damp dog.

O'Reilly started the engine and drove off, turning left at the end of the back lane. Barry now knew the layout of the village well. To get to the chapel and its attached Parish Hall, O'Reilly must drive from one end of Ballybucklebo to the other.

Barry looked at the rows of attached cottages that flanked Main Street on the Bangor side of the village's lone crossroads. He could have told anyone who asked which of his patients lived in which cottage. He'd made a lot of home visits since he'd started here in July.

He noticed that many of the homes sported holly wreaths on their front door. Small Christmas trees garlanded with fairy lights filled front parlour windows.

The car rolled to a stop for the traffic light. It was here in Barry's first week in Ballybucklebo that O'Reilly, infuriated at Donal Donnelly for stalling his tractor and making him miss several light changes, had roared at Donal, "*Was there a particular shade of green you were waiting for?*"

Barry chuckled. Funny how Donal had become so important in the life of Ballybucklebo.

"What are you chortling about?" O'Reilly asked.

"Donal," said Barry, not entirely untruthfully. "Donal and his schemes."

"Aye," said O'Reilly, "he's so sharp he could cut himself."

Barry, still smiling, looked to his left where the Maypole pointed a stiff finger at a dark sky. Ragged clouds, perhaps bearing snow, scudded before the brisk northeaster. He wondered if they might have a white Christmas. The last one he remembered was when he was seven and his father had taken him tobogganing on the hills of Bangor Golf Course.

He looked across the street to the Black Swan, where Mary Dunleavy was outside washing the front windows with a chamois leather she kept dipping into a bucket of sudsy water. She recognized the car, as every local would, and waved her chamois. He waved back.

The light changed and the car moved ahead slowly, its progress hindered by a small herd of black-and-white Friesians, their udders full, being driven leisurely along the road by a collie and a man on a bicycle. One cow lifted her tail and dropped a heap of steaming cow clap.

Even with the car's windows closed, Barry could smell the pungent aroma. Although the new rustic odor was perhaps less unpleasant than the old one of damp dog, at times he thought he'd be quite grateful to suffer from anosmia, a condition where the sufferer had no sense of smell. Barry had never thought he'd be grateful if Fingal lit his pipe. He was wrong.

Barry noticed that there weren't many pedestrians today. That wind was cold, and besides, few housewives would shop for any perishable goods on a Monday. They knew that anything for sale would have been left over since Friday and would not be fresh.

All the shop windows were decorated. There was spray-on snow, sprigs of holly, tinsel streamers, a cardboard Santa, paper chains of letters spelling "Merry Christmas," and a crèche attended by an angel with one wing, hovering by a string over the manger. All competed for the attention of the passersby. Main Street, Ballybucklebo, was like Donegal Square in Belfast, but in miniature and more personal.

Here in the village he might well have treated some of the shop assistants; most would know him by name, and they would go out of their way to be helpful. In Belfast he was often made to feel like no more than a device for carrying cash and perhaps leaving some in the store.

He loved this place more each day—its smallness, its tight community, its unhurried pace. He wondered how Patricia, a small-town girl herself, would feel about Ballybucklebo after her three years at Cambridge.

Three years. How much would she have changed after such a long time? He knew how much he himself had grown in the mere five months he'd been here. It would be unreasonable for him to expect Patricia not to be different, and yet—and yet he ached at the thought of the girl he had fallen in love with becoming another person.

He suspected from her lack of urgency about coming home for Christmas that the process had started after only three months. Perhaps after a couple of years she'd decide she'd outgrown a small-town GP.

The Rover's old heater was doing its best, but at the thought of losing Patricia, Barry shivered.

The university town wasn't large, but he knew she'd have the opportunity to meet any number of interesting people there, including, damn it, interesting young men.

Cambridge was a stone's throw away from London. He remembered being taken to the capital city as a child and being terrified by the noise, and the smell, and the traffic, and the sheer number of people on the streets.

Here in Ballybucklebo, where the aroma of cow clap lingered in the old Rover, he looked out at the rumps of several cows, and thought he was more likely to be pushed aside by a herd like the one ahead than be run down by a car. Damn it, he went to Belfast only when he really had to.

Patricia was different. She revelled in new experiences. She'd be stupid not to travel down to London. It was less than an hour's train ride to Liverpool Street station. After she'd seen Oxford Street and the Strand, how would she feel about Belfast, never mind Ballybucklebo, where Miss Moloney's was the only dress shop in the village?

As the car crept past her shop, Barry remembered that he must check to see if the results of Miss Moloney's blood tests were back. She'd be coming in to the surgery again, perhaps as early as tomorrow. He wondered if she'd added the extra inch to the waist of O'Reilly's Santa Claus trousers yet.

"Bloody cows," O'Reilly muttered. He honked his horn. One cow stopped and turned her head, staring with her soft velvet eyes while mindlessly chewing her cud. "Bloody cows," he said again and shook his head. "But if you choose to live in the country, you have to put up with them."

"It's better than fighting the traffic in Belfast, Fingal." Barry slumped back against the worn leather upholstery. And I'm not driving, he thought, nor am I in a great rush to get anywhere. His eyelids drooped.

"It is, Barry; it surely is."

Barry heard enthusiasm in O'Reilly's voice. When he blinked his eyes open, Barry could see why. The cowherd was ahead of the animals, waving his stick and shouting to make them take the road to the left, the road that skirted the housing estate and wound up into the Ballybucklebo Hills. The cowherd followed the last animal, touching his cap to the Rover and its occupants.

O'Reilly waved back. "Liam Gillespie's young brother," he said. He rolled down the window and roared, "Paddy. What's the word of Liam?"

"He's home and up and doing, thanks, Doc. He's not quite ready to go back to work yet. These are his beasts. I'm taking them home for milking."

"Good man ma da," yelled O'Reilly, seemingly oblivious to the honking of a car horn behind him. "Give him my best when you see him." He closed the window and was about to drive on, but before he could accelerate, a red Massey-Harris tractor towing a trailer piled high with manure left the same road the cattle were using and turned onto the Belfast Road immediately ahead of the Rover. "Bugger," said O'Reilly. He drummed his fingers on the steering wheel for a while and then said, "What can't be cured must be endured." It wasn't the first time Barry had heard the remark.

Barry was happy enough to sit as the car rolled along at tractor speed. "I was wondering," he remarked, "if we can't cure Fitzpatrick, does that mean we have to endure him?"

"It's my hope," O'Reilly said, "that we can get him to change a bit. I don't really care if he wants to give crushed primrose roots to folks with colds."

"They'll get better on their own anyway," Barry said, "and if it makes the customer feel better—"

"It's just like our black bottle. I do know that, but I'm still going to give him what-for for not using Miss Hagerty." O'Reilly had to brake as the tractor signaled for a right turn. He turned to Barry. "I'll not let him get away with it. Miss Hagerty's a seasoned professional. She deserves to be treated with respect. Damn it all, everyone does, at least until they give us cause to stop respecting them."

Barry was not surprised by that remark. He'd seen O'Reilly practice what he preached. "Do unto others, Fingal?"

"Aye. 'Before they do it unto you,' an old friend of

mine used to say. I agree, and it is time we did it to that man." O'Reilly's voice took an edge. "I could have lost Gertie and her baby."

Barry felt for his senior colleague. He could still recall having to deliver a face presentation and how he'd had trouble putting on rubber gloves because his hands were so sweaty. To be stuck with an undiagnosed breech hardly bore thinking about, and yet O'Reilly wasn't upset about being in a tough obstetrical situation. He was angry on behalf of the patient.

"I told you I'll call him . . . and I will." O'Reilly pulled over to the side of the road and parked behind a string of vehicles straddling the grass verge. "Stay, Arthur," he said. "Come on, Barry."

Barry turned up the collar of his coat against the wind that screeched over the sand dunes between the road and the shore. He narrowed his eyes as the wind brought fine particles of sand with it.

He hurried his pace to catch up with O'Reilly, who was already turning onto the drive to the one-storey building abutting the grey stone chapel.

The building brought back memories so clearly that Barry could see and hear the scene.

In September, shortly before Patricia had left to continue her civil engineering studies at Cambridge, Barry had walked past this chapel with her. He could remember asking her to explain its interesting architecture. He'd been holding her hand, and she'd let it go to shield her eyes from the midafternoon sun as she squinted up at the steeple.

"It's about two hundred years old," she'd said. "You can tell by the three-stage tower. It's called Early English detailing."

"Och, sure," he said, in a stage Irish brogue with a catch in his voice, "and don't the English get everywhere in this sorry country, even into Irish church steeples? Wirra, wirra, poor Ireland."

She laughed, then said, "Be serious, eejit. You asked me to explain. Do you want me to, or don't you?"

"You're the engineer," he said. "Please."

She pointed up to the tower. "You see how it rises from a sandstone base, with two lancet windows in each face?"

"Yes. Yes, I can." He'd had to screw up his eyes because autumn was approaching and the sun was low in the sky.

"Those circular windows above the pointed ones are called oculi."

"That's Latin for 'eyes.'"

"Right. That part supports the belfry. It's a fancy piece of work with louvered-arched windows set between pilasters and topped with balustrading and corner finials, those little minispires. Above them is the thin octagonal spire ending in a point surmounted by a cross. The classical three-stage church tower."

"Patricia," Barry said, impressed by her knowledge, "what in the world got you interested in this stuff in the first place?"

"I've always loved beautiful things."

"Like opera?"

"That's right . . . and impressive buildings. My dad understood and gave me books about architecture." She glanced down. "Have you ever seen a picture of the Leaning Tower of Pisa?"

"Everyone has."

"Did you ever wonder why it leans, and more importantly why it doesn't fall over?"

"Not really."

"I did. I wondered so much that I wanted to find out the answer. I wanted to know how to build things—"

"So you decided to become an engineer?"

"Right."

"And I admire you for it. I love you for it."

And when she'd kissed him her lips were warm and the world had gone away.

"Are you coming, or are you going to stand there looking up and waiting for the Second Coming?" yelled O'Reilly.

O'Reilly brought Barry right back into the chilly, windy world. Barry wished Patricia was here now with her warm kisses. Kinky had better be right. He missed Patricia, was chilled without her. Barry trotted ahead.

The chapel was solid, it was imposing, and—he silently thanked its builders—it provided shelter the moment he stepped into its lee.

O'Reilly was holding open the door, which he closed as soon as Barry stepped inside. Barry took off his coat. The central heating must have been going at full blast. He could hear what he thought might be a harmonium accompanying a children's choir. The sounds took him back to his childhood and Sunday school on Sunday afternoons. He smiled. He'd been expelled because he had once taken his pet white mouse to class and scared all the little girls.

As a child, Patricia had liked buildings, he thought. He'd been fascinated by animals.

Barry's nostrils were filled with the scent of incense. The last time he'd been aware of that aroma had been at the wedding of a Catholic friend the previous year. He'd thought Freddy, a classmate, was too young to be getting married. Maybe Freddy had been right, but Patricia had said to him at Sonny and Maggie's wedding in August that marriage wasn't in her stars—not yet.

Barry hung his coat on a peg and looked around.

He stood in a small vestibule with a parquet floor and wood-panelled walls like those in the great hall of his old school, Campbell College.

O'Reilly had opened one of a set of double doors, which Barry could see led to the hall proper. A wooden crucifix was fastened to the door lintel. "Right," said O'Reilly, "let's have a peek inside, see if we can root out Cissie and let her know we are men of our word."

32

As Children with Their Play

"Come in, come in." Reverend Robinson, who stood at the back of the hall, spoke softly. His voice was barely audible over the harmonium and the children's voices. Barry remembered meeting him for the first time at Sonny and Maggie's wedding.

"Mr. Robinson," Barry said in muted tones, marvelling at the presence of a Protestant man of the cloth in what in many parts of Ulster would be regarded as the territory of the Antichrist. "How are you?"

The minister smiled, shook his head, and held a finger to his lips.

Barry understood and nodded in agreement. He looked around and saw that he was standing in a single room. The walls were yellow-painted breeze block, and the triangular trusses supporting the roof were visible above him. Coloured paper chains hung from them in loops.

"Fear not," said he, for mighty dread had seized their troubled mind . . .

He smiled. So they were rehearsing "While Shepherds Watched Their Flocks by Night." His friends at primary school always called that one "While Shepherds Washed Their Socks by Night."

"Glad tidings of great joy I bring to you, and all mankind."

Some of the little boys clearly had as much feeling for the notes as he'd had as a child. Their off-key warblings were distinctly heard over the more tuneful efforts of their classmates.

Barry could remember his own childhood pageants. He'd been allowed into the choir but had received strict instructions to mouth the words silently. His music teacher, Miss Fanshawe, had seemed to be under the impression she was rehearsing the famous Belfast Harlandic Male Voice Choir instead of a group of youngsters.

The young woman who was conducting today was a distinct improvement over the angular Miss Fanshawe. She stood with her back to Barry. He could see shoulders, a narrow waist to which tumbled a single plait of long copper hair, slim hips, and a pair of shapely calves beneath the hem of her black knee-length skirt.

Barry was quite willing to remain silent and hope she would turn around once the carol was over. He'd very much like to see her face.

"To you, in David's town, this day, is born of David's line . . ."

He managed to stop staring at the woman and looked down to where Father O'Toole, wearing a rollneck sweater and corduroy trousers, sat at a harmonium below and in front of the stage. He pedalled furiously and thumped on the keyboard. Barry could see beads of perspiration on the priest's forehead.

"The heavenly Babe you there shall find . . ."

He glanced at the Reverend Robinson, who was smiling and keeping time with one hand. Considering the unrelenting sectarian hatred that disfigured so much of the Six Counties, the presence of these two men under one roof seemed to Barry to be a sign that there might be a flicker of hope for the future. It was a hope that the violence that had been done for centuries—and that could break out again in the name of that heavenly babe, the gentle Jesus meek and mild—would one day stop.

And it wasn't only the priest and the pastor who could get along. Barry saw rank upon rank of folding chairs that marched over a wooden-plank floor with a central aisle between the ranks.

Next Monday night those chairs would be filled with parents, grandparents, brothers, sisters, cousins, aunts, and uncles from both denominations. There'd be teachers from MacNeill Primary, the Protestant school that years ago had been endowed in the family name by an earlier Marquis of Ballybucklebo. They'd be sitting with the nuns who taught at the Catholic school attached to their convent of Our Lady of Perpetual Sorrows.

When would somebody wake up to the fact that one of the first steps to religious misunderstanding was to educate the children separately? Barry wondered.

He noticed Flo Bishop and Mrs. Brown sitting in the front row. Cissie Sloan sat between them. From back here he couldn't make out if Cissie was talking, but judging by the way her companions seemed to be listening to nothing but the music, perhaps she was, for once, resting her jaws.

"*Good-will henceforth from heaven to men Begin, and never ceeee-ease.*"

The conductor turned. Barry's eyes widened. He couldn't make out her features clearly, but she seemed to have an oval face and, as best he could determine, green eyes. He tried to get a better view by leaning forward, but soon he was aware that O'Reilly was saying something. He turned so he could hear.

"It's a good thing, goodwill," O'Reilly said sotto voce. "Mind you, I'm finding it hard to go heavy on the goodwill when it comes to Fitzpatrick." He sighed, "Still, it is Christmas, I suppose."

Clearly O'Reilly was still stewing over how to deal with the man. Barry said, "I agree," but he didn't think O'Reilly heard him. At that moment Father O'Toole called out, "Very good, children. Very good," and stood to applaud. When he stopped clapping, the priest said, "Now everybody run along, and we'll have a wee small break while the actors in the Nativity play get ready."

The children trooped off stage right. Barry recognized Colin Brown. As usual, one of his socks was at half-mast, halfway down his shin and crumpled over his shoe. His mother rose and went through a door at the side of the stage.

"They're really rather good," said Reverend Robinson. "I always enjoy children's choirs." He waved down to Father O'Toole, who waved back. "I must have a word with Turloch." He started down the central aisle.

"And there wouldn't be a kiddies' choir or any Christmas pageant," O'Reilly said, "but for those two and their predecessors, priests and Presbyterian ministers. There aren't enough kids of each denomination to make up separate choirs, but together there are enough to make one." He fished out his pipe.

"Not long before I came here, the two churches got together and decided that just for that once, in the spirit of the season, they'd get the chisellers together for a carol evening. There was some opposition, but the Presbyterian elders, the more Christian ones, managed to persuade their congregation to give it a try, and more power to their wheels, I say. When the service was over, everyone had enjoyed it so much that it was decided to make it an annual event."

"Why? Why would they do a sensible thing like that?" Barry frowned. "It seems unbelievable. Ireland's been divided for hundreds of years."

O'Reilly's voice suddenly became wistful. "Do you know what happened in nineteen forty-one? At Easter?"

Barry shook his head. "I was only six months old."

"The Luftwaffe bombed Belfast."

Jesus. Barry suddenly remembered Kinky telling him that O'Reilly's young wife had been killed in those air raids. "That's terrible, Fingal."

"Aye," O'Reilly said and looked away. Barry heard him sniff. When he turned back, his eyes glittered. He was sucking his unlit pipe, much, Barry thought, as a baby sucks its dummy tit.

O'Reilly continued, "Thousands of people were evacuated to the countryside. All over Ulster the barriers came down. Catholics sheltered Protestants and vice versa. A group of Catholics came to Ballybucklebo. It didn't matter. Everyone helped. Some of the evacuees were billeted in the Orange Lodge. When Christmas came, the priest of the time, Father Moynihan, wanted to have a carol service of thanksgiving, and he approached the minister, a Mr. Holmes . . ."

"That's wonderful." Barry felt a little lump in his throat. He abhorred sectarian violence and to hear O'Reilly's words had moved him deeply. "Thank you for telling me, Fingal." Barry knew how horribly that blitz had affected the big man.

O'Reilly shrugged. "The next year somebody suggested that, in for a penny, in for a pound, they'd go the whole hog and have a pageant, carols, Nativity play, and all. The two churches have taken it in turns year about to host the pageant ever since."

"That's marvellous."

"I think," said O'Reilly, shoving his pipe back in his pocket, "it's what the fellah who had his birthday at Christmas would have wanted. It's certainly why"—he pointed to the front row—"you'll see Father O'Toole and Mr. Robinson with their heads together and the wife of Bertie Bishop, worshipful master of the local Orange Lodge, sitting in a Catholic chapel hall happily chatting to Cissie Sloan, this year's secretary of the Ballybucklebo branch of the Catholic Women's League."

Barry looked. By the way Cissie's jaw was working, Flo wasn't so much being talked to as talked at. He laughed. "We came to see Cissie—"

"Aye," said O'Reilly, starting to stride down the aisle. "We did."

Barry followed. He noticed a beautifully wrought crèche that stood at the right side, and above the stage an engraved wooden arc announced: "Peace on Earth. Good will to all men." It must be a prop trotted out year after year, Barry thought.

"Hello, Flo. Cissie," O'Reilly said. "Grand to see you both."

The ladies, obviously deep in conversation, nodded back before turning to each other again.

Father O'Toole turned from his conversation with Mr. Robinson and held out his hand to O'Reilly, who shook it; then the priest offered his hand to Barry. "And what brings you two men of healing here today?"

"Cissie Sloan," said O'Reilly. "She wanted us to see how the preparations are coming along."

"She and the other ladies have done a marvellous job. The decorating's all done, so, and the choir is well rehearsed. The set needs to be painted and the play needs a bit more rehearsing, but Miss Nolan, bless her, is working like a Trojan. Here she comes now."

Barry could get a decent look at her. She was petite and slim, but well contoured beneath her white open-necked blouse. Her eyes, widely set above a snub nose, were hauntingly green. She walked with the erect fluidity of a catwalk model but without the exaggerated stride.

"Miss Susan Nolan," said the priest, "I'd like you to meet Doctor O'Reilly and Doctor Laverty."

The young teacher held her hands demurely in front of her skirt and inclined her head to O'Reilly and then to Barry. "I am pleased to meet you, gentlemen," she said. Her voice was soft, musical, and Barry thought he heard a hint of the distinctive County Antrim accent with its lengthened vowels. "Please call me Sue."

It was as far as she got.

Cissie had risen and invited herself into the conversation. "Begod, saving your presence, Father, it's a delight to see you both, Doctors dear."

Barry nodded to her.

"And how do you like the hall? I think it's decorated to perfection, and the stage set is nearly built—"

"I can see that," O'Reilly said. "Who's doing the—"

Barry wasn't sure if O'Reilly was going to say "carpentry" or "painting."

"Aye," Cissie said. "The backdrop, it's just roughed in now. It'll be the stalls at the back of a stable. Sammy McCoubrey, him that's a house painter by trade, is going to do animals' heads, a horse, and a couple of oxen hanging over stable half doors. Stage left'll be the front door to an inn." She nudged O'Reilly and said conspiratorially. "He'll do a big sign to go over the door, so he will. It'll say, Bethlehem Inn, in capital letters . . ."—Barry thought she sounded as if she was speaking in capitals—"for the sake of the slow-to-recognize-things brigade. There's one or two about, you know."

"I'm sure it will be wonderful, Cissie," O'Reilly said. "Wonderful."

If Fingal had been hoping to slow her down, Barry thought, Fingal might as well have chucked a few pebbles in the torrent from a recently breached dam.

"I was just telling Aggie . . . her backside's better now since her fall on the frozen milk . . . I was just saying to Aggie . . ."

Barry, who was still eyeing the teacher, caught her eye and mouthed silently, "My cousin with the six toes," in unison with Cissie. He was rewarded with a lovely smile, and he guessed Sue Nolan had already heard of the famous cousin.

"I was just telling her that this year's pageant'll be the best ever. Did you like the choir?" Cissie asked. "I think they're cracker, so they are. They do 'Scarlet Ribbons for Her Hair' a treat . . ."

"And I don't think they should do it at all." Flo Bishop stood foursquare, arms folded across her chest. "It's not a carol, so it's not. What do you think, Doctor O'Reilly? I know you approve, Father. It'd not be in the program if you didn't. I like it right enough, but it's not a carol and I think it should be carols only."

This could be interesting, Barry thought. Would a medical degree trump ordination in the Catholic Church on what seemed to be an ecclesiastical matter?

He wasn't given a chance to find out. Before O'Reilly could answer, Cissie bored on. "Aye, but it's lovely. The way your man Harry Belly Fronty done it would bring tears to a stone . . . wee girl not getting nothing for Christmas because her daddy was too poor . . ."

Barry well remembered Harry Belafonte's version, which had been released in 1956. He'd still been a schoolboy. Back then he'd never dreamed that he'd be a country GP with a senior colleague, a Doctor Fingal O'Reilly, who would be helping to provide presents for the children of a needy mother.

Cissie flowed on, with the force of a tsunami. "Him and his calypsos too. 'Day-o, Day-o, daylight come . . .' "

Barry saw Miss Nolan's lips moving and heard a soft sweet soprano. " 'And me wan' go home.' " She inclined her head to one side. He followed her along one of the rows between chairs until Cissie's voice was a muted muttering.

Susan Nolan turned, and he saw a look of sympathetic amusement on her face. It wasn't quite a smile, but the corners of her eyes creased and her nose wrinkled. It was most attractive.

"Thank you," he said.

"Cissie has a heart of corn, but she does go on, and she's been here at every rehearsal. I've listened to her a lot, and by the look on your face you've heard her in full flight too. I thought you could use a break."

"You were right." Barry laughed. "Oh, were you right. I know Cissie well. I think she was vaccinated with a gramophone needle."

He was gratified when Sue Nolan laughed. She'd probably heard the old chestnut before, but she was gracious enough to pretend she found it funny. He liked that. It was amazing how easily she had made him, a lad who was notoriously awkward with women, feel so at ease. "So," he asked, "how long have you been teaching here, Sue?"

"Since I finished at Stranmillis teacher-training college two years ago. I come from Broughshane in County Antrim . . ." So he'd been right about her accent. "It's a small place too. I like the country and I love it here. The children seem to want to learn and are so obedient."

"All of them?"

She laughed again. "Weeeelll, most of them. One or two . . ." She rocked her outstretched hand from side to side.

He noticed how slim her fingers were and that she wore no ring on her left hand. He knew its absence shouldn't be of any interest to him, but it was.

She raised her right eyebrow almost imperceptibly. "You know what boys are like."

"Boys like Colin Brown?"

Her chuckle was like very deep, warm chocolate. "Doctor Laverty, that would be breaching a professional confidence."

He leant closer to her and was aware of a subtle perfume. He lowered his voice. "Not from one professional to another."

She looked directly into his eyes and held his gaze for perhaps a second too long. "I suppose we could share secrets . . . professionally, of course." Laugh lines ran out from the corners of her remarkable green eyes.

Barry swallowed. He knew his pulse rate had quickened. "Indeed." Perhaps, he thought, I should get back to safer small talk. "And do you live in Ballybucklebo? I haven't seen you about the place." If I had, I would have remembered, he thought. She really was quite stunning.

"No," she said. "In term time I board in Holywood and take the train."

"That's only a couple of stops up the line," he said. "Not much of a commute." But there were good GPs in Holywood, so she'd be unlikely ever to be one of his patients.

"Where do you live in the holidays?"

"With my parents on their farm. The Glens of Antrim are quite close by. It's such a beautiful area . . ."

Barry had heard of the Glens, a high plateau scored by wooded glens and glacial green valleys that swept down to the sea. A friend of his at school had even hinted that there was something mystical about the place. It certainly had its share of ancient sites. He'd always meant to visit them.

"I've never been there, but I've been told it's lovely."

Sue Nolan looked at him intently, as if gauging his sincerity. Then she dropped her gaze to the floor and said carefully, "I'd be happy to show you round, although I'll be staying in Holywood until after the pageant."

Barry wished she would look up again so he could

see her eyes. Was this just a polite, seasonal invitation? People were always more hospitable at this time of year. Still, she was definitely not one of his patients, so there was no professional reason not to ask her out. And he seemed sure she was telling him she'd be amenable to such a suggestion.

He chided himself for even thinking such a thing, but she really was lovely. And damn it, he was a healthy young man, not a monk in holy orders. It hadn't been much of a struggle to say a chaste good-night to Peggy after the nurses' dance, but this Sue Nolan was different. It was a bloody good thing Kinky was so sure Patricia was coming home soon. And yet what if she didn't? Or what if she did and, perish the thought, had cooled toward him?

Barry pursed his lips, took a deep breath, and looked Sue directly in the eye. "I might just take you up on that one day . . . to have you show me the Glens. But right now the practice is very busy, and I'll only be getting a couple of days off."

She inclined her head. "Anytime. But right now I'm going to be busy too," she said, as she turned to glance at the stage where children were beginning to take their places. "I'd like to stay and blether," she said, "but it's time to start the rehearsal."

"Nice to have met you, Sue," Barry said. "I enjoyed our chat."

"My pleasure. Perhaps we can do it again one day, just not when we're working." She patted his arm, turned, and started to walk away.

He inwardly cursed himself for being too stupid to

ask for her telephone number. Then he remembered he would be seeing her again at the actual pageant, and he relaxed. There would be another chance to get the lovely Miss Nolan alone for a cosy chat if he felt so inclined—and to get her phone number. Just having it didn't mean he was going to use it, did it? He followed her back along the row to where Father O'Toole and Doctor O'Reilly seemed to be speaking to Flo Bishop and Cissie. But it soon became apparent that they were *listening* to Cissie.

"Are youse not staying for the rehearsal, Doctor O'Reilly? It's very good you know. Jeannie Kennedy's a great Mary, and . . . What?" She turned because a voice from the stage had called her name.

O'Reilly leapt into the breach with the force of a storming party. "Sorry we have to run on, Cissie . . . Flo. We're mightily impressed, aren't we, Barry?"

"Absolutely."

"Thank you, Doctor," Flo said, perhaps a little huffily, Barry thought. "And I still think you're wrong, sir. If we let 'Scarlet Ribbons' in this year, what'll it be next year? 'Rockin' Around the Christmas Tree,' for God's sake?" She blushed. "Sorry, Father."

"No apology needed," said Father O'Toole. "I don't mind including the occasional secular song if it's tastefully done, but there is a limit."

Barry hid his grin. So, O'Reilly must have decided that in a theological tussle with Father O'Toole, discretion was the better part of valour. Cissie one, Flo nil, in the great carol debate.

O'Reilly looked at Barry, nodded toward the exit, and started to walk along the aisle. Barry followed. When he was halfway to the door, the houselights were dimmed, and the stage lighting took over. Barry paused and turned.

He could see three children on the stage. A boy held a little girl by the hand. A second boy—Barry recognized Colin Brown—stood in the open doorway. So this must be Mary and Joseph. Barry recognized the little girl, Jeannie Kennedy. She'd had appendicitis in July. The boy was not someone he knew—not yet, anyway. Sooner or later he knew that like O'Reilly he'd meet everyone here.

The actors started saying their lines.

"Hello, Innkeeper."

"Who's there?"

"It's Mary and Joseph. We've come to be taxed."

Barry wondered, given the universal hatred of Ulster farmers for the Inland Revenue service, if that line might inadvertently cause a certain amount of muttering from the audience on the big night.

"Mary and Joseph?"

"Could we have a bed for the night? My wife's having a baby, and she's very tired."

"Well, the inn's full, but you can go into the stable." Colin's voice was calm and welcoming.

Barry chuckled. It wasn't quite the line Colin had said he was to use. Perhaps Sue Nolan had done a bit of a rewrite. Colin had delivered it well, so he must have recovered from his disappointment over not playing

Joseph. Oil must have been been poured on the troubled waters. Barry caught up with O'Reilly, and together they stepped out into the teeth of the gale.

"Jesus," said O'Reilly, "it's cold as a witch's tit. I'd fancy a hot whiskey, and I know Arthur'd enjoy a Smithwick's. Will we pop into the Duck on the way home?"

"Why not?"

"Just one then," said O'Reilly, "and in case you think I've forgotten, I haven't. When we get home, I'll phone Fitzpatrick. Arrange to see him." He turned up the collar of his coat. "And in the spirit of the season, I *might* even soften toward him a bit if he agrees to lay off picking on Kinky and recognizes how valuable Miss Hagerty can be. I'd not mind an apology from him either."

"What if you don't get what you want?"

O'Reilly's face darkened. "In that case I might just use one of his own prescriptions on him."

"Primrose root?" Barry chuckled.

"Not at all. Gunpowder."

Barry, knowing firsthand how short O'Reilly's fuse could be, felt a twinge of sympathy for Doctor Ronald Hercules Fitzpatrick.

33

Make Thick My Blood

"Will you come with me please, Miss Moloney?" Barry turned and walked back to the surgery, assuming that his patient was following. He wasn't looking forward to this consultation. When he'd first met her in August, Miss Moloney had struck him as acerbic and rude. She'd certainly terrorized her shop assistants, Helen Hewitt and Mary Dunleavy. And when he'd tried to suggest she might not be so ruthless with her girls, she had told him in no uncertain terms to mind his own business.

O'Reilly had once remarked that not all doctors and patients were perfect fits. He'd suggested that if Barry felt antipathy to anyone, it would be better for them both if he advised the customer to seek medical advice elsewhere. Perhaps he should consider that in this case. Of course, between Ballybucklebo and the Kinnegar, Miss Moloney's choices were a bit limited.

Barry wondered if Miss Moloney's acidity and Doctor Fitzpatrick's arrogance would make for a better match. Then he quickly dismissed the thought. He might not like the woman, but that was no reason to subject her to the dubious doctoring of Ronald Hercules Fitzpatrick. Like her or not, he would do his medical best for her.

"And how are you feeling today?" he asked, as he and Miss Moloney walked down the hall.

"I'm still very tired, Doctor," she said. Her voice, normally sharp and harsh, was quavery. He noticed how pale she looked. "I've no energy. I'm just not at myself at all, and I get short of breath."

He closed the door, waited for her to sit, then took O'Reilly's swivel chair. Barry was comfortable trying to fill it, at least figuratively; he knew he'd never have the physical bulk to fill it. He turned to the desk and picked up the laboratory report that had been delivered in yesterday's post. "I have your results here."

Miss Moloney shrugged. "I suppose you'd better tell me." She was listless and seemed to be uninterested. She stared at the carpet. "I hope it's nothing serious."

Something in the tone of her voice when she said "serious" belied her apparent lack of interest. Miss Moloney was scared. Barry frowned. He'd like to be able to reassure her at once, but even though he'd scanned the laboratory values and knew his diagnosis of anaemia was correct, until he knew the underlying cause he was in no position to comfort her.

At least not if he were to be honest. But did he need to be brutally frank? He hadn't been so at her first visit. It wouldn't hurt to prolong the deception a little longer. Barry smiled at her. "You're anaemic, Miss Moloney. Thin-blooded," he said. "That's why you're not 'at yourself.' " He leant forward. "The lab report shows nothing else wrong with your blood. It's just anaemia, and that's not very serious."

"But . . . but there is something wrong . . . with my blood?" She sat hunched in the chair and would not meet his gaze.

Perhaps if he told her she didn't have one of the lethal blood diseases, it would give her more reassurance. He smiled. "Yes, but it's not anything nasty like leukaemia. That also thins the blood."

"Leukaemia? Oh my heavens." This time she looked at Barry intently, and as she did her lip trembled and a tear ran down her cheek.

Good God, what had he said? Think, man. Say something. "No, no, Miss Moloney. There is no question of leukaemia. You have simple anaemia. I promise," he said, wishing he'd never mentioned the blood cancer.

Her fingers picked aimlessly at the fringe on the patterned wool shawl she wore over her grey coat. She sniffed, wiped her eyes with the back of one hand, and made an effort to sit straight. Then, hauling in a deep breath, she said quietly, "I'm sorry. I shouldn't have got so upset."

"It's all right, Miss Moloney. It really is." Barry looked as deeply as he could into her eyes. This was a very different woman from the termagant he'd met in August. He couldn't help but feel sorry for her. He lifted the report from the desk. "Would you like me to explain all of this to you, Miss Moloney?" he asked, hoping she'd say no. She was in no state to understand terms like "mean corpuscular haemoglobin concentration," "mean corpuscular volume," or "mean corpuscular diameter."

She shook her head. "I trust you, Doctor Laverty."

"Thank you." Barry felt warmed by her words.

"And," she said, "Miss Moloney's very formal. My name is Alice."

"Alice. That's a pretty name."

"Thank you," she said with a little sigh, "but apart from my sister in Millisle, nobody uses it anymore." She smiled at him. "I'd like you to, Doctor."

"Of course . . . Alice." And he thought if that wasn't an indication of her accepting him, he didn't know what would be. It pleased him. "Now"—he held the report so she could see—"I won't explain everything because there are all kinds of numbers here, but really only two matter. That one, the haemoglobin, is 12.2. It should be 14.8, and that one of 39 is very low too. It's called the haematocrit. It should be at least 42."

She craned forward to see. "And what do they mean?"

"They mean, Alice, that your blood is too thin because you are short of iron. Because your blood is thin, you get short of breath because the blood carries the oxygen you breathe to all of the body."

"I see," she said with a little frown. "Interesting."

Barry took her hand and held it in his palm with the back of hers facing upward. It was chill to his touch. He pointed to her spoon-shaped nails. "That's called koilonychia. It's due to iron lack too."

"I see." She took her hand away. She cocked her head to one side. "And why would I be short of iron?"

Barry tried not to frown. This was the bit where his prevaricating about whether she was seriously ill would be put to the test. It pleased him that she was so willing to trust him. He didn't want to lose that trust. He knew he had to be honest now. He took her hand again and bent toward her. "I'm not sure." He met her gaze with his and sensed she was strong enough to deal with uncertainty.

"Oh. Could it be serious?"

Don't lie now, Barry, he told himself. "Yes, Miss Molo . . . I mean Alice . . . yes, it could, but ninety-nine times out of one hundred, it isn't."

"I see." For the second time, she took her hand away and folded it into the other in her lap. "Thank you for being honest, Doctor Laverty. Not every doctor would have been. I know that." Her lip trembled again.

He congratulated himself for judging her correctly. Some physician has hurt her, Barry thought, wondering if she too could be one of Fitzpatrick's victims.

She sat stiffly. "I suppose you do know how to find out what's wrong?"

"Of course."

She pursed her lips. "Then let's get on with it."

"All right. It's not hard. I need to ask you a few questions, examine you today, and perhaps arrange an X-ray."

"What kind of questions?"

Barry put the form back on the desk. "You can be

short of iron either because you're not eating enough of it or you're losing blood. My job is to find out which one it is."

Her mouth opened in a silent "o." She frowned, then nodded as if agreeing with herself. "I see. Ask away then."

"Doctor O'Reilly told me he'd treated you for piles once." Barry was pleased he had remembered that detail.

"About three years ago. Nasty things." She curled her lip. "Itchy, very itchy, but Doctor O'Reilly gave me ointment and laxatives, and I've had no trouble since."

"Good." It sounded as if she had been afflicted with external haemorrhoids. Their apparent cure did not exclude the possibility of varicosity of the rectal vessels inside. He'd have a good look when he examined her. "You told me last time you were here that you are fifty-one."

"Yes. I'll be fifty-two in January."

She might not be menopausal yet, might be having heavy periods. Barry was about to ask, but a tiny alarm was telling him to wait, to ask first about matters that would not embarrass her. Older countrywomen, he had learned, could be reticent about discussing "female" symptoms. "Do you like your grub?" She certainly was a skinny woman.

"I like it well enough. I've three square a day, but small portions. I'm not a big eater. I live on my own—well, me and my cat and budgerigar—so I've no one to cook for." Barry could hear the resignation in her voice. Perhaps her loneliness explained why she had been so vicious with her staff of pretty, marriageable young girls. "Seeing it's just me, I can eat what I please," she continued. "I don't like eggs or green vegetables," she said. "I don't eat red meat, but I like fish and chicken."

"I see." So, Barry thought, she didn't eat enough of the three main dietary sources of iron, and what she did eat most likely provided insufficient iron. "And how long have you been using that diet?"

"Since I was a very young woman . . . in India."

"India? I didn't know you'd been there." Miss Alice Moloney, owner of a tiny dress shop in Ballybucklebo, had been to India?

"Oh, yes," she said. "Daddy took the whole family there in nineteen thirty-two. I was nineteen."

This was intriguing. "And what did your father do there?"

"He was with the Indian civil service. In Calcutta. They kept him on after independence in nineteen forty-seven." Her lips trembled again. "My sister and I had been born in Ballybucklebo, and she and I came back to Ireland after . . ."—her hand shook—". . . after he was killed in the Hindu Moslem riots in nineteen forty-eight."

Ulster is not the only place to be racked by religious strife, Barry thought.

She pursed her lips and forced a weak smile. "But it was a wonderful place for a girl to live. We had a huge bungalow, ponies, dances with the handsome young white subalterns in the Indian army . . ."

Barry for a moment wondered why she hadn't married one. Perhaps she had been in love, but her young lieutenant had been posted far away and they had drifted. It could happen. He gritted his teeth; he should know.

She was still reminiscing. "We had summers in the hills, servants galore . . ."

Which might account for the way she had treated Helen and Mary.

She looked away into the middle distance, and Barry wondered if she was seeing the Maidan or scenting the mudflats of the Hugli River. As a boy he'd loved the works of Rudyard Kipling.

"I loved India. Have you ever seen an elephant?"

"Well, yes, there was one called Sarah in the Dublin Zoo in Phoenix Park. And I've seen them at the circus."

She snorted. "Poor creatures. I meant a ceremonial animal splendidly caparisoned, with a howdah on its back and a mahout—that's the driver—sitting just behind its head."

"I'm afraid not. I've not been very far from Ireland."

Not even as far as Cambridge.

"You must travel, young man. Find out about other peoples. I thought the Hindus were fascinating." She giggled. "You'll probably think it's silly, but I even learned a bit of yoga. I used to be able to sit in the lotus position."

"I don't see anything silly about it."

"Thank you. There's a lot the East could teach the West. I've read a lot of Vedic philosophy in their texts, the Upanishads . . ."

Barry was embarrassed, not by her confession, but by how badly, after two very short encounters, he had misjudged Alice Moloney.

"And I found the idea of not eating meat very appealing. Even to this day I can't eat beef. Cows are sacred in India, you know. As I said, I'm not a big fan of green vegetables, but I do eat carrots and parsnips."

"I see." It was almost certainly the answer. How interesting, India. Vegetarianism. It certainly added up. Barry was tempted to call a halt there and then, but to do so would be to neglect his responsibility to her.

She could be losing blood either from heavy periods or, more ominously, from one of a number of disorders of the stomach and bowel—disorders that included cancer. He ploughed on. "Have you been having an upset tummy? Pain when you eat or after you eat? Have you thrown up any blood?" All symptoms of gastritis or an ulcer in the stomach or duodenum.

"No." She shook her head. "Nothing like that."

"Have you noticed any pain in your lower belly, change in your bowel habits, diarrhea, any black motions, any red blood?" Black stools, called melaena, were a sign of stomach or bowel bleeding high in the system. Red blood would come from lower. Piles, diverticulitis, ulcerative colitis, Crohn's disease, benign polyps, and more worryingly, cancer of the bowel could all produce those symptoms.

"I've no pains, and I don't think there's anything wrong with my motions. Mind you, I don't look very often."

"Not many people do, but I have to ask." Her

answers still didn't rule out a condition that was painless, like an early cancer.

"I understand, Doctor. What else do you want to know?"

Barry swallowed, coughed, and then asked, "What about your periods?"

She shrugged. "They were never heavy, if that's what you mean. They stopped about three years ago . . . good riddance to bad rubbish, if you ask me." She leant forward and put a hand on Barry's knee. "Now I have the hot flushes."

Barry did not want to complicate matters at this visit, so he made a mental note to have a chat with her about using small doses of ethinyl oestradiol to control her flushes. At the moment, however, her anaemia took priority. He looked straight at her and said, "If you've had no trouble with your periods, and they're not coming anymore, we can't blame them for you losing blood. That leaves only two possible causes for your iron deficiency."

"And what are they?"

"My best guess is that you're not eating the right things."

"I suppose."

He didn't want to worry her, yet he didn't like to be dishonest. "You could have something in your bowel."

She looked him straight in the eye. "Like cancer?"

It was something in her voice that made him ask, "You really do worry about cancer, don't you, Alice?"

"I should. I have good reason to."

Barry waited. She'd tell him if she wanted to.

"The word is that you're in love, Doctor."

He wanted to deny it, but he could already feel the heat in his face. And this interview seemed to be all about telling the truth. "I am." Bloody rumour mill. He loved Ballybucklebo, but there were some disadvantages to living here.

"I was once." The same dreamy look she'd had when she spoke of India flitted across her face. "He was a captain with Skinner's Horse. It was a famous cavalry regiment." The look faded, and her eyes glinted as she said, "His doctors lied to him."

"I'm sorry."

"They did. They told us he'd get better." She took a very deep breath. "He died."

"I am truly sorry, Alice." What a trite thing to say.

"Do you know what he died of?"

Barry shook his head.

"Leukaemia."

"My God." No wonder she'd reacted the way she had done. And no wonder she was concerned about cancer. Thank the Lord he'd been honest, and he would be honest again right now.

"Alice, I can't tell you that you don't have cancer. Not until all the tests are done, and for starters I'll need to examine you, feel your tummy for lumps, and do a rectal examination."

She curled her lip. "I hate those, but I suppose it's necessary."

"I'm afraid it is."

She rose, left her shawl and coat on the chair, and

headed for the screened examining table. "We'd better get it over with."

Barry examined her abdominally and rectally without finding anything. By the time he had stripped off his rubber glove, washed his hands, and written a prescription for ferrous sulphate, Alice Moloney was already dressed and standing by the chair. Barry also stood.

"Well, Doctor Laverty?"

Barry shook his head. "I can't find anything, Alice."

"You mentioned an X-ray?"

"A barium enema."

"Should I have one?"

"Yes. I'll arrange it. I'll try to get it done before Christmas."

"I'd appreciate that."

"Have you a phone at the shop?"

"No. I have one upstairs. I live over the place."

"Are you usually in at night?"

She made a wry face. "Where else would I be?"

Barry felt her loneliness, and now, having heard her story, he could understand its depth. He wondered what she had been like as a young woman in India. Probably just as vivacious and mischievous as Helen Hewitt was today. Perhaps everything that had happened in Calcutta accounted for Alice Moloney's antipathy to young girls. He could hardly blame her if she had a bitter streak. He sighed and put his hand on her shoulder. "I'm beginning to understand. Thank you for telling me your story, Alice."

"Thank you for listening, Doctor."

"All right. I'll have to phone the Royal, make an appointment for you."

"Would you?" She put on her coat.

"Of course."

"That's very kind." She flung her shawl around her shoulders.

"And here," Barry said, handing her a prescription, "take one of these every day. They're iron pills. They should have you right as rain in about two to three months."

"If there's nothing more serious," she said, then shrugged. "But I suppose we'll know that soon."

"We will." Barry opened the door for her. "I'll be on the phone in a minute. It might take a while to make the arrangements, so you go home now and I will phone tonight." He accompanied her into the hall.

He barely heard her thank-you because he was already dialing the number of the radiology department at the Royal Victoria Hospital. She was in luck. There'd been a cancellation for Thursday morning. If Barry could give his patient the pretest instructions and tell her to go to the department by ten A.M., Alice would have her test at eleven. He'd get a report by Friday. He'd phone her tonight and tell her he'd pop in on Saturday to give her the results. The less time she had to worry, the better.

He was humming tunelessly to himself when he replaced the receiver. Strange, he thought, before Alice had sat down, he'd already decided he did not like the woman. Now, having heard her story, he thought he understood her a lot better, and he could feel a great deal of sympathy for her spinsterhood. Life hadn't been easy on Alice Moloney. Not one bit.

Barry went into the dining room, where O'Reilly was in his usual place hiding behind the *Irish Times*. He put the newspaper down and greeted Barry. "I see there's to be a free vote in the British House of Commons on the twenty-first."

Barry took his customary seat. "What about?"

"To abolish the death penalty."

"I'd be in favour of that," Barry said.

"So would I," said O'Reilly, "with one possible exception. And the law will still be in effect this afternoon." He smiled at Barry to show he was only joking—at least Barry hoped Fingal was joking.

"I take it," said Barry, helping himself to a freshly baked roll and spreading it with butter. "I take it you are referring to Doctor Ronald Hercules Fitzpatrick."

"None other," said O'Reilly. "Pass the rolls." He took three. "We're seeing him at his surgery in the Kinnegar at two."

34

I Do Like to Be Beside the Seaside

Barry got out of the Rover close to a low granite-block seawall. He heard water lapping at its base. The tide was in. Drying clumps of bladder wrack, their serrated fronds studded with air sacs that gave the seaweed its name, kept company with the flat broad leaves of kelp drying on the wall's coping stones and on the gravel of the Kinnegar car park.

Boots crunched on the loose stones as O'Reilly walked around the car to join Barry. "Would you look at that?" O'Reilly was pointing to a leathery pouch with tendrils that spiraled from its corners and twined around a piece of kelp. "It's the egg sac of a dogfish."

"The locals call it a mermaid's purse," Barry said. "Yesterday's gale chucked it in here with all the other debris." He inhaled the salty scent, which he knew came not from the tide itself but from the beached seaweed already starting to decay.

He stared out to sea. The Lough was somnolent today, peacefully reflecting the blue of the arch of the sky. It was definitely the calm after the storm, but because they were on their way to beard Fitzpatrick, Barry wondered if it was also the calm *before* the storm.

He glanced back to where O'Reilly stood gazing

out over the water. "Look at that ferry," he said, "'butting through the Channel in the mad March days.'"

The boat was ploughing purposely to Belfast along the dredged and buoyed fairway in mid-lough. It reminded him of a coal boat he'd seen one day making its way to Bangor Harbour. He'd taken Patricia for a walk on the coastal path near Strickland's Glen on one of their first dates, and the wind had torn the smoke from the collier's stack to tatters and made Patricia's ponytail merrily dance and swing.

"It's John Masefield, by the way, and I do know it's December, not March," O'Reilly said. "I thought you'd be quicker off the mark to tell me."

"The poem is 'Cargoes,'" Barry said. He hadn't been interested in playing Name that Quotation. Not today. "Sorry, Fingal. Seeing the boat made me think about something else."

"Or someone else?" O'Reilly's voice was soft.

Barry nodded. "Patricia's going to try to get onto a ferry from England. At least I hope she is."

"Never worry. She will. Kinky's *never* wrong." O'Reilly had a very confident look on his face. "She could teach your man in Rome a thing or two about infallibility."

Barry had to smile. He felt somehow comforted. "Thanks, Fingal," he said, and he promised himself he would try to stop worrying. Not wanting to talk further, he turned resolutely back to the sea, looked past the vessel and over to the far side where the Antrim Hills rose dark and purple. A line of white edged their crests like a thin layer of Kinky's royal icing.

Close to the near shore a cormorant was perched on a black creosoted post that rose from its own mirrored reflection. The bird stretched its long snakelike neck and spread its wings wide to dry in the rays of the winter sun.

A screeching flock of terns, black skull-capped and swallow-tailed, milled around in the sky and, diving like members of a Stuka squadron, plummeted to the calm surface. So clean was each bird's entry that Barry couldn't hear any splashes.

"Stewing over it won't bring her here any quicker." O'Reilly's voice was gentle. He had clearly understood Barry's mood.

"I know, Fingal, and I wasn't worrying . . . well, not much. Honestly. I was enjoying the Lough. It's always been a special place to me. I grew up beside it. My folks' house in Bangor was on a little peninsula. I'd often go and sit on the shore when I wanted a bit of peace and quiet."

O'Reilly stooped at Barry's shoulder. He straightened up, holding a smooth pebble. He looked at Barry, then nodded. "I know what you mean. I think everybody has a special place, what Ernest Hemingway called a *querencia*."

"A what?"

"Every bull in a bullfight will find a place in the bullring where he feels safe, secure. He'll retreat to it when he can to escape from his tormentors. I don't think there's an English word that's quite as effective as *querencia*."

"Sanctuary?"

"Maybe, but I prefer the Spanish." He lowered his voice and said levelly, "Mine's across the Ards Peninsula. Strangford Lough. I go there if I feel a bit tormented. And now you're here, my boy, I can go there more often because I know the practice is in good hands."

Barry swallowed. "Thank you, Fingal." He was thanking O'Reilly more for the confidence than the compliment. Kitty had said O'Reilly was a hard man to get to know, and he had surprised Barry by opening himself up a little.

"I'll be taking Arthur there on Saturday. I could use a break. I'm really looking forward to it," O'Reilly said. Then, as if embarrassed at having confessed to needing some respite like any other mortal, he continued, "But that's Saturday. We've other work for today. Fitzpatrick's expecting us at two." He hurled the pebble out into the Lough. "Come on." He strode out of the car park and turned right along the Esplanade.

Barry kept pace. "What are you going to say to him?"

O'Reilly stopped. "I suppose I'll try to appeal to his better nature. If he has one. Which I doubt. I'm not quite sure how to start, but on the old *Warspite* the gunnery officer was under standing orders to keep an eye out for targets of opportunity."

"I don't understand."

"It was the navy's answer to Mr. Micawber. If you kept your eyes open, something to shoot at often turned up, even when you didn't expect it."

"You mean you'll play it by ear until Fitzpatrick gives you a lead?"

"I think so. I want to put him on the defensive. I remember when we were students one of the things I disliked about the man was that he was a bully. He was forever picking on junior medical students and student nurses. He even tried to bully Kinky."

"Not an endearing trait."

"There is one thing about bullies . . ."

"They don't like it when someone challenges them, like Kinky did."

O'Reilly laughed. "It's a braver man than I who'll take on Kinky when she gets her dander up. She'll stand up to anyone."

And if anybody else can stand up, it's Fingal Flahertie O'Reilly, Barry thought.

"And Barry, you know I don't like the man, I grant you that, but this is not personal. I was on a very sticky wicket with that breech, and it needn't have happened at all but for his arrogance. He'd bullied Miss Hagerty." O'Reilly's brow furrowed. His eyebrows met. His eyes narrowed and flashed. His nose tip paled. "He needs to practice better medicine. That man needs to be taken down a peg or two."

"I agree." He looked at Fingal's face and tried to measure the depth of his anger. Good heavens, he realized, I think I'm starting to feel sorry for Fitzpatrick.

"And another thing, Barry."

"Yes?"

"When I talk about me and the breech, *I* don't

really matter. It's our job. I managed, but both the mother and child were in unnecessary danger. I can't forgive *that*."

"I understand, Fingal." Barry shuddered. "It's a bloody good thing you were on call that night. I've read the theory, but I've never delivered a breech. They only occur in three percent of term pregnancies. I don't know what I would have done if I'd been there."

O'Reilly clapped Barry on the shoulder. "You'd have coped, son. You've a good pair of hands. I saw you deliver that face presentation in August."

Barry glowed at his senior's confidence.

He walked at O'Reilly's side as they turned a corner. "It's along here somewhere," O'Reilly said, peering as they passed at the numbers on a row of detached three-storey houses. "Ah, Number Nine," he said, stopping outside a stunted, ill-trimmed privet hedge. Beyond it stood a plaster-stuccoed house with paint peeling from the window frames. "The very spot. *Chez* Fitzpatrick." He strode through a gateless gap in the hedge. "Let's get this over with."

35

Chastise with the Valour of My Tongue

Barry read from a tarnished brass plate that was screwed to the wall.

Doctor R. H. Fitzpatrick, M.B., B.Ch., B.A.O.
Physician and Surgeon.
Surgery hours: 9 A.M. to noon, Monday
to Friday.

There was a bell push in the door frame.

"Now," said O'Reilly, "I'll do the talking, but if I ask for your advice—"

"I'll back you to the hilt."

"Good." O'Reilly shoved his finger against the button with sufficient force, Barry thought, to drive the whole fixture deeply into the wall. He could hear an electrical bell buzzing inside the house. O'Reilly did not remove his finger until the door was opened.

Fitzpatrick stood in the doorway. His pince-nez caught a ray of sunshine and flashed. His Adam's apple bobbed above his wing-tip collar as he said, "Fingal. Laverty. Do come in." He smiled with his narrow mouth, but his eyes were lifeless.

Barry followed O'Reilly into an ill-lit hall. A huge, ornately framed print of Sir Edwin Landseer's *Monarch of the Glen* hung slightly askew on one wall. The brown linoleum flooring was badly worn in places, and there was a distinct smell of floor polish.

"In here," Fitzpatrick said, opening the door to his surgery. Barry saw at once that the room was considerably smaller than O'Reilly's, and here too the floor was covered with brown linoleum. A leather-upholstered examining couch stood against a wall sheathed in paisley-patterned wallpaper. The couch was frayed at one corner, and its kapok stuffing leaked out. There was a hospital smell of stale disinfectant.

"My consulting room," said Fitzpatrick, with the pride of a duchess showing off her salon. "I rent it. I don't live here." He parked himself on a wing-backed chair behind a table that served as a desk. Both were on a platform that was six inches above the rest of the floor. He did not invite O'Reilly and Barry to take one of the three kitchen chairs arranged in a semicircle and facing the raised podium.

The floorboards creaked under Barry's feet as he moved off to the side so he could watch both men's faces.

"This is where my healing mission is accomplished," Fitzpatrick said smugly.

"There's a thing of beauty," said O'Reilly, "with every chance of being a joy forever. Healing mission, is it? And all I ever do is treat the customers."

Fitzpatrick sniffed. "We all have our own approaches to the art and science of medicine. I believe you said that was what you wanted to discuss, Fingal."

"Among other matters, Ronald. Among other

matters." O'Reilly moved past the row of kitchen chairs, stepped on the dais, and hitched one buttock onto the corner of the table so he faced Fitzpatrick. Had O'Reilly chosen to do so, he could have thrust his face up against the pince-nez.

Fitzpatrick leaned back, increasing the space between himself and O'Reilly.

Barry moved forward so he could see O'Reilly in profile. He at once recognized that his senior partner had reversed the psychological advantage Fitzpatrick would have had by being seated at a higher level than anyone else—usually his patients. Did Fitzpatrick bully his patients too? Barry wondered. Almost certainly.

O'Reilly was able to look down on his adversary. "Now," he said, pulling out his briar.

Barry waited to see how Fitzpatrick would respond. The first time they had met, he'd described smoking as a filthy habit.

"Don't you dare light that smelly thing in here," Fitzpatrick shouted. His Adam's apple bobbed.

"Sorry," O'Reilly said, putting the pipe back in his pocket. "Force of habit."

"And it's a foul one." Fitzpatrick wagged a finger at O'Reilly. "Foul."

"Och, well," said O'Reilly calmly. "We *all* have some strange habits. Even you, Ronald, I'd be prepared to bet."

Fitzpatrick lifted his pince-nez from his nose. "I beg your pardon?"

"Bet, Ronald. Bet. A wager between gentlemen. You've a *very* funny way of dealing with yours."

Barry had to admire how O'Reilly had taken that one word, "bet," to give himself the opportunity to begin to manoeuver. He waited to see how Fingal would develop the gambit and start putting Fitzpatrick on the defensive.

Fitzpatrick sat rigidly. "Are you perchance referring to our ten-pound interest in the outcome of the rugby match?"

"The very ticket," said O'Reilly calmly. "I waited for you for quite a while after my side had won the game, but you didn't show up."

"That was a matter of little import. I fail to see why a gentleman would be concerned." Fitzpatrick, sounding as though he was lecturing a dim pupil, slipped his glasses back on and lolled in his chair.

At the world "gentleman," Barry noticed O'Reilly's eyes narrow for a split second, but he gave no other indication of irritation.

"I saw no need to bother. Our side would have won, and *I* would have won but for your wretched dog. No rational person would have considered any bet still active after that."

There was another almost imperceptible eye narrowing, but O'Reilly's tones were honeyed, reasonable, when he said, "I grant you that. It was a bit naughty of Arthur. I'd have agreed with you and forgiven you the debt if you'd asked me . . . but it would have been polite to talk to me about it. Think about that, Ronald." O'Reilly leant back and waited.

So, Barry thought, Fingal's not going to blackmail Fitzpatrick by threatening to reveal that he had welshed on a bet, not yet anyway. But by the look on Fitzpatrick's face, he was worried about such a prospect.

O'Reilly leant forward and put his face close to Fitzpatrick's. With ice in his voice, he said, "But then, Ronald, manners never were your strong suit."

Barry sucked in a small breath through pursed lips and controlled his desire to smile. This was going to be worth the price of admission. Fitzpatrick was going to feel as if he had been put through a mangle by the time O'Reilly had finished with him, and Barry had a ringside seat.

Fitzpatrick jolted back in his chair. "What?" His voice rose by at least an octave. "How dare you, an oaf like you, O'Reilly . . . how *dare* you question my manners?"

"Because, Ronald, your manners, both social and bedside, badly need to be questioned." O'Reilly drew back an accusatory finger and levelled it at Fitzpatrick's breastbone. Barry thought Fingal was going to poke Fitzpatrick in the chest. Indeed, when O'Reilly repeated, "*Your . . . manners*," he jerked the finger forward and seemed only to stop its forward progress by an immense effort of will.

Fitzpatrick must have thought he was going to get prodded, for he rose and scuttled behind his chair.

"Sit down," said O'Reilly. "I'm not going to hurt you." He waited until Fitzpatrick had taken his seat and then said very quietly, "But I will, Ronald . . . I will if you ever *ever* again treat Mrs. Kincaid the way you did last week."

Barry had thought O'Reilly's voice was icy. Now it

was as cold as solid carbon dioxide, and his nose tip was of the same ivory hue.

"Perhaps I was a little terse with the woman." Fitzpatrick's hectoring tone remained.

"No," said O'Reilly, "you were boorish, and bullying, and a right bashtoon. You will not treat Mrs. Kincaid like that again, or by God . . ."

Barry remembered O'Reilly saying he would gut Fitzpatrick like a herring. Now from the look in the big man's eyes he was sharpening the knife, and—Barry glanced at Fitzpatrick—the fellow knew it. Fitzpatrick turned one shoulder, raised it, and tucked his head down, then held his hands in front of his face, palms out, as if he feared O'Reilly might strike him. Barry had to strain to hear Fitzpatrick whisper, "I'll be nice to her in future. I promise. I promise."

"You'd better be," said O'Reilly, as he rose and stood towering over the man, "because Kinky is a human being. She deserves to be treated like one, with as much respect for her feelings, her dignity, as a duchess, maybe more. Kinky works for her living."

"I . . . I said I'm sorry." Fitzpatrick's voice quavered.

Barry had expected O'Reilly to cow the man but had not anticipated that his collapse would come so soon. And remembering the other matters O'Reilly intended to raise, he knew his senior colleague was just warming up. Despite Fitzpatrick's nature and his questionable medical practices, Barry felt a twinge of pity for the man. Being in the way when O'Reilly was on the warpath was a very unpleasant place to be.

"And while you're in the mood for feeling sorry, I'd suggest you start being nice to Miss Hagerty too."

"The midwife?"

"No. The wife and consort of Brian Boru, last *Ard Rí*—that's high king—of Ireland." O'Reilly shook his head. "Of course she's the bloody midwife. She's one of the very best midwives, and if you hadn't dismissed her from the care of Gertie Gorman—"

Barry watched as Fitzpatrick summoned enough spirit to fight back. He dropped his hands and shoulder and pointed his chin at O'Reilly. Fitzpatrick raised his voice. "She was challenging my care in front of the patient. She contradicted me. *Me.*" He stabbed his narrow chest with his own finger. "I won't have that. I won't." His Adam's apple sank beneath the rim of his wing-tip collar.

Barry thought the man's larynx would never reappear.

O'Reilly's nose went from ivory to alabaster. His fists clenched and unclenched. He took several deep breaths, and started to jab with his finger, but clenched his fist at the last minute and pulled it back. "She was probably trying to save your bacon, to stop you making a bigger ass of yourself than you already are."

Barry could have sworn the man actually gobbled like a turkey. Certainly the wattles of his neck shuddered. "I won't stand for—"

"You will, Ronald. You will." Until now, Barry had never heard anyone speak so sharply as to make him suddenly visualize a naked stiletto. "Because of *you*, I had to deliver an undiagnosed breech in the patient's home. *You* were nowhere to be found. The baby could have died, and you know that as well as I do. The mother could have too.

"Bugger Hippocrates and his oath," he continued. "It's unnecessary. You're a doctor, man. Your responsibility is to your patients first, last, and everywhere in between. You don't need some mumbo jumbo about 'swearing by Apollo, Asclepius, Hygieia, and Panacea' to tell you what you should do, and if you don't recognize that, you should be in some other trade." The steel in O'Reilly's voice was razor sharp.

And he was right, Barry thought. The day he'd started seeing patients as a student, he had learned from his seniors exactly where his responsibilities lay.

Fitzpatrick's shoulders were heaving, but O'Reilly bored ahead. "You weren't even professional enough to phone me to enquire how your patient was. And, Lord preserve us, I doubt if you as much as considered saying thank you to Miss Hagerty for getting hold of me." O'Reilly shook his head slowly.

Barry had expected O'Reilly to finish with a line like, "And you call yourself a doctor?" but now the look on O'Reilly's craggy face was one more of pity than anger.

Fitzpatrick hung his head. His momentary counterattack had shriveled to nothing, and Barry thought the man himself had shrunk. "You're right, Fingal," he said. "I'm sorry. I am sorry." His voice was barely above a whisper. "I am very sorry." He sniffled, produced a large handkerchief, and blew his nose with a high-pitched honk.

O'Reilly smiled, planted his backside on the desk's corner, folded his arms across his chest, and said in his normal voice, "Well done, Ronald. Well done."

Barry was amazed at O'Reilly's sudden change from a frontal attack.

"It takes a big man to admit he's wrong, wouldn't you agree, Doctor Laverty?"

"I certainly would." Barry caught Fitzpatrick's look of thanks and smiled back.

"You know, Ronald," O'Reilly continued, "I don't know what made you such a bitter man, but I suspect there is a half-decent side to you. I'm quite proud of you for admitting you were wrong, and even a little sorry for you."

And although the remark could have been pure sarcasm, Barry could detect nothing but honesty in O'Reilly's words or the way he now sat, leaning back on one outstretched arm and idly swinging one booted foot.

Fingal Flahertie O'Reilly, Barry thought, you could somehow have summoned up some sympathy for Adolf Hitler. It was one of the qualities that made O'Reilly such a fine physician. Fingal would not have taken an instant dislike to Miss Moloney without finding out what had made her the way she appeared to be. O'Reilly might be quite proud of Fitzpatrick, but Barry Laverty was filled to bursting with pride in his senior colleague, and a little ashamed of himself for eagerly anticipating the destruction of Fitzpatrick. The man was more to be pitied.

When Fitzpatrick looked up at O'Reilly, Barry was

sure he could detect gratitude in the man's eyes. "Thank you, Fingal."

O'Reilly rose and stepped down from the podium. "No thanks needed. Just see to it that you keep those promises. Remember why you practice medicine."

"I will, Fingal. I will try."

"Oh, yes," O'Reilly said. "One other wee thing while we're on about doctoring. Where the hell did a man like yourself, trained at a reputable medical school—the same one I was trained at—where in the name of Baby Jesus in velvet trousers did you come up with some of your quack remedies?"

To Barry it looked as if Fitzpatrick was going to protest, but after a ferocious scowl had crossed his face and faded, he asked meekly, "Such as?"

"Gunpowder for infertility. Honestly." O'Reilly shook his big head. "Gunpowder. Do you know, Ronald, when I heard about this remedy, I had a terrible urge to put out the word that your patient had died."

"But you couldn't. It's not true. It would have been libel." Fitzpatrick's eyes bulged.

"Not if I'd told everyone that they'd tried to cremate him . . . and they were still looking for the back wall of the crematorium." He guffawed. "They'd have seen I was only joking."

Barry, who was caught completely off guard, burst out laughing. He was surprised to hear a dry wheezing chuckle coming from Fitzpatrick. "You haven't changed, Fingal," Fitzpatrick said. "You could always make a joke out of anything."

"Maybe," said O'Reilly, deadpan now, a hint of metal

once again in his tones, "but I'll not find it funny if you don't keep your promises."

"I will," said Fitzpatrick.

"All right," said O'Reilly, climbing back up on the platform. He offered his hand. "See you do."

Fitzpatrick shook the hand.

Barry could tell by the way Fitzpatrick gritted his teeth that he was the recipient of one of O'Reilly's paw-crushing shakes.

"And now," said O'Reilly, still holding on to the hand, "before Doctor Laverty and I head off, in the spirit of the season we'll wish you an early merry Christmas and a happy New Year." He let go the hand, and Fitzpatrick immediately massaged it with the other. "And if you have any difficulty keeping your New Year's resolutions, I'm sure Barry and I can help you, Ronald."

He turned to Barry. "Come along, Barry. Don't trouble yourself to get up, Ronald. We'll show ourselves out."

When they left the house and headed back to the car, the light was already fading. It was, after all, Barry knew, only a few days short of the solstice, and then the days would start to lengthen. Even though today was calm, he'd not be sorry to see the gentler spring days arrive.

"That was amazing, Fingal," Barry said, as they passed the army facility. "You really brought him to heel."

"He is a bit of a cur," O'Reilly said, "and at heel is where he belongs. I just hope he'll stay there."

"Don't you think you were a bit lenient? I thought you were going to threaten him with exposure because he'd not paid up on his bet."

"Och," said O'Reilly, stopping to light his pipe. "I didn't need to. He caved in more easily than I'd anticipated."

"And you're sure he'll behave in future?"

"No," said O'Reilly, "he'll bear keeping an eye on." He opened the car door. "Hop in."

Barry did.

The car lurched as O'Reilly climbed aboard and started the engine. Before he drove away, he remarked, "Not saying I'll tell the world he welshed, but him knowing full well I could, means that for a few weeks at least we still have a shot in our locker if we need one."

"Clever. I hadn't thought of that." Barry wound his window down as O'Reilly let go a cloud of smoke.

"Ah, well," said O'Reilly, "we can't always think of everything."

Barry stretched and yawned.

"Tired?"

"A bit."

"I hope it's a quiet night for you tonight, Barry."

Barry laughed. "It will be. I'm absolutely certain."

"Good Lord." O'Reilly turned and peered at Barry. "Are you getting the gift like Kinky? How can you be so sure?"

"Because, Doctor O'Reilly, because I'm not on call tonight. You are."

"So I am," said O'Reilly, looking ahead. "Having

a go at your man back there must have made me forget. It was a bit like getting prepared for a boxing match . . ."

"When was the last time you fought, Fingal?" Barry asked, remembering full well his colleague had boxed at Trinity and when he was in the navy.

"In the ring? Gibraltar in nineteen forty-five. I lost on points." He put the car in gear and drove off. "Otherwise about ten minutes ago with Fitzpatrick."

"I'd say you won that one."

"True, but I'd got myself primed to go ten rounds. When he threw in the towel early, it was a bit of a letdown . . ."

Barry realized something he'd suspected for a long time. O'Reilly actually enjoyed a good scrap, be it with Doctor Fitzpatrick or Councillor Bishop.

"And I was feeling so pleased with myself for such an easy win that I completely forgot who was doing what in the practice. I'm on call tonight, and I'll be doing the surgery tomorrow." He let go another huge cloud of smoke.

"When I was going on to Fitzpatrick about the gunpowder, I should have remembered that Gerry Shanks and his missus are coming in tomorrow. I wish I'd made Ronald confess that the treatment is useless. I could have told Mairead that he'd said so."

"So what will you tell her?"

"If it'll bring her to her senses so she'll let poor Gerry stop taking the stuff, I'll say Fitzpatrick agreed it was useless."

"But he didn't."

O'Reilly let go another cloud and laughed. "True, Barry, true . . . but a white lie's in a good cause, and what the eye doesn't see, the heart doesn't grieve over."

36

For They Shall Be Comforted

"I wanna sweetie. I *wanna* sweetie. I wanna *sweetie.*" The continuous chanting was high-pitched and grating.

At least, O'Reilly thought, not having been called out last night had given him a good night's sleep. He was able to face this morning's surgery, but it did seem as if the room had suddenly shrunk. The parents of the child yelling "I wanna sweetie"—Gerry and Mairead Shanks—showed no interest in controlling either of their two children. O'Reilly had noticed Donal Donnelly in the waiting room. Donal would be bringing news about the raffle, and while O'Reilly would give the Shankses their fair share of time, he did not want their consultation to be unnecessarily prolonged.

Four-year-old Siobhan stood beside her mother. Her face was scarlet, her scowl ferocious. "*I waaaana sweeteeeee.*"

The doctor ignored her and rose to intercept five-year-old Angus's assault on the trolley. "Here," O'Reilly said, pulling out his key ring. "Play with this." He gave it to the child, grabbed the boy's wrist, pulled him away from the collection of sharp steel instruments, and guided him back to his father. "Hang onto him, Gerry."

"Right, Doctor."

"I . . . want . . . a . . . sweetie."

O'Reilly stifled his urge to say, "No, you want a good clip round the ear." He did understand how difficult it could be for parents, particularly newcomers like the Shankses, to find babysitters. "I'll be back," he said, as he left the surgery.

He went to the kitchen, and said, "Kinky, could you nanny a couple of chisellers? I want to finish on time so I can get up to Belfast today to do my Christmas shopping."

"Bless you, Doctor dear, I will indeed. Just let me pop your lunch to one side."

He saw a plate of wheaten bread, butter, and cheese. Bloody diet.

"Will we go now, sir?"

He headed back to the surgery with Kinky at his heels. "Children, this is Mrs. Kincaid."

Kinky, big and comforting, beamed at them and held out her arms.

"I'd like you to go with her, and she'll give you some treats," O'Reilly said.

Siobhan's chant stopped. She moved across to where Kinky stood. Angus followed. As the boy passed, O'Reilly caught his shoulder. "My keys?"

Angus thrust them at O'Reilly and raced after Kinky and his sister, yelling, "Wait for me. Wait for me."

O'Reilly put the keys in his pocket and took his usual seat.

"I'm awful sorry about that, Doctor," Mairead said, "but you know what kiddies are like." She smiled fondly. "I dote on them, so I do."

"Och," he said, "to the raven her own chick is white." Which was the closest he could bring himself to saying, she could dote, but he'd just tolerate. He gave her a moment to think about what he had said.

Now that he was no longer distracted, O'Reilly took a good look at Mairead Shanks. Gerry had said his wife was a pretty wee thing. She was indeed. She could not stand more than five feet tall, and her short coppery hair was cut in a pageboy. That made him swallow. He'd managed not to think of Deidre for a few days, but she'd worn bangs like that, even though at Christmas 1940 the back and sides of her hair had been done in a reverse roll in the fashion of the times. He inhaled deeply and told himself to get on with his work.

"They can be a handful. I'm sorry, sir."

"Never worry," O'Reilly said, "Kinky'll keep them occupied until we're done."

She smiled. It was a gentle smile of full lips and pale green eyes set in an oval face. "Thank you, sir."

O'Reilly popped on his half-moons. "You'd like to have another wean?"

She nodded and managed a wry smile. "After you've seen my two you probably wonder why, Doctor, but yes, me and Gerry . . ."—she glanced at her husband, who reached across and took her hand—"me and Gerry'd like one more. Just the one."

O'Reilly nodded. "Gerry said it's been two years, and you've seen all the specialists and they can't find anything wrong."

Her eyes glistened. "That's right, sir."

"I imagine you've been asked a lot of personal questions, had a lot of examinations, and are getting pretty sick of tests."

She sighed. "You can say that again, sir."

"I'm not going to examine you, Mairead, and I've no more tests."

He saw her frown. Many patients believed that if they were not given a thorough physical examination, the doctor was not doing his job. "There's no need, honestly. You've seen some of the best specialists. If they found nothing, you don't expect a country GP to, do you?" Pretty much the same tack he'd taken with Gerry, who was nodding in agreement.

"If you say so, sir." She smiled again.

Sometimes, O'Reilly thought, the absolute trust country patients had in their medical advisors was unnerving, even to the extent of their being willing to follow weird advice from a man like Fitzpatrick. "I do," he said. "I'd rather chat with you."

"See, didn't I tell you that, dear, when I come home after I'd seen him, that Doctor O'Reilly just wanted to have a wee word, like?"

"Aye. You did so."

O'Reilly leant forward. "There's just a couple of

things to discuss." And despite the Ulster countrywoman's reticence about matters sexual, he decided to jump in at the deep end. "Gerry told me you'd been advised that you should only make love once a month."

She coloured and glared at her husband.

"Come on, Mairead," Gerry said. "How's the doctor going to help us if he doesn't know what ails us?"

"It takes all the fun out of it." Her voice was very soft. Her eyes brimmed over. "Gerry's been very patient, so he has." And she smiled weakly at Gerry through her tears.

O'Reilly pulled the half-moons down to the tip of his nose. "Mairead, I do understand. And I know it's a tricky subject, but I don't think the Lord invented sex just for making babies. I think he made it so two people in love could have fun too." He waited to let that message sink in.

She frowned, looked down, then looked back at O'Reilly. "You mean that, don't you, Doctor?"

"Of course." There was no need for her to know that there had been no courses in sexuality when he was a student and that his advice was based on his own experience, and it *had* been fun with Deidre and, damn it all, might very well be with Kitty. Pity she'd not be back until Christmas Day. He shoved the spectacles back up his nose. "Tell me, Mairead, what the doctors at the Royal told you."

She sniffed again and accepted the handkerchief her husband gave her. "They said they could find nothing wrong. That the two chisellers we already have was pretty good proof that things were working all right, just a bit slow this time, like. If there was something serious, I'd likely never have got pregnant."

"Do you think maybe the specialists could be right?"

She blew her nose. "Well, I suppose . . ." She sighed mightily. "But why is it taking so long? They told me the right days of the month to . . . do it"—she blushed and looked down—"and we have, so we have. And now you say on one hand you're just a country GP, but on the other you don't agree with the big doctors at the hospital." She looked from O'Reilly to her husband and back to O'Reilly. "I'm getting muddled, so I am."

"I don't think the doctor would tell you wrong, dear," Gerry said. "He shot straight with me, so he did, and you remember what Gertie told you about how he delivered her wee Noelle? I'd listen to the man, so I would."

O'Reilly nodded, grateful for Gerry's support. He steepled his fingers. "I don't agree, Mairead, because I do know that if you took one hundred couples like you and Gerry and they all started on the same day trying to have a baby, some would get in the family way in a couple of months, but it would be three years before most of them were pregnant. Three whole years. Some folks just take longer than others."

She looked up at O'Reilly, at her husband, and back to O'Reilly. "Honest to God?"

He nodded. "And the other thing I know is that if

all the tests are done and are normal, no amount of making love on the 'right day' will produce any more babies than making love when the mood's on you."

He saw Gerry smile.

"Right enough?" she asked. "That'll be a relief to Gerry. He's been very good, so he has. He's even taking what that Doctor Fitzpatrick told him to. It must taste terrible."

"The gunpowder? I must confess I'd never heard of that treatment before." And he sincerely hoped he never would again.

"Nor me," she said, "but Fitzpatrick swore by it."

"Funnily enough, I was just having a wee word with Doctor Fitzpatrick yesterday." Quite a few wee words in fact.

"Aye?" Gerry said. "What about?"

"Gunpowder, among other things, and he did tell me that maybe he was mistaken about it. We had a good laugh about it." And that is true, O'Reilly thought. Well, it is if it's taken a bit out of context, and if it helps Mairead, what's the harm in a white lie? "I don't think he'll be prescribing it again." He'd bloody well better not.

"It's certainly not done nothing for me, so it hasn't," Gerry said.

Mairead shook her head. "Maybe Gerry won't need to take no more?"

"What do you think, Mairead?" O'Reilly asked.

"You can stop, dear," she said. "You can start putting the sugar in your tea again."

"Thank God for that." He smiled.

"So what you're saying, Doctor O'Reilly, is for us to get on with our lives, don't do nothing special, and hope for the best?"

"That's right, and I know it'll not be easy, but it's the best I can suggest." He heard a screech and a yell. "What the hell was that?" O'Reilly leapt from his chair, crossed the room, and flung open the door. He could see into the dining room.

Siobhan sat at the table, a half-drunk glass of Kinky's lemonade in front of her, a mostly eaten sweet mince pie clutched in a sticky hand. Her eyes were wide. Kinky was holding a tearful Angus, who had four red scratches on his left forearm. Lady Macbeth crouched under the table, spitting and hissing.

"It's all right, sir," Kinky said, looking straight at O'Reilly. "The young man thought Her Ladyship's tail was a handle to grab her by, so. She disagreed. I'll take him out to my kitchen, give the scratches a wash, and he'll be right as rain."

"Thank you, Kinky." O'Reilly waited until she had brought the tearful lad into the hall. "Let's have a look." He took the arm and satisfied himself that Kinky was right. All it needed was a wash. "Carry on, Mrs. Kincaid," he said and winked at her.

O'Reilly felt a presence at his shoulder and turned. Mairead was there looking worried. "It's all right, Mairead. Angus got scratched by my cat. Mrs. Kincaid'll see to him."

She pushed past and followed Kinky and the little boy.

Typical mother, O'Reilly thought. Bless her.

He went back into the surgery.

Gerry was on his feet. He was frowning.

"Don't worry, Gerry. Angus has a wee scratch, that's all. Kinky and his mother are looking after him."

"How did he get scratched? Was it Siobhan?"

Typical father of two, O'Reilly thought. Whenever one child gets hurt, Da makes the other the prime suspect. "Not at all. It was my cat. Angus had a go at her, and as a famous French fellah once said, the animal is very evil. If you attack it, it will defend itself."

"If you attack it, it . . ." Gerry started to laugh. "I don't think that was any Frenchman, Doctor. I think you just made that up there now."

"I didn't, Gerry, but it's good to see you with a smile on your face."

Gerry glanced down at his feet before looking straight at O'Reilly. "Doc, I've a reason to smile. I want to thank you for telling the missus what you done. Maybe now she'll get a bit of peace of mind for a while."

"I hope so, Gerry."

"That Fitzpatrick, he'd her worried stiff, so he had." He grimaced. "And I'll not be sorry to see the back of that bloody gunpowder."

"I believe you." O'Reilly clapped the man on the shoulder. "You nip into the dining room and collect your wee Siobhan. Then go along to the kitchen and see to your wife and son and get away on home."

"I will, Doctor, and thanks again. All this no-babies business and the move here have been hard on Mairead. She's not made too many new friends yet."

"So why don't you and the missus bring the youngsters to the Rugby Club Christmas party next Wednesday? You'll meet a lot of folks; the wee ones'll meet other kids. It's usually a great ta-ta-ta-ra. It starts at five in the pavilion."

Gerry smiled. "That would be great, so it would. We'll be there."

O'Reilly followed Gerry into the hall and headed for the waiting room.

37

A Good Plot, Good Friends, and Full of Expectation

O'Reilly opened the waiting-room door. "Who's next?" He couldn't stifle a grin when Ballybucklebo's arch-schemer rose and said, "Me, sir."

"Come along then, Donal," O'Reilly said and headed back up the hall. He shut the door behind him. "Well?"

"It's all set, sir. Johnny Jordan'll have a great big turkey ready and . . ." He handed O'Reilly two five-pound notes. ". . . And when Johnny heard what it was for—he knows how to keep his trap shut so I explained just a wee bit to him—he wouldn't take no money."

"Jesus, Donal, I thought we were keeping this between you and me."

"Sure I only told him Eileen would win the turkey. Not how much she'd get."

"But even if that gets out and Eileen hears, she'll refuse—"

"Divil the bit will it get out, Doc." Donal winked and held a finger alongside his nose. "See, your man Johnny? He's a mouth on him like a steel trap when you tell him a secret, and anyway Johnny'd do nothing to hurt Eileen. He's a bachelor man but he used to walk out with Eileen before, and he never married once she was taken."

"Is that a fact?" Lord, O'Reilly thought, with the number of folks carrying torches—me, Kitty, young Barry, and now the local butcher—it might be time to organize a torchlight procession.

"Och, aye, mind you Johnny's no oil painting, but he's a heart of corn, so he has, and that shop of his makes a mint. Wee Eileen could do much worser for herself."

And that is one hare I'm definitely going to let sit, O'Reilly told himself. I don't mind helping Eileen out financially, but I am *not* taking on the job of matchmaker. "I'm sure you're right, Donal."

"I'm dead on, so I am, but it's not for me to tell her that he gave the bird for free. He can do as he sees fit. But it was decent of him." He chuckled. "It's a bit of a gag raffling off a dead bird, but it's not as funny as the story your man Niall Toibin told about the raffle of a dead greyhound."

"Toibin? The comic actor?"

"The very fellah."

Toibin was a marvelous raconteur, and Donal was no mean hand at telling a story himself, as O'Reilly had learnt at the wedding. He had certainly piqued O'Reilly's curiosity, but the doctor was content to wait to hear more. Knowing Donal as he did, O'Reilly understood that on occasions the man had a little difficulty thinking in reasonably straight lines.

"I need to tell you about what I've been up to first," he said. "And I hope you'll be pleased with this, sir." Donal handed O'Reilly a green ticket. It had a perforated line at its equator. Both halves were identical. Each bore the numbers 4444. "That's the winner there, and before you ask, sir, I've not sold four thousand tickets. They came in a roll that started at forty-three hundred, and that one there's the one you need." He grinned. "You know, Doc, I thought I was pretty smart coming up with the notion of how to rig this so the one we want will win the money. I never thought there'd be another way to be sure of winning a raffle."

"Donal, I've already told you I don't want to know how you're going to make it work."

"And I'm not for telling you, sir, but I *will* tell you about the dead dog."

"I'm all ears."

Donal grinned, showing his buckteeth. "There was a man away out in County Kerry . . ."

"Och, Jesus, Donal. Not another Kerryman joke?" O'Reilly curled his lip. He'd heard enough the-Irish-are-stupid jokes told by other nationalities and more than enough Kerrymen-are-stupid jokes told by other Irishmen.

"Not at all, sir. This story'll show you the exact opposite, so it will."

"That Kerrymen are clever?"

"Aye."

O'Reilly waited.

"There was a dog man out in County Kerry. He'd bought a mail-order greyhound for sixty pounds from a fellah in Dublin. When the dog arrived in Kerry it was dead, and your fellah needed to recover his sixty quid. He got it back by raffling the corpse."

"Donal, why would anybody buy a ticket when the prize was a dead greyhound?"

"Doctor O'Reilly, why would anybody buy a ticket for a dead turkey when you and I both already know who has the winning ticket? Number forty-four forty-four—that there's it—and it's going to be a big win, so it is."

The answer to Donal's question about why anybody would buy a ticket was obvious, O'Reilly thought. They didn't know the raffle was rigged. But they did know that there was a chance for a turkey and that seventy-five percent of the take would go to the holder of the winning ticket if all the numbers were the same. One thing was still unclear. "How do you know that it'll be a big win?" he asked.

Donal grinned, his buckteeth large in his mouth. "I got the tickets from the printer on Saturday, and I rounded up a clatter of the lads from the Highlanders for my salesmen."

O'Reilly could picture Donal recruiting fellow members of his pipe band.

"They've been working away like beavers and there's hardly a ticket left, so there's not. They're selling like the ones the fellah sold on the dead dog out in Kerry."

"Good man ma da," O'Reilly said. "Have you any at all left?"

Donal dropped a hand to his pocket and pulled out a few green tickets. He frowned as he offered them to O'Reilly. "There's a few, but why would you buy any when you know they can't possibly win?"

"Och," said O'Reilly, "put it down to the Christmas spirit. Folks would think it strange if I'd not bought mine like everyone else."

"Boys-a-boys," Donal said, respect in his voice, "but you're quare and sharp, Doctor. You're near as sharp as the fellah with the dead dog."

"Give me five." He gave Donal a five-pound note. Donal pocketed the money.

"Thanks, Doc. Now like I was saying, when the Dubliner that sold the dog took it to the station to put it on the train to Kerry, what do you think he saw when he opened up the basket the dog was in?"

"You've already told me the story's about a dog that's dead."

"As mutton, sir. But the Dublin man reckoned he could get away with it. Sure wasn't it only one of those thick Kerrymen he was dealing with? For one thing he'd be too stupid to ship the animal back and demand a refund." Donal held out his hand. "While I'm on about giving things back, give me the stubs, sir, and when you give Eileen her ticket, keep the stub for me. It can't win if it doesn't go into the hat."

"Fair enough." O'Reilly pulled out his wallet and put 4444 safely away. The other five he tore in two, gave Donal the stubs, and slipped the tickets into his jacket pocket. "Go on about the dead dog."

"The Dubliner reckons he can swear blind that it was alive when he put it on board. The Kerryman will have to believe the story, and if he wants his money back will have to chase after the railway company for damages and that could take forever. On goes the dog. Away goes the train."

O'Reilly smiled. "Go on."

"Meanwhile, the Kerryman has been telling all his pals at the pub about the wonderful dog. 'Begob,' says he, looking at the pub clock, 'it's tree tirty-tree.' "

O'Reilly marveled at how easily Donal slipped from his native North Down accent to the singsong cadences of the southwest of Ireland where, because there is no "aitch" sound in the Irish language, none is pronounced when English is spoken.

" 'Time I was off to the station to meet the four o'clock from Dublin,' he says. He gets there, takes off the basket, opens it, and . . ." Donal started back. His eyes widened. His voice dropped to a whisper. " 'Holy tundering mother of the sainted Jasus Christ himself, and all the saints above! The poor wee doggy's dead . . .' "

If Donal ever lost his job as a labourer, O'Reilly

thought, he'd have no trouble finding work in the theatre. The man was a consummate actor.

"'And me out of pocket sixty pounds.' But then"—Donal winked—"he has a wonderful notion. He closes up the basket. 'Seamus,' says he to the stationmaster, 'will you mind this basket for a wee while for me 'til I send a man round to collect it?' 'Aye, certainly.' 'And, Seamus, don't you let on it came in on this train. Tell the fellah it's off the six.' Then the Kerryman hoofs it back to the pub. The lads there are all agog to see the dog."

O'Reilly started to chuckle. "Pay me no heed, Donal. Go on."

"'Och,' says our hero, 'it'll not be here until the next train.' He takes a long pause, then says he, 'And I've been thinking on it. I'm getting a bit long in the tooth to be running such a grand dog so I've decided to raffle it. The winner can pick it up at the station off the six o'clock from Dublin.'"

O'Reilly nodded.

"'Two pound a ticket,' he says, and collects up the money from about forty men. They have the draw there and then. A lad from Knockagashel wins, and about five thirty off he trots to collect the dog."

"The recently late dog."

"Aye. The dear departed. Stiff as a plank. By now it's six thirty, and our lad's been home for half an hour when there's a powerful dundering on his door. It's the winner. 'You gobshite,' roars he. 'The feckin' dog's dead.' 'Jasus,' says our man. 'Dead is it? Dead?'

" 'As a feckin' dodo. You sold me a pig in a feckin' poke, you buck eejit.' "

" 'Tut,' says he, 'tut, tut, tut. Your man in Dublin swore he'd dispatched it alive.' "

" 'Well, the feckin' thing's dead. I have it outside in the basket. Do you want to see it?' "

" 'No, I believe you. Lord, but that's very sad.' And he looks all soulful. 'I'll not see you wrong,' says he. 'Not for one minute.' "

" 'All right then,' says the man from Knockagashel, and that's a brave ways away. The whole story may never get back, our hero reckons."

Donal stopped, fixed O'Reilly with a stare, and waited. Then, keeping his face expressionless, he said, "He pulls out three pounds from his pocket. 'The least I can do is refund *you* your stake, and an extra pound for your disappointment.' 'Grand, so,' says the Knockagashel fellah. 'I'll be off now and no offence taken.' "

Donal stopped and raised one eyebrow. "Now what do you think, Doctor? Was that Kerryman not a clever one?"

Before he had stopped laughing O'Reilly had to wipe his eyes with a large handkerchief. "He was indeed, Donal, and you were right about another thing too. There *is* more than one way to make money from a fixed raffle . . . but the principle's the same."

"How come?"

"The fellahs in the pub didn't know the dog was dead. Nobody except us and Johnny knows ours is rigged. So no more telling folks like you told Johnny. All right?"

"Mum's the word, sir."

"Good. Jasus, but that was a grand story." O'Reilly still had to chuckle. Donal had painted the scene so vividly. "If it was the films you were in, you'd have won an Oscar."

Donal smiled his mooncalf smile, a sure token he was pleased by O'Reilly's praise.

O'Reilly clapped Donal on the shoulder. "Now run away with you, Donal Donnelly, and give my love to Julie."

"I will, Doc, and don't you worry. Eileen will be one turkey and maybe a hundred quid better off come next Wednesday."

O'Reilly still had a smile on his face as he saw Donal out.

The next two patients shouldn't take long, he thought. And then lunch. Bread and bloody cheese. It might as well be bread and water. Still, he brightened at the thought, the Cotter's Kitchen would be open when he got to the city, and they did very tasty snacks.

He knew he shouldn't complain about Kinky's dietary restrictions on his behalf when he thought of how Eileen Lindsay must be struggling to feed her family on her shifter's wages. He sighed. He couldn't help her earn more, but at least her kiddies would get their presents from Santa courtesy of Donal Donnelly and a dead bird. He chuckled and shook his head. That Donal was funny, amoral, and another thing about the lad, the way he kept knocking Julie up, he didn't need any of Fitzpatrick's gunpowder to put lead in *his* pencil.

O'Reilly walked along the hall.

The only thing gunpowder should be used for, and smokeless powder at that, was to make shotgun cartridges. While he was in Belfast, he'd pick up a couple of boxes of Eley-Kynoch 5 shot from Braddel's the gunsmith in the Cornmarket. It would be silly to run out of shot two days from now when he and Arthur Guinness would go to Strangford Lough for a day's wildfowling. That was something he was really looking forward to.

He hardly recognized that he'd had to stop whistling "Zip-a-Dee-Doo-Dah" to yell "Next" into the almost deserted waiting room.

38

The Pelting of This Pitiless Storm

O'Reilly huddled behind the wall of a semi-collapsed sheep cot halfway along Gransha Point, a dogleg-shaped peninsula sticking out into the waters of Strangford Lough. He could hear both the swishing in the grass outside as it thrashed, and bent, and swayed, and the regular grinding sounds of waves breaking on the shingle of the nearby shore.

He wore a waterproof insulated jacket over a thick oiled-wool Baínín sweater, a woollen shirt, and string underwear. He had draped a folded towel around his neck under his shirt for extra waterproofing. His thigh waders covered tweed trousers that were tucked into sea-boot stockings worn over silk socks. The added layer made the rubber boots a tight fit. His soft-crowned tweed Paddy hat was pulled down to cover the tops of his ears.

He felt as inflated as the Michelin Man, but despite his layers he still shivered. The barrels of his twelve-bore shotgun chilled his left hand.

The gale from the south had blown up last night. In the predawn, the Lough was living up to its old Viking name, *Strangfjorthr,* the turbulent fjord. It was ill-tempered, dark, and blustering, and a far cry from its well-mannered summer self of calm blue waters dotted with silent islands. That was the face it usually showed, the one that had caused the native Irish to name the inlet *Lough Cuan*, the peaceful lough.

Sometimes O'Reilly thought of the place as a high-spirited woman who changed her moods as the winds blew. Changeable. He hummed a few bars of "La donna è mobile"—woman is fickle—and remembered sitting with Deidre listening to *Rigoletto,* from which the piece came, on his old 78s.

She'd been like that. Calm, serene, loving. But if he annoyed her, usually by being thoughtless, she had a temper that could send chills through him as the wind today was sending icy fingers through the cracks between the wall's wet stones. He shuddered and gripped his gun more tightly when a gust charged through the entrance to swirl and batter, then die within. Deidre's temper would build until he apologized, and then he'd hold her and she'd say she was sorry too.

Her smile then would be as friendly as the lights of a farmhouse across the bay. The folks over there would be up, he thought, the range lit, the kettle on for the tea, bacon sizzling in the pan. He'd not mind a bacon sandwich now.

The glow of the lights was masked. He knew their disappearance would mark the arrival of a rain squall sweeping in from the open sea. When it had passed, the lights would shine again. If only *she* would. If only. How often, he wondered, had he told other people there was no profit in ploughing the same furrow twice? He must stop dwelling on the past.

O'Reilly looked at the dark outline of Arthur. It didn't seem like twelve years had passed since O'Reilly had brought home a wriggling, chubby black ball, who'd chewed his master's slippers and buried his favorite pipe in the vegetable garden.

Buying the pup had been Kinky's suggestion. She was a very astute woman, was Kinky Kincaid. She'd known that in his role as the village doctor, O'Reilly could not allow himself to develop deep friendships but must maintain a certain professional distance. Nor were there many opportunities for female companionship. She'd sensed O'Reilly's need, and she'd been right in her prescription. Arthur—clumsy, good-natured, as fond of his Smithwick's as O'Reilly was of his Jameson—had been a staunch companion and loyal friend.

He bent and patted the dog. "For a while there, you big lump, you were my only friend." At least until the marquis and O'Reilly had grown closer, initially because of their work for the Rugby Club. Arthur looked up but rapidly looked away, as if to say, "Don't interrupt me. I'm busy."

O'Reilly noticed that the dog was sitting alertly, nose twitching, collecting the scents brought in on the wind. Arthur would smell all manner of things, but all O'Reilly could detect was the salty tang from the seashore.

Arthur whimpered, stiffened, and stared straight out through the opening and into the teeth of the gale.

O'Reilly strained to hear over the wind's keening. Yes. His grip on the gun tightened. Yes. He could hear a whicker of pinions. Closer. Closer. He slipped the safety catch off. He stared and against the grayness of the false dawn sky saw three darker shapes like flying beer bottles hurtling head-on down the wind. As the ducks raced overhead, he hunched low, hiding behind the stones, holding his breath until he selected a target, straightened, and in one fluid movement brought the butt of the shotgun against his right shoulder, swung to lead the bird, and squeezed the trigger for the right barrel.

It seemed as if no time passed between the crash of

the shot, the frantic flaring of two birds as in panic they clawed for altitude, and the fall of the third, its wings folded, its neck bent back. So rapidly did the wind carry the survivors to safety, there was no time for him to fire the second barrel.

O'Reilly sensed rather than heard the thump as his quarry hit the turf forty yards out from his hide.

Arthur was trembling, tensed like a panther ready to spring.

"Hi lost, boy."

The dog raced out of the cot.

O'Reilly broke the gun, extracted the spent cartridge, fished a new one out of his jacket pocket, reloaded, closed the breech, and put on the safety catch. He stared out over the rear wall, now able to see Arthur more clearly as the light grew brighter. He knew that the sun, even if it was hidden behind clouds, would be over the horizon and climbing behind the low hills inland.

He watched Arthur stop, lower his head, and then straighten with the duck in his mouth. Head and bird held high, tail thrashing, Arthur trotted proudly back. O'Reilly turned to face the entrance as Arthur came into the cot, sat without bidding at his master's feet, and presented him with a plump drake mallard.

O'Reilly took the bird. "Good boy." He patted Arthur's head. "That's better than a Wellington boot, isn't it? Go on now, lie down."

Arthur wandered over to a sheltered corner, flopped, and laid his square head on his outstretched paws. The look on his face could only be described as one of pure contentment. The American author Robert Ruark had been right, O'Reilly thought. There is no happier animal than a gun dog in bird season.

O'Reilly picked up a gamebag from the corner where he'd left it and put the duck into the outer string-mesh pouch. Inside the inner canvas pouch were half a dozen cold fried Cookstown sausages in buttered bridge rolls that Kinky had put up for him and wrapped in greaseproof paper before she went to bed the night before. Kinky would have no truck with any other brand of sausages. A large thermos held the coffee he'd brewed for himself this morning.

He felt the sting of rain on his face as a sudden squall hit. You're daft, Fingal O'Reilly, he told himself. Mad as a flaming hatter. Why would any man in his right mind be out in this bloody awful weather with no company but a black Labrador who's as crazy as you are?

And it wasn't a difficult question for him to answer. It was what he'd tried to tell Barry. The place gave him time away from his everyday world.

No matter how inured a doctor thought he had become to the suffering of his patients, any physician worth his salt still worried about them, particularly the really ill ones. There was often recompense from them in their gratitude, but not always. Some became hostile and angry when their physician failed to meet their sometimes hopelessly exaggerated expectations.

He smiled to himself. He'd told Barry the day he arrived in Ballybucklebo that the first law of medicine was never to let the patients get the upper hand. But there'd been one or two occasions lately when the redoubtable Doctor Fingal Flahertie O'Reilly had failed to obey his own laws.

Thank God they were only a small percentage of the practice, but there were a few patients who would try the patience of Job. The ones who made thoughtless demands for attention, often at night, for trivial complaints.

He'd not got back to bed until two o'clock this morning because Seamus Corrigan, a farm labourer who lived in a two-room cottage about three miles from the Gillespies' farm, had staved a finger on Tuesday mending a drystone wall. For four days he'd had every opportunity to come to the surgery, but no, the boul' Seamus had got a skinfull last night at the Duck, decided his finger was broken, phoned at twelve-thirty, and demanded a home visit.

O'Reilly had examined the man, strapped the finger—strained or broken, the treatment was the same—and driven home in a foul temper, convinced his own blood pressure had gone up about twenty points. Seamus was damn lucky he hadn't acquired a broken neck. It had been a bloody good thing O'Reilly had planned to be on the Lough this morning, although he was keenly aware that Seamus had deprived him of what little sleep the early rising would allow; he'd had to get up at four to get to Strangford in time for the dawn flight.

Would Seamus have been as disturbed about his finger if the telephone hadn't been invented and he had to walk or cycle through the gale to the surgery? Sometimes the telephone was a bloody menace. It ruled doctors' lives.

He certainly took great pains to conceal it from Kinky and Barry, but every time the bloody thing rang O'Reilly flinched until he could determine whether it was a social call or yet another medical emergency to sort out.

It was all part and parcel of his chosen career, O'Reilly knew, but all the petty irritations, all the strains, built and accumulated until like an overloaded steam engine, O'Reilly knew he needed to open his safety valve.

Some men could find that solace in the arms of their wives. He found his in this wild place where no telephones ever rang, no babies died of pneumonia, and no arrangements had to be made to ship distraught, pregnant, out-of-wedlock teenagers to England. Nothing of the mundane could intrude, and he could enjoy the solitude and the raw undistilled beauty of the place.

The truth was he didn't really care if he never fired a shot. The ducks were simply his excuse to come here despite the cold and the gale. He flinched as water trickled under his towel and down his back.

The last shower had passed by and the dawn was breaking. O'Reilly turned to look inland along the peninsula's length. A gap appeared in the clouds as the sun's upper rim, chrome yellow, climbed over the hills. The light of the day brightened as the narrow sliver grew into a great disk, its colour changing to an incandescent orange that painted the clouds with screaming scarlet. The earlier invisible grasses, now green with punctuation marks of russet benweeds, bowed and swayed and danced their saraband.

When he looked out over the water, the black sea slowly changed to battleship grey dappled with ranks of cream whitecaps.

The sun's heat began to warm him, and O'Reilly sensed his inner maroon-hued serenity, that peace he only ever felt here on Strangford, his *quereñcia*. It restored the soul as surely as running on the surface recharged the batteries of a submarine.

"And that, Fingal Flahertie O'Reilly"—he told himself—"*that* is why you're out here in this winter weather with no one but a bloody great Labrador for company." He bent and patted Arthur's head. Then he said to the dog, "Today I'd rather be here than back at Number One, even if"—he blew on his hands—"it'll be a damn sight cosier there."

He propped his gun against the stone wall, pulled the thermos from the gamebag, poured a steaming cup of coffee, and settled down to see what the rest of the Saturday might bring.

39

To Travel Hopefully Is a Better Thing

Barry, grinning like a Barbary ape, took the stairs two at a time, then brushed aside Kinky, who was saying, "I'm sorry I yelled up to you, sir, but I have a cake in the oven, so and—"

He grabbed the receiver. "Patricia? Patricia? Where are you?" Was she home in Newry already?

"Bourn."

Barry's grin collapsed. "Is everything alright?"

"Of course, silly. I just wanted to hear your voice." She sounded happy.

"It's been a while." He waited.

"I know that, and I know what you're going to ask, and don't get cross, but no I haven't had a chance yet . . ."

Damn. Damn. Barry kept his voice level. "Why not?"

"I've been staying with Jenny at her aunt's cottage. It's a beautiful old thatched place that was built in sixteen fifty-three, in a tiny place called Draycot near Slimbridge in Gloucestershire."

Here we go again, he thought, more chitchat. More avoiding talking about important things. "Where the ducks are. I know." Bloody ducks. Pity O'Reilly wasn't over there with his gun. Barry was having difficulty keeping his temper. This prevarication had gone on long enough.

"Slimbridge is an amazing place. They're real conservationists here. They've bred one species, the Hawaiian goose, back from near extinction."

"Good." But was she going to do something to save *him* from extinction, or was she going to let them fall apart?

"Barry, I'm trying to explain."

"I wish you would."

"I asked you not to be cross."

"Damn it, Patricia, I want to see you. It's hard not to get cross. You promised to come." He hesitated. "Are you sure you really want to come back to Ireland?" He waited. "Telling me you'd rather see a bunch of birds is a pretty lame excuse."

"I did want to see the waterfowl. I'm glad I did. I may not get another chance. And it's not as if you're free much when I do come home. You still have a job to do. I'd be bored half to death hanging around in Newry. There's nothing to do there."

"I can understand that, but O'Reilly will give me time off. He knows I need to see you." Barry was now sure that even though she had admitted to some reluctance to travel, she still wasn't telling him the real reason. "There's something else, isn't there?"

Her tone changed from placatory to matter-of-fact. "Do you want an honest answer?"

"Of course I do." Never mind *something* else; there must be *somebody* else. He closed his eyes and waited.

"I'm not sure I want to leave here."

Damnation. Barry took a deep breath. "Not sure? Not even for a few days? Why not?" This was starting to sound like last July, when she'd told him she was too busy with her career to fall in love.

"I've been doing a lot of thinking."

"Yes," he said cautiously. "About what?"

"About us."

Barry blew out his breath through pursed lips. "What about us?" For God's sake, man, he told himself, ask her. "Patricia, are you trying to tell me you've met someone else?"

"Yes and no—"

"Yes and no?" he cut in. "What the hell does that mean?"

"I'm trying to say, yes, I've met a lot of people and, no, nobody in particular, just a whole lot of really interesting people. Cambridge is full of folks from all over the world. Thinkers. Questioners." He heard excitement in her voice. "You hear all kinds of new ideas. Nobody lives in the past, not like—"

"Not like your average Ulsterman. And your new friends are all a damn sight more exciting than a country GP from a little town in the back of beyond. Is that it?"

"I didn't say that."

Barry's jaws tightened. "You might as well have."

"That's not fair."

"Why not? It's what I am."

"Barry, look . . . I've never been away from Ulster before. It's taken a bit of getting used to. I'm in some pretty tough courses and the competition is fierce here. There are only three women in the class, and we have to show everyone how good we are. It's hard work . . . but I've never been happier."

Jesus, and he'd been stupid enough to believe he'd been competing with a bunch of ducks. If it were only that simple. This was the side of Patricia that frightened him. This was the aggressive I'm-a-woman-making-my-way-in-a-man's-world Patricia. This was the nothing-is-going-to-get-in-my-way Patricia, not even you, Barry Laverty. It had been hard enough to accept this when she was living in Ulster, but he had tried and succeeded reasonably well.

He wondered how many of the "really interesting people" she'd met at the university shared her opinions, reinforced them, hardened them. Was it one of them who had told her never to accept money from a man?

"I see," Barry said, as levelly as he could manage, "and it's so exciting there, although term's over and you don't have any classes, that you can't bear to drag yourself away even for a few days to be with—" He was going to say "the man who loves you" but bit off the words.

"Christ, Barry, that's not true."

"Patricia, I haven't changed. You have. I don't think you want to see me." Barry held his breath. If she said he was right, his world would collapse.

"I do, Barry. I still love you." She spoke quietly.

Barry exhaled. He felt relief, but it was tinged with wondering if it was the truth. He couldn't quite bring himself to say, "I love you too." "Then why haven't you made an effort to get a booking to come home?"

"Because I couldn't."

"Couldn't? Come on, Patricia. How much effort does it take to make a ferry booking? A phone call or two?" He heard an edge creep into his voice.

Her words were more terse too. "I said I couldn't, and I meant I couldn't. Draycot's tiny. Jenny's aunt hasn't got a telephone. There's no travel agent here. Today's the first chance I've had."

"And?" He knew he should have apologized for his sarcasm.

"*And* as soon as I get off the phone, Jenny's going to run me to Cambridge to the travel agent there. I *am* going to try to get home."

Good. At least he'd be able to thrash all this out with her face-to-face. "Then why did you tell me you weren't sure if you wanted to leave?"

"Because you asked me and because it's true. I've all kinds of reasons to want to stay. Jenny's dad's got tickets to King's College Chapel for the Christmas Eve lessons-and-carols service. I'd love to go. I'm enjoying living in Bourn with my friend. Some of my other classmates and Jenny and I are going down to the Tate Gallery in London today, and after we've been to Cambridge they're planning trips to the National Gallery and the Victoria and Albert. Newry's a dump, and even though I love Mum and Dad, I've already told you I'd be bored stiff there."

He clenched his fist. The temptation was huge to lose his temper and yell. "*Then why don't you stay?*"

Barry forced his fist to uncurl. "When will you know for sure exactly when you are coming?"

"As soon as I've got my tickets, you'll be the first to know, Barry." She managed a small laugh and said, "After the travel agent and Jenny, that is. But I may not get a chance to ring for a day or two."

Here we go again. "Why not, for heaven's sake?"

"I told you; I'm going up to town today." That was a very English expression for going to London. "And we'll be staying with Jenny's sister in Chelsea until Tuesday morning. I may not get a chance to phone you until I'm back in Bourn."

"Patricia, London is full of public telephones. They're in red kiosks. If you've no money, reverse the charges. You can leave a message with Mrs. Kincaid if I'm not here. I really want to know when you'll be arriving." He pursed his lips. "Look, I'm sorry if I was a bit snappy, but I miss you like mad, and Patricia . . . ?"

"Yes, Barry?"

"I love you."

"You weren't snappy, just worried, I know that. And I will try to get time to phone, but I am going to be very busy, darling. I do love you."

He tingled at the words.

"Hang on . . . what? We need to leave? All right. Sorry, darling, Jenny wants to leave now. I've got to dash." And before he could tell her once more that he loved her, the line went dead.

He shook his head and replaced the receiver. Although she was finally going to make the arrangements, Barry now knew he'd been right to worry that after experiencing life in England she might be less enchanted with a small town in Ulster. That was something they would have to talk about once she got here, but there wasn't much point stewing over it now.

He climbed the stairs to the lounge and plumped himself down in his chair. His abandoned coffee was stone cold. He shrugged. It didn't really matter. He wasn't that interested in it anyway. Just as long as his romance wasn't going cold too.

He looked over into the corner, where Lady Macbeth lay curled up sleeping under the oddly decorated Christmas tree. She clutched a little red glass ball to her chest.

Three evenings ago O'Reilly had called for all hands on deck to trim the tree. Very splendid it had looked until Lady Macbeth decided the dangling ornaments were fair game. O'Reilly had conceded defeat and removed some of the temptations. The tree now stood with an angel at its apex. Baubles, tinsel, and fairy lights graced the upper branches, but there was a two-foot strip of tree between the glory above and the green, crepe paper–swathed butter box below, which was devoid of any decoration.

Gift-wrapped and bow-adorned parcels lay beneath the tree on a maroon cloth Kinky had produced. Barry glanced at the one he had bought for Patricia. Please hurry up and make a booking, he thought. I want to see your face when you open it.

Barry sighed, picked up the paper, and folded it to display the cryptic puzzle. He'd do that first, write his Christmas cards, and finish the half-completed letter to his folks. Then it would be time to pop around as he had promised and give Alice Moloney her test results.

He looked at one across. Seven letters. "Ripped after a party. Got the wind." He smiled. Sometimes the answer seemed to jump off the page. The word in question had to do with wind. Ripped meant torn. "After a storm" suggested putting the letter "a" after torn and you got "torna." A party was a "do." Answer: "torn-a-do." He wrote "tornado" in the squares and moved on to the next clue.

At least his mind was still working, even if his heart was as roiled as must be the grey seas of Strangford Lough.

"Jesus," said O'Reilly to Arthur, "we're not meant to get bloody tornadoes in Ireland. We've not seen a bird for the last couple of hours. It's so bloody windy they're probably walking." He moved closer to the wall and tried to get what shelter he could. If anything, the wind's force had increased, and it made a mournful whistling sound as it blasted through a crack.

The tide had risen and the waves were steeper and broke on the shore, sending spume flying over his shelter. He ducked, then felt the spray hit his waterproof jacket and another trickle of cold water penetrate his neck towel. He shuddered.

O'Reilly pulled the last three sausage sandwiches out of the gamebag, which now held two mallard. "Here." He tossed one sandwich to Arthur and took a great bite out of one of his own. "Best bloody bangers in Ireland."

He had no idea how long Cookstown, a small town in county Tyrone, had been producing sausages, but trust Kinky always to have a dozen in her refrigerator. They were always ready, she said, if she wanted to make toad in the hole. He could almost taste the pork sausages wrapped in a Yorkshire-pudding batter.

Kinky's store of sausages had come in handy the previous Saturday when Kitty rustled up that great fry after they'd come back from delivering Gertie Gorman's baby. He'd enjoyed the meal and he'd enjoyed kissing Kitty good-night when she left Number One to drive back to Belfast.

O'Reilly gulped down the last bite of the first sandwich and started on the second one.

Never mind how much he'd enjoyed her cooking and that kiss, Kitty had impressed him that night with her professionalism. He'd been disappointed when she told him he wouldn't be able to buy her another dinner because she was leaving on Monday to spend time with her mother in Tallaght.

The time apart had allowed him to question his decision to let her into his life. He was a man who normally never hesitated to make a decision, and so he wondered if the act of questioning in itself was an indication that he wanted nothing beyond friendship with Kitty O'Hallorhan.

He ducked again as another wave hurled spume across the cot. He was getting chilled through, and the salt water had drenched the remains of his sandwich. He threw it over the wall. You were in love with her when she was a girl, he told himself. She's told you she still cares. She's giving you a second chance, but it won't last forever. She told you that too. Should you chuck her away as you chucked away the soggy bread and sausage?

O'Reilly picked up the game bag and slung it over his shoulder. He lifted his gun from where he'd left it propped against a corner, unloaded it, and tucked it in the crook of his left arm. "Come on, Arthur. Enough's enough. Let's head for home."

With Arthur at his heels, O'Reilly turned his right shoulder to the wind and started back to where he'd left the Rover. He trudged over the springy turf toward the five-bar gate at the end of the lane down from the Portaferry Road.

The wind and spray stung his cheek. A small pool of peat-brown water lay in his path. He could have walked around its verge, but instead he strode straight ahead, feeling the mud at the bottom sucking at his waders.

Arthur splashed through the water. "You must be getting bloody cold too," he said. "A run'll warm you up a bit. Get on out." He watched Arthur gallop off nose to the ground, quartering, looking for scent.

He thought of Kitty's perfume last Saturday night, how handsome he had thought her, and—a little thing—

how the fine hairs had curled on the nape of her neck. He remembered how she'd wanted a good wine but had been concerned lest he think it too expensive. That had been considerate.

He still felt jealousy of the other men who had kissed her. Kitty was a mature worldly woman, and he knew there must have been others. He'd guessed as much when she made him taste one of her garlicky snails, made sure they'd both eaten garlic before her not-so-subtle offer to kiss him. And he would have, by God, given her more than a good-night kiss in the hall, if the emergency hadn't intervened. He bloody well would have.

His thoughts were interrupted by a harsh high-pitched craaking, and he saw a small brown bird with a long narrow beak flying away, jinking erratically from side to side. A snipe. He threw the gun to his shoulder, then remembered he had unloaded. O'Reilly chuckled at himself and shouldered the shotgun.

You can be like that sometimes, Fingal. Acting reflexively without always taking the trouble to think things through. You did it with the raffle. A great idea, but you'd not considered how to ensure that Eileen won. It took Donal to sort that out. You took on Fitzpatrick without a clear plan of attack and were lucky to get away with cowing the man.

Now why, he wondered, why am I having reservations about Kitty?

He stopped to open the five-bar gate; its hinges were rusty and it refused to budge when he pushed at it. He planted his feet, then rammed at the gate with all his strength, and this time it creaked wide open. He went through and shoved it shut.

Arthur came racing down the Point, leapt, and soared over the gate.

"Well done," O'Reilly said. "You cleared that obstacle with room to spare." His utterance made him see clearly that as far as Kitty O'Hallorhan was concerned, the only obstacle was himself and the fear of being hurt. You're an *amadán*, O'Reilly, he told himself. When she comes back up north, she'll have Christmas dinner at Number One. Either that evening, if he could get her alone, or shortly after, he'd ask her if she'd . . . no, by God, he'd *tell* her he was going to take her up on her offer to give him a second chance.

He opened the back door of the Rover, putting his gun and gamebag on the backseat. "Get in, Arthur. That's enough for today. Let's head back to Number One, get warmed up, and see how Barry's doing."

Dog and master got into the car.

Even before O'Reilly started the car's engine—and certainly well before the unreliable old heater had a chance to warm him up—O'Reilly felt the chill leaving his bones. He knew it was because while he looked forward to Christmas dinner every year, *this* year there was an added fervour. Kitty O'Hallorhan would be there.

40

Now in Injia's Sunny Clime, Where I Used to Spend My Time

"Thank you for coming, Doctor Laverty. I do appreciate you taking the trouble to visit me on a Saturday morning." Alice Moloney, wearing a maroon, knitted, midcalf-length dress and low-heeled brogues, stood beside a glass-topped wheeled trolley. She poured tea into a cup. "Milk? Sugar?"

"Just milk, please."

As she fussed with his cup of tea, Barry looked around the living room of her over-the-shop flat. The walls were papered with a cream flock paper. Prints by Edgar Degas and Claude Monet kept company with dried flowers in circular glass-fronted frames. A framed tapestry sampler of the Lord's Prayer in fine needlework—he guessed it was her own stitching—hung over the mantel of a gas fireplace. The little blue flames danced and popped.

Miss Moloney's budgerigar sat on its perch in a domed wire cage hanging from a cast-iron stand in the corner of the room. Barry had never understood the appeal of keeping anything in a cage, but couldn't deny that the little cobalt-blue bird was a handsome creature. Its white head and face were highlighted by a scarlet beak and piercing black eyes and surrounded by a black-and-white striped hood.

A very large, almost spherical tortoiseshell cat lay asleep on a Victorian side chair in front of a tablecloth-draped sideboard, where small ivory carvings, intricately filigreed brass boxes, and a kirpan in a silver sheath—souvenirs from India, he thought—were arranged with geometric precision beside a few cheap knickknacks. Barry wondered if the cup emblazoned with A Present from the Isle of Man, the little Scotsman doll in a kilt, and the miniature Nelson's Column were all mementos of less exotic places she had holidayed.

A two-foot-high live fir tree in a pot of soil sat undecorated in the middle of a heavy bog-oak table.

Only two Christmas cards flanked an ormolu clock on the mantel.

"Thank you." He accepted the cup and saucer and waited for Alice Moloney to finish pouring her own and be seated.

Perched uncomfortably on the edge of an armchair he recognized as Queen Anne, Barry looked at the chair's characteristic drake feet and sculpted cabriole legs. His parents, to whom he had just posted the long overdue letter, were interested in antique furniture, and he had absorbed a working knowledge of the subject listening to them and studying the illustrations in their books. This one, with its flared armrests, was typical of the early eighteenth century, and it was now upholstered in red velvet, a lace antimacassar draped over its back.

"Will you have one?" She pointed to a plate of scones.

"No, thank you, Alice. The tea's fine."

"Nasty weather we're having." She held the handle of her Royal Doulton teacup between her thumb and first three fingers. Her little finger was outstretched. Her hand trembled slightly.

"Indeed it is." Miss Moloney had been brought up as a gentlewoman in preindependence India. She would insist on observing the social niceties before getting down to business. He sipped his tea and continued to test his knowledge of eighteenth-century furniture.

The room was cluttered with reproduction pieces, but he was pretty certain that a dropleaf table against one wall was an original Sheraton. On the table he saw a collection of photographs in silver frames. The silver had been freshly polished, but the photographs were fading.

"Your family?" he asked, looking more closely at one of a moustached and bespectacled man, an older woman, and two younger women. They all wore prewar clothes. They were sitting under a canopy and were flanked by two bearded Indians wearing jodhpurs, long jackets, and turbans.

She rose, set her cup aside, picked up the picture, and handed it to him. "That's Havildar-Major Baldeep Singh and Subedar-Major Gurjit Singh. They were friends of Daddy's. That's Mummy and Daddy." She sighed. "Mummy never got over his death. She followed him two years later. We were back in Ireland then. In Belfast."

"I'm sorry."

"Thank you. It's all right." She pointed at one of the young women. "Ellen, my sister, the one who's in Millisle, was married, so I—that's me on the left—I was on my own."

Barry looked at the picture more closely. She had bobbed hair and a wide smile. As a girl Alice Moloney had been quite lovely, yet she had never married.

"I'm afraid young gels—that was what girls were called then—young gels didn't have much education before the war, and Daddy left a very tiny pension that dried up when Mummy died. I had been taught to play the piano, arrange flowers, and sew. I did that sampler above the fireplace . . ."

Barry smiled. He'd been right.

"I wasn't a very good cook or pianist, or flower arranger for that matter," she said, with a faint smile, "but I was good with a needle. So I took my share of the inheritance and bought the dress shop here."

"And you've been here since nineteen-fifty?" Living alone, with few if any friends as far as he knew. No wonder she had struck him as a bitter woman when he'd first met her.

"That's right." She took the picture back and put it in its place beside one that immediately caught Barry's attention.

"Good heavens. That's Mahatma Gandhi with your father."

"Oh, yes, he often came to visit. I think in some ways he was what got me interested in Hinduism. He was a lovely little man."

"You must have loved India."

"I did. Very much." She sighed. "It was quite the most fascinating place." As she spoke, she gazed fondly at one framed picture. It was of a handsome, smiling young man astride a polo pony. He wore a solar topee, the pith helmet beloved by the sahibs of the Raj, and carried a polo stick over one shoulder.

Barry was sure this had to be the captain of Skinner's Horse who had died of leukemia. He was glad he was soon going to be able to set her mind at rest about her own condition.

"The climate was warmer there, but I've grown very fond of Ireland too, even when it pours. It was kind of you to call on such a horrible day," she said, as she once more took her chair and picked up her cup.

"I promised I would. I knew you'd be worried until you heard the results of your X-ray, particularly after what you told me in the surgery."

"I am." She sat stiffly, her back ramrod straight, and for a moment Barry wondered if as a "gel" she'd taken deportment classes.

"There's no cancer in your bowel."

Miss Moloney swallowed, took a very deep breath, and putting her cup into the saucer, glanced at the young man's picture. Her tremor had vanished. She exhaled. "Thank you, Doctor. Thank you very much for coming straight to the point."

Barry had learned the technique from O'Reilly, who had told him months ago, "Every patient who goes for a test will have a secret fear they have cancer. The very first thing you tell them if you can when they come to hear the result is that it's *not* cancer."

"Your X-ray was perfectly normal." He pulled an envelope from his inside pocket and offered to show her the report. "You can read it yourself if you like."

She smiled. "That won't be necessary, Doctor Laverty. You are a very sensitive young man. I trust you. Thank you for setting my mind at rest."

Barry felt his cheeks redden.

"And thank you for asking if we could come up here. You saw when you came into the shop how busy it was. Sally McClintock's a good girl. I took her on last week. She'll manage by herself for a while without me, and the shop was *not* the place to talk about my medical condition. Not in front of those nosy parkers."

Barry laughed. He'd narrowly missed being trapped in a conversation with Cissie Sloan and her cousin Aggie, who were being served by Sally, a farmer's daughter he was treating for painful periods. He hoped Cissie would be gone by the time he'd finished his tea.

Miss Moloney shook her head. "When Cissie's finished blethering, the whole village will be convinced I'm terminally ill simply because she saw you coming up here with me." She smiled at him. "But I'm not, am I? I really am very grateful for you coming to tell me."

"All you'll need to do—"

A piercing shriek interrupted the sentence. Barry jumped and almost spilled his tea.

The budgerigar pecked at a piece of cuttlebone, preened itself, and shrieked again.

Miss Moloney went to the cage and made quick, gentle noises with her pursed lips. "Who's a good boy, then? Billy Budgie's a good boy. He is. He is. Billy Budgie's Mummy's good boy."

Billy Budgie's a noisy bugger, Barry thought, as he finished his tea and rose, but she obviously doted on the bird. "As I was saying, Miss Moloney—Alice—all you need do is keep taking the iron tablets. Eat lots of green vegetables, and if you can bring yourself to do it, eat more red meat."

"I will, Doctor. I promise. Will you excuse me for a minute?"

"I was going anyway."

"It'll just take a moment." She left the room.

Barry shrugged. He wasn't in a hurry. He went to the cage where the bird was now clinging to one of the wires. It cocked its head to one side and regarded Barry with one of its beady black eyes. "Nice bird," he said, and he pushed a finger through the bars to stroke the budgerigar's head. It struck with lightning speed. Barry felt its beak slice into his fingertip. "Ow." He pulled his finger away and sucked it, tasting the copperiness of his own blood. He looked at the finger. It was a small wound, but he had to wrap it in a hanky to stop the blood dripping onto the carpet.

He looked at the budgie and could have sworn it was grinning at him. He shook his head. He should have known better than to tempt the creature.

He heard Miss Moloney return. She handed him a parcel. "Would you please give that to Doctor O'Reilly? It's the pants to his Santa suit. I've let them out."

He took it with his uninjured hand, keeping the other behind his back. "I'll give it to him the minute I see him, Alice."

"Thank you." She opened the door to a small landing above the stairs. "Now, Doctor, I'll go and finish my tea before I go back to work. I'll wish you the compliments of the season today, but I'm sure I'll see you at the pageant."

"You will, of course." Barry took his overcoat from a peg and slipped it on. "Good-bye, Alice."

"Good-bye, and thanks again." She closed the door.

Barry went down the stairs and into the shop, relieved to note that Cissie had left. He greeted Sally and then took the short walk back to Number One. The gale was on its last legs, and the sign outside the Black Swan was swinging gently. It had been flapping back and forth when he'd passed it on his way to the shop.

Poor Alice. She probably needed a few minutes to collect herself before she went back to work. Having a worry removed could be unsettling. At least this time life had been kind. It hadn't always been, and all she had were her souvenirs, her memories, her photographs of what must have been her happy past, and precious little else. By the way she'd looked at his picture, Barry thought she must have loved the young captain very dearly.

Barry'd taken some snaps of Patricia in September and had had one enlarged. He kept it on his bedside table. The rest were in the table's drawer. If he did lose her, would he still have those pictures twenty-five years later? He'd rather not find out. He'd rather have her in the flesh. Barry took comfort from having spoken with her earlier this morning.

He quickly covered the distance to Number One, walking past the same rosebushes O'Reilly had once thrown Seamus Galvin into because he had asked O'Reilly to look at his ankle without bothering to wash his feet. Barry smiled. Fingal really was unique. He wondered what time his senior colleague would get home.

O'Reilly slung his full gamebag over his shoulder, grabbed his gun, got out of the Rover, and let Arthur out. As soon as O'Reilly opened the gate, Arthur rushed through and began noisily lapping at his water bowl.

"Thirsty, are you? I'd go a pint myself, but I'd need to get cleaned up first."

Arthur paid no attention, took one last slurp, and

disappeared inside his kennel to sleep, perhaps, O'Reilly thought, to dream doggy dreams reliving his great retrieves of the day.

O'Reilly walked to the back of the house, propped his unloaded gun against the wall, and sat on the grass to wrestle off his waders. Leaving them outside, he picked up his gun and let himself into the kitchen. After the bitter cold of the day and the old Rover's less than efficient heating system, the room felt stiflingly hot. Something that smelled delicious was cooking. He slipped off his jacket.

Kinky had her back to him. She turned. "Is it home you are, Doctor dear?"

"I am, and pleased to be, Kinky. It was bloody bitter on the Lough today."

"Begging your pardon, but you've no sense, sir." She tutted. "Yourself just over the bronchitis and going out on a day like that. You need your head examined, so."

"Come on, Kinky. You've seen me go out in worse."

"I have, but Doctor O'Reilly, sir. You're not getting any younger."

"None of us are, Kinky, but it was grand to get away from this place and away down to the shore. It's a great spot for a bit of contemplation."

She nodded. "Everyone needs a bit of peace and quiet once in a while."

"I'd a great day," he said, "and I did so much thinking that I think I've probably unravelled all the secrets of the universe. I was even thinking about you in the car on the way home." And indeed he had been ruminating that he'd not done enough to show support for her when Fitzpatrick had been so bloody rude.

"Away with you, Doctor dear." She smiled.

"No, it's true. I've not had a chance to tell you about it, but Barry and I had a word in Fitzpatrick's delicate shell-like ear on Tuesday. I thought over how it had gone, and do you know? I think I might just have managed to get through to the man."

Kinky grunted. "He's an ignorant spalpeen, so."

"That's certainly how he comes over, but I've a notion he's never been a very happy man and so he doesn't understand how important a bit of courtesy is to other people. I decided this afternoon that he prescribes all his weird and wonderful nostrums because he thinks that it'll make his patients love him."

"If you say so, sir, but I don't see what that has to do with me."

"Among other things, I told him he'd been bloody rude to you, Kinky."

"He was."

"You handled him very well, Barry says, and I never thanked you. You did a great job of protecting me, Kinky."

"Sure weren't you sick, and isn't keeping an eye to you my job?"

"No, it's not . . ." He saw how she lowered her eyes. "Your job is to run this house, but . . . Kinky?"

She looked up.

"I very much appreciate your attention to me and young Laverty." He saw her smile. "And I should have thanked you for handling Fitzpatrick, so Doctor Laverty and I made him promise to mind his p's and q's and be polite to you in future."

She sniffed. "Maybe he will and maybe he won't. My mother used to say, 'Neither give cherries to a pig nor advice to a fool,' but thank you for doing it all the same, sir, and the next time I see him I'll hold no grudge . . . as long as he behaves."

"Good for you. You're a powerful woman, Kinky Kincaid." O'Reilly sneezed.

Her eyes widened and there was concern in her voice when she said, "Is it another chill you've taken?"

"Not at all, there's nothing wrong with me today that a nice hot bath and maybe some of your broth for lunch won't cure."

She frowned. "I have some Scotch broth ready to be heated. Would that do?"

He took her in his arms and gave her a hug that lifted her feet off the ground. "Kinky Kincaid, you're a godsend."

"Put me down, sir," she said, as she laughed. "Put me down."

He did as he was asked and then stepped back to watch her fussing with her hair and straightening her apron. "I'll be off in a minute for a bath," he said, "but I need to get my gun cleaned first and get the ducks in my bag plucked and gutted."

"What birds have you, sir?"

"Two mallard."

She went to the oven. "Don't you worry about plucking the birds, sir. *You* see to your gun and go for your bath, so. *I'll* see to the ducks once I've taken my meringues out of the oven." She turned away, opened the oven door, and muttered, "They're coming on a treat." Then she turned back to O'Reilly and said, "And Doctor Laverty came in about ten minutes ago. He's upstairs, sir."

41

Feel the Pangs of Disappointed Love

O'Reilly, fresh from the bath Barry had heard being drawn half an hour ago, strode in in a scented cloud of Badedas.

Barry smiled. It was hard to picture tough-as-nails O'Reilly taking bubble baths, but soon after Barry started to work here, O'Reilly had confessed his liking for them. He'd even told Barry to help himself to the pine-scented bubble maker.

"'Home is the sailor home from the sea . . . ,'" said O'Reilly, parking his recently bathed, dressing-gowned, and slippered self into his armchair.

"'And the hunter home from the hill.' Robert Louis Stevenson." Barry set his puzzle on the coffee table. "Except you weren't on a hill. You were at Strangford. Did you have fun?"

"I had a great morning. So had Arthur." O'Reilly

took a pipe and matches from his dressing-gown pocket. "And I'm going to slough about for a while before I get dressed. It was bloody cold out there, and I need to get properly warmed up." He rose and stirred the fire before sitting again. "We went to Gransha Point. Do you know it?"

"I do indeed." Barry could see with perfect clarity a day in August when he had taken Patricia there for a picnic and but for a sudden summer squall would have made love to her for the first time.

"There's an old ruined sheep cot about halfway along . . ." O'Reilly busied himself lighting his pipe.

"I know." Barry closed his eyes.

They'd been lying on a blanket on the grass in its lee. If he tried hard he could almost hear the sea on the shingle, feel the warm summer breeze, nearly as warm as her breast. He'd unbuttoned Patricia's blouse and was caressing her when the storm struck. She'd risen and stood, arms raised above her head facing the wind and rain, her soaked blouse plastered to her and limning her breasts. He remembered exactly how her dark hair had been wind-tossed and how he had thought she looked like an Indian princess worshipping the lightning god. He opened his eyes again. "I know it very well."

"It's right under a flight path," O'Reilly said, "and makes a great hide. There's two mallard in the kitchen."

"I'm glad you had a good time," he said, although in truth he was only half concentrating on what O'Reilly was saying.

O'Reilly let go a huge blast of smoke. "So did Arthur."

And so will I when she finally gets here. She should have her tickets by now. He glanced at the door, hoping that in doing so the telephone would ring in the hall. Any minute now, he thought.

The first day we're both free I'll borrow Jack Mills's flat in Belfast while Jack's at work. Barry smiled. There'd be no sudden gales in there to interrupt them, and the urgency of his need for her made him tingle. He missed what O'Reilly had just said. "Pardon?"

"I asked what you'd been up to."

Barry coughed, then spluttered, "Well I, um . . . that is, it's been pretty quiet here. I went to see Alice Moloney and gave her the test results."

"Alice, is it?" said O'Reilly, sounding mildly surprised. "You getting to be friends with the old targe?"

"In a way. She's not so bad when you get to know her."

"You could have fooled me, but go on."

"She's had a pretty tough life. I can understand why she comes over the way she does."

"Really?"

"Did you know she grew up in India during the Raj?"

"No."

"Her dad was in the Indian civil service. He was killed there when she was quite young."

"I didn't know that. I'm sorry to hear it. It's always

tough losing someone you love." O'Reilly frowned. "I haven't seen much of Miss Moloney. Ordinarily I've had little call to frequent dress shops." There was a wistfulness in his voice.

"We went there to buy Kinky that green hat," Barry said. "Remember?"

"I do. That and a couple of professional visits are all I know of the woman. She's a very private person. I saw her for piles. I told you about them."

"I know. She has a simple iron-deficiency anaemia, and it was good to know that history. They might have been the cause if she still had them, but she doesn't."

"Good." O'Reilly set his pipe in an ashtray and said, "You were with me the second time I saw her, when she was having the vapours because of Helen Hewitt. That girl showed a lot of spunk after the way Miss Moloney persecuted her."

"Do you know, Fingal?" Barry said. "I can almost forgive Alice for that. She's had her own tragedies. I'm not surprised she's a bit bitter at times."

"What tragedies?"

"I told you her dad was killed."

"Barry. That's *a* tragedy. You said, 'tragedies.' What else happened?"

"She lost someone she loved. I think she loved him very much."

"Did she now?" O'Reilly looked away from Barry and out through the rain-streaked window. He stared for a while, then turned back and asked softly, "And who would that have been?" Barry saw sadness in O'Reilly's eyes.

"A young army captain. He died of leukemia."

O'Reilly turned back to the window.

Barry heard the phone ringing below. "I'm on call. I'll answer that," he said, glad of the excuse to leave O'Reilly alone for a few minutes, and hoping for the phone call he so much wanted.

Kinky, wiping her hands on her apron, was on her way from the kitchen to answer the phone. "It's all right, Kinky." Barry lifted the receiver. "Hello? Doctor Laverty here."

"Barry?"

"Patricia." Barry was sure his heart turned over. "Where are you now?"

"You'll not believe this."

For a second he hoped she would say the ferry terminal in Holyhead, but he realized she couldn't have got there in the few hours since they last spoke. "Try me."

"London. In Thomas Cook's."

"The travel agent?"

"Yes."

"Terrific." She had finally kept her promise. As soon as he knew her arrival time, he'd get straight onto Jack to see about borrowing his flat. He wanted no more storms interrupting them. "Wonderful, darling. When can I expect you?" He held his breath.

"Barry, I'm sorry. I don't know how to say this."

"What? Say what?" She was dissembling again.

There *was* another man. Barry's palms sweated. His mouth felt dry. He took a deep breath and said as levelly as he could, "Just go ahead."

"It's *all* my fault. I got so wrapped up in the fun *I* was having. I was selfish. I didn't think. I didn't bother getting on with buying my ticket soon enough."

Barry frowned. He wasn't sure if he could believe her. "Patricia, if there is someone else, I'll try to understand. Honestly."

"Don't be silly. I *love* you, Barry. I love *you*."

"But you're not coming, right?" Damnation. Bugger it. Well, by God, he might phone Jack anyway. Try to see him for a pint. Barry could use his friend's advice and his comfort right now.

"I'm afraid not. I've been to two travel agents in Cambridge. I've left it far too late to get a ticket. I am truly sorry, Barry. I really do want to see you. I love you."

Barry held the receiver away from his ear, looked at it, and wondered what the hell to say. He heard garbled, tinny noises coming from the phone. He put it back against his ear.

". . . Barry. Barry, are you still there?" He heard her urgency.

"Yes. And I'll not pretend I'm not disappointed, Patricia."

"I know. So am I, and I tried. I really tried. The Holyhead run was booked solid; so were both the Liverpool and the Heysham boats to Belfast. I even tried to get a spot on the Stranraer-to-Larne ferry . . ."

"But it's hundreds of miles from Cambridge to Scotland . . ."

"I know, but it would have been worth it, Barry. I do love you, and I feel terrible. I didn't know what to do. Jenny suggested we try Cook's in London. She thought perhaps they might have bought blocks of tickets to resell. They're the biggest travel agent in England. I'm here now. The agent was wonderful, but she said all their tickets were gone."

"At least you let me know straightaway. Thank you." *O thou that tellest good tidings to Zion,* he thought. Some bloody tidings. He told himself not to be sarcastic—at least not out loud.

"It was the least I could do. Not keep you hanging on hoping."

"Thank you." But, he thought, if you'd booked before you tore off to see those bloody ducks.

"The agent could see how disappointed I was, and when I told her why, she insisted I use her phone to make a quick call to you."

"Decent of her." He couldn't keep the edge from his voice. Jesus, five minutes ago he'd been fantasizing about making love to her.

"Barry, don't be like that. Please. I will call as soon as I get back to Bourn. Try to explain. Try to make it up to you."

From eight hundred miles away. Good luck. Barry rocked to and fro on his heels, inhaled, and then said, "Patricia, I've tried. God knows, I've tried to understand."

"Barry, I'm sorry. I'm sorry."

"I can guess how new and exciting Cambridge is. I thought Belfast was pretty cosmopolitan after Bangor and a boys' boarding school. I can see how you got carried away by all of that." And I still want to know who he is . . .

"Thank you, Barry. Thank you for trying to understand. I didn't forget about you, back home waiting patiently." There was a catch to her voice. "I do really want to see you. It has to be a ferry. I can't afford—"

"A flight. I've already offered to—"

"Barry, I've tried to explain . . ." He heard her voice more faintly saying, "I'll only be a second more. Please? Thank you." Then she said, "Are you still there?"

"Yes." His voice was flat.

"Easter isn't too far away."

"Right." The hell it isn't.

"The woman at Cook's said the flights to Belfast are booked, but if I go to Heathrow on Christmas Eve I might get a standby ticket. They're really cheap."

"It's worth a try, I suppose." Barry shrugged. He knew he'd not sounded very enthusiastic. He'd had enough of having his hopes raised and dashed.

"Don't you want me to?"

"Patricia, I can't tell you what to do." He'd almost snapped *suit yourself*. "I still want to see you."

"If I can't get one, the next term doesn't start until the fifteenth of January. Maybe I could come for the New Year . . ."

"Fine. Just let me know if you *are* coming, but I

can't be bothered with more 'I might be coming' stuff. Please don't do it to me anymore."

Her voice sounded stiff. "Very well. I won't."

He waited. He could hear muffled voices, as if she had her hand over the mouthpiece and was talking to someone else. "The agent says I've had long enough on the phone. I'll have to go."

"Fine. Have a lovely time at the Tate and the National . . ." Where the hell else had she said she was going to visit?

"Barry, don't sulk."

He ignored her and simply said, "Let me know what's happening so I can plan, and if I don't see you . . ."—and I know I bloody well won't, Kinky notwithstanding—"have a very merry Christmas and happy New Year." Although how happy for him it would be, if this was the preliminary symptom of a final rift, didn't bear thinking about.

"And you, Barry. I love you, darling."

"And I love you," he said, trying to sound enthusiastic, "but if the Cook's woman wants you off the phone, you'd better run."

He wasn't sure if he heard a tiny sob just before she said, "All right. I love you, Barry. Good-bye." The phone clicked dead.

Christ, that good-bye sounded awfully final. Barry sighed, replaced the receiver, and stood for a moment staring into space. Then he trudged back up the stairs.

42

I Feel My Heart New Opened

Lady Macbeth was curled up asleep in his lap. O'Reilly sat gazing into the grate. He watched as the ember patterns rearranged themselves, as a piece of coal, finally reduced to ash, collapsed, and the lumps it had been supporting tumbled lower in the grate. Black coals, cherry-red glowing cinders, and grey ash seemed to be an Impressionist's oils on a canvas and gave to his eyes the warmth the fire gave to his body.

He thought wistfully of Deidre roasting chestnuts in their room in Portsmouth, holding the handle of a perforated, circular brass plate and giggling when a chestnut burst from the heat. Learning of Miss Moloney's loss had brought his own grief back, despite his resolve to try to let Deidre's memory fade.

He'd been able to think of nothing else since Barry had gone to answer the phone, and he hardly bothered to look up when his young colleague returned. "A call from the sick and suffering?"

"No." Barry's voice was clipped, flat.

O'Reilly turned to him. "Christ," he said, "you look about as sour as an unripe gooseberry dipped in buttermilk. What's wrong?"

Barry shrugged but said nothing.

"Barry. What's up?" O'Reilly said. "Tell me."

"It was Patricia." Barry said. There was no life in his words. "She's not coming for Christmas." He took a deep breath.

"Not coming? Bugger." O'Reilly sat so straight that he dislodged Lady Macbeth. "Why the hell not?"

"I'm sorry, Fingal"—Barry snapped the words—"but if Kinky can't find passage for Patricia on fully booked ferries or a seat on jam-packed aeroplanes, it's a nonstarter, unless Kinky has a flying carpet in her cupboard. Patricia left it too bloody late to book." By the way he spoke and stood, shoulders hunched, jaw thrust out, O'Reilly knew that Barry Laverty, usually a placid young man, was not so much feeling let down as angry.

"I think," said O'Reilly softly, "there's more to this than just disappointment that she's not coming. Sit down, Barry. Tell me about it."

Barry slumped in the armchair. "I don't know where to start." He sounded more resigned than angry now. He put his hands, one clasping the other, between his thighs, pursed his lips, and let his head droop.

O'Reilly rose and walked to the sideboard. When he returned he handed Barry a whiskey. "It's early for a Jameson, but this is for medicinal purposes."

Barry looked up and took the glass. "Aren't you having one?"

O'Reilly shook his head. "I'm not the patient. You are." He sat again.

Barry didn't drink. "Fingal, you know how worried

I was when she went to Cambridge? Worried we'd grow apart?"

O'Reilly sat and looked at Barry. Let the boy talk, he told himself.

Barry swallowed. "I think we have." He looked into O'Reilly's eyes.

O'Reilly saw a young man pleading for reassurance that it wasn't so. "Why would you say that?"

"Because she's not coming, and she promised she would."

O'Reilly frowned. "It's hardly her fault she couldn't get a ticket. That's what you said." With a bit of luck it was just a storm in a teacup. Perhaps Barry was reading too much into it.

Barry clenched his teeth. "Not couldn't. Didn't want to."

"How do you know that? Did she tell you?"

"She didn't have to. First, she didn't have the money for a plane ticket. She had to wait to see if her dad got a Christmas bonus."

"Sounds reasonable to me."

"I thought so too . . . then. I offered to pay her way." Barry managed a wry grin. "You know the funny notions she has sometimes about men and women. I wasn't entirely surprised when she refused my offer. Maybe I should have seen it coming then . . . or pretty soon after."

"Why?"

"Why?" Barry held his glass in both hands and stared deeply into it. He shrugged.

God, O'Reilly thought, getting him to open up

was like pulling teeth without anaesthetic. "Come on, Barry. Why should you have seen it coming?"

He looked directly at O'Reilly. "I had to suggest she might like to try for a ferry. She won a scholarship to Cambridge. She's one very clever woman, but the thought had never occurred to her. Or she didn't want to think of an alternative to flying. I really think she doesn't want to come."

"Perhaps she was too preoccupied with her studies? You know how all-consuming a professional course can be." O'Reilly knew he was searching for an explanation that would comfort Barry.

"Right. All bloody consuming." Barry snorted. "Fingal, the Cambridge Michaelmas term ended on December the first."

"Oh." That was more worrisome.

"She'd left it far too late to book. She's just admitted that she got too wrapped up in herself." Barry shook his head like a dazed boxer. O'Reilly'd seen that often enough in the ring. "Fingal, she could have been here a couple of weeks ago, but she's made new friends over there. She wanted to go to some Wildfowl Trust place. She should have booked before she went there. It would only have taken a few minutes."

O'Reilly sat silently, his eyes never leaving Barry's face.

"She's in London now for a few days. She's going to art galleries, museums. Places like the Victoria and Albert Museum. What have we got in Belfast? A few mouldy dinosaur bones and a mummy in the Ulster

Museum? We can't compete. I don't think I can compete." He took a sip of his whiskey. "She'd like to do almost anything except come home to Ulster and see me. I'm not sure she isn't glad she can't get a ticket. For the last couple of weeks she's been going to come, then she's not going to be able to, then she is. I've been going up and down like a bloody yo-yo."

O'Reilly fished out his pipe and started to fill it. He needed a moment to think. Was Patricia simply being carried away by new experiences, or was Barry right? His own experience in practice had led him to believe that two people either grew together or grew apart. He didn't want to ask the next question because Ulstermen like himself and Barry were notoriously reticent about discussing their feelings. He lit his pipe. Want to or not, it must be asked. "Is she still in love with you, do you think?" O'Reilly let both eyebrows move up, but otherwise kept his face calm.

He thought perhaps Barry was going to say, "Mind your own business." So it pleased him that after a few moments, Barry said, "She says she is. She says she does still love me, but she's not behaving as if she did. If it were me I'd have been on the first available transport back home, unless I had a bloody good reason not to."

O'Reilly guessed what Barry feared that reason might be. It was time it was voiced. "And you're not sure if there's another fellah over there, are you, Barry? Is that it?"

Barry blew out his breath. "She swears blind there's not."

O'Reilly tapped his teeth with his pipe stem. "I don't know the girl very well, but she struck me as somebody who'd not lie to you about a thing like that." He waited to see if that would bring Barry any comfort.

Barry shrugged. Took a drink.

"Barry? How about you? Is there someone else for you?"

"Don't be daft." Barry looked away. "I ran a nurse home after the dance I went to last Saturday. Pretty girl, but not much going on on the upper deck."

"I hesitate to ask, son. How about that schoolteacher? You seemed to be getting on well with her at the rehearsal."

"She's a lovely-looking girl, and I'm sure she'd go out with me if I asked."

"Are you going to?"

"Do you know, Fingal, I just don't know. I'm so mad at Patricia I've thought about it."

"There's nothing wrong with that. I was going out with a girl once; then I met someone else. It happens."

Barry looked at O'Reilly quizzically before he said, "I thought we were right for each other. I still half do, but there is something else. I know her horizons have widened. When I met her she told me she had too much that she wanted to accomplish to have time to fall in love. I think now that she's had a taste of life beyond Ulster, she's recognized how tiny the place is and maybe how uninteresting a country GP like me is." He took another small sip. "I'm going to lose her." Barry looked at O'Reilly. "I honestly believe I am, Fingal." There was the kind of pleading in his eyes that O'Reilly had seen in the eyes of sick children who silently begged, "Make it better, Doctor. Make the pain go away."

O'Reilly stuck his pipe into his mouth. "You're probably entirely wrong, Barry . . ."

"For a time I was uncertain if it would matter if I did lose her. There are other pretty girls out there. Three years, mostly apart, is going to be a hell of a long time. I wondered if the whole thing was worth the candle."

"And is it?"

"I think so, Fingal, but—"

O'Reilly was sure he understood Barry's reservations, if only because he was having the same kind of feelings about Kitty O'Hallorhan. "But you wonder if you cut your losses now whether it might hurt less than it would if things fall apart later?"

"That's right."

"I'm afraid it will, Barry. There's no cutting your losses once you've opened yourself to somebody. None at all."

Barry's expression changed. His pained frown slipped into a look of concern.

"And I know that you know what I'm talking about—"

"But—"

"It's all right, Barry. It's all right. Kinky told me a couple of months ago that she'd told you that I'd been married."

Barry's eyes widened. He took a quick drink. "She what?"

"She told me. I think her conscience got the better of her."

"What did you say to her?"

"I thanked her."

"For breaching a confidence?"

"Barry, when you've known Kinky Kincaid as long as I have, you'll understand that woman never does anything without giving it a lot of thought. I knew if she'd told you it was because she trusted you and because she'd decided having you here was good for me." O'Reilly leant forward and touched Barry's knee. "She thought it would help you make up your mind to stay if you knew a bit more about the old ogre who ran the place." That's floored him, O'Reilly thought. He hasn't suspected that I am well aware of how I often come across to people.

"You're not an ogre, Fingal. Far from it."

"I can be. Seamus Galvin thought so when I chucked him into the rosebushes. You thought so when you watched me chucking him." O'Reilly chuckled at the memory and was gratified to see Barry smile.

"I nearly bolted and went to look for a job somewhere else."

O'Reilly sat back. "I'm very glad you didn't. Very glad."

"Thank you, Fingal. So am I."

"And it's not just because you're a great help in the practice . . ."

Barry blushed.

God, O'Reilly thought, but he was an easy man to embarrass. "Watching you and your Patricia got me thinking."

"What about?"

O'Reilly stood, walked to the window, and peered out at the tilted steeple and the ragged clouds tearing over it. He heard the rain thrashing against the windowpane. He turned. Barry was looking up expectantly. Perhaps, O'Reilly thought, listening to me has lifted his mind from his own troubles for a while. He just needs one more nudge. "When I lost Deidre . . ."—he saw Barry's eyes widen—"Deidre Mawhinney was my wife's name before we were married." He'd not spoken her name aloud for as long as he could remember, and it pleased him to have done so without great pain. "When I lost her I turned inward and decided never to open myself to another woman again."

Barry frowned and his eyes softened. "That's very sad, Fingal," he said softly.

"I do know that, Barry. I told you I was seeing someone. It was Kitty. Then Deidre came along. Poor Kitty didn't have a chance. I thought Deidre was perfect."

"I really am very sorry. I know how you must have felt. I'm like that about Patricia."

"I know. That's why seeing you last summer, so happy with that girl, made me take stock, and when Kitty reappeared . . ." He looked down at his slippers, then back at Barry. "I was *very* fond of her when I was a student . . ."

"I think she's a lovely woman. You're lucky she reappeared."

O'Reilly smiled. Now the boot was on the other foot. Barry couldn't help himself. If somebody needed advice he'd give it gladly. "Aye. I think you're right. It's taken me a while to recognize it, but between you and me, Barry, I'm ready to take a chance again, and when I do I'm going to risk getting hurt again."

Barry stood. "So what you're telling me is, don't despair. Keep hoping. Stay open to her, give Patricia the benefit of the doubt . . . but keep my options open with Sue Nolan?"

"No reason why you shouldn't be nice to her."

"I suppose, but keep trying with Patricia?"

"That's right. If she doesn't come, would you like to scoot over to England? You could have a week off after Christmas."

Barry smiled. "Thanks, Fingal. Let's see what happens . . ."

"And," said O'Reilly, pleased to see Barry smiling, "I do mean *after* Christmas. There'll be far too much going on here between now and then for you to miss."

"Indeed so," said Kinky, who walked in carrying a tray with two steaming plates of what O'Reilly knew would be her Scotch broth. "And the jollifications start tomorrow with the pageant." She set the tray on the sideboard. "I was thinking, Doctor O'Reilly, would you like the two mallard you shot today for your supper on Monday before the pageant? Maybe with a plum sauce?"

"I would." O'Reilly felt himself start to salivate at the prospect of roast wild duck. "But no more fowl after that, Kinky, until the turkey on Christmas Day, or Doctor Laverty and I will start to grow feathers."

43

Not Half So Surprised as I Am Now

Now there," said O'Reilly, "is a thing of beauty. Thank you, Kinky."

"It is how you like them, sir."

Barry inhaled. The scent of the roast wild ducks she had set before O'Reilly was overpowering. He sat forward and eagerly waited for O'Reilly to carve.

"And there's the plum sauce, creamed potatoes, and green peas. I'm sorry I had to use Eskimo frozen peas, but I boiled them with a dried mint leaf."

"No need to apologize," O'Reilly said, lifting the carving knife and fork.

Kinky headed for the door. "If you need me, give me a shout, sir. I'm having a pot pie in the kitchen, then I'll be in my room getting ready. And don't tarry. We've to leave at six-thirty. The pageant starts at seven, so."

"Here," said O'Reilly handing Barry a plate of

duck. "Help yourself to the vegetables, then bung them up here." O'Reilly had put slices of breast and two thighs on his own plate. Before even waiting to add the peas and potatoes, he lifted one little drumstick and popped it into his mouth. When O'Reilly pulled the bone out, it was as cleanly stripped of flesh as South American cattle when they wander into a piranha-infested river. "That," he said, "is tasty."

Barry passed the tureens. He sampled the duck meat. He'd never eaten wild duck before and found the plum sauce set off the flavour of a flesh that was drier and much less gamey than he'd anticipated. "You're right, Fingal. It is."

"Mallard's the best eating," O'Reilly said. "Widgeon can be a bit fishy. They eat eel grass."

"How do you think a Hawaiian goose would taste?" Wasn't that the bird Patricia said had been brought back from near extinction at the wildfowl place?

O'Reilly stopped his fork halfway to his mouth. "Anybody who killed one of those craythurs wouldn't get a chance to try eating it. The folks at Slimbridge would have his guts for sausage skins and—" He frowned. "Are you still stewing over your Patricia? You said she'd gone there."

"A bit." Barry ate another slice of breast and watched as O'Reilly, whose own helping of duck had disappeared, grabbed the carving set and laid into the second bird. "She might have got a ferry ticket if she'd not gone bird-watching. I wish she hadn't."

Now the second bird was dissected, Barry noticed that O'Reilly's helping was considerably more than what was left on the serving plate. "If wishes were horses, beggars would ride," O'Reilly said. "Pass the plum sauce."

Barry smiled as he passed the sauceboat. "You're right. I should stop feeling sorry for myself. I think I will take you up on that offer to go to England after Christmas."

"If," said O'Reilly, "she doesn't show up here and surprise you."

Barry shook his head. "I'll believe it when I see it." Barry finished his duck. "Is there a scrap left, Fingal?"

"Aye. Pass up your plate."

Barry did.

O'Reilly returned it. Two small slices and one thigh. Barry shook his head. "I'm enjoying my *wee* bit of bird," he said. He waited to see how O'Reilly would respond.

"Good." He pushed his plate away. "In that case, you'll not mind if I go shooting again."

You're hopeless when it comes to taking a hint, Fingal Flahertie O'Reilly, Barry thought. He finished his helping.

"Come on," said O'Reilly. He picked up his plate and the peas and potato tureens. "Bring the sauce dish and your plate through to the kitchen."

When Barry had finished his meal, he followed O'Reilly's lead and carried his dirty plates out to the kitchen.

"I'll get our coats," O'Reilly said, putting his utensils in the sink.

"There was no need for that, Doctors," Kinky said. "I could have seen to them after we got back. But thank you both." She was wearing her winter coat, white buckskin gloves, and her green hat, her best green hat. It had been a present from her doctors in August, and she'd worn it to Sonny and Maggie's wedding.

"The minted peas were lovely, and the duck was wonderful, Kinky. Truly wonderful," Barry said.

"Thank you, Doctor Laverty." She inclined her head graciously.

"It's the truth, Kinky," O'Reilly said, handing Barry his overcoat and opening the door. "Come on. Out to the car."

Barry could see frost on the grass sparkling in the light from the open door. He shut it and followed O'Reilly and Kinky, hearing their footsteps crunching along the lawn. The moon, two days past full, blazed against a black velvet sky, yet even its brightness could not mask the icy fires of Polaris, Castor, and Pollux, and Aldebaran high overhead, and Sirius low on the southeastern horizon.

He hummed, out of tune, the old carol, "It Came upon a Midnight Clear." His breath hung in visible clouds, and the tip of his nose tingled. On a December night much like this, 1,964 years ago, a boy child was born in Bethlehem of Judea.

From the middle distance he could hear the pealing of the chapel bells summoning all to the reenactment of that night, although back then, he thought, the wise men travelled to the event on camels, not in an elderly Rover.

The Parish Hall was packed. The curtains were closed. The houselights were up. Row upon row of folding kitchen chairs were occupied by what Barry reckoned must have been the entire population of Ballybucklebo and the surrounding townland. People stood in the aisle and at the back of the room. The hum of conversation was deafening.

O'Reilly stopped and scanned the crowd. "There's Eileen Lindsay and two of her kiddies second row from the front. Last seat on the right side. Behind those nuns. Come on, I need to have a word with her." Barry and Kinky followed as O'Reilly, like an icebreaker in the Arctic seas, forced his way through the throng.

Progress was slow. O'Reilly was stopped by a pale-faced man wearing a tweed suit. "Liam Gillespie," he explained to Barry.

The man who'd needed a splenectomy, Barry remembered.

"Doc," said the big man, "I never got to thank you properly for what you done for me."

"Are you all better?" O'Reilly asked.

"I am, sir."

"That's all the thanks I need. Merry Christmas to you, Liam." O'Reilly didn't wait to hear the response.

A few rows further forward, they were stopped

again. Councillor Bertie and Mrs. Flo Bishop perched on opposing aisle seats, presumably to give them that little extra room. As O'Reilly was about to stride past them, Bertie leaned to his wife and said sotto voce, "I'm not sure I like it here with all these papists, Flo. All them nuns and all."

Flo immediately leant closer to him, and Barry distinctly heard her hoarse whisper. "Houl' your wheest, Bertie Bishop. It's Christmas, so it is." She looked up and clapped her hand over her mouth before removing it and saying, "I never seen you there, Doctor O'Reilly." She glowered at her husband. "Sometimes Bertie doesn't think before he opens his big trap."

"Evening, Flo." Barry couldn't tell from O'Reilly's expression if he had overheard their exchange about papists. If he had, he was clearly willing to ignore it. "Great turnout," he said. "It's good to get the Orange and Green together once in a while, isn't it, Bertie?"

Councillor Bishop shrugged.

"I kept you a seat, Mrs. Kincaid." Flo stood and moved into the aisle.

"Thanks," Kinky said. "I'll see you at the front door when it's over, if that's all right, Doctor O'Reilly." She started to shuffle sideways past Flo.

"Of course, Kinky." O'Reilly moved on.

Their progress, Barry thought, was as erratic as a metal ball bearing in a pinball machine, bouncing from Kieran O'Hagan, who insisted on showing Barry his healing thumbnail ("It's coming on a treat, sir"), to Julie and Donal, where O'Reilly stopped.

Barry thought how lovely she looked. She was wearing the same cream suit and maroon blouse she'd worn as her going-away outfit. He guessed it was what would be called in these parts her Sunday best.

"I got your blood work in today, Julie. Everything's grand. Come and see us in a month."

"Thank you."

Donal winked, grinned, and nodded his head to the row immediately in front. "I see Eileen's here."

"I'll be having a word." O'Reilly said, moving on.

"Doctor O'Reilly." It was Reverend Robinson. He wore a rusty black serge suit and his starched dog collar. "The marquis and I have kept seats for you and Doctor Laverty over there." He pointed.

"Thanks. We'll be with you in a minute, Reverend." O'Reilly went to the front and walked past a row of seated nuns. Barry followed. He thought all their faces looked freshly scrubbed. They conversed, one with the other, in low undertones, the younger ones occasionally darting glances at their mother superior, a tall hawk-faced woman whose constant smile belied the severity of her aquiline features.

O'Reilly went to the second row.

Eileen Lindsay smiled at him and stood up. "Doctor O'Reilly."

Barry glanced down. Neither of her stockings was laddered. He hoped the money she was making now that she was back at work was helping her to make ends meet.

"How are you, Eileen?"

"Very well, sir."

"And how's Sammy?"

She smiled. "Nearly better. Maggie's minding him tonight so I can bring wee Mary and Willy."

Barry saw her two children, each sitting primly, Mary in a frilly skirted frock, Willy in short pants and his school blazer. A rip in the left-hand pocket had been repaired with neatly placed stitches. Sometimes, Barry often thought, a good seamstress might make a better fist of sewing up human cuts than would a physician.

O'Reilly pulled out his wallet. "I've a wee present for you, Eileen."

"A what?" She frowned. "Why? What is it?"

"Don't get all hot and bothered," O'Reilly said. "We're having a raffle at the Rugby Club party on Wednesday."

"Doctor, I can't afford to throw away money on a ticket. It's tight enough these days."

"I know that, but your man over there, His Lordship, he bought a wheen and gave them to me. 'Fingal,' says he, 'hand these out to a few decent folks.' Here's yours, Eileen." He removed it from his wallet, tore it in two, and put the stub back in his wallet.

Barry saw her take the green ticket. "I . . . will you say thank you to him for me, sir?"

"I will," said O'Reilly. "You'll be there for the draw?"

"I'll try, sir," she said, and she bent and whispered something in his ear. Barry wondered what.

O'Reilly nodded. "Good lass."

"May I have your attention? May I have your

attention?" An amplified, tinny voice assailed Barry's ears. He looked up to see Sue Nolan standing on the stage in front of the curtain. She held a microphone in her right hand. Her copper hair was down and glistened in the glow of the footlights. Somehow, he thought, her four-inch patent-leather stiletto heels were a bit at odds with her severe academic gown, but they accentuated the curve of her calves very well. "Thank you. The pageant will start in five minutes. Five minutes. Will you all please take your seats?"

"Come on, Barry." O'Reilly walked back the way he had come, stopping for a moment to say, "Evening, Father," to Father O'Toole, who sat at the harmonium beneath the stage. He was simply dressed in his black cassock. The Christmas pageant was not a religious ceremony, so he was able to forgo the splendour of copes and chasubles and the rest of the liturgical vestments.

"What did Eileen want?" Barry asked.

"It's the tradition at the party for parents to bring their own kiddies' presents to put in Santa's sack. She wanted to tell me that if she came she'd be able to bring some things for her three. I'd been concerned that she'd be too short of cash for that. I'm glad she let me know. Can you imagine how a wee one would feel if Santa had nothing for him?"

Barry shuddered.

"And she said to thank you again for getting Maggie to babysit."

Barry took a leaf from O'Reilly's book, remembering what he'd said to Liam Gillespie. "Sure Fingal, if

Sammy's getting better and Eileen's coping, that's thanks enough." He surprised himself by seeing that it was the truth.

As soon as they had crossed the centre aisle, Barry saw two empty front-row seats. Barry took his between O'Reilly, who was immediately immersed in conversation with the marquis of Ballybucklebo, and the Presbyterian minister.

He heard the rattle of the curtains being opened and the first bars of "Silent Night" being played.

Conversation died. The houselights dimmed. The set for the Nativity play was revealed in all its glory, with painted stable, animals, and a sign reading: Bethlehem Inn.

Miss Nolan stood centre stage in front of the children's choir, her arms outstretched, her hands raised above her shoulders. She really did have very good legs.

"Silent Night" died away.

She counted, "One, two, three." Then the harmonium played, and sweet voices rose in the first verse of "O Little Town of Bethlehem."

Miss Nolan kept the beat with her hands.

Barry closed his eyes and remembered the pageants when he was a boy. He half envied Colin Brown, who later would play the innkeeper. Barry had never risen above the rank of third shepherd, a nonspeaking role.

Barry became aware of a rhythmic disturbance that was somewhere between a low rumbling and the noise of a ripsaw. He turned. Good God, O'Reilly was fast asleep, head thrown back, mouth wide, his snores in danger of overpowering the children. Barry leant across, nudged his senior colleague in the ribs, and whispered loudly, "Wake up, Fingal."

"What? Huh?" O'Reilly opened his eyes, blinked, and closed his mouth. "Thanks, Barry. I must have nodded," he said quietly.

By the time that little drama had been played out, the carol had finished, the applause had died, and the choir was well into "Good King Wenceslas," known universally in Ulster as "Good King Wence*less*lass."

Barry watched, enjoying the expressions on the faces of the choristers as well as sneaking occasional glances at O'Reilly to make sure he'd not nodded off again, and admiring the fluid way Miss Nolan's body moved as she conducted.

The carol ended. Barry joined in the applause.

Miss Nolan turned to the audience and bowed on behalf of the children. She must have spotted Barry, because, looking him directly in the eyes, she smiled at him and her right eyebrow arched upward.

Barry smiled back. She was quite lovely, and Christmas spirit be damned, Kinky's reassurances not withstanding, and O'Reilly's admonishments of Saturday aside, he was going to try to get a word with her later.

The applause died and she addressed the room. "My lord, ladies and gentlemen, We beg your indulgence. It will take a few moments for the choir to leave the stage and for the players to take their places. While that is going on, I will set the scene."

A woman—another teacher, Barry assumed—appeared from stage left and began to shepherd the children off as the curtains were jerked closed.

Miss Nolan, who must have known the words by heart, began to recite, "And it came to pass in those days, that there went out a decree from Caesar Augustus, that all the world should be taxed . . ."

Barry, who believed he had left religion behind, found he had a lump in his throat and a prickling behind his eyelids as she told the story. In his mind he repeated the words with her. As a concession to the Protestants present, they were the majestic words of the King James Bible, which he had made no conscious effort to learn but had absorbed in his childhood, and knowing those words was as much a part of Barry Laverty as his blue eyes and his fair cow's lick.

He looked to O'Reilly, and to Barry's surprise the big man's lips were moving too. They were forming the same words that Barry was hearing from the stage: ". . . into Judea, unto the city of David, which is called Bethlehem, to be taxed with Mary his espoused wife, being great with child . . ."

The pulleys creaked, the curtains opened. It came as no surprise to Barry that a group of shepherds near the back of the stage sat around a pen of live sheep. Such props would not be hard to come by in Ballybucklebo.

A spotlight focused on Joseph, who wore open sandals and a white robe tied at the waist with a piece of rope. The same cordage must have been haggled to tie a chequered hanky round his head for a kaffiyeh. Micky Corry led a live donkey by its halter.

Jeannie Kennedy, wearing a long blue dress up the front of which padding of some sort had been stuffed, rode sidesaddle. She clutched the donkey's mane and looked to Barry as if she were terrified she might fall off.

The party stopped outside the door over which hung the Bethlehem Inn sign. "Oh, dear, Mary. Everywhere's full. Maybe this inn will have a room." The lines were delivered in a flat monotone.

"I hope so, Joseph."

Joseph knocked on the door.

It was opened by Colin Brown. He was bareheaded and wore a grey robe that looked to Barry as if it might have started as one of Mrs. Brown's dresses. He sported a blue-and-white striped butcher's apron.

"Hello, Innkeeper."

Colin's smile was beatific, his words enunciated loudly and clearly. "Who's there?"

"It's Mary and Joseph. We've come to Bethlehem to be taxed."

"Mary and Joseph?"

Barry had harboured a tiny doubt that Colin might try to pull some stunt. Now he relaxed. The little play was going perfectly.

"Could we have a bed for the night? My wife's having a baby, and she's very tired."

Colin's voice was soft, welcoming. "Well, Mary"—he emphasized the word "Mary"—"I've no room at the inn, but of course *you* are welcome to go into the stable."

Barry stiffened. That wasn't how he remembered the script.

"Of course you can, Mary," Colin said. Then he turned to Joseph and yelled, "But as far as I'm concerned, Joseph, you dirty wee gurrier, you miserable little gobshite, *you can just feck off.*"

There was such a communal in-drawing of breath that Barry thought the walls of the hall might bow inward.

He glanced at the stage where the players, all save the innkeeper who had a wicked grin, were frozen as in a tableau vivant. Mary's eyes were wide. Joseph looked as if he were ready to kill. A shepherd was on his feet yelling.

It must have scared one of the penned sheep because the animal cleared the hurdle as easily as a horse named Battlecruiser, who Barry remembered from the Ballybucklebo races, had cleared the perimeter hedge of the racecourse.

The sheep collided with the donkey. Barry heard an enormous bray. The donkey, with Mary clinging to its mane, ran at the door to the Bethlehem Inn and knocked the innkeeper flat on his back before disappearing into the wreckage of collapsing scenery.

He knew he shouldn't, but Barry couldn't stop laughing. He felt a tugging at his sleeve, turned, and heard O'Reilly yell above the row, "Come on, Barry. I need a hand. The mother superior's fainted."

44

Things That Go Bump in the Night

Barry, still laughing, jumped to his feet. He was deafened by the noise. After the initial shock, everyone was voicing an opinion. People across the aisle were standing and craning forward to see what was happening.

O'Reilly was heading down the row of chairs. Barry saw the reverend grimace, and he realized O'Reilly must have stood on the man's toes. Barry followed. Trying to ignore the racket, he excused himself as he forced his way past a pain-faced Reverend Robinson. Then he crossed the centre aisle and stopped at the rear of a scrum of nuns. Some were standing; others were bending over what was apparently the supine body of the mother superior.

All he could see was a kneeling O'Reilly and a pair of laced-up black boots sticking out through the edge of the throng. Barry thought of the ruby-slippered feet of the Wicked Witch sticking out from under Dorothy's house in *The Wizard of Oz*.

"Excuse me . . . excuse me." He edged forward until he stood over O'Reilly, now in his shirtsleeves because he'd used his jacket as a pillow.

Mother Superior's narrow face was ashen. Her breath came in little panting gasps. Her wimple was awry, and strands of grey hair had escaped from under its band. Tiny beads of sweat clung to her upper lip among the fine hairs of a faint moustache.

O'Reilly held the woman's limp wrist. He was taking her pulse.

"Fingal?"

O'Reilly looked up. "Simple syncope," he said. "Fix her up in no time. Hold her head so she can't twist away."

Barry knelt.

O'Reilly bent over to rummage in one of his jacket pockets and pulled out a small glass bottle. He looked expectantly at Barry, who put a hand to each of the nun's temples and then nodded at O'Reilly.

The fumes of the smelling salts O'Reilly held under her nose made Barry's eyes water. He'd have used a hand to wipe them away if both weren't occupied restraining the mother superior. He was surprised by her strength.

Her eyelids flew open like two camera shutters. Her eyes were unfocused.

O'Reilly removed and recorked the bottle. Barry released her head.

"Where am I?" she asked in a weak voice. She stared at O'Reilly. "You've no beard," she said. Barry heard her puzzlement. "Saint Peter, you've no beard. Glory be." She crossed herself. "Can I come in?"

She thinks she's at the pearly gates, he realized. As her question closely paralleled Joseph's recent inquiry of innkeeper Colin Brown, Barry awaited O'Reilly's reply with some trepidation. While he didn't think his colleague was likely to say, "Feck off," with Fingal you never could tell.

"I think," said O'Reilly, "you've a decade or two to wait before you'll need to ask that, Mother. You fainted, that's all."

"Fainted?" She shook her head. "I see." She stared at the nearest nun and said severely, "And what are *you* staring at?"

Barry saw the young woman blush. "We were worried, Mother."

"I see. Thank you, Sisters"—her tone was clipped, commanding—"I would suggest you all take your seats."

As the nuns shuffled away, she tried to sit up, but O'Reilly put a hand on her shoulder. "Just lie there for a few minutes. We don't want you to be keeling over again."

She let her head fall back on the jacket. "Thank you."

Barry stood. The noise had lessened. Most people were sitting down. He turned and looked at the stage. All the children had vanished. The sheep pen was still there, and most of the original inhabitants now seemed to be their usual placid selves. Four men were reerecting the inn's front, although he could see that the sign was smashed beyond redemption.

Father O'Toole clambered up onto the stage, took the microphone, and said loudly, "My lord, ladies and gentlemen. Can I have quiet please?" He waited. "Please?" His Cork brogue was as soft as his request.

The noise gradually died.

"Thank you." He lowered his voice. "That was a bit unfortunate, so, but he's only a little boy, and little boys do make mistakes. You'll agree to that." He waited.

Barry heard one of the nuns mutter, "Sure he's only little, so he is." He assumed that the low buzz coming from the rest of the audience was likewise one of agreement.

The priest's gaze swept around the room. "Before you condemn the lad, remember, as I remember what our Lord said in the Gospel according to Matthew, 'Judge not that ye be not judged.' "

Barry saw heads nodding. The hum rose in volume.

"A child let himself get carried away, that's all." The priest held his left hand out, palm to his audience, fingertips to the roof. "All I ask is that 'he that is without sin among you, let him cast the first stone.' "

Barry turned and looked up the hall. He was concerned that Bertie Bishop, the staunch Orangeman, might object to the Catholic priest taking charge. Most of the audience was still standing, but Bertie, who must have retaken his seat, was struggling to rise. Flo was holding on to his arm and clearly remonstrating with him.

A harsher northern accent caught Barry's attention, and he turned to see that the Reverend Robinson was now on the stage, not needing the mike, but speaking in his best pulpit voice, the one Kinky had said "let his listeners feel the spits of him six pews back." "All the children and Miss Nolan have worked very hard, so let's give Colin a fool's pardon, a Christmas reprieve. Let us *all* take our seats." His gaze was directed at Bertie Bishop, who subsided.

There was a scratching of chair legs on the wooden floor.

"Please bear with us," the minister said. "It's going to take . . ." He turned to one of the men working on the inn front.

Barry recognized Donal Donnelly's red thatch.

"About another ten minutes, your reverence." Donal sounded confident.

"About ten minutes, so I'll ask you to be patient, and very soon we'll be able to return to our portrayal of a night in Bethlehem of Judea and see again why we keep Christmas. We keep it to celebrate the birth of the Saviour who came to earth to take away the sins of the world."

"Thank you, Reverend. Well said." Father O'Toole beamed out over the audience. "I think the Saviour'd be happy to take away young Colin's sin of envy. Don't you?"

There was a long silence, then a swelling murmur of assent, above which O'Reilly could be heard bellowing, "Hear! Hear!"

Barry felt a tugging at his sleeve.

"Doctor Laverty?" Cissie Sloan, her hair obviously coiffed for the occasion, her floral-patterned dress freshly laundered, was pulling at him with one doeskin-gloved hand. "Miss Nolan says could you or Doctor O'Reilly please come backstage? And it can't be himself because he's still busy with the nice nun, so he is . . ."

Barry saw she was right. O'Reilly still knelt beside the mother superior.

"So it'll have to be yourself . . ."

"What's up, Cissie?"

"Wee Jeannie, her that's Mary, and she's a lovely Mary, isn't she?"

Barry started to walk toward a door that led to the back of the set, with Cissie in hot pursuit.

"Wee Jeannie bumped her head when the donkey bolted, and I don't think there's a more stupid animal, so I don't . . ."

Barry held the door for Cissie before he climbed four wooden stairs.

". . . Except maybe my cousin Aggie Arbuthnot, you remember her, Doctor?"

Barry, now standing in the dimly lit wings, raised his eyes and thought about six toes and was surprised when Cissie rang the changes and continued, "The one I think could use an anenema."

"Doctor Laverty. Thank you for coming." Sue Nolan had taken off her academic robe. She wore a powder-blue cashmere sweater, which, he noted, she filled very well, and a black pencil skirt.

Barry knew he should be concerned for the patient, but his first thought—O'Reilly's comforting conversation of Saturday night notwithstanding—was how to get rid of Cissie and have a few moments to get Sue's phone number. "Cissie says Jeannie bumped her head."

"That's right. I have her lying down in a side room.

If you'll come with me?" She turned and Barry started to follow.

"You'll not be needing me no more, Doctor, will you?"

He didn't need an excuse to get Sue alone. Cissie wanted to go.

"It's fine, Cissie. I can manage."

"Good, for I want to see the rest. My wee lad's one of the shepherds, so he is. He's a good wee lad. Not like that Colin Brown. I'll bet when his da's done with him, he'll be taking his meals standing up for a few days."

Barry grimaced. She was probably right. He didn't like corporal punishment—he'd been beaten at his boarding school—but he couldn't see how Colin could avoid being smacked. Oh, well, it would be over quickly, and the lad would be his usual self in no time flat.

"My Hugie, my husband, would have taken his hand to our wee lad if it had been him. Aggie says . . ."

Barry didn't wait to hear the pronouncements of cousin Aggie. He followed Sue Nolan. As he did, he heard hammering from stage left and rattling as someone closed the curtains.

When he entered the side room, he saw bookshelves lining the walls. Freestanding bookcases were arranged in ranks along the middle of the parquet-floored room. It must serve as a library.

Sue stood beside a low couch against the far wall where the Virgin Mary lay with a pillow propping up her head. The belly under her dress was no longer swollen, so Barry surmised that the same pillow had been used to simulate her pregnancy. He sat on the edge of the couch. "Hello, Jeannie." He remembered how sick she'd been last summer with an appendix abscess. It was quite remarkable how easily children could recover.

"Hello, Doctor Laverty." She grinned and pointed to a facecloth on her forehead. "I hit my head a quare rattle, so I did, when the donkey ran into the wall of the inn."

Barry removed the damp cloth. There was a bump right above Jeannie's left eye. It was about an inch in diameter and was raised for a quarter of an inch above the surrounding skin of her forehead. The skin was shiny and turning a dusky shade of blue. It was probably nothing more than a bruise, but Barry had once missed a diagnosis of bleeding inside the skull. He was not going to take any chances now.

He rummaged inside his pocket for a pencil torch. "I'm going to examine you, Jeannie."

"That's all right."

"And before I do, I'm going to ask you some questions, like what day is it?"

"Don't you know, Doctor?" He heard concern in the child's voice and a soft laugh from Sue.

"I do," he said. "I want to know if you do."

"Sure it's Monday. It's four days before Christmas." She looked around her. "And this here's a wee room in the Parish Hall, so it is."

Barry smiled and explained to Sue, "She's not disorientated. That's a good sign. Now . . ." He shone the light into one eye, pleased to see the pupil constricting.

In less than five minutes he had completed a neurological examination and was relieved that, as far as he could tell, everything was normal. He stood. "You'll be fine, Jeannie. Just a bit of a bump."

"So she can act out the scene?" Sue asked.

"Of course."

She bent down to Jeannie. "Come on then. Let's get you ready." Barry watched as she smoothed down Jeannie's dress, produced a brush, and brushed the little girl's hair. "Off you trot," she said. "Take your place with Joseph in the stable. We'll not need the pillow or the donkey because we're going to start after the birth of Jesus."

"Good. I'll maybe have a baby one day, but I'm never getting back on one of them donkeys, so I'm not."

Barry smiled at her vehemence.

"Fair enough," Sue said. "When the curtains open, start from 'It's not a bedroom, Joseph, but it will do rightly.' "

"Yes, Miss." Jeannie left.

"Thanks, Barry," Sue said. He saw how she smiled. It was an intriguing smile.

"My pleasure," he said. "I thought before Armageddon struck, your kiddies were doing very well."

"They are fun," she said. "I—"

Before she could continue, Father O'Toole appeared.

"Are you ready to go, Sue? The natives are getting restless out front, and the set's jury-rigged."

"Excuse me, Barry," she said. "I'll just be a minute."

Damn it. The moment to get her phone number was gone. Perhaps that wasn't such a bad thing. He knew he'd be devastated if he found out Patricia had given her number to another man.

"Why don't you stay, Barry, and watch from the wings?" Her eyebrow lifted. He swallowed. "I'd like that," he said. "Very much."

Sue vanished and the priest left. Barry walked to the wings above the doorway. He stood silently watching Sue Nolan positioning her charges, and he smiled when she ran across the stage and joined him. "It's a good thing the innkeeper's not needed for the rest of the play."

Barry grinned at her.

She held a finger up to her lips.

He heard applause and the rustling of the curtains, and he watched in silence, aware of her nearness and her light perfume.

The children acted the old story of the nativity of the Christ Child; of heavenly hosts and shepherds abiding in the fields; of stars in the east and wise men. Barry recognized many of the little performers as patients he had seen in the surgery.

The curtains were drawn on the final scene. "Barry," Sue said, as they waited for the applause to die down. "I've to conduct the closing carol."

"Off you go."

Her voice was soft. "Will you wait here for me until it's over? I'm leaving for Broughshane as soon as the performance is over. I'd like to wish you a Merry Christmas properly."

He knew he should say no, find some excuse, but instead he said, "Of course." And why not? She was going away that night.

She stretched up and kissed his cheek. "I'll not be long."

He whistled under his breath and felt the place she had kissed. It was a good thing she was leaving tonight. He watched her cross the stage and marshal the combined forces of the actors and the choir.

The curtains reopened. The choir stood stage left; the actors, stage right. Shepherds and wise men knelt before Joseph and Mary, who in her arms held a dolly wrapped in swaddling clothes.

Sue Nolan took the mike. The footlights outlined her. Damn, but she did have *very* good legs.

"My lord, ladies and gentlemen, 'Our revels now are ended.' Well, almost. There's one last carol, and we invite you to join in the singing. Father O'Toole?"

The harmonium played the introductory chords. Barry listened to the piping of the children onstage and the singing of the entire audience. He silently mouthed the words.

Once in royal David's city
Stood a lowly cattle shed,
Where a mother laid her baby
In a manger for his bed.

45

Jolly Gentlemen in Coats of Red

O'Reilly took one peep into the waiting room. Holy Mother of God. It seemed to him as if there were more people in there than you'd see at an international rugby match. He'd never get them all seen in time to go to the Rugby Club party that night. He closed the door and walked quietly back to the dining room where Barry sat finishing his coffee and reading the *Belfast Newsletter*.

The paper rustled as Barry looked up. "There's an interesting article here, Fingal. Canada's dropped the old Red Duster, and now they have a new red and white flag with a red maple leaf on it."

"Wonderful. I'm happy for them, but we have a bigger problem. How many home visits have you to make?"

"This morning? None. Why?"

"Because the entire populations of Ballybucklebo, the townland, and for all I know the Outer Hebrides and parts of the Isle of Man are in our waiting room. I need your help."

O'Reilly had deliberately said "our," and he was gratified to see Barry smile. It was good the lad felt that way about the practice.

"Is there a flu epidemic, Fingal, or—?"

"No. It's the same every year on the last day the surgery will be open until January. I've always shut down, except for emergencies, two days before Christmas. The locals know that, so everyone and their cat comes in. Some *will* have a recent complaint that's blown up last night or today, but the rest want to get prescriptions refilled at the last minute, or they have vague aches and pains seen to in case they might flare up and spoil the holidays. I think some just come in to say, 'Merry Christmas.' It's been like this every year I've been here. I have a theory about why it happens."

"Why?"

"I think it goes back to pagan times. The country folks, professed Christians as they may be, haven't left all their pagan roots behind."

"You mean like . . . like Kinky and her gift?" Barry asked.

"Exactly." The boy's still worrying about his girl, O'Reilly thought. Then he said, "Yule marks the winter solstice, the time when the days start to lengthen and the year has turned. People used to clear out their rubbish so they could start the New Year with a clean slate. I think there's a sort of communal health spring-cleaning too. They come in to leave behind whatever has ailed them this year."

"I wouldn't have thought of that."

"It took me a year or two to work it out, and I could be wrong . . ."

"You, Fingal? Never."

O'Reilly laughed and said, "Less of your lip, young Laverty." Inwardly he was pleased to see how Barry's self-confidence, so badly rattled when he was facing a possible malpractice suit in August, had grown enough that he was able to risk teasing his senior colleague. "I did think I was wrong once . . . in 1956 . . . but I turned out to be mistaken about it."

Barry laughed. "To err is human," he said.

"Alexander Pope. And 'to forgive divine.' But there'll be no forgiveness for us from the customers if we don't get into the trenches right quickly."

Barry didn't hesitate. "Fair enough."

His response pleased O'Reilly. Barry would have been quite within his rights to say it wasn't his turn to take surgery today.

"So I'll work in the surgery," Fingal said. "You work in here, Barry. Just keep going down to the waiting room and yelling, 'Next!' until the place is empty."

"All right, but even with two of us working, some folks are going to have to wait forever to be seen."

"Not at all." O'Reilly shook his head. "I'll show you. Come on." He headed for the waiting room with Barry at his heels. O'Reilly opened the door a crack and allowed Barry to peep in. "Do you still think Fitzpatrick's a threat?"

Barry shook his head and grinned.

That was one less thing for the boy, who was a congenital worrier, to fret over. O'Reilly flung open the door. "Gooood morning, all."

"Good morning, Doctor O'Reilly." It sounded like the roar of the supporters when a winning try has been scored.

"Right. Listen to me. There's one hell of a lot of you

here. Doctor Laverty's going to help out, but it's still going to take time." He waited for the muttering to die down. "I have a couple of suggestions. First. Is there anyone here just to wish us a merry Christmas?"

There was a muted chorus of "Me, sirs" and "I am's."

"It's very nice of you, very civil indeed, so Doctor Laverty and I thank you and wish you the same in return." He hoped they'd get the hint. O'Reilly waited and watched Kieran O'Hagan hold the outside door open for his wife Ethel. He noticed Kieran was carrying a brown paper–wrapped parcel. "I don't mean to be ungracious, and I know some folks have been like the three wise men and are bearing gifts."

The room was filled with chuckling.

"If you are, go round to the front door. Mrs. Kincaid will be happy to accept them and say thank you very much on our behalfs." As several other people rose and left, O'Reilly continued. "Rather than have you all hanging about for two or three hours—or more, because Doctor Laverty and I will break for lunch . . ."

"I hear your Santa suit needed letting out, sir," a voice from the back of the crowd observed. It was greeted by a round of laughter.

"I'll let that pass in the spirit of the season, Connor O'Brien." O'Reilly waited. "And are you in for your usual very deep injection with a big needle?"

"I am not, sir." Connor's voice sounded anxious. "No, sir."

The second round of laughter was louder than the first.

O'Reilly thought to himself, Barry thought I'd been joking when I told him my first law: *Never let the patients get the upper hand.* "So rather than hanging round, I want a third of you—and you all know who came in early and who came in late—to go home and come back at one o'clock, unless you reckon you're so sick you need to be seen at once."

Even as the procession started to file out the back door, O'Reilly yelled, "Who's first?" Then he waited until Agnes Arbuthnot had risen. " 'Morning, Aggie," he said, then turned and headed for the surgery.

He heard Barry's loudly spoken "Next" and felt confident that his assistant, who he hoped would stay on as a full partner next year, would do a first-class job in the dining room.

O'Reilly parked the Rover and let Arthur out. He'd really enjoyed his late afternoon run on Ballybucklebo beach. The big dog had slept in the car, while O'Reilly made two home visits that had been requested in the middle of the morning. Barry had stayed in Number 1 to deal with the patients who returned after lunch.

"Into your kennel."

Arthur obeyed.

O'Reilly let himself into the kitchen. Kinky had her back to him. She mustn't have heard him come in. She was taking small sausage rolls on a baking tray from the oven and putting them on a wire-mesh rack to cool. The smell of the freshly baked pastry was tantalizing.

"Hello, Kinky." He snaffled a hot roll and juggled it from hand to hand.

"Doctor O'Reilly, sir." Kinky turned and stood foursquare with a hand on her hip. "I'd have thought my leek-and-potato soup at lunchtime would have been enough, so."

"Och, just the one roll won't hurt," he said, popping it whole into his mouth and making little puffing breaths. It was still too hot.

"And no more," she said. "Flo Bishop asked me to help cater for the party, and I'll not have all my hard work eaten before it leaves this house."

"All right." O'Reilly looked round. "Holy Moses," he said, surveying the laden shelves, "is it the five thousand you're going to feed? What are all these things?" He waited for Kinky to explain. She took great pride in her culinary skills, and it pleased her when people showed an interest in what she had cooked. And, O'Reilly thought, if he distracted her, he might be able to pinch another sausage roll. They were delicious.

"Well, sir," she said, "that there's a plate of ham sandwiches, and those are egg mayonnaise. Here are two trays of sweet mince pies . . . keep your hands off the sausage rolls, sir."

O'Reilly felt suitably chastened. He knew he should have known better than to try to outfox Kinky in her own kitchen. "Sorry."

She pointed. "That's a cold baked ham wrapped in foil. And do you see those terra-cotta pots covered with aluminium foil held down with a red rubber band?"

"I do."

"Six are my smoked salmon paté, and six my smoked mackerel paté."

O'Reilly started to salivate at the thought of her smoked mackerel. "Come on now, Kinky. It's the season to be jolly. One more roll? Please?"

"'Tis a terrible man you are, Doctor O'Reilly." She smiled. "All right, but just the one." She looked up at the wall-hung kitchen clock. "Doctor Laverty's changed and ready. He's in the lounge. You'll need to change and get your Santa suit. I've put it in a canvas holdall, and I've polished the boots." She smiled. "You can see your face in them . . . but if I was you, sir," she chuckled, "I'd not bother looking."

O'Reilly laughed so loudly he sprayed a fine dust of pastry into the air. "You're one sharp woman, Kinky Kincaid."

"Aye, so, and sure isn't it the season to be jolly?"

"It is. By God, it is." For a moment in his mind he was happy in the long-ago season in Portsmouth, and he decided that in Deidre's memory he'd make this Christmas, for himself and for those around him, the merriest ever.

"So when you go upstairs, will you ask Doctor Laverty to come down? I'm sure he'll not mind helping me load the boot of your car."

"I will." He stretched out his hand to the rolls.

"I said *one* more . . . sir."

O'Reilly was still smiling when, dressed in his best tweed suit, brown boots, overcoat, and paddy hat and carrying the bag containing his outfit, he climbed into the Rover. "Everything on board, Kinky?"

"It is, so."

"All set, Barry?"

"Aye."

O'Reilly fired up the engine. "Then off we go."

As he drove he thanked the Lord it wasn't snowing or icy, because to get to the rugby clubhouse in time for the party he'd have to get a move on. He did. The Rover might be old, but there were plenty of horses under the bonnet. He paid no attention to Barry's occasional sharp in-drawings of breath when the car leant into a sharp curve.

O'Reilly parked outside the front door of the clubhouse. "Go on in, Kinky," he said. "Get your troops mobilised to empty the boot."

The back door slammed.

"Out, Barry. Open the boot and start giving Kinky a hand. As soon as we're unloaded, I'll run this thing to the car park; then I'll meet you in the changing room."

Barry left, the boot door creaked open, and O'Reilly watched Barry, carrying the ham, and Kinky, with a plate of sandwiches, heading for the pavillion. Outside the corridor of light coming from the open front door, the night was pitch-black.

O'Reilly sat and watched the partygoers arrive. There was Alice Moloney, and . . . sweet Mother of Jesus! . . . she was in deep conversation with Helen Hewitt. They must have called a truce if not an entente cordiale. Good.

He recognized Willy Lindsay, his sister Mary, and praise be, Sammy, who was holding on to Eileen's hand. O'Reilly, safe in the knowledge that in a very short time she was going to win the raffle, reckoned he knew how Ebenezer Scrooge felt when he sent the boy to buy the biggest goose and deliver it to the Cratchetts.

The Shanks family had made it. Terrific. Gerry was holding Mairead, his arm around her waist. He smiled down on her while they both ignored their two children, who were yelling happily and dashing about like a pair of collies rounding up sheep. By that smile O'Reilly inferred that it was indeed sugar Gerry was now having in his tea.

Kinky reappeared. She was accompanied by Flo Bishop, secretary of the ladies' committee, and committee members Aggie Arbuthnot and Cissie Sloan.

He wound down his window. "Do you need another pair of hands?"

"Not at all, thank you, sir," Kinky said.

"Is it yourself, Doctor O'Reilly? Fit and well you're looking." He got no chance to answer as Cissie charged on. "You'll be Santa again this year. *Well* . . ." He heard how righteously indignant she sounded. "I hope you've only a lump of coal for that wee gurrier Colin Brown, because—"

"Cissie Sloan," Flo Bishop said, in a voice that could have come from a regimental sergeant major of the Irish Guards. "Give over your colloguing, and grab those pots."

He closed his window.

When they had finished emptying the boot, O'Reilly drove around the back and parked. Then carrying his bag, he rushed back to the pavilion and in through the back door to transform himself into Santa Claus—or Father Christmas, as he was known in Ulster.

He opened the carryall, half undressed, and laid his tweed jacket and suit pants on a bench. "'*Vesti la giubba*,'" he sang. "On with the motley." He took out the red trousers, recently enlarged by Miss Moloney, and pulled them on. "Ho, ho, ho." He took his wallet from his tweed suit and, along with his pipe and tobacco pouch, shoved it into the pocket of his red trousers. Then he sat and hauled his black knee-boots on. Kinky really had worked on them.

Barry came in. "I'm starting to get used to these Ballybucklebo hooleys," he said, "and this one has the makings of what you'd call a fine ta-ta-ta-ra."

"Getting going, are they?"

Barry parked himself on a bench. "When I came in, the noise was deafening. A gramophone was playing Bing Crosby singing 'White Christmas.' People had to shout to be heard over the music. Children were running about like dervishes, screaming, laughing, and yelling. You can hear it in here."

O'Reilly had no trouble agreeing with Barry. "And how's Kinky making out?"

"She was in her element behind a couple of trestle tables. I've never seen grub like it."

"I," said O'Reilly, "like the sound of that."

Barry had a tinge of wonderment in his voice. "I counted eight cold roast hams, four cold roast turkeys that must weigh at least twenty pounds apiece, three topside roasts of beef, two cold joints of mutton . . . I can't remember everything."

"And how about 'Three French hens, two turtle doves . . .' "

" 'And a partridge in a pear tree'?" Barry laughed. "I didn't see any of those, but I saw hills of dried dates stuffed with marzipan, dunes of dried figs, and a small mountain of chocolate-covered cherries." Barry smiled. "Nobody's going to die of starvation. People are filling their faces. And"—Barry handed O'Reilly his red fur-trimmed coat—"all the kiddies keep charging over to a Christmas tree and staring at a bulging sack, so come on, Santa. Everybody's waiting."

"Right." O'Reilly put on the coat. He lifted his suit pants and jacket, rummaged through all the pockets, and laid his valuables on the bench. He handed Barry his tweed suit. "Shove that in a locker."

O'Reilly cinched the black patent-leather belt with its silver buckle round his waist. "How do I look?"

"You need your beard."

O'Reilly bent and pulled a huge white beard from the bag, and with two curved wires he clipped it around his ears.

"You're him to a tee," Barry said. "At least you're

the version made popular by Coca-Cola advertisements since nineteen thirty-one. The jolly old elf."

O'Reilly adjusted his beard. "But there was a real Saint Nick. He is the patron saint of children, bankers, pawnbrokers and mariners . . . I always had a soft spot for him when I was at sea." O'Reilly lifted his valuables from the bench and stuffed them in his red pocket. "I'd not want to leave those unattended in here," he said. "Saint Nick was the patron saint of murderers and thieves too."

"Busy chap," Barry said. "After today's two surgeries I can sympathise."

"But you enjoyed being busy, didn't you?"

"I did, Fingal." Barry was looking into O'Reilly's eyes. "Just like you."

"I'll not deny it." O'Reilly adjusted the hang of his coat and said something he had believed for a long time. "There's not much point practicing medicine if you don't enjoy it. You might as well be a . . . I don't know . . . a civil servant stuck in some dreary office."

"I know."

"And I'm having no truck with anything dreary tonight." He headed for the door. "'Kiddies' gifts first, then the raffle, and then by God, a large Jameson for me. I'll have earned it by then." Which he had to admit to himself wasn't entirely true. He enjoyed playing Santa so much he'd have paid for the privilege.

46

Surprised by Joy

With Barry following, O'Reilly strode along the corridor. He opened one of the doors leading to the main hall. The noise was palpable. Raised voices all but drowned out the lyrics of "All I Want for Christmas Is My Two Front Teeth" coming from a loudspeaker system. O'Reilly could hear childish squeals and the clatter of running feet. Barry was right. The hooley was getting going nicely, and O'Reilly was pleased—he really enjoyed a good party.

Barry said, "See? Didn't I tell you?"

"It's warming up all right."

O'Reilly looked around the room. Colourful streamers hung from the ceiling, and the Christmas tree stood glittering in one corner. Beside it an empty armchair awaited Santa. Donal Donnelly was bending over the bulging sack by the chair, tucking something inside. Presents for some chiseler. Father O'Toole, who usually looked after receiving the gifts, must have asked Donal to help out. Was there anything in this village that didn't involve Donal?

"There's the marquis chatting with Sonny and Maggie," O'Reilly remarked to Barry.

"That's a sprig of yellow gorse in her hatband. It was two wilted geraniums the first time I met her."

"And you thought she was *craiceáilte*. Crazy."

"A woman who said she'd headaches two inches *above* her head? Don't you think I'd every reason to?"

O'Reilly laughed. "But you learned better." You've learnt a lot of things, Barry Laverty, in five months. I'm proud of you, son, O'Reilly thought.

The music changed to Bing Crosby's "Christmas in Killarney." "*The holly green, the ivy green . . .*"

"And sure isn't that a pretty picture too, all those folks standing around in groups? Do you know, Barry, it makes me think they look like islands in the sea, and from time to time one or two folks, like canoes on a voyage of exploration, cast off from their own shores, make a short voyage, and land on another atoll to see if the natives are friendly."

"That's poetic, Fingal."

"You mean I'm a poet . . . and I don't know it?"

Barry groaned. "I heard that in kindergarten."

O'Reilly laughed. "I'm glad you learnt something there, son." He saw the marquis detach himself and head for the doorway in which the two were standing. "Now I've about five minutes before I have to go on because here comes His Lordship looking for Santa." O'Reilly stepped back and opened the door more widely.

"Fingal. Laverty." The marquis offered O'Reilly his hand.

"John." O'Reilly shook the hand and noted that Barry kept a respectful silence.

"All set at your end, Fingal?"

"I think so, as long as Donal has the sack ready."

"He has. So give me a couple of minutes to arrange your grand entry, and you're on." The marquis vanished into the hall.

O'Reilly took one last look before letting the door close. Gerry and Mairead Shanks were listening to Cissie Sloan, and the two little Shanks were playing tag with Colin Brown and Micky Corry. There was more to this Rugby Club party than having a good time, he thought. It was serving tonight to introduce the Shanks to Ballybucklebo, and if the way they were giggling and laughing was anything to go by, it had been a place for Colin and Micky to bury the hatchet with each other. Begod, Fingal, he told himself, if Fitzpatrick were here I'd offer to buy the man a drink.

He was letting the door close when he saw Gerry Shanks again. This time O'Reilly frowned. He tried to remember exactly what he'd said when he'd suggested Gerry and his family come to the party. It came back to him. "Mother of Jesus."

"What's up?"

"I've just had an awful thought. You remember the Shankses?"

Barry smiled. "The gunpowder man?"

"Aye. They're out there with their kids. They're new here. I told them to come to the party."

"What's wrong with that?"

"I forgot to tell them to bring presents for their own kids."

"Jesus, Fingal. It would be a disaster if Santa had nothing for them."

"Don't I know it. To be ignored by Santa in front of the entire village? They'd be devastated." Think, O'Reilly. You made the mess, you fix it.

"What'll we do, Fingal?"

O'Reilly looked at Barry. "We?"

"Of course, we. I'll help however I can."

"Good man ma da." O'Reilly was still trying to find a solution when Barry asked, "Could I maybe drive to Ballybucklebo and buy something?"

"No, the shops will be shut. Everybody's here." And Bangor and Holywood were too far away. Think, O'Reilly. Think. Got it. "Have a word with Phyllis Cadogan."

"Billy-the-asthmatic's mother?"

"The Cadogans run the newsagent's, and they stock Dinky Toy cars, little dollies, and stuffed puppy dogs. Maybe she could get there, open up, and get back here in time with some things."

"Right. I'm sure I saw her."

The door opened. Bing Crosby's velvety voice, made harsh by the loudspeakers, crooned, *"I'm dreaming of a white Christmas . . ."*

Donal shut the door. "The marquis sent me to switch off the music. Gramophone's in the committee room, and he says once the music stops, Santa's on."

"All right." O'Reilly made sure his beard was properly attached. "And Donal"—O'Reilly pulled out his wallet—"here's the stub you wanted." He handed over the stub of Eileen Lindsay's raffle ticket.

Donal palmed it, winked, and started back along the corridor.

"I'm off, Fingal." Barry let himself into the hall and left the door ajar.

Bing Crosby was wishing "May your days be merry and bright," but he didn't get any further. Donal had done his job.

O'Reilly took a deep breath, flung the door wide, and strode into the hall.

The cheers that greeted him were, if anything, louder than the earlier racket. He bowed and began his progress, as slowly as he could. The more time he gave Barry, the better. Bugger. He'd lost Barry in the crowd, and could only hope he would find Phyllis Cadogan quickly.

O'Reilly climbed onto his chair and roared, "Ho, ho, ho!"—sentiments he did not exactly share. "It's good to be back in Ballybucklebo with presents for the children." All of them, please God, if Barry gets a move on. "Let me see who's first." He opened the sack, pulled out a parcel, and read the label. "Callum Sloan, get you up here this very instant." There was applause, and O'Reilly's "Ho, ho, ho!" rang out over the noise.

"Ho, ho, ho! Come on, Colin Brown. Your turn. There's room in my sack for your prezzy, even if there didn't seem to be much room at your inn." The laughter was subdued. No one, it seemed, wished to embarrass the boy. As Colin walked forward, he blushed until his face was almost as red as Santa's tunic. O'Reilly enveloped the boy in an enormous bear hug, hoisted him onto his knee, and handed him a gift-wrapped parcel. "Try to be a good boy next year."

"Yes, Santa. I promise."

O'Reilly solemnly shook the boy's hand to seal the agreement.

Colin walked away. The applause was deafening. Maybe that's put the wee lad's stock up a bit, O'Reilly hoped.

He scanned the room. Phyllis was heading purposefully for the door. O'Reilly noticed her husband surrounded by their five children waiting their turns. Get a move on, Phyllis. Please. Fingal O'Reilly had to get on with things here.

"Jeannie Kennedy, where are you?" he roared. Crisis notwithstanding, he really enjoyed being Santa, and he had room to regret he'd never been able to play it for children of his own.

Up she came, shining in her frilly party dress. Hair was neatly brushed and held in place with a green Alice band.

"Ho, ho." He lifted her onto his knee. "Have you been naughty or nice this year, Jeannie?"

"Nice, Santa. And my pet pig has too."

O'Reilly remembered running from the sow last July when he and Barry had visited her parents' farm. He'd thought the animal was chasing him, but in reality she had only wanted her snout scratched.

"Good, but she's not getting a present. You are." He handed her a parcel. "Off you trot." He set her back on the floor and put his hand into the sack, which was a great deal emptier than it had been fifteen minutes ago.

O'Reilly glanced to the Shanks. Gerry had his arm around Mairead's shoulder. Their two children stared at Santa with obviously eager anticipation. Angus was grinning widely and turning to say something to his younger sister. She clapped her hands and jumped up and down. It wasn't difficult to infer that he'd been reassuring her that their turn would come soon.

It was still far too early to expect to see Phyllis returning. "Lucy MacVeigh." O'Reilly called.

A little girl was brought forward by her mother. She was sucking her thumb and resisting her mother's efforts. As she neared O'Reilly, she started to cry. He towered over her from his seat, and to the child he must have seemed huge.

O'Reilly immediately slipped from his perch and knelt before little Lucy, bringing his face down to her level. He whispered to her. She stopped crying, slowly fingered his Santa's beard, and started to giggle. O'Reilly did not stand up until Lucy had shyly accepted her gift and she and her mother had moved away.

Ten minutes later O'Reilly thrust his hand deeply into a sack that seemed to have collapsed for lack of contents. He looked over to the still-closed hall door. What the hell was he going to do?

He stuck his hands deeply into the pockets of his jacket and felt something. Saved by the bell. He grinned and didn't hesitate to decide what to do. "Are the Shanks children here?" O'Reilly boomed. "Angus? Siobhan?"

He could see Siobhan clinging to her mother. "I know you're here. I saw you," Santa called. "Come out, come out, wherever you are."

Gerry took each of his little ones by a hand and led them forward. The silence in the hall was so deep O'Reilly could feel it. Gerry stopped in front of O'Reilly. "Here they are, Santa."

"Come here, the pair of you," O'Reilly said. He held out his arms and then embraced Siobhan in the crook of one and Angus in the other. "Welcome to Ballybucklebo."

He saw Phyllis pushing her way through the crowd, waving to attract his attention. Too late. If she gave him some toys now, the little Shankses would see and the illusion would be shattered. He'd better get on with it.

O'Reilly disengaged his right arm and put his hand into his pocket. Before he produced his surprise, he said, "Mrs. Claus and the elves were very, very busy this year. She said to say she's sorry they didn't have time to wrap your presents. Anyway, they'd run out of paper at the North Pole."

He pulled out the presentation pen and pencil set he'd taken from his jacket after he had changed into his Santa suit. He spoke loudly. "Here you are." He handed the pen to Angus and the propelling pencil to Siobhan. "Merry Christmas."

The two piped, "Thank you, Santa," and the way

Gerry stood smiling broadly was worth more than any presentation pen and pencil set. O'Reilly raised his voice. "Ho, ho, ho!" he roared. "Ho, ho, ho! Merrrrry Christmas!" Then he raised both arms above his head, extended his hands palms out, and in the immortal words of Tiny Tim, said, "God bless us, every one."

The applause and cheering, which started as a dull rumble, eventually became so loud that they must have scared the jackdaws from their roosts in the big elm trees at faraway Ballybucklebo House.

O'Reilly left the sack on the floor and headed for Barry. "That," he said, "in the words of that great Irish-born duke of Wellington after Waterloo, was 'the nearest run thing you ever saw in your life.' "

"Fingal, that was most generous—"

"Balderdash." He shook his head. "Christmas is for the kiddies. How could I let a couple of them get hurt?"

Barry whispered under his breath, "Suffer the little children . . ."

"Stop mumbling, Barry. Come into the hall with me. I've still got to be Santa 'til I get out of here." O'Reilly turned and faced the crowd. He waved and waved and roared, "Merrrrry Christmas!" as he sidled to the door.

The minute Barry had joined him and the door was closed, O'Reilly ripped off his black belt and started to unbutton his coat. "I have to get out of this suit. It's like being in one of those Scandinavian saunas, so be a good lad and get me a Jameson." Without waiting for a reply, he strode off, yelling, "I'll be back as quickly as I can. I don't want to miss the raffle."

Back in his tweeds once more, O'Reilly headed for the hall.

Come, they told me, pa rum pum pum pum . . . blared from overhead.

He made a beeline for Kinky, who stood behind two trestle tables. The roasts Barry had described had been reduced to bony skeletons. There was no sign of Kinky's sausage rolls. A couple of lonely sandwiches, their edges curled, lay on a plate.

There were a few nuts, some sad-looking mandarin oranges. It looked as if Barry's confident assertion that nobody was going to die of starvation might be proved false.

" 'Twas a Grand Santa you were, Doctor O'Reilly." Kinky smiled at him from behind her table.

"Hungry work," he said, still looking at the tables. "Was it a swarm of locusts went through here?" He sighed. "Is there a bite left in the house for when we get home?"

"Better," she said, stooping and straightening up. She handed him a plate laden with beef, turkey, ham, and sausage rolls. "I didn't bother with anything sweet," she said. "Those Santa pants will be a size smaller next year, or my name's not Kinky Kincaid."

"It's not," O'Reilly said. "It's the angel of mercy. Bless you, Kinky." He accepted the plate.

"The cutlery's on the next table," she said, "so you

go along, and I'm going to see Cissie and Flo and Aggie in the back. The three of them worked very hard, and we've set a bit aside for ourselves in there, so."

"Thanks, Kinky." His thanks were heartfelt. Not only had she thought to save some grub for him, she'd not gone to get her own until he'd been seen to. That woman would have been a marvellous mother.

O'Reilly grabbed a knife and fork wrapped in a paper napkin from the next table and headed to where Barry stood in conversation with the marquis.

"Here, Fingal." Barry handed him a glass. "It's a double, and by the way I thanked Phyllis. She said it was no trouble as long as the kiddies got some kind of present."

"Good man." O'Reilly, full plate in one hand, grabbed the whiskey from Barry. "*Sláinte.*" He drank and turned to the marquis. "My lord."

"Fingal, I saw what you did for those children. That was generous, most generous."

"Most generous," Barry added.

"The club will make it up—"

"The club will do no such thing," O'Reilly said very quietly and very seriously. "I'd prefer if no fuss is made. I did what I had to, that's all. And it was my mistake in the first place, inviting them without telling them to bring presents." If you bugger something up, you bloody well fix it, he thought. My father taught me that. The old man was right.

"I'll respect that," the marquis said.

"Thank you." O'Reilly took a hefty swallow of his drink. "Now, John, we've one more piece of business, and then we can all get on with the party." He balanced his glass on the side of his plate, ignored the wrapped cutlery, and used his fingers to pop a slice of ham into his mouth. "Can you get the raffle up and running?"

"Naturally. You enjoy your supper." The marquis turned and headed for the front of the hall.

O'Reilly thought, as he savoured a piece of roast beef, in about ten minutes Eileen Lindsay'll have the wherewithal. Jesus, he loved Christmas. He swallowed the beef and tried a piece of turkey.

The marquis, standing at the front of the hall, was demanding silence. "Ladies and gentlemen," he boomed. "Ladies and gentlemen, if I might have your attention?"

Conversation gradually died as people turned to see what was happening.

"Could Johnny Jordan please come forward?"

The crowd parted to let through a jolly-looking, red-cheeked, bald-as-a-coot man of about thirty. He stood beside the marquis and held aloft a very large turkey.

"Mother of God"—Barry heard a woman's voice from nearby—"that thing's mother must have been an ostrich. It's twenty pounds if it's an ounce."

"Johnny here has very kindly donated this bird for our first annual Christmas raffle."

Polite applause.

"The club can always use cash . . ."

"Hear, hear . . ."

"So we decided to sweeten the pot. Naturally the winning ticket gets this magnificent bird."

Johnny held it higher.

"But we wanted more people to buy tickets, and so we decided to gamble. The odds are long, but if the winning ticket's numbers are all identical, the holder will also win seventy-five percent of the money collected, which is . . . Donal?"

"One hundred and ninety-five pounds, my lord," Donal said, from where he stood off to one side.

There was a communal in-drawing of breath and several muted "ooohs" and "aaahs."

"Will Donal Donnelly and Councillor Bertie Bishop please come forward now?"

The two men appeared. Donal carried a hat. The councillor looked fit to bust with pride.

"Give the hat a good stir, Donal."

Donal tilted the headpiece forward so everyone could observe how thoroughly he was mixing the ticket stubs. "Ready, sir," he said.

"If you please, councillor?"

Bertie Bishop made a great show of rolling up his sleeve. Then, imitating a music hall conjuror, he said, "My lord, ladies and gentlemen, see, there's nothing up my sleeve but my strong right arm."

"Makes a change," a voice called. There was good-natured laughter.

Bertie closed his eyes, plunged his hand into the hat, and produced a single ticket. He handed it to the marquis of Ballybucklebo.

"And the winner of the turkey is . . . whoever holds ticket number 4444. I repeat, 4444."

Everyone applauded and looked all around to see who the lucky winner was.

O'Reilly tried not to look smug. He looked for Eileen. She was laughing as she and her brood moved to the front. She handed the marquis her ticket. "Here, sir." She turned to her children. "See, you'll get your turkey now."

O'Reilly watched the wee ones jumping up and down. He realized that the significance of the numbers all being the same had not dawned on Eileen.

The marquis read it, beamed, and stooped to her, saying, "I'm sorry. I don't know your name."

"Eileen. Eileen Lindsay, sir," she said. "Thank you very much."

"Don't thank me. It was the luck of the draw."

She beamed at him. "It's very good luck then, sir. A big turkey and all."

"It's more than that, Eileen."

She looked puzzled.

"I think, people," the marquis roared, "in case anyone has not noticed, the ticket numbers are identical. That means—"

There was a great joyous shout of approval.

"Congratulations, Eileen." He handed her an envelope. "The money's in there, and will you please give Eileen her bird, Mr. Jordan?"

"Thank you, sir. Thank you, everybody." She gathered her children around her and told them. "It's going to be the best Christmas ever. The very best."

Johnny Jordan moved forward as Donal started making his way toward O'Reilly. He recalled Donal saying he suspected Johnny had a crush on Eileen. The man certainly looked excited, almost as excited as Eileen herself. "Eileen." He offered her the bird. "Here's your turkey. Congratulations."

"Thank you." She leant forward to take it. "And thank you for donating it."

He was holding something over her head. It was a sprig of mistletoe.

"I'll settle for a Christmas kiss." He kissed her firmly and soundly. He looked breathless when he stopped.

Everyone waited silently to see what Eileen would do.

She didn't slap his face. Instead she said, "Shame on you, Johnny Jordan."

He blushed deeply and hung his head.

She took the mistletoe from him, held it over *his* head, and kissed him back. Then she said, "It's a very big bird and you a bachelor man. Would you like to come to us for your Christmas dinner?"

His obvious assent was drowned by the cheers.

Donal had finally arrived, still carrying the hat he'd used for the draw. "Didn't I promise you, Doctor, sir?" he said with a bucktoothed grin.

"You did. Well done, Donal, and the timing's very good," O'Reilly remarked. "Tomorrow's Christmas Eve, so Eileen will still have time to shop. Santa will come to her house after all."

"I'm pleased about that, sir. She and her chisellers

deserve to have a merry Christmas. I'm glad I could help, so I am. Julie's pleased too."

O'Reilly bent closer and said, sotto voce, "How *did* you do it?"

Donal offered the hat to both O'Reilly and Barry. "Take a ticket."

O'Reilly did. Barry did. He showed his to O'Reilly. Both tickets read 4444.

"I told you I got them from a printer friend of mine. Sure, as well as the ones we sold, didn't I have him run off a couple of hundred all the same, and didn't I put only those stubs in the hat?"

Barry laughed.

O'Reilly guffawed so loudly that people turned around to see what was so funny. He put an avuncular arm around Donal's shoulder. "I wonder about you sometimes, Donal," he said. "It's only the Lord who is meant to move in mysterious ways."

47

It Came upon a Midnight Clear

The stern, fifteenth-century nonconformist Martin Luther would not have approved of O'Reilly's suggestion, but then, Barry thought, it was unlikely the old Puritan would have approved of O'Reilly at all.

"Why don't we go to midnight mass?" O'Reilly asked. "Father O'Toole does the service very well." He finished another mouthful of his Christmas Eve dinner.

"I'd like that, Fingal," Barry said. "I'd enjoy that very much."

"Good. And we'll ask Kinky if she'd like to come. Even if she is a Presbyterian, she's very broad-minded. You know now—you were at the pageant—that there's quite a tradition here of ecumenism, particularly at Christmas, and I think Kinky approves."

"Even if Bertie Bishop doesn't?"

"But Flo does. We'll see her there." Then O'Reilly, who had once pronounced the adage "Eating time is eating time, and talking time is talking time," nodded, grunted, and applied himself with vigour to devouring his share of Kinky's roast goose. She'd ignored his instructions about no more fowl.

Barry was glad she had. He was quite content to savour his own meal in silence. It *would* be pleasant to bring in Christmas by going to midnight mass, he decided. It would make a change from sitting up past midnight and listening to the Festival of Nine Lessons and Carols broadcast by the BBC from King's College Chapel. When he'd lived at home, his parents made listening to it a family Christmas tradition. Ever since he'd turned nine, his parents had allowed him to stay up for it.

He exhaled hard through his nose. King's College? Humbug. Barry didn't want to be reminded of anything to do with Cambridge. One of the reasons Patricia had given for staying there was that her friend Jenny's father had got tickets for this year's service.

Fair enough, it must be spectacular to be there in person. He remembered how, as a boy, once the service was over, he'd been allowed to open one Christmas present. Then, after a small piece of Christmas cake, he was bundled off to bed to try to sleep, because everybody knew there'd be no presents in the pillowcase at the foot of the bed for any child who stayed awake. Oooh, the anticipation, but for a little chap the very late night had always produced the effect his parents had hoped for. Sleep came quickly then.

But tonight, after the mass, would he be able to drop off? Barry sighed. He was missing Patricia, still worried about her. Would he lie awake picturing her in the chapel at King's College and, despite her reassurances, wondering who she was with?

He speared a piece of roast parsnip and looked around as Kinky came in.

She was carrying the iced, beribboned, and decorated Christmas cake on a large plate. It was accompanied by a serrated cake knife. She set them on the sideboard. "For later," she said.

Barry wondered if Kinky observed the same tradition as his folks, who cut the cake—"opened it," as the locals said—once they had come back from church.

"Mrs. Kincaid, you've done yourself proud," O'Reilly said. "The chestnut stuffing and applesauce set off your goose to perfection. Perfection."

"And," Barry added, "the roast potatoes were simply marvelous. Thank you, Kinky."

"I'm glad you enjoyed them, sir. I roasted them in the fat from the goose." She put the cake in front of O'Reilly. "I learned that trick from my mother down in *Béal na mBláth* in West Cork . . .

"Where the Big Fellah was shot?" Barry asked.

"Michael Collins himself, God rest him." Kinky paused. "He was a darlin' man, so." She lifted the plate on which rested the wreckage of the goose. "We always had a goose on Christmas Eve, but my aunty preferred to serve salted beef." She peered at O'Reilly's florid complexion. "I believe, sir, too much salt is not good for the blood pressure, so. Not even on Christmas Eve. That's why I never do it."

O'Reilly laughed. "All right, Kinky. You're right."

"That's why," Kinky continued, "I've had tomorrow's ham soaking since eight o'clock last night, and I'll take it out at eight o'clock tonight.

"Twenty-four hours? Why so long?" Barry asked.

"To get *all* the salt out before I boil it tonight and then roast it tomorrow along with the turkey."

"How long will the boiling take?" O'Reilly pushed his now empty plate away.

"A ten-pound ham at twenty minutes per pound?" Kinky frowned and looked up before saying, "Three hours and ten minutes, so."

"So if you start boiling it at eight, you'll be done by eleven-thirty?" O'Reilly enquired.

"I will, sir. Why?"

"Doctor Laverty and I are going to midnight mass.

I know you usually go with Flo Bishop, but this year we thought you might like to come with us."

She pursed her lips and furrowed her brow. "I'd like that," she said. "I've to finish the house cleaning, but I'll be done in time."

"House cleaning? On Christmas Eve?" Barry said. "It seems a bit of an extra chore to me."

"Oh, no, sir," she said quite seriously, "it's no trouble at all, at all. Country folks everywhere in Ireland do it. It's for the same reason we leave a candle burning in the front window."

"Why's that, Kinky?"

"Our Lord came at Christmastide once before. He'd nowhere to stay. You'd want the house to be ready if he comes again." She looked him directly in the eye. "And not only him. You never know *who* might be coming to stay tomorrow."

Barry felt tingly. The locals would say he felt as if a goose had walked over his grave. A strange idea, considering he'd just finished eating a goose. Kinky couldn't mean Patricia, who'd already told him that coming home wasn't physically possible.

"Well," said O'Reilly, "you carry on, Kinky, but don't worry that Miss O'Hallorhan'll be staying. She's just coming for the dinner."

"There'll be plenty for all. I'll see to that," she said, still looking at Barry. "And there'll be room here even if there was no room at the inn once—"

O'Reilly chuckled and said, "Twice, if you count the pageant."

"True, sir, but at Number One we'll be ready no matter who comes." She lifted the cake. "But we'll not be ready if I don't go and get on now."

"Leave the cake, Kinky." O'Reilly had half risen.

"Sure, sir," she said, moving the plate out of his range. "I think maybe we should observe another of my mother's traditions. We'll open the cake tomorrow morning when the three of us get back from the mass."

Although the moon was not many days past full, there was no moon glow nor any stars to be seen when O'Reilly parked at the chapel. Barry got out and inhaled the scent of the sea borne on a chilly northeaster. The bells in the steeple pealed, chimed, and merrily ding-donged in the out-of-sequence cadence of hand-pulled church bells. He could picture the ringers hauling on the bell ropes.

He opened the car's back door for Mrs. Kincaid; then they both followed O'Reilly through the high-arched, oak front door and into the narthex. Incense filled the air. Inside the chapel, someone was playing the harmonium. Saint Columba's was too small to afford an organ.

"That's Bach's Toccata and Fugue in D Minor," O'Reilly remarked quietly, as he removed his hat and stepped aside to give a parishioner access to the font of holy water. The man dipped his fingers, crossed himself, and genuflected toward the altar.

O'Reilly led the way into the nave, nodding greetings to those seated patients he recognized and receiving their nods and smiles in return. The place was packed.

It was unlike his senior colleague, Barry thought, but Fingal indicated a pew one row from the back. Ordinarily he'd head straight for the front of anything and expect space to be made for him. He bowed to the altar and sidled into the half-empty pew. Barry bowed, followed O'Reilly, and let Kinky bring up the rear. Barry took his seat and for a few moments closed his eyes and lowered his head.

He opened his eyes and sat up. "Good evening, Doctor Laverty." He turned to see that he was seated beside the Finnegans—Fergus the jockey, his brother Declan, and Declan's French wife Mélanie. "*Joyeux Noël*," she said. It was too dim to see Declan's face clearly, but Barry knew it would be nearly expressionless because of his Parkinson's disease.

Barry struggled but managed to say, "*Et à vous et votre famille, Madame.*" French had not been Barry's long suit at school.

"*Merçi, Monsieur le Docteur.*"

Barry nodded his thanks, smiled, and looked around.

The chapel was small, intimate. There was no transept. The chancel was separated from the nave by three low steps, at the top of which was the communion rail. Behind it on his right side was a dark wood lectern; to his left, the pulpit. The communion table, immediately behind the low wooden railing and in front of the altar, was flanked by two enormous wrought-brass candlesticks. Barry reckoned they must be at least five feet tall. In each candlestick a large white wax candle flamed and cast fluttering shadows, as tiny draughts swirled into the church from the open door. Candles seemed to burn everywhere; they illuminated the garishly painted wooden crucifix that hung from the far wall and inclined out over the altar.

The harmonium music died, and as it was reborn as the first chords of "Once in Royal David's City," the congregation rose. Barry turned to watch the processional.

Father O'Toole led. He was resplendent in his red cope with a gold midback seam running up the centre and splitting at shoulder-blade height into two arms that reached the tips of his shoulders. Beneath he wore a surplice, white for Christmas. In his vestments, he personified the panoply of the Catholic church so denigrated by the Nonconformists, yet so much a part of the ancient ritual.

He was immediately ahead of two altar boys in white surplices. Each swung a censer, and as they passed, the aroma of incense became more powerful. The members of the little choir—six boy trebles, four altos, eight tenors, and four basses—were robed in white, but sported scarlet, ruffled, high collars. Each held his hymnbook before him.

Father O'Toole stopped just before the altar rail, turned, and faced the congregation. His right arm was outstretched above his head. The choir filed into their stalls behind the altar rails to Barry's right. The hymn ended, and as all the Catholics present crossed themselves, the priest made the sign and said, "*In nomine Patris, et Filii, et Spiritus Sancti.*"

Barry, who had had to pass an examination in Latin to gain admittance to medical school, had no trouble translating, "In the name of the Father, and of the Son, and of the Holy Spirit."

He joined in the communal "Amen" and sat along with everyone else.

The service continued with a greeting, an invitation to partake in an act of penitence, and a communal confession.

"*Confiteor Deo omnipotenti, beatae Mariae semper Virgini . . .*" and on until the final "*mea maxima culpa.*"

Barry found the sonorousness of the Latin words for "I confess to Almighty God, to Blessed Mary ever Virgin," right through to "my most grievous fault," dignified and comforting even to him, an agnostic.

The priest pronounced the prayer of absolution.

The congregation responded in song. "*Kyrie eleison . . . Christe eleison . . .*" Their heartfelt tones carried a palpable feeling of relief for sins forgiven and for the promise of the new day and, at this season, of a new year to come. He remembered O'Reilly's explanation for why the last surgery of the year had been packed with people getting rid of their old year's ailments.

Barry looked around at the backs of the heads of familiar people. Donal's carroty tuft beside Julie's shining gold. Miss Moloney's pepper-and-salt, Helen Hewitt's red. He smiled as he glanced sideways to see Kinky's shining silver half hidden by her green hat. He noticed the Reverend Robinson and his wife. The Presbyterian service would have been over hours ago. Barry was not surprised to see the minister. He and Father O'Toole golfed together every Monday.

"*Gloria in excelsis Deo. Et in terra pax hominibus bonae voluntatis . . .*"

"Glory to God in the highest. And on earth peace to men of good will . . ." What a shame, Barry thought, that in September the second Vatican Council had published its report recommending that mass be said in the vernacular. There was a wonderful resonance to the Latin mass. But whether Latin or English, perhaps if only for this night, the men and the women of this congregation were all of good will, and peace did fill this hall.

Barry Laverty, outsider until five months ago, felt himself being silently absorbed by the body of the village while he was wrapped in the serenity and mystery of the ancient, changeless mass.

"*Adoramus te. Glorificamus te.*" We worship Thee. We glorify Thee.

The Gloria ended, and the priest held silence for several moments.

After a short prayer, a lay reader, a man Barry recognized by his bulbous red nose as Mr. Coffin, the undertaker, walked to the pulpit and read from the book of Isaiah. "For Zion's sake I will not keep silent, and for Jerusalem's sake I will not rest . . ."

Barry allowed himself to flow with the congregation, rising, sitting, and kneeling with them as the service demanded.

He recited the prayers that he knew as best he could with his schoolboy Latin.

He sang the familiar hymns as best he could in his off-key voice.

He listened to the old words, the words he'd heard as a child, read as a boy and as a young man until they were part of his fabric. He could whisper them in concert with the reader.

"Behold a virgin shall be with child, and bring forth a son, and they shall call his name Emmanuel, which being interpreted is, God with us . . . And he knew her not till she brought forth her firstborn son: and he called his name Jesus."

Barry Laverty closed his eyes and pictured Christmases past, happy and safe in the fold of his family, and he wondered about Christmases yet to come. He hoped they would be celebrated here with his new, larger family in Ballybucklebo. He knew his eyes were not entirely dry.

When the time came, neither Barry nor O'Reilly nor Kinky took communion, as they were not confirmed in the Catholic faith. Barry watched the procession to the altar rail, noting the reverence of the communicants as each received the bread and wine. He saw Kinky with a gentle smile on her open face.

O'Reilly looked somehow different, and it took Barry a moment to realize that the man's ordinarily craggy and wrinkled visage had somehow become smooth and frown-line free. Soon the service ended, as the priest faced the congregation and said, "*Ite, missa est.*" Go, you are dismissed.

Barry rose with the rest of the worshippers and joined lustily in the recessional hymn.

God rest ye merry, gentlemen,
Let nothing you dismay,
Remember Christ, our Savior,
Was born on Christmas day . . .

Because they were in a rear pew, Barry, O'Reilly, and Kinky were among the first to leave the church.

As Barry stepped out into the dark night, the chill nipped at his cheeks, his nose. Yet Barry's heart was warmed by the joyous pealing of the bells above and the gentle swirling of the snowflakes that tumbled from a pitch-dark sky and told him that when he awoke later this morning, Christmas 1964 would indeed be white.

48

Glorious Morning Have I Seen

The pealing of the chapel bells summoning the faithful to morning mass woke Barry. He rubbed his eyes, rolled out of bed, stumbled to the attic window, and opened the curtains. The glare being reflected from the pure white carpet that covered O'Reilly's back garden forced Barry to narrow his just-awake eyes. The snow that had fallen last night had not begun to melt.

There'd be no snow where his parents were celebrating Christmas, not in the middle of the Australian summer. He had no other relatives in Ulster, so he might have been spending a lonely Christmas on his own had he not been lucky enough to land this position at Number 1. It wasn't just a job. Barry had been made to feel as much one of O'Reilly's peculiar family as Arthur Guinness—whose tracks Barry could now see leading from his kennel to the hidden vegetable garden where the apple trees bowed low under their snowy burden.

Some branches had been torn from the horse chestnut tree by the weight of the snow. It didn't seem like five months had passed since revellers at Seamus Galvin's going-away party had sought shade under its leafy boughs. That was the day he had made his decision to stay on as O'Reilly's assistant. He had no regrets about his choice.

Beyond the tree, looking like a fine painting, the white roofs of the houses behind Number 1 Main Street drew an irregular margin against the rolling Ballybuckebo Hills. From the chimneys the smoke rose vertically into an azure, cloudless sky, the black smudges the only blemishes on the cleanly rendered canvas.

Barry hoped the country roads wouldn't be closed. He was looking forward to the marquis's open house later today. Still wondering who he would see there,

Barry wandered to the bathroom. Ten minutes later, he was scrubbed and dressed and heading downstairs.

O'Reilly sat at the head of the dining room table. He grinned, rose, and held out his hand. "Merry Christmas, Barry."

Barry walked to the head of the table and shook O'Reilly's hand. "Merry Christmas, Fingal." The grasp was not one of O'Reilly's bone crushers. "And thank you for having me here."

"Rubbish." O'Reilly released Barry's hand. "You live here, don't you? You work here?" The words sounded harsh, but O'Reilly's grin did not fade.

"Yes." He was a hard man to thank for anything. At least, as Barry was learning, that was how O'Reilly liked to seem to be.

"Get your breakfast into you; we've a busy day ahead of us." O'Reilly spooned Mrs. Kincaid's homemade strawberry jam over warm buttermilk pancakes.

Barry went to the sideboard. There was barely room for the chafing dish among the paper-wrapped, bottle-shaped parcels, all of which had been delivered by grateful patients two days ago. The parcels stood out like a row of sunflowers in a densely packed field where Christmas cards were multihued pansies.

Barry served himself and poured a cup of tea. "Busy? I thought the shop was closed today." He took his accustomed place.

"Of course it is, you eejit." O'Reilly dabbed a red smear from his chin. "I'm on call today; you're not, but that doesn't mean you won't be busy."

"Fine." If Patricia had been coming, Barry might

not have acquiesced so easily, but what the hell? "What do you want me to do? Walk Arthur? Wash the Rover?"

"Don't be daft. The water would freeze."

Lord, Barry thought, he thinks I'm seriously offering to wash his car.

"We'll walk Arthur together," O'Reilly said. He bent, reached under the table, and produced four wrapped parcels. "I brought these down from under the tree." He pushed two to one side, moved one closer to himself, and slid the last the length of the table. "Yours."

Barry lifted the parcel with its red bow and read the message on the tag. O'Reilly's bold pen strokes read: *To Barry Laverty, the finest assistant I could wish for. With my very best wishes and my thanks, Fingal.*

Before he could open the gift, Kinky appeared. She was wearing her coat and best hat.

"Merry Christmas, Kinky," Barry said.

"*Nollaig shona agus dia dhuit, Dochtúir Laithbheartaigh.* Merry Christmas and God be with you."

"Thank you, Kinky. Are you off to church?"

"I am, so. The turkey's on, the ham's on, and they'll come to no harm. They've to cook for hours yet."

"Have you a minute before you go?" O'Reilly asked.

"Just a shmall little one. The service starts at ten, and I want to get there early to get a good pew. Reverend Robinson's always in good form on Christmas Day."

"Here," said O'Reilly, rising and handing her two

parcels. "One's from me. Maybe the other's from Saint Nick." He grinned.

"Thank you, sir. I appreciate this very much . . . especially today."

Barry frowned. "I don't understand. Why 'especially'?"

"Because, sir, tomorrow is called Boxing Day because it's the day servants usually get their Christmas boxes."

Barry at once understood. Typical of O'Reilly to ignore that social distinction and treat Kinky, as he had told Fitzpatrick to, as a human being worthy of respect.

She smiled at O'Reilly. "I'll open them now then?"

"You'll not know what's inside if you don't." O'Reilly sat again and started to attack his pancakes. "Can't have these going cold."

"True." She nodded, then examined the tags. "This one's from you, sir." She took off the wrapping paper with great care and folded it neatly. "It'll come in handy next year," she said to herself. She opened a flat white cardboard box.

Barry smiled. He already knew, courtesy of Alice Moloney, what was in there.

Kinky took a midnight blue silk scarf from a nest of green tissue paper. "It's beautiful. Thank you, sir." She put it back in the box and set the box on the table. "Now for the other. And it's not from Santa. It's from you, Doctor Laverty, dear."

Barry smiled, hoping she would be pleased. He silently blessed Alice for telling him that O'Reilly had bought a blue scarf and then advising Barry about his own choice. The transition in that woman, he thought, from harpy to pleasant human being had been quite remarkable.

Kinky went through the same ritual of saving the paper and finally produced a green silk scarf. "It's lovely." She bent and dropped a tiny kiss on Barry's cheek. "Thank you, Doctor Laverty. Thank you very much."

"My pleasure," he said, then blushed.

Kinky looked from one scarf to the other. "You two gentlemen have put a poor Cork woman in a fix, so."

O'Reilly swallowed his mouthful. "No, we haven't. Wear the green one today because it goes very well with your hat. There'll be no offence taken by me."

"Thank you, sir." She picked up both boxes. "I'll be running along, but I'll be back in an hour or so."

"Enjoy yourself," O'Reilly said. "We'll be here just in case there are any emergencies." Barry heard the anticipation in his senior colleague's voice and saw the brightness in his eyes when he said, "Kitty's coming down this morning."

Barry sighed and wished he was waiting for Patricia to arrive.

"I'll go then and thank you both for my presents. They're *álainn*."

"*Álainn,* that's beautiful to you, Barry," said O'Reilly, once Kinky had left. "And it's a high compliment coming from Kinky. She really likes her scarves." He squinted at his own parcel, picked it up, and shook it against his ear as a child would, Barry thought.

"And what could be in there? Have a look."

"All right." O'Reilly tried to rip the wrapping off, but a couple of strips of Sellotape resisted his initial assault. He sliced through them with his knife, picked up the oblong box, and flipped it open. His eyes widened as he extracted a briar with a straight stem and a pale, sandy brown bowl. He whistled on the intake of breath. "Thundering Jesus, that's a Dunhill Tanshell," he said. "Thank you, Barry. Thank you very much."

Barry inclined his head.

O'Reilly rummaged in his pocket and produced his tobacco pouch. "I'll have to break it in"—he started filling the bowl—"and there's no time like the present."

Barry smiled. The man in the local tobacconist's had been most helpful. He'd said Dunhills were the Rolls-Royces of pipes and not to be put off by the pale colour. With use it would develop a patina of great beauty. "Glad you like it," Barry said.

"Mmmfh," O'Reilly agreed, the new pipe clamped between his teeth. He held a lit match over the bowl. Its flame dipped down as he drew, and puffs of smoke escaped from between his lips. When it was drawing well, he said, "It is a beauty." He let go his customary blue cloud, took the pipe from his mouth, and pointed the stem at Barry's parcel. "Thank you."

Barry's pleasure was as great as O'Reilly's obvious delight.

"Your turn, Barry."

Barry lifted his gift and noticed again the words *the finest assistant I could wish for.* His chest expanded. He removed the paper. One word on the box, Hardy, was enough to tell him of the treasure inside. He opened the box and took out a single-action fly reel. The manufacturers were the ne plus ultra in rod-and-reel building. This was the first Hardy reel he had ever owned. "Fingal, it's wonderful. Thank you. Thank you very much. I can hardly wait to try it on the Bucklebo." It didn't seem very long ago that the villagers, at the going-away party for the Galvins, had given him a beautiful fly box full of hand-tied trout flies.

"Ask the marquis." O'Reilly said. "You'll be seeing him at his open house."

The front doorbell rang.

"Will you see who that is, Barry?"

"But you're on—" Barry bit off "call" and rose. He went into the hall and opened the front door to be greeted by Donal and Julie Donnelly. By their glowing cheeks, both were perfectly well. "Good morning," he said. "What can I do for the pair of you on Christmas Day? Nobody's sick, I hope?"

Donal shook his head. "Not at all."

Barry smiled. "Good. And I'm not buying any raffle tickets."

Donal laughed. "Good one, sir. I'm not selling none, and you can't do a thing for us," Donal said, lifting his cap. "Me and Julie just wanted to wish you and himself the compliments of the season and hope that next year will be a very good one for the both of youse, so it will." He handed Barry a parcel. "Julie's a quare dab hand in the kitchen, so she is. Her granny was Scottish and it's her recipe for shortbread, and"—he winked and lowered his voice—"we all know himself has a sweet tooth."

Barry took the parcel. "That's very kind of you. Thank you, Donal. Julie. A very merry Christmas to you two, and a very happy New Year . . ."—he glanced at Julie's tummy—"to you *three*."

Julie laughed. "Thank you, Doctor Laverty. Enjoy the shortbread." She tugged at Donal's hand. "Come on, love," she said. "We don't want to be late for the service . . . Good-bye, sir."

Barry stood in the open doorway. He was cold without a hat and coat, and yet there was a feeling inside him that was toasty warm.

He recognized Councillor Bertie and Mrs. Flo Bishop walking to church along the opposite pavement, and he called, "Merry Christmas." He was rewarded by a smile from the councillor, a return of his greetings, and a reminder from Flo. "We'll see you and himself tomorrow at our open house. It starts at one."

"Right. Thank you," said Barry, wondering how his liver was going to stand up to all the festive good cheer. He had forgotten all about the Bishops' party, but he was damn sure O'Reilly hadn't. It wouldn't be worth mentioning.

He stepped inside and went back into the dining room. "Shortbread from Julie and Donal," Barry explained, setting the parcel on the table. "They just came to wish us—"

"A Merry Christmas." O'Reilly shook his head. "We're going to hear a lot of that today, and do you know what?"

"What, Fingal?"

"It never sounds trite or hackneyed to my ears."

"I know what you mean." It was funny how much a little show of gratitude made working with people so worthwhile.

"Come on," said O'Reilly, "let's go up to the lounge."

The time between Kinky's leaving for church and her return passed quickly. There were no calls. O'Reilly was putting on their second LP of the morning—part of a three-record set of Herbert von Karajan conducting the Berlin Philharmonic in Beethoven's Sixth Symphony—when Kinky stuck her head around the door and announced, "I'm back, so."

The doorbell rang again. "Go and get your hat and coat off, Kinky. I'll answer it," O'Reilly said and then headed for the stairs.

Barry heard the roar from below. "Kitty. Kitty O'Hallorhan. Merry Christmas. Come in, come in. Let me take your coat."

"It's nippy out there," she said.

"Let me look at you in that powder-blue twin set." Pause. "By God, Kitty O'Hallorhan, you look good enough to eat. Give me a hug."

Barry heard what sounded like a kiss, then Kitty's

chuckle. "Coming from you, Fingal, that's a rare compliment."

"I meant it. Now, do you want a cup of tea? Some shortbread maybe?"

"No, thank you."

"Then go you on up to the lounge. The fire's lit. Stop footering with your overcoat. Go on with you and get warm."

"But, Fingal, I—"

"Upstairs, woman. You said it was nippy out. I'll not have you die of exposure in my house."

Barry heard Kitty chuckle. "All right and Merry Christmas, Fingal," she said. Then he heard the sound of footsteps ascending.

Barry moved from his armchair and took a straight-backed chair before they came into the lounge. He rose when Kitty entered. "Merry Christmas, Kitty. Have a pew."

She took one armchair. "Please sit down."

Barry sat. O'Reilly charged past and bent down beside the half-naked tree. Lady Macbeth jumped onto Kitty's lap. She stroked the animal's head. The cat, wearing a red ribbon round her neck, butted her head against the caressing palm and purred mightily.

"Listen to that," said O'Reilly, straightening up, "but pay her no heed. It's for her own good that a cat purrs. She's trying to ingratiate herself."

Don't tell me he's jealous of the cat, Barry thought. He'd never seen O'Reilly look at anybody or anything as fondly as he gazed on Kitty.

Kitty seemed to be oblivious. She turned to Barry. "Nice to see you again, Barry."

"It's been a while."

"I had a week's holiday. I went and spent it with my mother. She gave me the twin set. Mum lives in Tallaght. It's a bit south of Dublin. I drove back up to town last night."

"And about time too," O'Reilly said. "We've missed you."

"Och, sure, Fingal," Kitty said, "doesn't absence make the heart grow fonder?"

"Ahem," said O'Reilly, clearing his throat. "Ha-hm. I have something for you, Kitty." He handed her a long parcel.

"Thank you, Fingal. That's very sweet."

"Sweet, my aunt Fanny Jane. It's Christmas." O'Reilly lifted his shoulders.

Lord, Barry thought, you'd probably drop dead, Fingal, if you thought anyone suspected you've a soft side.

She looked at Fingal, said nothing, and opened her parcel. "My God," she said, looking at the label of a bottle of red wine. "It's a Lafite Rothschild '61. That's a noble vintage year. You haven't changed much, O'Reilly, have you? You were always a romantic bugger." She kissed his lips, then said, "I hope you'll help me to drink it?"

O'Reilly spluttered and his face reddened.

Barry looked away. He didn't want to embarrass O'Reilly further, and he desperately wished someone was kissing him.

Kitty stepped back. "And I have a wee something for you, but it's downstairs in my coat. You'll get it when we come back from His Lordship's."

O'Reilly rose. "Now," he said. "It's eleven-thirty. Things kick off at the marquis's at twelve. We don't have to be there exactly on time, and we've a couple of calls to make first so we'd best get going."

Calls? It was news to Barry. "Who've we to call on, Fingal? Nobody's phoned."

"Didn't I tell you the first week you were here? Sometimes it's the ones who don't call that need the visit."

"Oh. Right." There was no arguing with that.

Before Barry could ask who they'd be visiting, O'Reilly was heading for the stairs with Kitty on his heels.

Barry followed, hoping the calls weren't to patients, and he saw Kinky bustling down the hall. He was still three steps from the bottom of the stairs when she opened the front door. He stopped and looked over the heads of O'Reilly, Kitty, and Kinky.

"Och," she said, "and would you look at that? What a lot of wee dotes."

There were three children standing on the front steps. He recognized Colin Brown and Jeannie Kennedy. The third, a girl he guessed was twelve or thirteen, had her back to the doorway. She raised her hands above her head and, with both index fingers extended, began to conduct.

We wish you a Merry Christmas . . .

There were more than three children singing. A boy with a strong voice and a lisp could be heard over the rest.

We with *you a Merry* Chrithmath . . .

Barry came down and stood where he could see the front path. For the second time in two weeks he was reminded of *The Wind in the Willows*, one of the favourite books of his childhood. The children carol-ing could have been the dormice singing for Rat and Mole. The youngsters' cheeks were rosy, their mouths wide, and their eyes serious. Their breath made small clouds of vapour on the still air.

We wish you a merry Christmas . . .

The tall girl conducted energetically. Her long, black hair spilled out from under a green and red striped, woolly bobble hat. She faced Colin and Jeannie, and behind them were Micky Corry, Eddie Jingles, who was well and truly over his pneumonia, and Billy Cadogan, the asthmatic.

And a happy New Year.

There were more Barry could call by name. He felt proud to be able to recognize so many.

Oh, bring us a figgy pudding . . .

The carollers grinning started and Barry realized why when Mrs. Kincaid headed back toward her kitchen. She was going to fetch treats for the singers.

Oh, bring us a figgy pudding . . .

Fine snow drifted slowly down, winter's white sub-stitute for summer's dandelion puffs, and like icing sugar it powdered the shoulders of new overcoats, multihued woollen toques, and the flat tops of dun-coloured tweed caps.

. . . and a cup of good cheer.

The black-haired girl held up her hands and turned to stare at O'Reilly. Barry was struck by the darkness of her eyes and the length of her eyelashes, where a single, large snowflake had lodged. She turned back to her choir and with more forceful movements of her arms exhorted the voices to greater efforts.

We won't *go until we get some; we* won't *go until we get some . . .*

Kinky appeared, pushing a trolley laden with plates of sweet mince pies and a steaming bowl of dark liquid that Barry knew would be hot Ribena Black Currant Cordial.

Barry joined in a round of applause when the carol ended. Then he stepped aside as Kinky invited the children into the hall.

All but the dark-haired girl queued for their mince pies and hot drinks. She held up a collecting tin with UNICEF on its label.

Barry pushed a pound note through the slot in its top. The United Nations International Children's Emergency Fund was a worthy cause.

"Merry Christmas, Doctor Laverty," she said.

"Well done, Hazel Arbuthnot and all the rest of you," O'Reilly said. "Aggie's daughter," he remarked to Barry, who couldn't help wondering if Hazel had an extra toe like her mother.

O'Reilly put a five-pound note in the tin. "That's from Miss O'Hallorhan and me."

Hazel made a small curtsey. "Thank you, sir."

"Well done, all of you," he said, ignoring the chorus of thank-yous. "Now Kitty, Barry, we've calls to make, so get your coats on. I've to get a wee thing." He stepped into the dining room and then reappeared clutching a bottle-shaped, paper-wrapped parcel. "Hold that." He handed it to Barry and shrugged into his coat.

"Who are we going to see, Fingal?" Barry wanted to know.

"Declan and Mélanie Finnegan, then Eileen Lindsay. They all live on the estate."

Barry glanced first at the bottle he was carrying and then to O'Reilly. "And will we be bringing food and wine and pine logs too?"

"No," said O'Reilly, "I'm not Good King Wenceslas and you're certainly not my page, but with his Parkinson's disease Declan doesn't get out much, and he always enjoys a wee half-un with his Christmas dinner."

Barry wondered if this was the first Christmas O'Reilly had made this kind of call, but decided it almost certainly was not.

"Come on," said O'Reilly. "Time we were off."

Kinky looked up from dabbing at the coat of a small boy who had spilled his juice. "Then run along, make your calls, and enjoy His Lordship's hooley," she said. "But I'll expect you all back by five, not a minute later. I'd not want the dinner spoiled."

49

The Corridors of Power

"*Ne dites plus, Mélanie. C'était notre plaisir.*" O'Reilly had sent Kitty and Barry out and was saying good-bye to the Finnegans. And it *had* been his pleasure to see Declan's stiff smile and Mélanie's obvious happiness to have the opportunity to speak her native French. The operation Declan had undergone earlier that year had not cured his Parkinson's disease, but it had certainly improved it.

"*Joyeux Nöel et une bonne et heureuse année, Docteur O'Reilly.*"

"*Et à toi, Mélanie.*"

She closed the door behind him, and he started to walk along Comber Gardens to catch up with Kitty and Barry. Somehow, he thought, the street seemed less dingy today. Perhaps it was the covering of snow. Perhaps it was the happy shouts of children. Mary Lindsay sat on a small toboggan, and while Willy Lindsay pulled, another boy pushed. The sled's runners crunched through the snow. They didn't pay him any attention. And why should they? They were having fun. He hoped Sammy was enjoying himself too, and that was something he'd find out as soon as they made their call on Eileen.

Barry and Kitty stopped where a group of children

were building a lopsided snowman on the footpath. "That's a good one," Kitty said. "I like the way they've given him a smile."

O'Reilly looked at the upturned, curved row of small pieces of coal at the bottom of the snowman's head. Anne-Marie Mulloy—he'd treated her last year for chicken pox—was sticking in a carrot for its nose between the larger lumps of coal that were the eyes. "Whose dad is short a bowler hat," O'Reilly asked, "and a Glentoran scarf?" He wondered if the items might belong to Gerry Shanks, but saw no sign of either of his kiddies.

O'Reilly pulled out his old briar—the new Dunhill was in his other pocket—and he looked at the pipe's bowl burnt black and irregular by years of use. "Here, Malachy." He offered it to a hatless boy in a grey coat. "Stick that in your man's gob. He doesn't look right without a pipe."

The boy dashed a snot track from his upper lip with one hand as he grabbed the pipe in the other. "Thanks, Doctor O'Reilly. That's wheeker, so it is. Thanks a million." He turned and pushed the pipe into the middle of the snowman's mouth.

"That's more like it," said O'Reilly, chuckling as he led his companions to Number 31.

The air was crisp and the smell of burning coal was strong. When O'Reilly looked up, he could see that every chimney in sight was smoking. There was no central heating in any of these houses, but at least the occupants would be keeping warm today.

O'Reilly pounded on the front door frame so hard

that the holly wreath fixed to the door shuddered and swayed. Realizing he had overdone the announcement of his arrival, he stopped hammering and stamped his feet as he waited.

Eileen Lindsay opened the door. "Doctor O'Reilly? Is everything all right?"

"Of course, Eileen. We just came to wish you the compliments of the season. Can we come in?"

"Please." She stepped aside.

"This is Miss O'Hallorhan."

Eileen made a tiny bob. "Pleased to meet you." She closed the door. "Go on into the parlour. Can I get youse anything? A cup of tea in your hand? A wee half-un? Maybe an eggnog?"

"No thanks, Eileen," O'Reilly said. "We've only popped in for a minute to see how Sammy is." He led Kitty to the parlour, and Barry followed along.

A fire blazed in the grate. Three empty red felt stockings lay on the carpet, and O'Reilly could see the hooks in the mantel from which they had hung. An unlit red candle surrounded by a holly wreath sat in the middle of the mantelpiece.

Johnny Jordan and Sammy sat on the floor at the control box of a Hornby Dublo 00 electric train, an engine, two passenger coaches, and a guard's van. The train cars made a high-pitched clattering as they ran around and around an oval track. "How's about ye, Doctor O'Reilly?" Sammy asked.

"I'm fine, thanks, Sammy. How are you?" O'Reilly nodded to Johnny, who smiled. Donal had been right. The man was no oil painting. His bald pate glistened in the light coming in through the window. His smile was very wide, and O'Reilly noticed that two of his lower incisors were missing. "Doctor," he said, lowering his head slighty.

Sammy stopped the engine and showed O'Reilly his arms. "My rash is all gone now, so it has, and I'm not swollen up no more."

"Good."

"But Mammy wouldn't let me go out yet. She says it's too cold. Willie and Mary's gone to throw snowballs, so they have."

"I know. I saw them. Do you mind not going out?"

Sammy grinned. "Nah. Santa brung all three of us bicycles . . . but you can't ride a bike in the snow. Anyway I'd rather play with Johnny and my new train set."

O'Reilly tousled the boy's hair. "Good for you." O'Reilly was delighted, and the best part of helping the Lindsays had been watching Donal work the fiddle. Admit it, Fingal, he told himself, that kind of scheming has always appealed to you. "Right then," he said, "we'll be off." He steered Kitty to the door. "A Merry Christmas to this house," he said. "A very happy New Year."

The chorus of returned greetings was still ringing in his ears as he closed the front door.

O'Reilly held open the back door of the Rover for Kitty. "Next stop, Ballybucklebo House. We're running a bit late but His Lordship won't mind, and by the time we get there the party should be in full swing."

"I don't care if we're a bit late. Please drive carefully, Fingal," Kitty said, as she got in. "Sammy may think it's too snowy to ride a bike, but if there are any cyclists out today . . ."

"And you don't want to think of anybody in a ditch on Christmas Day." He started the engine. "All right. Careful it is."

The boughs of the monkey puzzle tree in front of the Rover were bent low, their prickly leaves sheathed in softness. There were a lot of parked cars. Quite a few were Rolls-Royces, Bentleys, and Daimlers. O'Reilly had to park some distance from the big house, but the drive had been cleared.

The snow, glistening as it reflected the rays of the low winter sun, lay almost unblemished on the lawns. The only imperfections in the white smoothness were tracks of birds' feet. O'Reilly narrowed his eyes. At least three pheasants had been there. With a bit of luck the marquis would have a shoot in January.

O'Reilly looked at Kitty. Her eyes were sparkling and her cheeks ruddy, and he had a sudden desire to push her down and roll her in the snow, ignore her laughing protests, and then hug her to warm her up. Instead he took her soft leather gloved hand in his.

"I love days like this," she said, "and we haven't had many for quite a while." She held his gaze.

"More's the pity," he said, and he smiled down at her when she smiled up at him and squeezed his hand. He looked away but held her hand more tightly. The lower windows of the Georgian front of the big house were festooned inside with evergreen branches and holly sprigs. By God, if there was a mistletoe sprig somewhere about the place, he'd get her under it before the day was over.

He led his little party up the wide front steps. Inside the portico the big front door was open and led to a marble-floored entrance hall.

"Hang on, Fingal. Hold this, please." Kitty handed him a shoe bag she was carrying. In no time she was standing in a pair of elegant grey-suede stiletto heels. "Can I leave my boots here?"

"I don't see why not," O'Reilly said.

He heard a low creaking and turned to see a pair of mullioned glass doors being opened by a middle-aged man in a morning suit and grey gloves. O'Reilly recognized His Lordship's butler.

"Good morning, Thompson."

"Good morning, Commander O'Reilly, and a Merry Christmas."

"The same to you."

"May I take your coats?"

O'Reilly, Kitty, and Barry shed their outerwear. "Fingal," Barry asked quietly, "he called you Commander?"

O'Reilly smiled. "Your dad and I weren't the only Ulstermen on the *Warspite*. Thompson was gunnery chief petty officer then. He won a Distinguished Service Medal at Cape Matapan." And bloody nearly lost his left foot, O'Reilly thought.

Thompson, now laden, began to carry coats and scarves to the coat stand.

"If you'll excuse me, I'll get these hung up. His

Lordship's expecting you, and you know your way, sir." The butler limped away with the pile of coats.

"Come on then," said O'Reilly, "the party's along this way."

Kitty stopped. "Hang on," she said. "I want to get a good look." She stared up at the arched cathedral ceiling. "It's not every day a girl gets an invitation to the lord of the manor's place."

O'Reilly smiled as he watched Kitty scan the oil paintings that adorned the walls. There were a great many portraits of earlier holders of the title, almost all of whom had iron-grey hair.

"Good God," she said, pointing to a painting of a periwigged soldier in a tricorne hat and scarlet coat who stood leaning against a caparisoned horse. "That could be Sir Joshua Reynolds's painting of Captain Robert Orne. I've seen it in the National Gallery in London."

"It *is* a Reynolds," O'Reilly said, remembering that Kitty dabbled in painting. Somehow, he thought, I'll give good odds she does more than merely dabble.

He heard footsteps approaching.

"My God," Barry said, "it's O'Brien-Kelly."

O'Reilly looked down the hall. Two young men were approaching. He recognized Sean, the marquis's soldier son, and Sean's senior officer, Captain O'Brien-Kelly. The captain, who had been in Ballybucklebo in August, was in O'Reilly's opinion a buck eejit of the first magnitude. "This should be interesting," he told Kitty, and before he could explain further, Sean was offering his hand. Almost as tall as his father, he had the same facial features, the same iron-grey hair.

"Merry Christmas, Doctor O'Reilly."

"Merry Christmas, Sean. On leave?"

"For a week. I brought my captain with me for a day or two at the pheasants. This is Captain . . ."

"O'Brien-Kelly," O'Reilly said, looking the man right in the eye. "We've met.

"Captain, Sean, may I present Caitlin O'Hallorhan and Doctor Laverty?"

Barry shook hands with Sean and then said to O'Brien-Kelly, "We've met."

O'Reilly turned to Kitty. "Caitlin O'Hallorhan. Lieutenant, the honourable Sean . . ."

"It's Sean, and may I call you Caitlin?"

She smiled. "I'd prefer Kitty."

"Kitty it is."

"And," O'Reilly continued, "this is Captain O'Brien-Kelly. He's a great fan of Irish thoroughbreds." O'Reilly struggled to keep a straight face. This was the man Donal Donnelly had sold Irish half crowns to for much more than they were worth. Donal had persuaded him that because the coins had a horse embossed on them, they were medallions specially struck to honour the great Irish thoroughbred Arkle.

"Delighted," said O'Brien-Kelly. "And jolly pleased to see you again, O'Weilly. Didn't get a chance to say cheewio. Had to leave in wather a wush after the waces."

The poor man must believe that pronouncing his *r*'s as *w*'s adds class to his speech, O'Reilly thought.

"Something to do with a bookie . . . Honest Sammy Dolan, as I recall," Barry said innocently.

Something to do with the marquis having to pay off O'Brien-Kelly's gambling debt, O'Reilly remembered.

"Indeed," the captain said. He quickly changed the subject. "I never had a chance to thank you, O'Weilly."

"Thank me?" O'Reilly frowned. He'd been quite prepared to be sworn at for introducing O'Brien-Kelly to Donal.

"Well, when I went to sell those coins to the chaps in the wegiment—recoup a bit, as you might say—an Irish officer, not Sean here, told them that all I had was some worthless Irish currency." He smiled widely. "The chaps twigged at once, but they seemed to think it was all a gag and that I was no end of a comic."

O'Reilly guffawed mightily.

"That's wight. No end of a joke, weally. The chaps do enjoy a bit of fun at a senior officer's expense, so my stock's been very high since. That's why I owe you my thanks."

"My pleasure." O'Reilly said, as he thought, will wonders never cease? He'd characterized O'Brien-Kelly as the classic Anglo-Irish upper-class twit, yet the man was able to laugh at himself. He'd give the captain points for that, even if he was a bit dim.

O'Brien-Kelly, clearly dismissing O'Reilly, turned to Sean. "Now, Sean, are we going to see that gelding?"

"Yes. Please excuse us." Sean bowed to Kitty, smiled at O'Reilly, and led O'Brien-Kelly toward the front doors.

O'Reilly grinned and shook his head. "You know, Barry," he said, "I'll be damned if I can remember who said the Lord looks after drunks, children, and idiots, but there went living proof."

"I think," said Barry, "it was attributed to Bismarck."

"Wonderful," said Kitty. "Now are you two going to stand there all day playing Brain of Britain, or are we going to a party?"

50

Come and Go, Talking of Michelangelo

Together they entered a large high-ceilinged drawing room. O'Reilly guessed there were fifty or sixty people standing in groups or sitting on comfortable armchairs and loveseats that were distributed in a seemingly haphazard manner throughout the room. This was, next to the Ballybucklebo races, the social event of the year, and certainly the women present were all dressed in their Sunday best.

Above the sound of conversations, rising and falling as waves in a narrow inlet, occasional roars of laughter rose like whitecaps on their crests.

He led Kitty and Barry to the fringes of the party. In the background he could hear a gramophone playing Vivaldi's *Four Seasons*.

He accompanied the music, pom-pomming happily.

A man standing on the periphery turned and saw O'Reilly. "Merry Christmas, Doctor."

"Merry Christmas, Constable Mulligan." Judging by his blue three-piece worsted suit, the village's single police officer was off duty. "Have you seen the marquis?"

"Yes, sir, I seen him proceeding in an easterly direction toward the library, but he said he'd be back, like."

O'Reilly recognized the man approaching the constable. The undertaker's nose bore a large rhinophyma, a blockage of the ducts of the sebaceous glands. The result was a red bulb that O'Reilly thought might have made Rudolph envious.

"Merry Christmas, Doctor O'Reilly."

"Merry Christmas, Mr. Coffin."

"How's about ye, Christopher?" The constable beamed and began engaging the undertaker in a spirited conversation. O'Reilly knew the two had struck up a friendship after Seamus Galvin's going-away party in August. "Great to see a white Christmas, so it is."

"Right enough, but I hope it goes quick. It's a bugger to get a hearse through it . . ."

O'Reilly left the two men chatting happily. "Let's mingle," he said, taking Kitty by the elbow. His tummy rumbled. He caught a whiff of the delicate scent of a potpourri of dried flowers and noticed a ceramic pot on a side table near the fireplace. The table also bore full silver cigarette boxes, bowls of nuts, boxes of Bendick's Bittermints from Bond Street, plates of shortbread, and marzipan-stuffed dates. O'Reilly had a soft spot for marzipan-stuffed dates. He changed course to head in their direction.

The Bishops were chatting to Sonny and Maggie. A large sprig of holly was tucked into the band of Maggie's purple felt hat. He noticed that in honour of the occasion she was wearing her false teeth.

None of them had seen O'Reilly, who was intent on reaching the stuffed dates. He decided he'd stop to chat a little later, but he hesitated when Bertie Bishop said to Sonny, "Anyway, says I to your man, 'If you think I'm paying two thousand pounds for that horse—two *thousand*—you need your head examined, so you do, because—"

A roar of laughter from the far side of the room drowned out the councillor's words. Whoever it was who was so amused had a giggle that could fillet a herring at ten fathoms.

"You were just right, Bertie," Sonny said and smiled at Bishop. "The brass neck of your man, to think he could put one over on you . . ."

So, O'Reilly thought, Bertie's not the only one suffused with the Christmas spirit. He knew that Sonny did not hold the councillor in high esteem, and he had good reason not to, but for today anyway he was willing to let bygones be bygones.

"Fingal." It was Barry's voice. "I thought you could use some sustenance."

O'Reilly turned and saw Kitty holding something in a white paper napkin. Barry had finished offering a plate of smoked salmon to her and was now holding it in O'Reilly's direction. "Good lad." He snaffled two slices of buttered wheaten bread covered with thin red portions of lox. He admired the pale green capers on top of the smoked fish and popped the first slice whole into his mouth. His words were muffled when he said, "'For this relief much thanks.'"

"*Hamlet*," said Barry. "Here. Have another."

O'Reilly took one. It was a delicate soupçon, but he really fancied a stuffed date. He shoved on to his goal near the fireplace, confident that Barry and Kitty were following.

They skirted the loose group where Father O'Toole, Reverend and Mrs. Robinson, and Miss Moloney were listening to Fergus Finnegan, captain of the rugby fifteen.

"I reckon this new lad Michael Gibson's going to turn out to be a better outhalf than Jack Kyle was."

"I'm not so sure," Miss Moloney ventured. "My father used to take us to the games before we went to India, and I kept going after I came back to Ulster. I went up to Belfast and saw Kyle at Ravenhill in nineteen fifty-three. He was at his peak then . . ."

O'Reilly waited. Anything to do with rugby football interested him, particularly when a woman had an obviously educated opinion on the subject.

"Against France?" Fergus said.

"That's right. He made a break, sold two magnificent dummies, and scored a try that people still talk about."

They did indeed, O'Reilly thought, impressed that Miss Moloney understood the game's finer points. He'd been at Ravenhill himself, and to watch Kyle run, jinking like a snipe through the French defence, had been a moment he would never forget. And Jackie Kyle himself a doctor.

There was a note of respect in Fergus's voice when he said, "Right enough, but I reckon we should give Gibson a year or two. That boy has talent. It's sticking out a mile, so it is." He moved a little closer to Miss Moloney. "Every year a bunch of the lads from the club charter a bus and go down to Dublin for the international games. Would you like to be put on the list, Miss Moloney?"

Her eyes sparkled. "I'd love it, if I can get away from the shop . . . and it's Alice, by the way."

Good for you, Alice Moloney, O'Reilly thought. He moved the last two steps to the table.

"My goodness," Kitty said, looking around, "this *is* grand. This is very grand."

"Nothing but the best if you travel with O'Reilly," he said. "It is cosy, isn't it?"

"It should be," she said, "Look at the size of that fireplace."

O'Reilly inhaled deeply, and the smell of burning wood mingled with the aroma of pipe tobacco and cigars.

A huge log burnt on black andirons in a cavernous fieldstone fireplace. The grate was flanked by inglenooks with benches. Two ceramic fire dogs, white-and-black painted Dalmatians, sat erect with supercilious grins on their glazed faces.

Kitty chuckled. "It makes the gas fire in my flat look a bit puny."

The Four Seasons had finished. It had been replaced with another piece he recognized, Mozart's Thirty-ninth Symphony. O'Reilly had to strain to hear because the noise level in the room was now much higher. Old Doctor Flanagan, who had sold O'Reilly the practice, had called alcohol the universal social lubricant. He was right.

O'Reilly helped himself to a stuffed date and looked around to see if he could find a waiter. He'd not object to a bit of oiling of his own gears. No luck. He reckoned he knew how the garrison must have felt in the besieged town of Mafeking during the Boer War: cut off from supplies and very thirsty.

He helped himself to another date and turned to see Kitty scrutinizing a portrait above the Connemara marble mantel. It was of a much younger marquis wearing the dress uniform of the Irish Guards.

"I think that's an Annigoni." Kitty's voice had dropped to a whisper.

"It is. My father commissioned it," the marquis said.

"Jesus, Your Lordship," O'Reilly said, "don't creep up on folks like that. As Kinky would say, you gave me such a surprise I near took the rickets."

"I didn't think anything could shock you, Fingal," the marquis said with a grin.

"My lord." Barry made a small bow.

"Laverty. Nice to see you, and it's *very* nice to see you back, Miss O'Hallorhan. I recall you were here for Sonny's wedding."

"I was, and it's Kitty, please, my lord."

"Kitty. It's a very friendly name." He gazed at her face. "I must say you are looking lovely today."

O'Reilly wasn't quite sure whether to swell with pride or feel a tiny stab of jealousy. The marquis, who wasn't much older than O'Reilly, had been a widower for eight years and was a charismatic man.

"Thank you, sir," she said and smiled.

He noticed how graciously Kitty accepted the compliment. She didn't blush. Kitty O'Hallorhan, he could tell, was well used to compliments.

"Now," said the marquis, "I will try to get a proper word later, but soon I must go and greet my other guests. I think you know most of them, Fingal."

"I'm sure I do, and if I don't, haven't I a mouth between my nose and my chin?"

The marquis laughed. "I don't think you'll have to introduce yourself to that colleague of yours, Fingal." The marquis nodded toward Ronald Hercules Fitzpatrick, who stood beside the decorated tree at the far end of the room where two of the marquis's dogs, an Irish setter and an Irish wolfhound, slept beneath the branches. Good God, Fingal thought.

"I thought you might like to meet a fellow medical man under social circumstances. The Kinnegar's not far, and it used to be part of the estate before my father sold it to pay death duties for his father. Grandpa lived to be a hundred and one, you know, and I'm afraid my dad didn't outlive him by much."

O'Reilly, stifling his surprise at seeing Fitzpatrick, looked at the marquis and saw in him a living symbol of the age-old history and permanence of a place like Ballybucklebo.

"I'll have a word with him." O'Reilly resolved to go speak to Fitzpatrick soon, but not until he'd had a drink. Fitzpatrick was talking to a very tall man with an aquiline nose who sported a monocle in his left eye. "Who's that, John?"

O'Reilly had to wait to hear the answer. Once the laughter died, the marquis said, "Sir Aidan Creighton-Dwyer-MacNeill. He's a baronet. We're related distantly. His father was a MacNeill from the Antrim branch of the family. They have quite a large farm near Ballymoney. He married Annie O'Sullivan. She's one of *the* O'Sullivans, and they boast John L. Sullivan, the boxer, from their Tralee branch and Maureen O'Sullivan, the actress, who comes from their Roscommon connection. She's Mia Farrow's mother, you know . . ."

The marquis frowned. "Sometimes I do go on about genealogy. Families here do tend to get a bit complicated. A second cousin of ours had to be sent to Purdysburn mental hospital about twenty years ago."

"I'm sorry to hear that," Barry said.

"It was a long time ago and"—the marquis chuckled—"Dolores really was quite gaga. She had a habit of presenting strangers with her dentures."

Just a bit more speeding up. The marquis beckoned to a uniformed maid, who was carrying a tray of full glasses. "I really must circulate now, but please make yourselves completely at home, and a very merry Christmas to you all."

"Jameson, Doctor O'Reilly?"

Mafeking had been relieved. O'Reilly grinned. "Of course, Margaret." He helped himself. He recognized her because he'd treated her for mumps when she was eight.

The maid offered her tray to Kitty. "Madam?"

"Are those Buck's Fizz?" Kitty pointed to champagne flutes with an orange-coloured liquid inside.

The maid nodded.

"Thank you." Kitty took one. "Champagne and orange juice. Just the job for Christmas Day."

"Sir?" The maid offered the tray to Barry.

He took a fizz. "Thank you."

"Cheers," Kitty said and sipped. "I like the marquis. He's even more charming than he was at Sonny and Maggie's wedding."

O'Reilly decided, peer of the realm or not, when it came to Kitty O'Hallorhan he'd keep an eye on John MacNeill, 27th Marquis of Ballybucklebo.

"He is a good man," O'Reilly said, and lack of mistletoe be damned, he encircled Kitty's waist with his arm, pulled her to him, and gently kissed her lips. "Bless you, Kitty, for being here. I . . ." God Almighty, he was within an ace of telling her he loved her, but he couldn't quite summon the courage. "I wish you a very merry Christmas." Damn it, Fingal, he thought, tell her, you great lummox. But as he bent to say the words, he realized that Barry was within earshot and Sonny and Maggie were rapidly approaching. He decided to hold his tongue.

"Merry Christmas, Doctor dear," Maggie said. "Doctor Laverty."

"And you remember Miss O'Hallorhan?" O'Reilly said.

"I do." Maggie cocked her head and looked at Kitty appraisingly. "It's a nice outfit," she said, "but I prefer the one you had on for my wedding."

"If I'd known, Mrs. Houston, I'd have worn it." Kitty chuckled.

O'Reilly was impressed that Kitty had remembered Maggie's married name. "We popped in with Eileen Lindsay this morning. You'll be glad to hear Sammy's completely better and the Lindsays are having a wonderful Christmas."

"That is good," Sonny said. "Very good. I'm pleased."

"You two were a great help when he was sick, Maggie. I mean it." O'Reilly said.

"Och, sure, wasn't it Doctor Laverty's idea?"

O'Reilly saw Barry smile. And rightly so. The lad was

learning there was more to country doctoring than making diagnoses and writing prescriptions. There was pleasure to be taken from helping folks get on with their lives.

"And anyway," Maggie continued, "the babysitting was nothing. What made it for her was winning that raffle, so it was."

O'Reilly nodded. He felt rather pleased with himself.

"Och, sure, and wasn't it a Christmas miracle?"

"It was, Maggie." O'Reilly picked up another stuffed date.

"And run by Donal Donnelly." Her smile was very wide when she leant over and whispered, "And me never knowing that Donal was an angel."

She knew it had been fixed, or more likely she knew Donal.

"But we'll say no more about it, will we, Doctor dear?"

"Not a word, Maggie. Not a word."

She winked at him and turned to Sonny. "Right, dear. Time we were running along. My turkey needs attention, and the General and your dogs have been on their own long enough."

No doubt, O'Reilly thought, Sonny's five dogs and Maggie's battle-scarred cat, Sir Bernard Law Montgomery, would be dining on turkey today too. "Safe home," he said.

"And to you, Doctor," Sonny said, and with his arm protectively round Maggie's waist, he started to steer her to the door. "We'll see you all tomorrow, I hope, at the Bishops' open house."

"You will," said O'Reilly. He turned to Kitty. "Could you make it down for that?"

She shook her head. "Sorry, Fingal. Some of us have to work."

He shrugged but inside he felt as keenly disappointed as he knew Barry must be about Patricia not coming today. "Can't be helped. I understand, and perhaps—"

O'Reilly got no further. He glanced around the room. The latest gale of laughter, a mix of guffaws, belly laughs, and giggles, seemed to be coming from a group surrounding the tall cadaverous-looking Doctor Fitzpatrick. The man was grinning like a mooncalf and clutching his pince-nez in his left hand.

"What the hell—?"

"I think," said Barry, "that your old university friend is holding court."

"We should go and listen," O'Reilly said, taking Kitty's hand. "Come on."

"Excuse me, excuse me, excuse me." He forced his way past several strangers. He knew that Kitty and Barry were following in his wake. He brought his party to a standstill at the back of the group surrounding Fitzpatrick.

"Merry Christmas, Father O'Toole."

"Doctor."

"Compliments of the season, Reverend, Mrs. Robinson."

"Doctor O'Reilly. Doctor Laverty. Miss O'Hallorhan."

He heard Barry saying, "I'm glad the iron pills aren't causing you any trouble, Alice," and then heard Miss Moloney wishing Barry a merry Christmas.

It was like a family reunion, and wasn't that what Ballybucklebo was? And wasn't he very glad to be a member of that family?

Fitzpatrick's harsh voice carried. He was well into his story. "Anyway, the patient trusted the doctor, and he took his gunpowder every day, quite religiously . . ."

He took his *gunpowder*? What was Fitzpatrick doing?

"Every day . . . for six months . . . six whole months."

O'Reilly looked around. The audience had grown and seemed to encompass every one of the partygoers. The marquis, his son, O'Brien-Kelly, and Sir John MacNeill were at the far side of the crowd. There were Bertie and Flo. He smiled at them and they smiled back.

"And then . . ." Fitzpatrick lowered his voice. "And then the poor man died."

There was a sudden communal in-drawing of breath, and the silence following was broken only by the notes of the final movement of the Mozart symphony.

"And do you know what happened next?"

O'Reilly was impressed. Fitzpatrick certainly knew

how to hold an audience. He would be a difficult candidate to argue with in an election.

"They tried to cremate the corpse."

"And a very good idea," Mr. Coffin called.

"Wheest, Christopher," Constable Mulligan whispered in a loud voice.

"You're right, sir. It did seem like a good idea, but . . ."—Fitzpatrick swept his gaze around the room—"but to this very day they're looking for the back wall of the crematorium."

O'Reilly joined in the universal laughter and applauded with the others. He minded not at all that Fitzpatrick had pinched the line he himself had used when he'd chastised Fitzpatrick for using gunpowder as a treatment. Fair play to the man. O'Reilly let go of Kitty's hand and shoved his way to the front. He grabbed Fitzpatrick's hand and shook it. "Well done, Ronald. Well done."

"Thank you, O'Reilly. Coming from you that means a lot."

"Och, it's Christmas Day."

"So a Merry Christmas to you, Fingal, and I hope we all have a very happy New Year." He slipped the pince-nez back on his narrow nose and swallowed so his Adam's apple bobbed.

"I couldn't have said it better myself," O'Reilly said.

He felt a tapping on his shoulder and turned to see Kitty. "Excuse me, Ronald," she said.

"Certainly, Kitty."

"Fingal, it's four thirty . . ."

"And we have to go, or Kinky will baste me instead of the turkey." O'Reilly smiled at Fitzpatrick. "I've to go and say thanks to His Lordship; then we'll be off. Enjoy yourself."

"And when you get home," said Fitzpatrick with a small bow, "please wish Mrs. Kincaid a merry Christmas from me."

51

"Presents," I Often Say, "Endear . . ."

Barry was still amazed by the apparent transformation of Doctor Fitzpatrick. He had thought that seeing the light on the road to Damascus only happened in the Bible. But if the tousling O'Reilly had given the man last week had produced this change, then more power to his wheel.

He followed O'Reilly and Kitty across the back lane and into the garden. He could see lazy flakes drifting down and glistening in the glow from the nearby street light. As he and the other two walked through O'Reilly's dark garden, all he could hear was the crunching of shoes and boots in the snow. There were no traffic noises coming from the road, no chapel bells, no children's voices, no mewling of gulls, no lowing of beasts. Nightfall and snowfall had cocooned Ballybucklebo in a web of gentle silence.

There was no sign of Arthur. O'Reilly did not seem concerned, so it was unlikely that the dog had managed to roam.

It was nippy in the garden, but as soon as he was in the kitchen Barry had to take off his coat. And the cooking smells . . . oh, the aromas. His mouth watered.

"Nice to see you all home on time." Kinky, wreathed in a cloud of steam, closed the oven door and straightened up. She held a turkey baster in one oven-mitted hand. "The bird's coming on a treat. I'd not want it too dry from overcooking."

"I'm sure it'll melt in our mouths," O'Reilly said. He stood holding a bag that Barry knew contained Kitty's high heels. Kitty removed her coat and her fur-lined ankle boots. She slipped into her heels.

"And by the way, Doctor Fitzpatrick said to wish you a merry Christmas."

"By the Lord," she said, "will wonders never cease?" She looked at Kitty. "Pop your boots in the corner there, Miss O'Hallorhan."

"And I'll hang my coat in the hall." Kitty started to leave but hesitated when Kinky said, "Doctor O'Reilly, sir. I've a little job for you and Doctor Laverty."

"What?" O'Reilly asked. "I hope you don't expect me to bake the ham."

Kinky laughed so much her chins wobbled. "No, sir. I do not." Barry thought she sounded like a mother reassuring an eight-year-old that he'd not be expected to run the mile in four minutes. "Even though I am a *bit* behind with the cooking."

And that was the first time in five months Barry had ever heard Kinky confess to anything less than perfection. Somehow it made her even more admirable.

"I've been back and forth like a fiddler's elbow answering the door to all the folks who've come to wish this house a merry Christmas." She used her forearm to shove an errant wisp of hair out of her eyes. "I know people do come round every year to thank yourself, sir." She pointed at O'Reilly with the baster. "I know some folks came to the surgery on Wednesday with gifts, those who'd not been here before came today, and now there's *two* doctors here, every last visitor brought *two* bottles. There's enough whiskey in the dining room to have emptied Jameson's distillery, aye, and made a dent in the stock of Bushmills as well."

Barry saw O'Reilly's huge grin. The bottle they'd taken to Kieran O'Hagan would not be missed.

Kinky put the baster down on the counter and rattled a saucepan on the stovetop. "Boiled potatoes. They'll be ready to drain and start roasting in ten minutes," she muttered to herself. Then she continued to instruct O'Reilly. "I'd appreciate it, sir, if you'd take all them bottles upstairs." A saucepan lid rattled. She turned and tipped it so steam could escape. "Christmas pudding. It'll be done in another hour." She turned back to O'Reilly. "You can see, sir, I'm just a tad busy here. If you'd put them in the sideboard in the lounge . . . I'll need the sideboard in the dining room to put things on when I bring dinner through, so."

Kitty handed her coat to O'Reilly. "Hang that in the hall, Fingal, on your way to the dining room, please."

She sounded as if she'd been asking O'Reilly for that kind of little favour for years and, Barry noticed, O'Reilly accepted the coat as if he'd been doing it for years—and enjoying it.

Kitty rolled up her sleeves. "Mrs. Kinkaid, can I not give you a hand?"

"Bless you, Miss O'Hallorhan, that's very kind, so." Kinky pointed to three laden plates. "But if you'd just take the Christmas cake, the sweet mince pies, and the meringues through and set them on the sideboard once the doctors get it cleared, that would be help enough, thank you very much."

There was a finality in her thank-you, that edge that Barry interpreted as, Too many cooks spoil the broth, and saving your presence, Miss O'Hallorhan, this is *my* domain. He wondered if perhaps Kinky Kincaid, who for years had regarded Fingal Flahertie O'Reilly as her property, was feeling a bit jealous.

"I understand completely," Kitty said. "I'm a guest here. It's *your* kitchen, Kinky."

Nice peace offering, Barry thought, amazed as always at how astute women could be at sensing undercurrents.

Kitty picked up two laden plates. "I'll come back for the meringues. Lead on, Fingal."

O'Reilly headed for the hall with Kitty following. Barry saw Kinky watch her departure. There was a hint of a smile on the Cork woman's round face. She opened the oven again and pulled the lower rack halfway out. Barry admired the ham. Kinky had scored the fat into diamond patterns, and in the centre of each stood a clove. "Coming on nicely," she said, before pushing it back inside and closing the oven door.

"It looks lovely, Kinky."

"I think it will be," she said, "if I'm given peace to get on."

Barry took the not-too-subtle hint and went to help O'Reilly.

Barry stood at the fire, which was burning brightly in the grate. He bent and patted Arthur Guinness's head. The Labrador and Lady Macbeth, who must have declared their own Christmas truce, shared the hearth rug. Barry noticed that the cat had shed her ribbon.

"And the lion shall lie down with the lamb," O'Reilly said, from where he stood putting the last of the liquid gifts into the sideboard.

"Try 'the calf and the young lion and the fatling together,'" Barry said. "Poor old Isaiah is never quoted correctly."

"You're right, but how in the hell could you call that skinny wee white cat a fatling?"

"I see your point." Barry straightened.

Arthur looked up questioningly, as if to say, "I was enjoying that. Don't stop."

"We always let Arthur in for Christmas Day," O'Reilly said, which accounted for his absence from the back garden, Barry thought. Leaving an armchair for O'Reilly, Barry took the plain chair close to where Kitty sat in the other armchair. She'd set a small gift-wrapped parcel beside her. Barry had seen her pull it from the pocket of her camel-hair overcoat just before they'd all come up here. She kicked off her high heels and recrossed her legs. "They may be smart, but those shoes pinch my feet." She bent and massaged her toes.

Barry said nothing, but he was impressed by how obviously at home she must feel. He glanced through the window where outside snowflakes tumbled gently, white eiderdown feathers illuminated by the light spilling from the room and by the nearly full moon.

"I'll draw the curtains," O'Reilly said.

Barry had enjoyed watching the flakes swirl and dance, but now that they were hidden he felt the warmth of the familiar room. And it wasn't so much the heat from the fire as the feeling of belonging, of being cosily at home. Never mind lions and fatlings; he, Barry Laverty, once so intimidated by Doctor O'Reilly, no longer saw him as his senior. And just as Arthur and Her Ladyship were enjoying each other's company, so was Barry enjoying Fingal's. He just wished Patricia was here to make it a perfect evening.

O'Reilly, now back at the sideboard, asked. "Who wants what?" Then he quickly saw to drinks for Kitty and Barry. "I'm not a great enthusiast of mulled wine," he announced, pouring himself an enormous Irish. "And I'm glad you two aren't either."

"If I'd known you had it, I'd have asked for it,"

Kitty said. "I've always enjoyed shoving the red hot poker in." She accepted her gin and tonic.

There was a twinkle in her eyes, and Barry couldn't be sure if she was serious or was taking a hand out of his senior colleague. O'Reilly harrumphed and gave Barry a small whiskey, then went to the half-decorated tree. "Only a few more to go," he said, lifting a parcel. "One for you, Barry, and"—he lifted two more—"one apiece for Lady Macbeth and Arthur Guinness."

Barry looked over at the single gift-wrapped present that remained lonely beneath the tree. He knew only too well that the tag read: "To Patricia Spence." He sighed. There was nothing marked "From Patricia."

"Here," said O'Reilly, handing Barry two gifts. "Open Arthur's and your own, and I'll see to Her Ladyship."

"Right." Barry set the brown paper–wrapped parcel with the Australian stamps on it on the carpet and unwrapped Arthur's present. He burst out laughing. It was a pair of child-size Wellington boots.

"What's so funny?" Kitty asked.

"Do you remember, Kitty, at Sonny and Maggie's wedding how Fingal gave me a job to do? My first unsupervised one?"

She frowned, then smiled. "You'd to look for the other half of a pair of wellies because Arthur had stolen one."

"That's right."

"And I thought," said O'Reilly, "that if he had his own pair to play with, he might leave other people's alone."

Barry took the boots to the dog. "Merry Christmas, Arthur."

Arthur opened one eye, his eyebrow shot up and twitched mightily, and he sniffed his gift. Then he promptly went back to sleep and snored.

"Ungrateful beast," said O'Reilly, setting a small opened tin beside Lady Macbeth. She awoke, stretched, and arched her back so highly that Barry thought she almost folded herself double. Then she straightened, lowered her head to the tin, and suddenly sprang backward as if she'd put her nose against an electric fence. Tail fluffed, she advanced very slowly and sniffed again, padded at the tin with one paw, sniffed again, bent, and started to eat.

"What's in the tin, Fingal?" Kitty asked.

"Anchovy fillets," he said. "I thought she might like them."

"She certainly seems to. You'd think she'd not eaten for a week the way she's wolfing them down."

"I hope she enjoys them," said O'Reilly quite seriously. "And Arthur doesn't know it yet, but the wellies are only a joke. There's a big marrow bone in his doghouse for him. I don't see why animals can't enjoy a special day too. After all, there were plenty of them in the stable that first Christmas. Ours should get their frankincense and myrrh. Mind you," he grinned, "I'm fond of Arthur and Lady Macbeth, but not fond enough to bring them gold."

And you are a wise man, Fingal, Barry thought, even if you're not a Magus.

O'Reilly took his seat. He nodded to Barry's parcel. "So what's in there?"

Barry pulled off the brown paper. A book. *Fishing Round the World* by the American writer of westerns, Zane Grey. Barry was definitely pleased. He'd always wanted to read it, and with no surgery to run for the next few days—and no Patricia—he'd have all the time he needed. "It's from my folks," he said.

"Your turn, Fingal," Kitty said, handing him the small parcel beside her. "I promised you'd get it when we got home." She smiled. Barry saw her watching O'Reilly expectantly.

His eyes widened. "Mother of God," he said, when his gift was revealed. "Holy, thundering mother of Jesus in a gold lamé frock. You're a genius, Kitty O'Hallorhan. A certifiable genius." He rose, pulled her to her feet, enveloped her in a great hug, and kissed her firmly.

Barry could see why Kitty was a genius. Lying on the table beside O'Reilly was a Parker fountain pen and propelling pencil set.

O'Reilly let her go, held her at arm's length, stared into her eyes for just a bit longer than Barry thought necessary, took her by one hand, and said, "Thank you, Kitty. Thank you very much." O'Reilly frowned. "But how did you know?"

"If you want to know anything in this house," Kitty said, "I'm sure Mrs. Kincaid can help."

Except, Barry thought, when it comes to knowing if certain people would be coming home. Yet somehow

Barry's happiness at seeing O'Reilly so comfortable with Kitty softened his own disappointment.

O'Reilly laughed. "Kinky told you?"

"She did. She knew about the presentation from the Rugby Club, and what Santa did at the party, and . . ." Her voice softened. "I think what you did for those kiddies was very sweet. Mind you, I'd have expected no less from you. You always were a softie." She stood on her tiptoes and kissed him. "What you did was wonderful," she said.

"Ha-hmm." O'Reilly cleared his throat, looked at her, and then said, "Kinky's wonderful."

Barry heard footsteps and turned to see Kinky standing in the doorway. Several wisps of hair straggled across her forehead, where Barry noticed a few beads of sweat. "I am not, so," she said. "I'm sorry, but dinner's five minutes late."

"Kinky," said O'Reilly, rising, crossing the floor, and grabbing her around the waist to whirl her around once. "Kinky Kincaid, if you were a week late at the pearly gates, Saint Peter would wait for you. We'll survive five minutes." Barry heard the growling of his senior's stomach.

"Well, you may survive," she said, "but if you don't put me down, sir, and get yourself and Miss O'Hallorhan and Doctor Laverty down to the dining room, my turkey vegetable soup will get cold."

And, Barry thought, in the world of Kinky Kincaid, housekeeper *sans pareil,* that would be a catastrophe. He rose, headed for the door, and said in a fair imitation of O'Reilly, "Come on, you two. I'm famished."

52

A Feast Fit for a King

"This table," said O'Reilly, looking at the place settings, "is a thing of beauty."

Barry had to agree. The best cutlery was arranged on either side of green, woven placemats. To the right of each setting lay multicoloured Christmas crackers. Waterford crystal glasses sparkled in the light. Crisp white linen napkins were embraced by silver napkin rings.

O'Reilly, to Barry's surprise, didn't grab his seat but instead ushered Kitty past him. As he pulled out a chair to the right of his usual place at the head of the table, he said, "Please sit here, Kitty."

"Thank you."

"And you, sir. Under the table," he said to Arthur Guinness, who had followed them downstairs.

Arthur sighed mightily and obeyed.

Lady Macbeth had made herself at home on a chair in front of an extra place set to Barry's immediate left. He wondered who it was for. Perhaps an empty place at the table was a Cork custom with which he was not familiar, like having a candle burning in the window last night. He refused to believe that Kinky, fey though she might be, still thought that Patricia would show up.

He sighed as deeply as Arthur had, then waited

until O'Reilly was seated. As Barry took his own chair, he heard O'Reilly say to Kitty, "Will you try the wine? I don't normally drink much of this stuff, but today's dinner is special."

Indeed it is, Barry thought, looking around.

A bright red cloth covered the dining room table. The centrepiece was a set of angel chimes. Heat rising from the lit candles made a canopy spin, and as it did so, cut-out angels struck bells, causing them to tinkle. Barry swallowed. His mother had owned one just like it. Above the ringing, he heard the clink of bottleneck on glass.

"It's a Montrachet," O'Reilly said, "to make up for the one we didn't get to finish at the Inn. See if you like it."

Kitty spun her glass and sniffed its contents before sipping. "That's very good, Fingal," she said and held out her glass. The wine gurgled.

O'Reilly poured for himself and then said, "Shove your glass up here, Barry."

Barry did so, then waited for O'Reilly to fill his wineglass and return it.

"Now," said O'Reilly, holding his glass aloft, "a toast. It was one of my father's. Here's to us. Who's like us . . . ?" He winked at Barry.

Barry and Kitty both joined in. "Damn few, and they're mostly dead." Glass clinked against glass; then they sipped the wine. Cold, crisp, and dry, Barry thought. He was no oenophile, but he found the wine delicious. He chuckled, then asked, "Why *that* toast on Christmas Day, Fingal?"

O'Reilly roared with laughter. "Because, young fellah, it's the only one I know that's fit for mixed company."

Kitty said. "You should have heard him, Barry, when he was a student."

"I can imagine."

Kitty chuckled. "You don't know the half of it."

"Och, sure," said O'Reilly, "and haven't I mellowed?"

"Just like good wine," Kitty said. She raised her glass. "To the doctors of Ballybucklebo."

Barry smiled and sipped. At least she hadn't suggested, "To absent friends."

Barry took his serviette out and laid it on his lap. He peeked inside the ring. A hallmark of a harp surmounted by a crown told Barry this was Irish silver like the set his mother kept for best. So many memories of Christmases past.

"Now," said O'Reilly, "Kitty, Barry, Merry Christmas. Raise your glasses again with me. We don't say grace in this house, but I will say, God bless us, every one." He drank.

"Indeed," said Kinky. Her tray was laden with steaming soup plates and an extra bottle of wine. She slipped the wine onto the sideboard and then served Kitty first. "I know who said that, Doctor O'Reilly, sir. I've read the book, so." She stared at his tummy. "*Tiny* Tim. Here's your turkey soup, sir, and I hope next year we'll be asking Miss Moloney to take your Santa suit in again."

She set O'Reilly's plate before him, moved around

the table, and then gave Barry his soup. "And yours, Doctor Laverty. It's my own turkey-vegetable-barley soup. I hope you enjoy it."

"That's delicious," Kitty said, "but I thought you'd need the turkey carcass to make the stock."

"Lord bless you, no, Miss O'Hallorhan. I use the giblets—the heart, liver, and gizzards—and the wings. Nobody eats turkey wings."

"Well, it is truly wonderful, Kinky."

"Hear, hear," mumbled O'Reilly, his mouth full.

Barry savored his helping. But he wondered where he was going to find room for the entire meal. He knew the turkey course was to come, and hadn't Kinky been getting her Christmas puddings ready a couple of weeks ago when she'd found one had eaten a hole in a stainless steel bowl?

He glanced at the sideboard. The plates of sweet mince pies, the Christmas cake, and the meringues were tucked in between ranks of Christmas cards and two flanking holly wreaths that encircled lit candles. The meringues were soft, white, sugary, whorled cones, each one fixed to the next by a layer of whipped cream.

Get through all that, Barry Laverty, he told himself, and *you'll* be taking your new pants to Miss Moloney—to be let out.

"I'll be back with the bird soon," said Kinky, as she left.

O'Reilly muttered something like "Thanks" through a full mouth.

Barry had nearly finished his soup when he heard the front doorbell ring. Who in Hades would be at their door at dinnertime on Christmas Day, with the snow coming down hard enough to stop traffic? He exchanged a quick glance with Fingal, whose eyebrows were raised.

"Are we expecting anyone?" said O'Reilly.

"Doctor dears." They heard Kinky's shout through the noise of pots and pans clattering meaningfully. "Can one of youse see to that?"

Barry glanced at O'Reilly, who was starting to rise. The man had his Kitty here. Let him enjoy her company. "Kinky clearly has her hands full. I'll go, Fingal."

He heard O'Reilly yell after him, "Don't worry, Barry. When Kinky brings in the main course, we'll set up a plate for you and pop it in the oven. If it's a patient, fix 'em up quick and ask them if they've eaten."

The sound of Fingal's and Kitty's laughter followed him as he crossed the hall and opened the door to a small figure shrouded in a huge duffle coat with the hood up. The light from the hall illuminated the swirling snow—it was a scene from a snow globe. A car engine receded, red taillights heading toward Belfast.

"Can I help you?" The stranger stepped forward, and Barry noticed the limp. Jesus Christ. "Patricia? Is that you?"

"Barry."

He felt his heart swell.

She stepped through the doorway, dropped her case, and threw back the hood of her coat. "I'm sorry I've led you such a song and a dance. I really am." She moved close to him.

He held her and kissed her, hard and long, and the sweetness of her . . . She was here . . . His heart sang. She was here. He moved back a little. "How did you . . . ?"

She was a little breathless when she said, "I've had hell's delight getting here. I took the travel agent's advice and went to Heathrow."

"But I thought all the flights were full."

"I was lucky. I got a standby seat midmorning. Dad picked me up at Aldergrove airport. I've been in Newry with my folks—"

"Why didn't you phone? Jesus, Patricia, you might have let me know."

"I tried, Barry. Honestly, I did try. Everything happened so fast. I just had time to call Dad from London before I got on the plane. I was going to phone as soon as I got home, but in Newry it's snowing heavily enough to beat Banaher. The telephone lines have been down since noon—"

"Ssshh," he said, taking her into his arms again and kissing the top of her head.

"I wanted to let you know I was here, in Ulster, for Christmas. Dad said to wait until tomorrow, but I had to come and see you today." Her voice cracked. "I just had to."

"It wasn't your fault. I understand. How did you get here?"

She smiled. "My dad's a poppet. He's got an ancient old Land Rover that'll get through anything. He said to wish you a merry Christmas, but he needed to start for home before the snow got any heavier." She kissed Barry again, stood back, looked deep into his eyes, and said, "I love you, darling."

"I love you, Patricia." Barry's hands trembled as he reached for her shoulders and said, "Let me help you out of your coat." She was here. It was the best Christmas ever. He didn't even notice what she was wearing as he hung up her coat, took her hand, and led her into the dining room. "Look who's come," he said.

"Why, Miss Patricia Spence," said Fingal. "What a pleasant surprise. Come in, come in. You've only missed the soup course. Sit yourself down."

Barry clung to Patricia's hand and stared at her oval face, her almond eyes, her lips.

The room was silent and when Barry finally looked up from Patricia's face, he could feel three sets of eyes on his. "Jesus, Barry," O'Reilly said, "are you going to keep the poor girl standing there all day?"

He wasn't sure if anyone heard his mumbled "Sorry" through the laughter, but it didn't matter. Kitty was leaning under the table, shooing Lady Macbeth off the extra seat. O'Reilly was busy uncorking the second bottle of wine and pouring Patricia a glass. Arthur lumbered out to sniff Patricia's hand and give it a welcoming lick.

"Thank you, everyone," she said, and then she sat down. "I didn't mean to intrude."

Barry saw the nape of her neck beneath her ponytail and longed to drop a butterfly kiss there.

"Intrude, is it?" said Kinky, as she appeared in the doorway and set her tray on a clear spot on the tabletop. "There's enough here for twice the number. Merry Christmas to you, Miss Spence. That's *Nollaig shona dhuit* in the old tongue." She looked hard at Barry, and he knew by her look what she was thinking: So you didn't believe your girl was coming?

Kinky sniffed, then unloaded tureens and small bowls, identifying the contents of each as she put them on the table. "Mashed potatoes, brussels sprouts. Carrot-and-parsnip mix. Bread sauce. Gravy." She set a pile of dinner plates on O'Reilly's placemat. "I'll be back with the bird."

"You'll not starve in this house, Patricia," O'Reilly said.

She laughed, a sound Barry had longed to hear for what had seemed like an eternity. "I'm more likely to explode. Mum had *our* dinner ready for two o'clock."

"Just nibble a bit then," said O'Reilly. "It'll please Kinky to see you eating. And you'll take a glass of wine, won't you?"

"Please."

He handed her the glass he'd already poured. "Now, I think I'll just pop to the kitchen and help Kinky with the ham." He rose, then quickly sat again, as Kinky appeared bearing the turkey on an ornate silver platter the size of a child's sleigh.

"Here it is," Kinky said proudly. It was a big bird. The skin of its breast was browned to a deep gold and striped with strips of fatty bacon. She set the plate in front of O'Reilly, stood back, folded her arms across her chest, cocked her head to one side, admired it, and said, "Johnny Jordan did us proud again this year. It's a young one. It should be easy to carve. I hope you all enjoy your meals, so."

"Kinky, you've outdone yourself this year. That is the most magnificent sight I've ever seen. Now, Mrs. Kincaid, that bird's been enough for you to carry. I'll be back in a second with the ham."

"If you say so, sir," she said with a smile.

In a minute he was back, a ham on an oval plate in one oven-mitted hand.

For the second time that day Barry admired its glazed outer skin marked with a diamond pattern of crisscrossing dark lines and studded with myriad cloves.

Kinky wiped her hands on her pinafore. "I've just the sherry trifle to take out of the fridge, and the pudding out of the boiler." She looked at the still-standing O'Reilly. "And will you warm the brandy, sir, to pour over the pudding so you can set it alight?"

"Of course."

"There's a sprig of holly and a bowl of brandy butter on the kitchen shelf." She let the hem of her apron fall. "So, sir, Miss O'Hallorhan, Doctor Laverty, Miss Spence, I'll wish you all a very merry Christmas, hope you enjoy your meal, and I'll be off to change. I'm having my dinner with Cissie Sloan and her family this year. She's a very good cook even if she is a bletherskite."

"Not yet," said O'Reilly.

Her eyes widened. "Is there something wrong with the meal, sir?"

O'Reilly sounded very serious. "Only one thing."

"What?" She tensed and raised her shoulders.

O'Reilly's grin was huge. "You, Mrs. Kinky Kincaid, you've done all the work, and we've not had a chance to thank you yet."

Hers shoulders sagged, and Barry could sense her relief.

"So, Kinky"—he poured a glass of wine—"take that in your hand." He reached over and moved a chair by the sideboard to the table, dislodging Lady Macbeth for a second time. "Come round here and sit for a minute. I want you to have a drink with us, and here"—he handed her an envelope—"that's a wee tangible thank-you from Doctor Laverty and me."

Kinky bobbed and sat on the chair O'Reilly held out for her. "Thank you both."

Barry wondered how much money was in the envelope—and how much his yet-unasked-for share was. Damn it, he didn't begrudge her a penny. He looked at Patricia. To have her here to share Kinky's Christmas feast was all he could have wanted. Whoever had said, "Money isn't everything," was right. He reached under the table and took Patricia's hand, feeling its cool softness.

O'Reilly, who was still standing, bent and filled his glass, then raised it. "Now everybody, Kitty, Barry, Patricia"—he peered under the table—"and you, Your Ladyship, and you lummox, Arthur Guinness, here's to Kinky Kincaid."

Barry reckoned that four people saying, "Kinky Kincaid," in unison, accompanied by "Aaaaghow" from Arthur, made a very respectable noise. It certainly stimulated Lady Macbeth, who leapt onto the table, only to be deposited on the floor by O'Reilly.

Kinky blushed and stuttered her thanks.

O'Reilly inclined his head. "Now get that wine into you, Kinky. I'll carve the turkey and the ham, and while I'm at it, will you tell us all exactly what's on the plate and in the bird?" He picked up the carving knife and fork. "White or dark meat, Kitty?"

"Both, please."

He nodded and began to carve the breast. "Come on now, Kinky. Tell us all."

Kinky took a sip of her wine. "Well," she said, "around the plate are roasted potatoes and parsnips. Those little thingys are chipolata sausages. In the neck end of the bird I've put pork and chestnut stuffing, and in the vent end my usual sage and onion and breadcrumbs, so."

"That's amazing," Kitty said. "However do you get it all done, Kinky?"

Kinky took a sip of her wine. "It's just a matter of planning."

So, Barry thought, was the D-day invasion. One hell of a lot of planning.

Patricia took the words from his mouth. "I think you're a marvel, Mrs. Kincaid."

"*Think*?" said O'Reilly. "I bloody well know it. Have done for years." He handed a plate to Kitty. "Help yourself to the trimmings. Patricia?"

"Just a teeny helping, please. I've already had one Christmas dinner today, Mrs. Kincaid."

Barry sat patiently waiting for O'Reilly to serve

Patricia, then him. O'Reilly's own helping, Barry thought, would have fed two. Barry added bread sauce and vegetables to his own already heaped plate.

Kinky finished her wine and rose. "I'll be leaving—"

"Not just yet, please," Barry said. He got to his feet "I have a toast of my own." He hesitated, trying to find exactly the right words for what he wanted to say.

"Get on with it," O'Reilly called. "Your dinner's getting cold."

"All right." He bowed his head, then spoke clearly. "Here's to Kinky Kincaid, the best housekeeper in all Ireland . . ."

"Hear, hear," O'Reilly said.

"To Fingal O'Reilly, my colleague . . . and my friend . . ." He stared at O'Reilly, who was nodding a silent agreement.

"To Kitty O'Hallorhan. May Number One Main Street see lots more of her next year . . ."

"Thank you, Barry." Kitty was smiling at O'Reilly.

"To Arthur and Her Ladyship. May their Christmas truce persist . . ."

No luck with that one. As if on cue, Lady Macbeth took a swipe at Arthur's nose, but missed. Barry had to wait until O'Reilly had finished laughing before he could continue. "And to Patricia. May her studies go from strength to strength . . ." He stared at her and smiled. "And may the road between Cambridge and Ballybucklebo rise up to meet her when next she makes the journey . . ."

"At Easter, and I will book in time. I promise."

He nodded in agreement.

"And to us all in this room. May nineteen sixty-five be the best of New Years and the happiest."

And happy and at peace with the world, Barry Laverty sipped his wine, and inside he smiled.

Afterword

by Mrs. Kincaid

Dia dhuit. Hello. It's December the twenty-sixth, and I've a chance to take more of a breather than usual. All my life, because my mother drilled it into us children, Boxing Day was the day that thank-you letters had to be written, even if one was to an auntie who lived next door and had given you a string vest that you didn't want in the first place. So here I am sitting at my kitchen table with a pen in my fist and this writing tablet before me, but it's not for thank-you letters.

This year, glory be, I'm going to break with that tradition. Doctor O'Reilly says I can use the telephone to talk with anyone I don't feel like writing to. He did say there was a condition, so. I was to use the time saved to sit down and give you some more of my recipes.

He says that Taylor fellah who spins these yarns has had a lot of letters since I put my recipes in his first two books. One nice lady from America said she'd tried my mock turtle soup, and by the hokey it was better than the recipes she'd got from four other cookery books, so.

I have the time to do it because I'll not be cooking today. My doctors are away to Flo Bishop's hooley, and when they come home I've a fridge full of cold turkey and ham. I took the meat off the bones this morning, and the carcass and the hambone are boiling away so I can make stock. Ould Arthur'll get the hambone later, and I've some turkey treats put aside for Her Ladyship. The wee dote.

Himself says for me to give you a clatter of Christmas recipes, and that's not as silly as it sounds even if Christmas Day is over. Of the things I'm going to tell you about, Christmas puddings and the Christmas cake are traditionally made the year before in Ireland. I made my Christmas cake last August, but ever since the pudding ate my steel bowl, I'm not so sure about doing them too soon either. I think they can wait a while.

You'll see when you read on that this year I'm making a change from just giving you quantities in pounds and ounces, cups and spoonfuls. Your man Taylor's first book was translated into German, Dutch, and Russian—how in the name of the wee man you translate "not come within a beagle's gowl" is beyond me—but there's been a request for me to use these newfangled grams for the sake of the continentals. Now I can't convert measures, but when that nice schoolteacher lady Miss Nolan comes back next term I'll get her to give me a hand.

Whether you follow the old measures or the newfangled ones, here are the recipes. I hope they turn out well for you.

Ulster Christmas Recipes

• *Sweet Mince*

225 g/8 oz/1 cup vegetarian suet
225 g/8 oz/1 cup Bramley apples, peeled, cored, and chopped finely (These apples are grown in County Armagh, so if you cannot find any, use any apples that you like.)
115 g/4 oz/½ cup candied peel, chopped
225 g/8 oz/1 cup of seedless raisins or yellow raisins
225 g/8 oz/1 cup currants
175 g/6 oz/¾ cup Demerara sugar
1 teaspoon mixed spice or allspice
zest and juice of an orange
60 ml/2 fluid oz brandy

Mix all the ingredients together. Pack into sterilised jars and seal. Store in a cool dark place until you want to use it.

This makes about 1.8 kg/4 lb/8 cups of sweet mince, a traditional Irish filling for individual mince pies, served warm at Christmas. It has been used in my family down through the ages, and originally it did contain meat. Now the only meat present is in the suet, and for the sake of vegetarians like Miss Moloney I have used vegetarian suet.

• *Brandy Butter*

Here's another wee Christmas speciality of mine which goes down a right treat with your mince pies or your Christmas pudding, and it's made in no time at all.

115 g/4 oz/1 stick unsalted butter, softened
115 g/4 oz/½ cup confectioner's sugar
2 tablespoons boiling water
3 tablespoons brandy

Cream together the butter and the icing sugar. Beat in water and brandy until smooth. Chill until needed, and serve with hot mince pies or Christmas pudding.

• *Christmas Cake*

225 g/8 oz/2 sticks butter
225 g/8 oz/1 cup soft brown sugar
225 g/8 oz/1 cup plain or all-purpose flour
225 g/8 oz/1 cup each: currants, raisins, muscatel raisins, and seedless raisins
115 g/4 oz/½ cup each: glacé cherries and mixed peel
55 g/2 oz/¼ cup ground almonds
1 teaspoon mixed spice or allspice
½ teaspoon cinnamon
½ teaspoon salt
4 eggs
grated rind of one lemon and one orange

Preheat oven to 140 C/275 F/gas mark 1. Grease and line an 8-inch cake tin so that the paper extends above the sides by 1 inch.

Cream together the butter and brown sugar until light and fluffy. Add eggs one at a time, beating in well. Stir in the almonds, flour, salt, and spices. Finally add the cherries, dried fruit, and rinds. Pour the mixture into the prepared tin. Bake for 3 hours. Check for readiness by inserting a thin skewer. When it comes out clean, the cake is done. Cool on a wire rack, and store in an airtight container until you are ready to ice it.

• *Royal Icing*

3 egg whites
575g/20 oz/2½ cups confectioner's sugar, sieved
1½ teaspoons liquid glycerine (optional)
3 teaspoons lemon juice

Lightly whisk the egg whites, adding the sugar at intervals. Beat well until the icing reaches soft peaks. Add the glycerine (if using) and the lemon juice.

• *Marzipan*

150 g/5½ oz/⅔ cup ground almonds
140 g/5 oz/¾ castor or white sugar
juice of ½ lemon
glycerine, 10 drops approximately
almond or vanilla essence, to taste

Mix together the ground almonds and sugar. Gradually add the lemon juice and glycerine until you get a marzipan texture. Flavour to taste with almond or vanilla essence.

• *Icing the Cake*

Place the Christmas cake on a cake plate or foil board. Dust hands with flour and work surface with a little icing sugar. Knead the marzipan (see accompanying recipe) until soft. Roll out half of it to fit the top of the cake and the rest to fit round the sides. Brush the cake with warmed apricot jam and place the marzipan on top. Cover with a tea towel, and leave for four days before covering with the royal icing (see accompanying recipe).

You can buy marzipan and royal icing or make your own. But whichever you do, please make sure that after you put the marzipan on the cake, you leave it for four days to dry out before you go putting on the royal icing, or you'll spoil it, so.

• *Christmas Pudding*

175 g/6 oz/¾ cup soft bread crumbs
400 ml/1¾ cups milk
300 g/10½ oz/1¼ cups castor or white sugar
250 g/9 oz/1 cup suet
175 g/6 oz/¾ cup plain or all-purpose flour
½ teaspoon salt
1½ teaspoons nutmeg
175 g/¾ cup grated carrot
250 g/9 oz/1 cup currants
250 g/9 oz/1 cup raisins
175 g/6 oz/¾ cup mashed potato
75 g/2½ oz/¼ cup candied peel

3 eggs, beaten
4 teaspoons treacle or molasses

Heat milk to boiling point and pour over crumbs in a very large bowl. Add the sugar and leave to soak for ½ hour. Mix in all the other ingredients, except eggs and treacle, mixing very well. Finally add the eggs and treacle and beat very well. Put mixture into greased bowls, cover and steam for 4 hours. Continue to add boiling water from time to time to ensure that it does not boil dry. Makes one very large (2¾ litre) pudding or two small ones (1½ litre).

You can use special bowls with their own lids, or else cover the bowl with aluminium foil. I use greaseproof paper, then brown paper, and I tie it on with string, making a handle with the string. If you haven't got a doctor handy, you do need to be very careful with the boiling water, so.

The pudding matures and tastes much better if you can remember to make it one year to 6 months before you need it.

On Christmas day steam for a further 2 hours. Turn out and garnish with a sprig of holly.

• *Brandy Sauce*

55 g/2 oz/4 tbsp butter
55 g/2 oz/¼ cup plain or all-purpose flour
570 ml/20 fl oz/2½ cups milk
55 g/2 oz/¼ cup castor or white sugar
¼ cup brandy

Melt the butter and stir in the flour. Cook for 2 minutes and stir in the milk. Bring to the boil, stirring all the time. Simmer gently for 10 minutes. Stir in the brandy and sugar, and serve with Christmas pudding.

Now, that's that done. I'm going to have a nice cup of tea and read a book I got for Christmas from my sister Ailech, who lives in Rosbeg in County Donegal. It's called *The Reivers* and it's by William Faulkner. I did so enjoy his *As I Lay Dying*.

And to you I wish success with your cooking and *an Athbhliain shona dhuit*, a Happy New Year to you all. No doubt you'll be hearing from me again soon. Sometimes I wonder if that Taylor fellah's ever going to dry up. He's as chatty as Cissie Sloan.

Slán agat.

Farewell,
MRS. KINKY KINCAID
Housekeeper to
Doctor Fingal Flahertie
O'Reilly, M.B., B.Ch., B.A.O.
1, Main Street
Ballybucklebo
County Down
Northern Ireland

Author's Note

Doctors Taylor, Laverty, and O'Reilly, Mrs. Kinky Kincaid, and their friends and patients are very pleased to welcome back readers who are already acquainted with Ballybucklebo. They hope that you will enjoy meeting old friends and making fresh ones, visiting familiar places, and exploring new ones. You have seen the townland in summer and autumn. This time it is winter, Christmas is coming, and the geese are getting fat.

For readers new to rural Ireland in 1964, perhaps a word of explanation from the author might be helpful. To you I offer the following.

I had just finished a novel, *Pray for Us Sinners,* a follow-up to *Only Wounded,* a collection of short stories, both concerning the 1969–1994 Ulster Troubles.

Concurrently I had been writing a monthly humour column in *Stitches: The Journal of Medical Humour,* where Doctor Fingal Flahertie O'Reilly and the residents of Ballybucklebo first appeared in 1995. My editor at Insomniac Press read my column and suggested that the characters might form the foundation of a novel. The idea of writing about something lighter than internecine strife was appealing, so *An Irish Country Doctor* began to take shape.

Once it was finished, I completed *Now and in the Hour of Our Death,* the sequel to *Pray for Us Sinners,* but when that was done I discovered that I was much more fond of pre-Troubles Ballybucklebo than I was of sectarian strife–torn Belfast and County Tyrone. I decided to follow the further doings of the cast of *Doctor* with *An Irish Country Village. An Irish Country Christmas* is the third volume of the series.

In writing the series I have used the Ulster dialect. It is rich and colourful, but often incomprehensible to one not from that part of the world. For those who may have difficulty, I have taken the liberty of appending a glossary (page 633). I have been sparing in my use of the Irish language, which is not spoken by most of the citizens of Northern Ireland.

The setting is Ballybucklebo, a fictional village in County Down, my own home county. The name came from my high-school French teacher who, enraged by my inability to conjugate irregular verbs, yelled, "Taylor, you're stupid enough to come from Ballybucklebo." Those of an etymological bent may wish to know what the name means. *Bally* (Irish, *baile*) is a townland—a mediaeval geographic term encompassing a small village and the surrounding farms; *buachaill* means "boy"; and *bó* is a cow. Thus *Bailebuchaillbó,* or Ballybucklebo, means the townland of the boy's cow.

Since the publication of the first two novels I have been amazed by the number of my Ulster friends who insist on trying to pinpoint Ballybucklebo as a real village in North Down. It is clear that the old

Irish pastime of chasing moonbeams is not yet dead.

In my darker works I strove to make the setting and events historically accurate. *The Irish Country* stories take some liberties, and in Ballybucklebo time and place are as skewed as they are in Brigadoon.

The purist will note that the southern shore of Belfast Lough is devoid of sand dunes. Further round the County Down coast at Tyrella, there are dunes aplenty. No salmon river called the Bucklebo flows through North County Down. The nearest is the Shimna River in the Mourne Mountains, not far from Tyrella. Everything else is as accurate as extensive reading and memory permit.

I have also taken liberties with Ulster politics. Some say fiction is an outward expression of the author's wishes. In this work I have portrayed a tolerant place that the majority of people in the north of Ireland would have wanted. Sadly, in that small country in the sixties it could not have existed. The ecumenical spirit exhibited by those on either side of the sectarian divide in Ballybucklebo had little chance to flourish in Northern Ireland—although it could have, but for the bigoted intransigence of a very few people. Fortunately, as I write, it seems that those days are gone forever.

I will not miss them, but I do miss the rural Ulster I have portrayed and the Ulster people; indeed I missed one so much that I have returned to Ireland after thirty-seven years in Canada to be with her.

I know the place I have come back to has changed.

The farms and villages still look much as they did, but the simplicity of rural life has been banished by the Troubles and the all-pervasive influence of television. The automatic respect for their learning shown to those at the top of the village pecking order—doctor, teacher, minister, and priest—is a thing of the past, but men like O'Reilly were common when I was a very junior doctor. And on that subject, may I please lay to rest once and for all a question I am frequently asked? Barry Laverty and Patrick Taylor are *not* one and the same. Doctor F. F. O'Reilly is a figment of my troubled mind, despite the efforts of some of my Ulster friends to see in him a respected—if unorthodox—medical practitioner of the time.

Lady Macbeth *does* owe her being to a demoniacally possessed white cat, Minnie. Arthur Guinness is a reincarnation of a black Labrador with the same name, now long gone, but who had an insatiable thirst for Foster's lager. All the other characters are composites, drawn from my imagination and from my experiences as a rural GP.

Today's medical graduate would not recognize the conditions under which medicine was practiced in the sixties. Only five years earlier than this story the link between thalidomide and birth defects had been established. In 1963 the first cadaver kidney transplant had been performed in Leeds, and in 1965 cigarette advertising was banned from British television. It was not until 1967 that Doctor Christiaan Barnard gave Louis Washkansky the first heart transplant. This was followed by the first heart-lung transplant in 1971. We had to wait until 1978 for the birth of the world's first baby conceived by in vitro fertilization.

Diagnostic tests were rudimentary, both in the laboratory and in imaging departments. In 1979 Godfrey Hounsfield was awarded the Nobel Prize in Medicine for the invention of computerized axial tomography, the CAT scan. The eighties, the decade that saw the identification of the AIDS virus, was also the time lasers began to appear in operating rooms.

By today's standards, medicine was in its infancy, and much depended on the clinical skills of the Doctor O'Reillys. They practiced a very different brand of medicine on real people, whose feelings and lives were as important as the diseases that afflicted them.

Doctor O'Reilly has asked me to tell you he hopes you will have as much fun in Ballybucklebo as he has.

PATRICK TAYLOR
Cootehall
County Roscommon
Republic of Ireland

Glossary

The Ulster dialect, properly called Ulster-Scots, is rich and colourful but can be confusing. Like all patois, Ulster-Scots is not one bit shy about adopting useful phrases from other dialects. For example, the reader should not be surprised to find examples of Cockney rhyming slang here.

acting the goat: Behaving foolishly.
apples and pears: Cockney rhyming slang for stairs.
argy-bargy: Voluble disagreement.
arse: Backside (impolite).
aunt Fanny Jane, my: Nonsense.
away off and chase yourself: Go away.
away off and feel your head: You're being stupid.
away on: I don't believe you.
bamboozle: Deliberately confuse.
Banagher, to beat: Exceed any reasonable expectations.
bangers: Sausages.
banjaxed: Exhausted or broken.
banshee: Female spirit whose moaning foretells death.
bap, to lose the: To be temporarily out of control.
barmbrack: Speckled bread.
bashtoon: Bastard.

beagle's gowl: Very long way; the distance over which the cry of a beagle can be heard.

bee on a hot brick: Running round distractedly.

bee's knees: The very best.

bee's knees, he thinks he's the: He's conceited.

bigger fish to fry: More important matters to attend to.

bind: Cure diarrhea or cause constipation.

bit my head off: Expressed anger by shouting or being very curt.

bloater: Salted and smoked herring.

bletherskite: Nonstop talker.

blow you out: Tell you to go away.

bob, a few: One shilling; a sum of money.

bodhrán: Irish. Pronounced "bowron." A circular hand-held drum.

boke: Vomit.

bollocks: Testicles (impolite). May be used as an expression of vehement disagreement or to describe a person you disapprove of; for example, "He's a right bollocks."

bonnet: Hood of a car.

boot: Trunk of a car.

both legs the same length: Standing about uselessly.

boul': Bold.

bowsey: Dublin slang, drunkard.

boys-a-boys, boys-a-dear: Expressions of amazement.

brass neck: Impertinence, chutzpah.

bravely: Feeling well.

breeze blocks: Cinderblocks

bunk, done a: Ran away.

buck eejit: Imbecile.

bun in the oven: Pregnant (impolite).

cailín: Irish. Pronounced "cawleen." Girl.

call the cows home: Be ready to tackle anything.

capped: A cap was awarded to athletes selected for important teams. Equivalent to a letter at an American university.

carrageen moss: An edible seaweed.

caubeen: Traditional Irish bonnet.

casualty: Emergency room.

céili: Irish. Pronounced "kaylee." Party, usually with music and dancing.

champ: A dish of buttermilk, butter, potatoes, and chives.

chemist: Pharmacist.

chiseller: Dublin slang, a small child.

chuntering: Talking nonstop.

clabber: Glutinous mess of mud, or mud and cow clap.

clatter, a brave: A large quantity.

colloguing: Chatting about trivia.

conkers: Horse chestnuts. Used to play a children's game.

coortin': Paying court to. See also *walk out with*.

cow's lick: Tuft of hair that sticks up, or hair slicked over to one side.

cracker: Excellent (see also *wheeker*).

craking on: Talking incessantly.

crayture: Creature. Equivalent to North American "critter."

craytur, a drop of the: Whiskey.

crick in the neck or back: Painful strain.

crúibins: Irish. Pronounced "crubeen." Boiled pigs' feet, served cold and eaten with vinegar.

cure, wee: Hair of the dog.

dab hand: Skilled at.

damper: Device for restricting the flow of air to a coal or turf fire to slow the rate of burning.

dander: Literally, horse dandruff. Used to signify either a short leisurely walk or anger. For example, "He really got my dander up."

dead on: A strong affirmative or excited acceptance of good news. Equivalent to "I totally agree" and "That's marvelous."

dibs: A claim upon.

didny; didnae: Did not.

divil: Devil.

divil the bit: None. For example, "He's divil the bit of sense." (He's stupid.)

doddle: A short distance or an easy task.

do-re-mi: Money. Equivalent of North American "dough."

dosh: Money.

dote: Something adorable.

dote on: Worship.

do with the price of corn: Irrelevant.

dozer, no: No fool.

drill-the-dome boys: Medical slang, neurosurgeons. See also *nutcracker*.

drouth, raging: Pronounced "drewth." Alcoholic.

drúishin: Irish. Pronounced "drisheen." Dish made of cows' blood, pigs' blood, and oatmeal. A Cork City delicacy.

dudeen: Short-stemmed clay pipe.

dulse: A seaweed, which when dried is eaten like chewing gum.

dummy tit: Baby's pacifier.

duncher: Cloth cap, usually tweed.
dunder: Forcible thump.
Dun Laoghaire: Port near Dublin. Pronounced "dun leery."
eejit: Idiot.
egg-bound hen: A hen with an egg that cannot be laid stuck in the oviduct. Applied to a person, it suggests extreme distress.
fag: Cigarette.
fall off the perch: Die.
feck, fecking: Dublin corruption of "fuck" and "fucking."
fenian: Catholic (pejorative).
field, the: A place where Orange Lodges and bands congregate after the Twelfth of July parade.
finagle: Achieve by cunning or dubious means.
fist of, to make a good: Do a fine job.
fit to be tied: Very angry.
flex: Plug-in cable of an electrical appliance or light.
flies, none on: Smart. Streetwise.
flying: Drunk.
fornenst: Besides.
foundered: Chilled to the marrow.
full of it: Being either stupid or excessively flattering.
gander: Take a look at.
get (away) on with you: Don't be stupid.
get on one's wick: Get on one's nerves.
give over: Stop it.
glipe, great: Stupid or very stupid person.
gobshite: Dublin slang used pejoratively about a person. Literally, dried nasal mucus.

good man ma da: Expression of approval.
grand man for the pan: One who really enjoys fried food.
great: The ultimate Ulster accolade; can be used to signify pleased assent to a plan.
grotty: English slang. Run-down and dirty.
guard's van: Caboose.
gub: Mouth.
gub, a good dig in the: A punch in the mouth.
gurrier: Dublin slang. Street urchin.
guttersnipe: Ruffian.
hairy bear: Woolly caterpillar.
half-cut: Drunk.
hand's turn: Minimum amount of work.
having me on: Deceiving me.
head staggers: Making a very stupid decision. Literally, a parasitic disease affecting the brains of sheep and causing them to stagger.
heart of corn: Very good-natured.
heifer: Young cow before her first breeding.
heels of the hunt: When everything has been concluded.
hirstle: Chesty wheeze.
hit the spot: Fill the need.
hobby-horse shite, your head's full of: Literally, sawdust. You're stupid.
holdall: Canvas sports bag.
hold your horses: Wait a minute.
hooley: Party.
hoor: Whore.
houseman: Medical intern.
how's (a)bout ye? How are you? Or good-day.

humdinger: Something extraordinary.

I'm your man: I agree to your plan and will follow it.

in soul, I do: Emphatic.

in the stable: Of a drink, already paid for before being poured.

jar: An alcoholic drink.

jaunting car: An open, high, two-wheeled vehicle. The passenger accommodation was two benches, arranged along either side so the passengers sat with their backs to the cart bed. By the 1960s it was rarely seen except in the most rural parts of Ireland or as a tourist attraction.

jigs and reels, between the: To cut a long story short.

knackered: Very tired. An allusion to a horse so worn out by work that it is destined for the knacker's yard, where horses are destroyed.

knickers in a twist, in a knot: Anxiously upset.

knocking: Having sexual intercourse.

Lambeg drum: Massive bass drum carried on shoulder straps by Orangemen and beaten with two sticks, sometimes until the drummer's wrists bleed.

length and breadth of it: All the details.

lepp: Leap.

let the hare sit: Leave the thing alone.

like the sidewall of a house: Huge, especially when applied to someone's physical build.

liltie: A madman. An Irish whirling dervish.

load of cobblers': In Cockney rhyming slang, "cobblers' awls" means "balls." Used to signify rubbish.

lough: Pronounced "logh," almost as if clearing the throat. A sea inlet or very large inland lake.

lummox: Stupid creature.

main: Very.

make a mint: Make a great deal of money.

moping: Indulging in self-pity.

more power to your wheel: Very good luck to you; encouragement.

muggy: Hot and humid.

mullet, stunned: To look as stupid or surprised as a mullet, an ugly saltwater fish.

Mullingar heifer, calves like a: Cows from Mullingar were said to have very thick legs.

my shout: I'm buying the drinks.

near took the rickets: Had a great shock.

no dozer: Clever.

no goat's toe, he thinks he's: Has an overinflated sense of his own importance.

no spring chicken: Getting on in years.

not as green as you're cabbage looking: More clever than you appear to be.

not at myself: Feeling unwell.

Not at the match: Not altogether sane.

nutcracker: Neurosurgeon.

on eggs: Extremely worried.

Orange Order: Fraternal order of Protestants loyal to the British crown.

Orange and Green: The colours of Loyalists and Republicans, respectively. Used to symbolize the age-old schism in Irish politics.

ould goat: Old man, often used affectionately.

out of kilter: Out of alignment.

oxter: Armpit.
oxter-cog: To carry by supporting under the armpits.
pacamac: Cheap, transparent, plastic raincoat carried in a small bag.
Paddy hat: Soft-crowned tweed hat.
Paddy's market: A large, disorganised crowd.
pan loaf: Loaf of ordinary bread.
peat (turf): Fuel derived from compressed vegetable matter.
peely-wally: Scots. Under the weather; unwell.
pelmet: Valance.
penny bap: A small bun, usually coated in flour.
petrified: Terrified.
physical jerks: Gymnastics.
piss artist: Alcoholic.
poke: Have sex with; a small parcel.
pong: British forces slang for "stink."
pop one's clogs: Die.
poulticed: Pregnant, usually out of wedlock.
powerful: Very.
power of: A great deal of.
praties: Potatoes.
punter: Gambler, particularly on horse races.
quare: Ulster pronunciation of queer. Very strange.
randy: Sexually aroused.
randy as an old goat: Very sexually aroused.
raparee: Originally an unskilled labourer. Now used pejoratively for a ne'er-do-well.
rapscallion: Ne'er-do-well.
raring to go: Eager and fully prepared.

recimetation: Malapropism for recitation.

registrar, medical: Trainee physician equivalent to a North American resident.

reverse the charges: Call collect.

right enough: That's true. Used interrogatively, is that true?

rightly: Very well.

rightly, it will do: It's not perfect but will serve well enough.

roast: Verbally chastise; *not* pay humorous tribute to.

ruddy: Euphemism for "bloody."

rug rats: Children.

run-race: Quick trip to, usually on foot.

script/scrip: Prescription.

scunner, take a scunner at or *to:* Dislike someone intensely and bear a grudge.

scutch grass: Coarse grass found growing in salty soil.

semi: Semidetached house. Duplex.

shebang, the whole: Lock, stock, and barrel. Everything.

sheugh: Bog.

shit, to: To defaecate.

shite: Faeces.

shufti: Army slang. A quick look at.

Sinn Féin: Literally, ourselves. The political party of the Irish Republican Movement.

skitters: Diarrhoea.

skiver: Corruption of "scurvy." Pejorative. Ne'er-do-well.

skivvy: From "scurvy." Housemaid.

skinful, to get a: To get drunk.

sliced pan, best thing since: Presliced, then wrapped, pan loaf was reintroduced after the Second World War. To be better than it was the acme of perfection.
slip jig: Traditional dance.
slough about: Laze around.
smacker: Pound.
snotters: Runny nose.
soft hand under a duck: Gentle or very good at.
solicitor: Attorney, but one who would not appear in court, which is done by barristers.
sore tried by: Very worried by or very irritated by.
spavins: A disease of horses resulting in a swayback.
spunk: True grit. Nerve.
sponge bag: Toilet bag.
stays: Whalebone corset.
sticking out: Very good.
sticking out a mile: Absolutely the best.
stocious: Drunk.
stone: Measure of weight equal to fourteen pounds.
stoon: Sudden shooting pain.
stout: A dark beer, usually Guinness.
strong weakness: Hangover.
take a gander: Look at.
take your hurry in your hand: Wait a minute.
taste, a wee: Amount. Small amount, not necessarily edible.
ta-ta-ta-ra: Dublin slang, party.
there: Used for accuracy or immediately. Examples: That there dog; that dog. There now; now.
thick: Stupid.
thick as champ: Very stupid.

thole: Tolerate or put up with.
thon: That.
thrapple: Throat.
throw off: Vomit.
thrupenny bit: Three-penny coin.
tinker's damn, don't give a: Could not care less.
toty: Small.
toty, wee: Very small.
tousling: Roughing up.
tried, to get: Become agitated about.
turf accountant: Bookmaker.
up the spout or *pipe:* Pregnant.
walk out with: Pay court to. See also *coortin'*.
wean: Pronounced "wane." Child.
wee: Small, but in Ulster can be used to modify almost anything without reference to size. A barmaid and old friend greeted the author by saying, "Come on in, Pat. Have a wee seat and I'll get you a wee menu, and would you like a wee drink while you're waiting?"
wee buns: Very easy.
Wellington boots, wellies: Knee-high rubber boots patterned on the riding boots worn by the Duke of Wellington.
whaling away at: Beating.
wheeker: Very good.
wheen: A large number of.
wheest: Be quiet.
wheezle: Wheeze in chest.
whet (wee): Alcoholic drink.
whin: Gorse.

whippet: Small, fast, racing dog, such as a mini-greyhound.
willy: Penis.
won't butter any parsnips: Will make absolutely no difference.
worser: As bad as it is possible to get; much more so than worse.
you're on: Agreed to, or to indicate acceptance of a wager.
your head's cut (a marley): You are being very stupid, and your head is as small and as dense as a child's marble.
your man: Someone who is not present but is known to all others there.
youse: Ulster plural of you.

Turn the page for a preview of

An Irish Country Courtship

PATRICK TAYLOR

Available now from
Tom Doherty Associates

A FORGE BOOK

Put the Car Away

O'Reilly was looking forward to getting home. He chuckled and would have rubbed his hands together had he not been steering. He drove past Palace Barracks and into Holywood, the only Irish town other than Ballybucklebo to have a Maypole. Not much farther to there now.

And Kitty would be coming down on . . . damn it all, why not ask her to stay for the whole weekend? He grinned and let go a blast of smoke from the pipe he'd lit only seconds after getting into the car. He would ask, by God. As an old bachelor—well, old widower—he had forgotten until five months ago how enjoyable it was to be in the company of a woman, and a bright, feisty, bloody good-looking woman at that.

He'd tell Barry to take the weekend off, and would give Mrs. Kincaid a few days as well. She had a married sister, Fidelma, and nieces and nephews down in County Cork. Fidelma's husband, Eamon, farmed near Beal na mBláth. O'Reilly'd speak to Kinky tonight. By God, he would.

He sang to himself:

Oh love is pleasing and love is teasing
And love is a pleasure when first it's new . . .

He accelerated, knowing he should stop thinking of Kitty O'Hallorhan and concentrate on his driving. The traffic was light, but the roads were still slippery despite their having been salted and sanded.

On the far side of Holywood he hit a right-hand corner and felt the back end of the Rover start to go. O'Reilly wrenched the steering wheel into the skid, hoped to God nothing was coming the other way, and by brute effort forced the car back on course. He grunted and muttered, "Bloody slush."

The spire of the Ballybucklebo Catholic church loomed to his right. O'Reilly turned into a sharp left and headed for home, where he'd get his supper and a Jameson. He'd settle down in front of a big fire, get stuck into a plate of cold ham and turkey, see how young Barry was, and . . . "*Christ Almighty*."

He wrenched the wheel to the right, slammed on the brakes, and rammed the heel of his hand on the horn. Someone was wheeling a bicycle across the road in front of the car. He hauled the wheel back left, but this time nothing could bring the big car out of the skid. An unstoppable juggernaut, it crabbed ahead, missing the cyclist by inches. The crunching as the car's nose slid into the ditch underscored the horn's blaring. Steam hissed as it jetted from the radiator. O'Reilly sat rigidly now that the movement had stopped. "Bugger," he muttered.

Ignoring the steam, he put the car in reverse and floored the accelerator. Perhaps he could get the old Rover to limp home. The engine howled, the back tyres screeched, and the stink of burning rubber filled his nostrils. He decelerated, then tried again, with exactly the same results. "Bugger," he said again, switching off the engine and pounding his fist on the steering wheel. "Hellfire and damnation."

O'Reilly grabbed a torch from the glove compartment and climbed out. The Rover's nose was well into the ditch, and the rear tyres had dug muddy trenches and thrown twin plumes of darkness onto the skid marks behind. "Blue blazing buggery." He'd have to leave the car and walk home. When he got his hands on the buck eejit with the bike—

"Excuse me, Doctor sir."

Donal Donnelly stood in front of O'Reilly. Donal's duncher was pushed back over his carroty hair, and he scratched his scalp. His other hand held his self-decorated bike of many colours by the handlebars.

O'Reilly roared, "Donal? Donal bloody Donnelly, you great glipe, you unmitigated *amadán*. What in the name of the sainted Baby Jesus in velvet trousers were you doing crossing the road? You've put me in the fornicating ditch."

"Makes a change," Donal said.

"You impertinent—" But O'Reilly had already seen the funny side. He'd lost track of the number of times his driving had forced cycling locals, including Donal, off the road. He cleared his throat and tried to scowl at Donal, but then he said, "Fair play. Touché. You're all right, Donal? Not hurt?"

"Och, I'm grand, so I am, sir, but when I came to see how you were, I took a quick gander up front. There's a brave dent in the bonnet of your motor; I think the radiator's banjaxed. She's stuck in thon ditch too. I doubt we'll no' get her out the night."

"I'll have to leave her, get someone to bring a tractor round tomorrow and drag her out."

"I'll get hold of Charlie O'Hara first thing," Donal said. "He's got a big Massey-Harris. Charlie's a good head. He'll see you right in the morning, sir."

"Thanks, Donal." O'Reilly remembered his promise to Kitty. "I need another favour too."

"Fire away."

"If the road's better tomorrow could you drive Miss O'Hallorhan's car up to Belfast?"

"Aye. In soul, I could. Me and Julie's going down to Rasharkin to see her folks. It would save us the train fare to Belfast."

"Pop round about nine. I'll give you directions—and a couple of quid."

"I'll be there, sir." Donal fidgeted. "Would you like a lift home now, sir?"

"You've no car."

"No, but I've the bike, so I have. You could sit on the crossbar, like."

O'Reilly roared with laughter. He'd not been transported sitting sidesaddle on a bicycle since he was a chiseller, but why not? "You're on," he said, and with very little effort the archtrickster of Ballybucklebo was soon trundling along the road with the village's senior medical practitioner clutching the bike's crossbar.

"Home, James, and don't spare the horses," O'Reilly roared. "I want to know the state of play at Number 1."

Donal wobbled near the snowy ditch, but regained

his balance, and Doctor Fingal Flahertie O'Reilly threw back his head and in his mellifluous baritone belted out, "Daisy, Daisy, give me your answer, do . . ."

He and Donal were finishing the final chorus, "But you'd look sweet upon the seat of a bicycle built for two," when Donal stopped, put one foot on the ground, and said, "Here y'are, sir. Home sweet home."

"Good night, Donal. Thanks for the lift."

"Doctor O'Reilly?" Donal asked quietly.

"Yes, Donal."

"It's dark and it's cold and this is no place for a chat, but I'm sore troubled by a wee money matter."

"Julie and the photographer?"

Donal shook his head. "No. It's to do with a horse."

"A horse?" O'Reilly pricked up his ears. When Donal was involved with racing greyhounds or horses, there was usually a bob or two to be made. "Tell me more."

"It's too long a story, sir. I promised Julie I'd be home—"

"Tell me when you pop round tomorrow."

"Would Friday suit, sir? Like I said, Julie and me's going down to Rasharkin to see her folks for a few days." He lowered his voice. "She'll be with me tomorrow and I'd rather not talk about it in front of her."

O'Reilly laughed. "Fair enough. Friday morning it is. I'll be waiting with bated breath." He leaned closer to Donal and lowered his voice. "I hope it's a good story, Donal."

"Huh. It is not, so it's not. It's all about shares in a horse, you know."

"Shares?" O'Reilly frowned. "In a horse?"

"Aye. And Councillor Bishop. My boss."

"Donal Donnelly, come inside this minute. I want to hear all about—"

"Saving your presence, Doctor O'Reilly, I really need your advice, sir, but I promised Julie—"

"All right, all right. Go on home, but I'll expect you tomorrow at nine and at ten on Friday."

"I'm your man, sir. Thank you. Good-night, sir."

O'Reilly stood for a moment chuckling and watching Donal's departing back. Shares in a horse *and* Bertie Bishop? He'd look forward to hearing *that* story.

When he let himself in, he could hear Kinky clattering about in her kitchen. Off with his overcoat and down the hall he went. "How are you, Kinky?"

She turned from the counter where she'd been rolling out pastry. "Grand, so. And yourself, sir?"

"I could be better. I've bent the Rover."

She made sympathetic clucking noises.

"Och, sure it could have been worse. There's not a scratch on me."

"Praise be."

"And how was Flo's?" he asked.

"The *craic* was ninety." She chuckled and her three chins wobbled. "Cissie Sloan could make a cat laugh when she gets a head of steam up." She wiped her hands on her apron. "She was very interested in what I knew about Doctor Laverty and his lady friend too."

"What did you tell her?"

"Not a word. Sure what I knew was no more than what Flo told me. Poor young man."

O'Reilly sighed. "Aye."

"And it's all over the village by now."

"At least," O'Reilly said, "it's unlikely to be malicious."

Kinky nodded. "He's liked well enough, so."

And that, O'Reilly thought, coming from Kinky, who had a firm grip on the pulse of Ballybucklebo, is praise indeed. "You're a sound woman, Kinky Kincaid," he said. He nodded up to where two pairs of Barry's pants were hanging to dry on the bars-ropes-and-pulley device, then pointed at her cooking. "And you work too hard." He smiled. "How'd you like a few days off this weekend? See your family?"

She put a hand on her hip. Her eyes narrowed. "Would Miss O'Hallorhan be coming down?"

O'Reilly felt the blush start. "She would."

Kinky turned back to the counter and with a fine brush began to paint egg yolk onto the pastry. "I'd need to leave on Wednesday, sir, to travel all the way to Cork and get back by Sunday, but I'd like to see Fidelma and Eamon and theirs. I'd have to phone her to see if it's all right."

"You know where the phone is. Go on and ask your sister if it'd be all right for you to go on Tuesday. Make a decent holiday of it. I know it's a fair stretch of the legs from here to Beal na mBláth. Train to Belfast. Change stations. Train to Amiens Street Station in Dublin. A different station for a train to Cork City, another to Clonakilty. Then what?"

"Eamon'd pick me up in his motorcar."

"Great. Barry and I can manage." He stepped behind her and gave her a pat.

She spun round. "Don't you be taking liberties, sir," she said, but her grin was ear to ear. "And you'll not need to worry. I'll leave this turkey pie and plenty of other stuff in the fridge and instructions for heating them. And I've tonight's cold supper ready in the dining room, so."

"You're a marvel. Thanks, Kinky." A thought struck. "Has Barry eaten?"

Her smile fled. "He has not. That boy is sore wounded."

"Has he told you himself about Patricia?"

"Before I left to go to the Bishops', I asked him what the matter was. He was very low." Kinky looked O'Reilly straight in the eye. "But he did not have to tell me. Nor did Cissie. I already knew."

Fingal felt goose bumps start, as he always did when Kinky exhibited her uncanny ability to know things she had no way of knowing. Mrs. Kinky Kincaid was fey.

"I did see it coming, the poor *garsún*."

"Is he upstairs in the lounge?"

"He is not. Nor is Miss Spence. He was there when I came home, but he got called out. When he came back, he gave me another pair of pants to wash, apologized for that, and said he was going to bed." She sighed deeply. "I think he's in his room licking his wounds."

O'Reilly sighed. "I wanted to talk to him after I'd had my supper. I could have taken him up a bite too."

"I think, sir, if you'll take a woman's advice, you'll leave him be tonight. I think Doctor Laverty is the kind of man to bottle things up. A private sort of a kind of a person, so. I do think he will want to talk to you, but not until he does be good and ready."

O'Reilly pinched his nose, considered Kinky's opinion, and then said, "You're right, Kinky. I'll let him come to me." He patted his tummy. "And I'll go and see what's in the dining room."

An Irish Country Christmas

Trade Paperback: 978-0-7653-2072-8 • Paperback: 978-0-7653-6685-6

"Has all the charm of Taylor's previous books and adds Christmas warmth without sacrificing credibility."

—*Publishers Weekly*

An Irish Country Girl

Trade Paperback: 978-0-7653-2073-5

"A bang-up storyteller who captivates and entertains from the first word."

—*Publishers Weekly*

An Irish Country Courtship

Trade Paperback: 978-0-7653-2175-6

"Patrick Taylor has become probably the most popular Irish-Canadian writer of all time."

—*The Globe and Mail*

A Dublin Student Doctor

Trade Paperback: 978-0-7653-2674-4

"Taylor masterfully charts the small victories and defeats of Irish village life."

—*Irish America* magazine